The Shadow of Elisabeth

Michael Pearson

HEINEMANN : LONDON

William Heinemann Ltd
Michelin House, 81 Fulham Road, London SW3 6RB
LONDON MELBOURNE AUCKLAND

First published 1990
Copyright © Michael Pearson 1990

A CIP catalogue record for this book
is available from the British Library
ISBN 0 434 58666 8

Printed and bound in Great Britain
by Mackays of Chatham plc, Chatham, Kent

For Sue

Acknowledgements

Since this novel covers broad areas, it has required much advice from others. I would like to give special thanks to Professor M. R. D. Foot, author of the official and prestigious *The SOE in France* for reading the manuscript and suggesting corrections; Wendy Baker for her guidance in the fashion scenes; Trainer Hugh Collingridge and Jenny Justice for their checking of the racing passages; Bernard Hunter, who has represented so many celebrated actors and actresses, for viewing the chapters concerned with the artistes' agency business; Llyn Evans for scanning the shipping sections; Dr John Avison for his comments on certain medical aspects; Sir Brooks Richards, prominent in the SOE, for advice on Secret Service procedures; and my old friend Kernan Gorman, a native of New York, for his general guidance.

I am grateful, too, to those who have discussed the book with me over a period such as Tess Sacco and Julian Bach, my wife Susan, my son Robert, my daughters Tess and Kate, my son-in-law Derek Wakefield and my friend who have given me such valuable support.

In particular, I must emphasise my thanks to Laura Longrigg, who has edited the book quite brilliantly, seeing its potential at the idea stage, and providing a firm but highly creative hand in the writing of it.

One

It was the quality of that silence he would always remember – almost opaque, like mist. Shock had stripped the scene of all reality. They stood round the bare table in the cottage and tried to understand what they were being asked to do.

It was dusk and there was a fire, since even in late May the evenings were cold that high on the Massif, and the flames threw distorted moving shadows of them on to the walls. All of them were tensed, hardly breathing, as they watched Duncan, their *réseau* leader, prepare five strips of paper of equal shape and size – then draw a cross on one in pencil.

He screwed the strips into little balls and put them into the fine felt hat that matched his cover as a surveyor of roads. It was a good cover, for surveyors of roads have reason to travel.

He shook the hat to mingle the balls of paper – then held it out to Sonya. 'You go first,' he said.

She was alarmed, taken by surprise, but contained it quickly. 'Why me?' she asked calmly.

Duncan shrugged. 'Someone has to start,' he said. 'I'll draw first if you'd prefer.'

'No, I will,' she said. But still she hesitated, her hand suspended.

'Go on,' Duncan urged gently. 'Pick one.'

Anyone watching through the window might have thought it was a game, the kind people play at parties. What made it different was that a woman was going to die. The question to be decided was who was going to kill her.

'What if I can't do it?' Sonya asked. She was very cool, very blonde, very angry.

'You can,' Duncan insisted. 'Any of us can. It'll be very very hard but we can. We've done it before.' Jesus, Charlie thought, he means kill people.

'Germans,' Sonya retorted. She snapped the word, but she was still calm. 'Not Elisabeth,' she said.

The name, spoken aloud for the first time, was like a blow in the stomach. Charlie felt a sudden sharp pain.

Duncan winced. 'We did it when it was necessary,' he said. 'Do you doubt it's necessary now?'

'Without a court martial,' Max put in accusingly.

'Without a court martial,' Duncan agreed. He was in the army. Being in a secret service didn't alter that. You didn't question orders. 'You've read the signal,' he said. Max had. They all had – because at first, when Duncan had come lumbering heavily down the narrow staircase, he hadn't been able to speak.

They knew that upstairs he had been in radio contact with London. The invasion was imminent. Throughout France, the Resistance – the Armée Secrète – had been put on alert. Operations were being geared to it with increased attacks on communications. Their job was to direct a sector around the Vercors Massif which, with its sheer white cliffs, dominated the plain of the Rhône Valley between Grenoble and Valence.

It was remote mountain country, thickly forested, that could only be reached by narrow, winding roads tunnelled through the limestone – ideal, therefore, as a base for the Maquis, and for contact with London or Algiers unhampered by detector vans.

During the past week, radio traffic had become heavier and they were ready for anything in the way of orders. At least that's what they'd thought until they saw the devastated expression on Duncan's face; and Leah, close behind him, dwarfed by his great bulk, looking as though she'd seen a ghost. She was always fragile, but she seemed to have shrunk, her cheeks hollowed. Leah was the radio operator. She knew what Duncan knew.

Each in turn had read the signal and tried to absorb those shocking, unbelievable words. Leah had written the message in plain language under the coded letters as usual. It was stark in its emphasis of the huge danger that faced all the circuits, the nightmare that someone had informed, been 'turned'.

It happened – at times with the most trusted friends – and then it was lethal. Many of their people had been shot or transported to camps in Germany to face God knows what. But Elisabeth? It was unthinkable – especially to Charlie. For almost a year he'd been her lover, and she had transformed him, enlarged his vision, ambitions, perceptions, shown him sensations and feelings he didn't know he had.

She had affected the others, too, in different ways. If any of them had been asked to name the comrade they most admired – most loved, even – they wouldn't have hesitated. She was older than the rest of them and had lived a life that was way beyond their horizons – an elegant sophisticated Parisienne in her mid-thirties, famous as a broadcaster, married to a banker, on first-name terms with people they'd only read about. She had even interviewed Hitler.

By contrast, they were all kids. Even Duncan was only twenty-five. Charlie was twenty. He had fallen in love with her the moment he saw her but, brash and overconfident though he was, had expected nothing.

Two lovers couldn't have been more different. She was a goddess from another world, like one of those film stars she knew. As for him – well, when your father works in a drugstore on Second Avenue, you don't expect you'll ever be President of the United States. You think maybe you might own a shop. A real big deal would be two shops. That was how he thought before he met Elisabeth. Now, all that was changed. He planned to be a man of influence, make a fortune. She had made it seem so easy.

He could never figure out quite what she saw in him. 'Raw material,' she had explained mockingly when he asked her, adding more seriously: 'You know, Charlee, you can never tell what makes a woman feel passionate for a man. Look around and you see beautiful girls quite mad about the oddest, plainest, dullest of men.'

And this was the woman they had been ordered to execute. Without court martial. Forthwith. Repeat forthwith. Death to appear in action or by accident to protect sources. Confirm.

Max was staring at Duncan from beneath hooded lids. He was lugubrious, spare with words. 'It's a basic right,' he insisted quietly, 'to answer one's accusers.'

Duncan nodded his big head. Rights didn't come into it. 'The order's precise,' he said. 'Just show me any options.' He threw the signal down in front of him. 'Go on, Max,' he urged, 'I'd give anything for a choice.'

Max knew what it said. They had explored all the possibilities, faced Duncan's idea of staging this terrible, macabre ballot. Max just sat motionless and silent, elbows on the table. 'Do you deny that it's possible?' pressed Duncan. 'That she's been turned, I mean?'

Max stared at him, unblinking. 'Well, isn't it possible?' Duncan persisted. For Charlie, it was beyond belief, but once Duncan had raised the spectre it couldn't just be shrugged off. They'd learned that the Gestapo had found Elisabeth's daughter. It was a common technique for dealing with the Resistance. A wife, a child, a husband. The most fervent patriots had been broken by the impossible conflict. The death or mutilation of a daughter – how could a mother accept that?

They'd urged her to fly out to England, but she had refused. It was vital she stayed in France, she said. They suspected she was planning a rescue, bribing the right people, perhaps, using influence from the past. That's how Elisabeth thought.

'Well?' demanded Duncan.

Max hesitated. 'It's possible,' he conceded.

Duncan thrust the hat towards him. 'Then take one,' he commanded. Max still paused. Then, very slowly, he reached out and took one of the balls of paper.

'Remember what we agreed,' Duncan told them. 'We won't speak of the lots we draw. Only one person will ever know the exact truth. But we'll share it, as a firing squad does. All our hands will be on the gun.' Leah uttered a sound that could have been a sob, bitten back. Duncan glanced at her and she seemed even smaller. She was not just shocked. She was tired. She had been up most of the previous night at her radio transmitter. He didn't talk of where the gun should be used – but if it was to be in action, the scope was obvious. They were due to attack a train to Grenoble the next night.

He turned once more to Sonya. 'Now,' he said. This time she didn't hesitate. She put her hand into the hat and removed a paper ball, opening it with trembling fingers. Duncan was watching her, as she knew, daring her to display relief or despair. She looked at it, then met Duncan's gaze – and none of them knew.

He offered the hat to Leah and she reached inside it with her thin, delicate arm – then undid the paper, holding it close to her stomach. She blinked as she looked at it, but that could have signified anything. As a radio operator, she would not normally be on the next night's raid, but that was a detail no one seemed to have thought about.

Then Duncan did a strange thing. He drew the next lot himself, leaving Charlie until last. It was a gesture, Charlie guessed, partly to his age, for he was the youngest, but mainly because they all knew what Elisabeth meant to him. The duty would be overwhelming for any of them. But for Charlie it would be herculean and obscene, and scar him for life.

4

Duncan would have spared him this if he could, but the five of them had shared all the dangers, covered each other under fire. No one could be excused.

As Duncan offered the hat to him, he smiled, with sad sympathy, urging courage. Charlie looked at the small ball of twisted paper – alone now in the bottom of the hat. At first, he couldn't touch it. He imagined opening it, and seeing the cross. Jesus, how he needed that little ball of paper to be blank. Never had he wanted anything so much. He prayed, though he wasn't much of a believer. Please God, if you're there. Just this once.

'Charlie,' said Duncan softly, 'take the paper out of the hat.' Charlie forced himself to obey, feeling a sudden revulsion as he touched the paper. He thought he was going to be sick. For a few seconds, he couldn't undo it, and just held it within his fingers in a kind of mental limbo.

'Charlie,' Duncan pressed again, 'you've got to know.'

But he didn't have to. Not then. For Elisabeth returned sooner than expected. She stood looking at them from the doorway, with the beret on the side of her head and a red scarf round her neck, dressed like any woman her age in the towns around the Massif. But she couldn't help being chic, like something out of *Vogue*. She would have been chic in a sack.

'Hallo,' she said brightly. 'What are you all looking so gloomy about?'

Charlie savoured her as she stood there, taking in everything he loved about her. That waist, still narrow despite the child. The black hair, once tended in the best Paris salons, that she wore short now. The legs, so beautifully curved and slender despite the thick wartime stockings. The brown eyes, with that look of amusement, as though the whole of life was really rather funny. She was very French, very cynical, a bit wicked, but tolerant of any human fault except cruelty.

Later, he couldn't recall if anyone answered her question, for her arrival only gave him a respite. Nothing was changed. He didn't open the ballot paper until late that night, and then he saw what he had feared. It bore the pencilled cross.

Two

Every year or so she would call him back across the Atlantic. The summons didn't come suddenly, but grew within him slowly, like a mild but worsening pain.

Even when it became persistent, it was not urgent. One year he resisted for as long as two months as a test: if he was to be haunted, he wanted to know the limits. Not that it was marked by eerie elements of hatred or revenge. There were no evil spirits. There were memories, of course, very vivid ones, with every minor detail brilliant in his mind of what she wore, the way she looked, her tone of voice. The call was a needing, really, a hunger.

There was no guilt. He had all the answers to guilt. He was a soldier. He was under orders. Jesus, if he could have disobeyed them, he would have done. He'd thought of it enough times – of firing wide, maybe, or shooting to wound. That would buy time, but she would still have to die.

Charlie had faced up to that during the terrible twenty-four hours he had spent with her before the raid. If she truly had been 'turned' one thing was certain: Duncan and the others would be taken, as he himself would. The whole network involved thousands of Resistance men, and if the enemy were warned of their plans the casualties would be immense.

At times he'd played with the notion that he hadn't killed her, that it had been a German bullet. They had been under heavy fire in darkness. The noise was deafening; they were being raked by Spandaus, and the mortar shells were dropping all round them.

But he knew he was kidding himself. He could still feel the trigger as he squeezed it, could still recall the Sten gun shaking in his hands. He would never forget that. How had he made himself do it? How had he obeyed that obscene order?

By pretending it wasn't her. That was the trick. By forcing himself to accept illusion. She's a target, he had kept repeating, like the straw-filled dummies they had used in training. A target. A target. A target.

Thank God he hadn't been able to see her eyes, for then he would have been paralysed. As it was, she was a vague figure ahead of him. Nothing was clear on that black horrendous night. It was very quick. Two seconds of rapid fire, then, oh Jesus, a brief thinning of the clouds; the opaque outline of a half-moon. Enough for him to see her – lying in the mud near the railway cutting, very still, in an awkward position with one leg doubled up beneath her. She wasn't a target then, she was Elisabeth, and he had felt an overwhelming need to go to her, to make a final peace. But the enemy were closing in. No time for last rites. They had had to get out fast.

The odd part was that afterwards, back at the cottage on the Massif, no one mentioned her. He remembered Leah laying the table for breakfast. She just set five places instead of six.

Usually they talked a lot after an operation, going over the hairy moments. By God, that was a near one, they'd say. But that morning they were silent most of the time, sitting over their coffee.

After several weeks had gone by, they started talking about her again, wondering what she would have thought of something, recalling a joke she had made, advice she'd given, the way she laughed, for she was always laughing. Even then, though, no one spoke of execution. She had died in action, hadn't she?

Often they said they missed her. Charlie missed her as if she were a limb he had lost. He still wasn't whole – even now, sixteen years later. Couldn't be, could he, or he'd have been able to resist the call.

Charlie didn't always return to the Massif, to the grave in the small cemetery under the high rocky outcrops they called Les Trois Pucelles. Oddly, the grave didn't move him much. He felt closer to her in the places where they had been together – not just there in the Grandes Alpes. He had gone to Paris with her on one mission. Another time, they had been pulled out for a couple of weeks to London.

Even more, he needed the others who had been with her. He would usually find Leah in London, go talk to Sonya in Paris, catch Max if he wasn't in Hollywood, take a train to Newmarket to meet Duncan.

It wasn't always as tidy. Sometimes just two of them would meet; sometimes there would be three. Occasionally, every two years or so, they would all get together for a proper reunion, like the one planned for two days' time in Paris.

Once Charlie had taken Philana with him – early on when they had only been married for a couple of years – but it hadn't worked. 'You're like the Mafia,' she told him. 'It's as though you've got your own secret bond.'

Philana couldn't quite define what she was facing, but she feared it, though she pretended to shrug it off. It was very sad about Elisabeth, she said, but many others had died in action, too, and she hadn't heard of anyone else forming secret societies.

'Reunions are common enough,' Charlie had responded carefully.

Philana had just looked at him with those big eyes – like deep blue water. She didn't have to put it into words. Their meetings weren't like other reunions. 'When they've been together,' Annette, Duncan's wife, had confided to her, 'I feel as if I'm married to a man from Mars. Everything's different. His attitudes, standards, priorities. Then he settles back again to life on the planet Earth.'

2

'How long will you be in Europe?' Philana asked. She was pouring coffee, so her eyes were averted as she spoke.

'About a week,' Charlie answered. 'Maybe ten days. The usual.' It was easier now in 1960 and he could go by jet in only a few hours. At first he had travelled by ship – five days each way without counting the time he was there.

He looked out of the window of the dining room. It was a fine day, the sun striking the trees in Central Park. He didn't want to meet her eyes either. This was delicate territory, one of those minefields that exist in marriages.

'The Godfather returns,' she said. She looked at him then, a slight smile hovering round her lips. She was half teasing, saying she didn't like it, but she would put up with it. She was Greek. Greek wives were brought up to accommodate their husbands. She was right, too. If they *were* like the Mafia, he was the Godfather. Charlie seemed to have taken over the leadership from Duncan.

'You'll miss Father's charity dinner,' Philana went on. 'Marlene'll be there. And Greta. And the Vice-President probably.

Pity you couldn't have gone over later.' She was playing with him. Greta Garbo never turned up at charity dinners.

Charlie shrugged. 'There's never a good time. You'll tell him I'm sorry, won't you?'

The children came in with Mona, the nurse. 'Daddy's going to Europe,' she told them, 'to see his friends from the war.' She turned to Mona. 'Is Harry waiting?' she asked, referring to the chauffeur.

'Yes, Mrs Dawson.'

'Better not keep him.' She smiled at Rhona and Tim. 'Give Daddy a big kiss.'

Charlie took his son and his daughter on his knee in turn and told them to be good and look after Mummy for him – what fathers say. 'I'll see what I can find for you in Paris,' he said, 'something really snazzy.' As the children left the room he met Philana's eyes. 'For you, too, honey,' he added.

'If you have time.' She gave him a soft smile. 'Something for me to look forward to – as well as your return.'

He was fortunate. She was a good wife. Pretty, in a soft way: a natural ash blonde, rare among Greeks and highly prized, with hair that wasn't made to stay tidy – and big blue eyes, that she could keep from blinking for a while, as actresses learned to do.

That morning, she was using her eyes as well as words for the nuances. Everything she said had an edge to it. She was just making her point – a woman of spirit, even with her Greek background. There were always grey areas. For some wives it was another woman. Her mother had warned her to expect it, absorb it. The nature of men. She would have found it hard if Elisabeth had still been alive – intolerable, in fact. She still found it hard, though she knew this was unreasonable. After all, Elisabeth was dead.

Charlie knew how she felt, wished he could have shared with her something of the emotional hunger that overtook him at times. But they had tried that. The odd part was that, but for Elisabeth, they would never have met. It was at a smart New York dinner party, the first he had ever attended, given by Marie Cayzer – the opening of the door for him, just as Elisabeth had predicted. 'Get into Marie's good books,' she had said, 'and in New York you'll find everything will happen.'

Charlie had seen a newspaper picture of Marie taken at a society function – very poised, hair up in an elaborate coiffure, wearing a diamond necklace. It was like a photograph he had seen of Elisabeth at some pre-war gala. He had found this daunting enough. Elisabeth had shaken her head with a little smile, like a teacher with a pupil she favoured but found a trifle dense. 'We're all just women,' she said, 'even if we're wearing armour. Not much different really from the girls in the villages. Never be daunted, Charlee, by the externals.'

Even so Charlie was daunted by Marie Cayzer, which is to say he had been back in Manhattan for all of twenty-four hours before he summoned up the courage to call her – enough time to realise how much Elisabeth had changed him. He was plagued by a sense of anguish. His parents had given him a great welcome – a big party in the small apartment where he'd been raised, with all the family and friends from the neighbourhood, and slightly slurred speeches by his father and uncles about his service for Uncle Sam.

There'd been mention of a job at the drugstore, of how Mr Weinberger had declared that Charlie was just what the business needed – maybe the very man who might step into his own shoes when the time came. Well, who could tell?

Charlie had responded as he should and they had all applauded his words of modest appreciation, but he had felt a little deceitful – and remote. Deeply fond, grateful, loving; but an outsider viewing them from a different world – a world in which he could attack an enemy train as an officer in the US Army; in which he could telephone a woman like Marie Cayzer and be greeted with a little cry of welcome.

'I find this quite uncanny, Mr Dawson,' Marie Cayzer declared in her soft Boston accent. 'Only this morning I was thinking of Elisabeth, grieving for her again. And here you are on the phone within the hour. She wrote me a while before she died – a very short scribbled note. She was in London, she said, which was how she could write, with a young comrade called Charlie, who I suppose was you.'

'I was flown out to London with her,' he said.

'Then we must meet, mustn't we, Charlie? In fact, I'm having a dinner party tonight where there'll be several people who'd love to meet you. Is there any chance you could come?'

'I'd be honoured, Mrs Cayzer,' said Charlie.

'That's wonderful then. Eight o'clock. Black tie.'

She treated him like a guest of honour at a gathering that included a four-star general, three senators and their wives, a famous Broadway actress, and Costa Mastorakis, who controlled a huge shipping fleet. Marie placed Charlie, clad in the tuxedo he had bought that day, on her right hand with Philana Mastorakis on his other side.

'I admired Elisabeth Ferrier more than any woman I've ever met,' Marie declared. 'She died a heroine, didn't she, Charlie?'

'She certainly did, ma'am,' Charlie agreed.

'Were you there when it happened?' asked the general suddenly.

'I was, sir. We were raiding a train on the way to Grenoble just before D-Day. The plan was to blow up a section of the track as the train went over it. But they were waiting for us.'

'And?' persisted the general.

'Madame Ferrier was killed.' Charlie felt harrowed as the wound reopened. Oh God, he thought, he's going to ask exactly how and that'll plunge me back into the black void.

But Costa Mastorakis intervened. He had been watching Charlie intently from across the table. 'What was this unit you were in?' he asked in heavy tones.

'The OSS, sir,' Charlie answered. 'Though I think that now they call it the CIA. We were working with the British SOE and the French BCRA, merged under one command for operations in France.'

The butler removed his plate and Charlie looked down at the rows of silver cutlery that would have terrified him a couple of years before. But he and Elisabeth had played the dining game. She had made him go through the basics of meeting important people – refusing, with much laughing, to give herself to him until he answered her questions correctly. 'How can I sleep with a man who doesn't know what fork to use?' she teased. 'A lady's got to have *some* standards, don't you think?'

Mastorakis was still studying him. 'Must have taken nerve,' he said. 'Did your nerves bother you?'

Charlie gave a modest shrug. 'Same as anyone fighting, sir, I suppose.'

'Now that's the biggest understatement I ever heard,' put in Marie. 'You were a hero, Charlie. Why not admit it?'

Beneath his thick brows Mastorakis's dark eyes were serious as he pondered Charlie's answer. 'It's not the same,' he growled. 'In a regiment, you've got other men around you. It's structured, controlled by line of command. But you were like bandits, weren't you, Mr Dawson?'

Charlie forced a laugh. 'You could put it that way, sir. Stole a couple of horses once.'

Mastorakis nodded. 'Must've needed initiative, fast thinking.'

'Costa,' Marie cut in, 'you really must stop monopolising my guest. If you want to talk to him so earnestly you should ask him to lunch.' She gave Charlie a wink that he only just caught.

After dinner, when they all retired for coffee to Marie's ornate sitting room, Philana again sat next to him. They'd had little chance to talk at table, but now they were alone for a moment. 'My father likes you,' she said. 'Have you made plans yet about what you're going to do?'

He shook his head. 'Give me a chance,' he said. 'I only got back to America yesterday.'

'That's what Father's going to give you. A chance. I hope you'll take it.' A little smile appeared on her face. 'You were in love with that Elisabeth, weren't you?' She saw the flash of pain in his eyes. 'Sorry. I've said the wrong thing. Will you forgive me?'

He shrugged. 'I didn't realise it was so obvious.'

'It wasn't to anyone else, but I was sitting next to you, and I noticed your hands on your lap. They were clenched as you spoke of her. Look, Father's coming over to join us now. Well, I told you, didn't I?'

Nearly sixteen good years had passed since then. Charlie had soared up through the Mastorakis organisation, and then broken away to form his own company with its own ships. He had managed this without too much ill-feeling between him and Mastorakis. They disagreed on policy. Charlie was convinced the future lay with mammoth tankers, but the old man was cautious. What would happen in the bad times that always haunted shipping men? The two of them got on well enough, though. There was trust between them, and they had a deal. If anything happened to his father-in-law, Charlie would move back to head up the main company. Mastorakis had no sons, and both of them knew that Charlie had always held a trump card. She was sitting opposite him now at breakfast.

'What time's your plane?' asked Philana.

'Twenty hundred,' he answered. 'That's eight o'clock.'

'Can we have a cocktail here before you go?' The sharpness had left her voice. She wanted him to go feeling close to her. So did he.

'That's a good idea,' he said.

'Then I'll drive out to Idlewild with you, and see you get off safely.'

'You're full of great thoughts this morning.' He folded the *Times*, then went to her and kissed her gently on the lips. 'I'm a lucky feller.'

It was a play they quite often acted out on the days he left for Europe, with the same changing pattern, the complaint in her tone becoming compliance, becoming 'I love you'. He'd always return from Europe very easy, very affectionate – freed for a while, as she tended to think of it, though it seemed a strange concept.

Others too had been marked by the war. She knew of men who woke up screaming in the night. Charlie didn't wake up screaming. He came back with presents carefully chosen, obviously in love with her, and passionate. Her friends considered her fortunate. But his departure always made her uneasy, caused her to wonder if this time it might be different, if indeed he would come back at all.

3

Rain was slanting across the tarmac of Orly Airport as the Comet landed. Somehow, he never thought of Paris in the rain. To him it was Elisabeth's city where the sun always shone, where people sat out in cafés.

The weather changed nothing. It was the first proper reunion they had had for two years, with all of them present, and Charlie was excited. Maybe, he reflected later, he sensed that this time would be different from any of the others.

Sonya was waiting for him in the main hall. Groomed as usual, not a hair out of place. A suit, tailored with no sign of a crease. She looked like an actress, always ready for the camera to roll.

She was warmly affectionate, though, with people she liked. She put her arms round his neck and clung to him for a second. Then she held him back from her so that she could study him. 'You're looking well. Good trip?'

'Great,' he answered. 'Been reading a big story in a French

newspaper about the Lanier trial. By Sonya Mason, it said, known throughout France for her human touch. Name seemed familiar. Don't I know her? I asked myself.'

'Too well, I think,' she answered with a grin, as they headed for the exit. They always picked up exactly where they had left off – as though they saw each other once a week.

As they walked to her car she said: 'Leah's flying in tonight. She'll be dining with us. Max and Duncan are arriving tomorrow.'

She put the car in gear and nosed out into the traffic, heading north up the autoroute to Paris.

'It's gripping stuff,' said Charlie. 'That trial story. You're getting good, honey.'

'Want a favour?' she queried. 'Go on like this and I'll roll over like a puppy.'

'I mean it. It's deep. Touches the note. No kidding.'

'It's good to have a fan,' she said. 'They call me in if a story's running dull. Passionise it, chérie, Claude says. Passionise it.'

'So that's the magic ingredient. Works better than all other powders. You deserve your success, you know.' It was considerable; Sonya's name was almost as famous as Elisabeth's had been, with a column twice a week.

'You think Elisabeth would approve?' She was smiling softly as though they were sharing a secret mutual joke.

'She'd love it,' he said, before adding lightly: 'Well, maybe not quite this good.'

'Now, Charlie, there was nothing like that about her, was there?'

'You're right,' he agreed. 'No envy. Envy's not positive. Just go out and do better, she'd say.'

Sonya braked hard as a small Citroën CV2 cut close in front of her, careering on its soft springing. 'She gave me such a lot,' she went on. 'Confidence, a belief in my potential – though how she knew, I've no idea. And Claude, of course. That was a gift and a half. Not many kids who want to write for newspapers get that.' She gave a sad, wry laugh. 'Remember how I agonised about contacting Claude – whether it was fair to approach him?'

Charlie remembered all right. They'd been sitting in a café near the Place de la Madeleine. It was the closest Sonya had come to speaking of the real cause of Elisabeth's death.

The other three had come to him separately with similar

questions – as though seeking his permission since he had been closest to her. Elisabeth had spoken to all of them about friends of hers they should contact after the war – people who could help them with the plans they had discussed with her. There was much time on the Massif. Days, even weeks of waiting. They had all become very close.

He had told them Elisabeth would expect it. 'Always do what's needed. She often said that.' And he'd done the same himself when he contacted Marie Cayzer.

Sonya, though, was the first to enjoy the impact of Elisabeth's power. Claude Duclos was the editor-in-chief of *France Aujour-d'hui*. Then about forty, he had inherited the paper from his father. He was a connoisseur of fine art, of politicians, celebrities, beautiful women; a man of great influence.

Elisabeth had spoken of him a lot, and Charlie, always jealous, had asked if Claude had been her lover. She'd responded with a disappointed smile. 'What a question, Charlee! I must stop you, you know. If I don't, you'll be pressing me about every man I ever mention. And what do others matter, after all? You and I are what matter. Now listen to me. Claude Duclos is an old friend. He's been very important to me – taught me my trade, you might say.'

He was important to Sonya, too, though it was a rough ride. From the first, he had overwhelmed her. On the phone, when she'd said she could lunch with him, she had heard him tell his secretary to cancel his date for that day unless it was at the Elysée Palace. 'Only the President of France could come before a comrade of Elisabeth,' he told Sonya.

It was heady treatment, if a trifle flamboyant. Sonya's back-ground wasn't like Charlie's. Her father was fairly affluent – a lawyer in the Paris office of a big American corporation. Her mother came from a good *grand bourgeois* wine-growing family.

Even so, Sonya was only twenty-three and Claude Duclos was looking at her as she was brought to his table in Maxim's inner room as though she was the most lovely woman he'd ever seen. He wasn't good-looking – dark and wiry with ample rather greasy black hair combed back fairly tight from his forehead – but he was animated and enthusiastic.

He told her at once that she was beautiful. 'A rare bonus,' he said. 'It would have been quite enough for you to have fought with Elisabeth. Did you really carry a gun?'

Then he interrogated her – very deftly, with much charm, meeting her eyes. He asked about Elisabeth's death, about where they'd been and how it had happened.

When she finished, he said: 'I think Elisabeth was right to encourage you to write. You've got a good eye. You can describe things well – even sad ones. It must have been hard to talk of that raid. You obviously loved her.'

'I did. She was an amazing woman.'

He smiled. 'I did too. And I'll back her hunch. We'll start work tomorrow. Now we'll go to my apartment. I have one of the best collections of modernists in Paris.'

Sonya could hardly believe her ears. That old gambit. 'Does the job depend on it?' she asked caustically.

He laughed – a man who'd had many women. 'A casting couch?' he queried. 'Of course not. We're going to make love, I think, but not if you don't want to.'

'We're *not* going to make love,' she insisted hotly. 'I don't even know you.'

He gave another laugh – gentle but not patronising. Already he was making love to her. 'That's a good reason,' he said. 'I'll give you another. Never sleep with the boss. Elisabeth would agree completely.'

'Did you sleep with her?' she retorted sharply.

He looked pained – and ignored the question. 'There's another rule, isn't there? Don't let a man think you're easy.'

'I can think of a better one, Monsieur Duclos.' She paused. 'Wait till you're married. That's what my mother would say.'

'A wise lady,' he said, amusement in the slight movement of his shoulders. 'All right, we'll wait till you're married. Meanwhile, I'll show you my pictures. I promise my behaviour will be exemplary.'

And it was. The apartment was superb, with a view of the Seine and Notre Dame. The paintings were breathtaking, for their number as much as their quality, including Matisses, Picassos, Braques, Klees.

He made no move to touch her – not even by casual error as they walked from room to room or strolled out on to the balcony. When he brought her a brandy in the huge sitting room, his fingers didn't touch hers.

They just talked and looked at each other. It was the voice mainly that affected her. Half the time she didn't hear what he

16

was saying. He made no propostion, but he knew the effect he was having on her, understood the timing of her emotional clock. When at last he got up and went into his bedroom, she followed him.

'You didn't wait till I was married,' she said afterwards.

'I couldn't,' he answered. 'There was an explosion. We're going to be very close, Sonya, as I was with Elisabeth.'

'So you *were* lovers.'

He sighed. 'You don't have to be lovers to be close.' He leaned over her and began to kiss her mouth tenderly. 'You haven't asked me if it was good, if it pleased me,' he whispered.

'Do women always ask you that?'

'It was more than good. Wonderful.' He got out of bed. 'I fear I must get back to the paper. My chauffeur will take you wherever you wish to go. Come to the office at ten o'clock tomorrow and we'll get you to work.'

The next day he received her immediately and briefed her. Two hours later he summoned her back to the luxurious office, furnished like a drawing room, that contrasted so sharply with the newsroom that adjoined it. Visitors walked through that great open space – where a hundred men and women were pounding typewriters, talking on the phone, calling for copy boys – to find themselves in tranquillity, with magazines laid out neatly on a table, a couple of sofas, a neat, leather-topped desk.

Duclos was standing with his back to the door, looking out of the window into the Boulevard Malesherbes. 'Have you done what I said?' he enquired without turning.

'Yes,' she answered. He had ordered her to spend the morning in the cuttings library reading Elisabeth's articles from her last year of writing.

'Now tell me why she was so good.' His tone was abrupt, businesslike.

'Well . . .' she began. 'She was very good. No question about that . . .'

'Why?' The word was snapped out.

She became confused. 'It's hard to define. Her articles are compelling, of course . . .'

He turned round then. 'Go back to the library. Study again every piece you've read. Tear them apart, line by bloody line. Take all day. Find me a word you can cut without damage, that's even wrong. Analyse the excitement. She could make a man walking along a road sound exciting – but how? Do you think it was luck? Don't come back until you can at least discuss it. That is, if you ever want to be sent out on a story. Now you must excuse me. I've a paper to produce.'

Sonya stared at him. 'How dare you speak to me like that?' she demanded.

His eyes were cold. 'Because you've wasted the morning,' he answered. 'Well, haven't you?'

She didn't reply – just turned and hurried through the news-room, tears of anger and humiliation streaming down her cheeks. She called a cab – then changed her mind and went back upstairs to the library. She did as he'd ordered. Word by word. Hour after hour.

She began to recognise phrases Elisabeth had used in their long talks on the Massif – phrases that somehow she'd missed earlier in the morning. Sonya realised how much she had learned during those deep discussions – about grand design, purpose, principle. Now she glimpsed how she could put it all into practice. Claude was right, after all.

Charlie remembered how that first day had ended for her. She hadn't gone back to see Claude – a petty gesture of revolt. She'd returned to her apartment to find four dozen roses waiting for her. They didn't really surprise her. Nor did the note: 'I've thought of you all day. Please dine with me. I'll call for you at eight.' It conformed with the sweet-and-sour picture she had of him. How to handle a woman, Lesson Two. She wouldn't dine with him, of course, that much was certain. But, inevitably, she did.

'A lot of water has gone under the bridge since then,' Sonya said as they headed down the Avenue de la Porte d'Ivry, out of the suburbs and into the city proper.

'How is Claude?' Charlie enquired.

'Fine,' she answered in an offhand tone. 'There are other girls now, of course, though we're close, you could say. Maybe it's like it was with Elisabeth – as he said it would be.' She flashed him a smile that was marked with sadness. 'I've booked you into the Bristol as usual.' It was a pleasant hotel, not too ostentatious, and quite close to her apartment.

A few minutes later, she turned into the traffic of the Place de la Concorde. 'It's going to be fun, isn't it' she said, 'seeing them all again? There's just one thing I always think is rather sad.'

'What's that?' he asked.

'Elisabeth won't be there. She'd have loved it, wouldn't she?'

'Maybe she will be there,' he said. 'In a way.'

Three

On her way out, Leah stopped for a moment at her desk and looked again at the design that lay there. She put down the small suitcase of Moroccan leather and perched thoughtfully on the swivel armchair without removing her coat. She took up a pencil. The dress was simple – full to the calf with the nipped-in waist that had marked her collection last month, but with changes. An inch off the hem, a bit more interest at the bodice, a neckline that was deeper and darted. Still not right, though. She began to shade in some more pleating.

The door opened, and the chatter of the girls in the workroom outside became louder. Hugo stood there. 'You're going to miss your plane, darling, unless you leave right now. That can wait, let's face it. We've only just got through the last collection.'

She grinned a bit sheepishly. 'Just got an idea, that's all.'

'You should be giving your mind a rest – at least until you've seen the new fabrics at Frankfurt.' She was flying on to the Interstoff Exhibition in Frankfurt after the reunion. Everyone in the creative side of the fashion business went to the Interstoff in May for fabric and colour ideas.

Leah got up, took hold of her case, moved to the door and kissed Hugo gently. She knew he hated these meetings, but they didn't happen often. 'You do realise, don't you,' she said gently, 'that I'd never have met you if it hadn't been for Elisabeth?'

'I know,' he said with a sigh of affectionate boredom. 'And no one might ever have heard of Leah Grant. You always get like this before you meet that lot. Anyone would think you were going to some kind of ceremony. It's just a reunion, darling.'

'It is a ceremony,' she insisted softly.

He shrugged with a smile. 'There's a taxi waiting. If you don't go now you'll miss the first hymn.' He took her case and walked with her through the fitting room. Her attention was caught by one of the girls working on dummies, but Hugo checked her gently. 'Not now,' he said.

Monica, in charge of the showroom upstairs, waved to her as

they hurried through towards the entrance. Leah stopped to speak to her, but Hugo eased her on into the street and held open the door of the waiting cab. 'By the way,' he said, 'don't think I'm not aware of what we owe Elisabeth.'

She leaned forward and kissed him again. 'Bless you,' she whispered. She sat back in the cab as it headed along the King's Road and smiled at Hugo's strong-armed way of getting her off. For the best part of fifteen years now he had been the strength behind her, running the business, handling debts, finance, creditors – at first working with her part-time; then, as heady success swept them forward, the business needed his full commitment and he dealt with the press, her presentation, and organised the collections.

Elisabeth had talked often about his father, Ben Jordan, and about the fashion business Leah hoped to start. She was impressed by the simplicity, the sheer fun, of the sketches Leah drew on the Massif – more for therapy at first than anything as ambitious as a career. Elisabeth detected the talent, predicting a big future for the right kind of collection aimed at the young. 'Things are going to be different,' she said. 'Until now, it's always been the woman of forty who has dictated fashion. In the future, mass production and new fabrics will make good cheap dresses possible – not just the blouse and skirt that was all most young girls have been able to afford. I tell you what. This pendant . . .' round her neck she wore a miniature gold bar on a fine chain, joking sometimes that she carried it so she would always have something to sell 'I'll lend to you to take to Ben Jordan in London. He'll back your business, give you the money you need to get started.'

'But why?' asked Leah.

Elisabeth had not answered the question. 'He will,' she insisted. 'You'll see. Meanwhile, if anything happens to me, you're free to take it from my things.'

Like the others, Leah had done as Elisabeth suggested. She found Ben Jordan Financial Services in the London telephone directory and called at his office.

'Have you an appointment?' asked the receptionist. 'He won't see you without one.'

'Perhaps you'd give him this envelope,' said Leah.

The girl shrugged. 'Won't make any difference. Not without an appointment.'

'Perhaps,' said Leah, 'but would you please take it to him?'

The girl flounced out, but when she returned her manner was more respectful. 'He'll see you at once,' she said.

Ben Jordan was sitting at his desk swinging the pendant with a sentimental smile on his florid face. He was a large, grey-haired man of about fifty with eyes that seemed strangely soft for a financier – though he was the first Leah had ever met.

'So you were with Elisabeth,' he said, 'and she advised you to contact me. Well, what can I do to help?'

He listened carefully to her plans, then stood up. 'Let's go and look at this shop you've found.'

'Now?' she asked.

'No time like the present.'

In Reception, he told the girl: 'When my son comes in, ask him to join us at this address.'

It was the speed that Leah found astonishing. Mr Jordan and his son, Hugo, looked round the shop, called on the agent and negotiated the lease.

'That's settled then,' Jordan declared. 'I'll provide any money you need, which I'll lend you at low interest providing my firm can own ten per cent of the project. Hugo here will look after the business side so you can concentrate on the clothes. Is that acceptable?'

Leah looked at Hugo, then in his early twenties, maybe a year older than her – a bulky man with unruly fair hair, bright blue eyes and an expectant grin. 'I suppose so.' She giggled. 'I don't believe any of it.' Then she added: 'I'm sure Hugo will do very well – providing he can cope with me.'

'I can cope with you,' he said firmly.

The cab came to a halt by the glass doors of the terminal and a porter took her bag. As they walked into the main hall she heard her name being called on the loudspeaker. She took up the phone at the BEA desk.

'Sorry, darling,' said Hugo. 'There's a crisis. Monty called. AMC want to change their order. They want to go lighter on Freda and much heavier on Anastasia. Also they want to bring forward delivery.'

'They can't,' Leah wailed. 'We're tight as it is. Hugo, we're talking twenty thousand garments.'

'More than that now, darling. Over thirty thousand.'

'Then it's impossible.'

'It's possible,' Hugo insisted. 'It's got to be possible for AMC.' Associated Merchandising Corporation was the biggest buying organisation in the world, supplying department stores everywhere. 'And he wants a design change to Anastasia – a small one, he says.'

'No!' she pleaded. 'I know Monty's changes.'

'Yes,' Hugo said firmly. 'You've got to talk to him. Come right back now. I've re-booked you on a morning plane and called Sonya.'

'No, Hugo.'

'Don't worry, you'll make the reunion.'

She replaced the phone with a sigh. 'A cab, madam?' queried the waiting porter. 'How did you guess?' she said and followed him out of the terminal.

2

The second phone rang on Max's desk. 'Hang on a moment, Bob,' he said and picked it up. 'Sally, I'm in the middle of speaking to – '

'It's Romy from the South of France,' his secretary cut in. She was under orders to interrupt him whenever Romy called – even if he was talking to Sam Goldwyn himself.

'Hello, Romy darling,' Max said, covering the mouthpiece of his other phone. 'Lucky you called. I'm just talking to Robert in Hollywood. Coincidence, eh? He's offering a hundred and fifty plus eight per cent of the gross and Cary Grant. Started at five. Could mean a quarter of a million. Only Liz has ever got that much. I think we say yes, don't we? It's a great script. Well, that's the problem. They want to start shooting next month.'

Sally came in. 'Betty called, but I told her you'd gone already,' she said.

He nodded and beckoned her to stand beside him. 'Can you change your plans, Romy? You're a trouper, darling. I bet it's lovely down there, isn't it? The bougainvillea out? I'll never forget the day I first saw you on the terrace there, with that mass of purple beside you and all that blue, blue sea. Well, I *am* a romantic. Take care, darling.'

He put the phone down, and went on talking to Robert. 'Bob, I'm having trouble with Romy. Can you help me a little more?'

As he spoke. Max ran his hand idly up the inside of Sally's

thigh, fondling the soft skin above her stockings. 'Well, Romy's big enough, Bob,' he went on, 'and that role's absolutely made for her. She'll kill 'em, Bob. Bet you a grand she gets nominated. Well, how about another two per cent? OK, one then and maybe we've got a deal. I'm off to Paris in a moment, but I'll call you Friday to confirm.'

He replaced the phone and looked up at Sally, his fingers still between her legs. 'You're excited,' he said. 'So am I. You're a lovely girl, Sal.'

She shrugged coolly. 'Maybe you should stop doing that to me. You'll have to leave in five minutes.'

'There's time.'

'No there isn't. Can we have dinner Friday?'

'Sure.' He began packing his briefcase with scripts to read on the plane.

'Unless Romy sends for you?'

He looked up at her, pained by her tone. 'What worries you so much about Romy, Sal?' Romy was the only client she was jealous of, though there were others who were prettier, younger, sexier.

'I wish I knew why she was quite so special,' Sally said.

'She's one of our stars, my first client. You know that. A very big first for a young agent who didn't even have an office.'

'There's more, though, isn't there? I love you, Max. I know you very well. There's something you haven't told me.'

'You've chosen a fine moment to start this, haven't you? We'll talk Friday.' He saw the look in her eyes. 'Honey, how many times have I told you the story? I met her through Elisabeth. They were friends. It's as simple as that.'

'Nothing's simple when it comes to Elisabeth,' said Sally. 'She was dead by then. At least, that's the theory.'

He winced. 'Don't speak like that. Elisabeth was a very great lady. I wrote Romy that Elisabeth had suggested I get in touch.'

'And she invited you to La Galère with all that bougainvillea and the blue, blue sea.'

'Right.'

'And she said she'd like you to handle her career even though you had no experience.'

'She took a bit of persuading. And I'd had *some* experience.'

'As a teenager.'

'The idea of young blood attracted her. She'd got a stuffy old agent she'd had for years. Now, may I go to Paris?' She still wasn't satisfied. 'Sal, you're a gorgeous girl, the colour in my life,' he said and kissed her. 'I don't want you worrying about Romy, because I'm crazy about you.'

'You're going to make me a star?' she asked sarcastically, but smiling now.

'You are a star, darling,' he said. 'My star.' He kissed her again. 'Friday,' he said and hurried out of the office.

3

At first it was pretty well like their previous reunions in Paris: very easy almost at once, as though sixteen years couldn't have flashed by leaving them all in their mid-thirties – the age Elisabeth had been when she had seemed so knowledgeable and wise. It was only when Duncan arrived that everything changed.

They were drinking champagne in Sonya's fabulous apartment in the Palais Royal, with its split-level sitting room and its windows overlooking the Palais Gardens. As always, they would be dining at L'Ambroisie in the Place des Vosges, where they had celebrated the night they 'liberated' Paris – though the menu was more elaborate now.

Duncan was late, but even before he came Charlie felt again the uneasiness that had dogged him a little ever since his plane had landed. For a moment, he stood with his back to the window and watched the other three. Leah, a trifle thin, as though she was living on her nerves, was eagerly explaining something to the others. With maturity she had lost the look of a startled fawn, but the dark haunting beauty had remained. Max, with more weight now but still lugubrious, deadpan, still holding his body motionless as he spoke so fluently; Sonya, elegant, maybe a little packaged, but with the kind of presence Elisabeth had displayed. Everyone looked up when she walked into a restaurant.

Leah saw Charlie watching and smiled. He raised his champagne glass to her and sipped a silent toast, then wandered over to them.

'I was just saying what Hugo did yesterday,' she said. 'Pretended he didn't mind me coming, even rushed me off to catch the plane – then called me back to deal with a huge changed order that I found he'd known about all day. He didn't think I could cope with it in time to be here. Isn't that unbelievable?'

Charlie laughed. 'Devious. But you're here, so it obviously didn't work.'

A childish grin was on her face. 'It'd take more than that to keep me away,' she said.

'You always did have everyone fooled, honey. That quiet, little-girl look. Seems Hugo still doesn't realise who he's got. Not that I blame him. He resents what he can't share. Philana doesn't like it either.'

'Sally's the same,' Max put in, his face jowly and immobile. 'Romy bothers her, but she can't figure out why.'

'I suppose we're a bit like a family,' Sonya said, 'with the same kind of secret language. Instead of a common childhood, we've got an experience.'

The doorbell shrilled and Sonya left the room. Then Duncan stood there, like a friendly giant, with huge shoulders, huge head. He kissed the women, embraced the men. 'A bit held up this morning,' he apologised. 'Contretemps with Annette on the gallops. Got a good colt, but he's not been working as well as he should. Big race next week. How can I waste my time in Paris? she asks. Then, would you believe it, there's a call from Prince Khalid's racing manager. His Royal Highness will be in Newmarket tomorrow and desires to review plans for his horses. Annette's delighted. Now, she says, you really can't go, can you? Ah, thank you, my love.' He took the glass of champagne Sonya handed him. 'Boy, do I need this!'

'So how come you're here?' asked Sonya.

Duncan sipped the champagne and grinned. 'Nothing was going to stop me coming to Paris.'

'Not even Prince Khalid?' Sonya queried. For Duncan, Elisabeth's friend Prince Khalid had provided the same kind of opportunity that Romy had given Max. The Sheikh's horses were top class, the material of solid winners. Just having some of them, and bringing them on properly, had been enough to ensure that Duncan's stable became one of the biggest in Newmarket.

'Not even Prince Khalid,' Duncan confirmed. 'Anyway Annette's as good as I am. She'll have him eating out of her hand. Are we dining at L'Ambroisie?'

'Of course,' said Sonya.

'The Feuilletés de Truffes?'

'Naturally.'

Duncan beamed and put his arm round her waist. 'Amazing

how close we always feel – as though we'd only left the Massif a week ago.'

The look of pleasure faded from his face. 'You know, something disturbing happened last week. I lunched at the Special Forces Club, sat next to Steve Swinburne. He told me about Elisabeth's daughter, Nicole. Things haven't gone well for her. Her father died five years ago – bankrupt.'

'Bankrupt?' said Max. 'He was a banker. Whoever heard of a bankrupt banker?'

Duncan shrugged. 'He made some mistakes. It can happen to bankers, too.'

'How old would Nicole be now?' asked Leah.

'She was four at the time,' Sonya answered, 'so she must be about twenty.'

For Charlie, the revelation came as a shock, though later he wondered at the force of his reaction. He had heard a lot about the child from Elisabeth, knew she had lived with her grandmother in Annecy – under an assumed name and a cover story that wasn't good enough, it seemed, since the Gestapo had taken her. She'd been freed, they heard, once she had no further value as a hostage. But Charlie had never thought of her as grown-up, still seeing her as a four-year-old, as though she were in a timewarp.

The thought of her as a woman disturbed him. His uneasiness became anxiety. 'Did Swinburne say where she was living?' he asked carefully. Swinburne had been one of their section officers in London.

'Not exactly,' Duncan answered. 'He'd heard she was working as a waitress in a café in the Boulevard Saint-Germain.'

'A waitress!' echoed Sonya. 'Elisabeth's daughter?'

'Did he say which one?' queried Charlie. The Boulevard Saint-Germain was a Left Bank centre of intellectuals and artists and there were many cafés.

Duncan shook his head. 'I think he'd have known if it was Les Deux Magots,' he said, naming the most famous.

'We'll find her,' said Sonya, 'and see what's needed. I'll get someone on to it first thing in the morning. Now we'd better be moving or we'll be late for our table.'

Four

It was past two o'clock in the morning, and many tables in the café were now unoccupied as Charlie watched Elisabeth's daughter. The experience astonished him, evoking a mixture of acute emotion and sheer wonder. It was like seeing Elisabeth as a girl of twenty.

Enough people still lingered to give life to the place – the hum of conversation, the odd burst of laughter, waitresses moving about with trays. There was the smell of coffee, cigarette smoke. Charlie savoured it all as he sat engrossed by the girl.

After dinner, he had gone back with the others to Sonya's apartment and talked for an hour or so before the party ended with plans to meet for lunch.

Sonya had noticed Charlie's preoccupation. 'Don't worry,' she said as he left, 'we'll find her fast enough tomorrow.'

But he wasn't willing to wait. Also he felt a strange need to meet the girl first on his own. Elisabeth was his. He needed to share her with the others, for they gave substance to his memories. But she didn't haunt them as she haunted him. They were bonded by her, but she didn't wake them up at night.

He hadn't planned to go to the Boulevard Saint-Germain. But as he strolled towards his hotel, he saw a cruising cab and stopped it more by instinct than design.

The search wasn't easy. He asked for her at seven cafés, to be met each time with a shake of a head. As he entered the eighth, he was starting to wonder if the rumour had been unfounded.

A waiter greeted him and Charlie was just about to ask the usual question when he saw her. There were no doubts, for the likeness to Elisabeth was too marked. She was serving a table at the back of the café. Deliberately, he chose a place nearby.

She approached him, an order pad in her hand, and he found himself looking up into Elisabeth's eyes – deep brown, speckled, with the contours of large almonds, set slightly askew. She was aware of his study, but clearly it wasn't unusual. Men often studied her. Her tone was sharp only when she had to repeat her question: what could she get him? It was late. She wished they would all go home. A wisp of hair had escaped across her forehead and she brushed at it with the back of the hand that held the pencil. Her face was a trifle angular like her mother's, with the same high cheekbones.

Then suddenly the girl smiled – displaying a look of friendly but cynical amusement that he recognised. She had rendered him speechless, it seemed. What did he want to drink? Please, monsieur, a girl has things to do. A cognac? Of course.

After she set the glass before him, he just watched her – serving customers, swopping comments with the other staff, often highlighted by a laugh. She looked younger than twenty, Charlie decided. The girl had small features, sharply formed as though they were crafted in porcelain, with a quick smile that lit up her face.

At last he signalled to her and she came over to him, assuming he wanted his bill. 'I wish to ask a personal question, mademoiselle,' Charlie ventured as he took out his wallet. 'I'm looking for a girl named Nicole Ferrier and I think you may be her. Am I correct?'

He saw her alarm. Who was asking? The police perhaps? What had she done? He smiled to reassure her. 'I knew Nicole's mother,' he said. 'I served with her in the Resistance. You're very like her.'

She was giving nothing away – no sign of emotion at the mention of her mother. She just studied him without speaking. 'The Resistance?' she said. 'But you're not French, monsieur.'

He nodded with a smile. 'I'm American. We worked with the Resistance. Surely you knew that, mademoiselle.'

She knew well enough. She just wanted him to talk while she absorbed what he had said. There was an odd challenge in her eyes, in her stance. She was holding herself upright, her head high, as though about to make a public declaration. 'She was killed,' she said.

He nodded. 'I was with her.'

This was a shock for her. 'When she died?' she asked.

'Yes.'

A suspicion of tears, cleared quickly, again with the back of her hand. 'I've met no one before who was with her, monsieur,' she said.

'Then I think we should have a talk, don't you?' Charlie suggested. 'What time do you finish here?'

She glanced at a clock on the wall. 'I could probably leave in a minute. We're not busy. I'll ask the *patron*.'

'Is there somewhere we could go?'

She shrugged. 'My room.' She saw his expression and giggled. 'A bench on the Quai? It'll be chilly at this time of night.'

Charlie handed her a ten-franc note from his wallet to pay for his cognac. 'Go and ask the *patron*,' he said.

2

Her room was small and rather shabby, with peeling wallpaper and chipped paintwork. It was above a shop on the third floor of an old building in the Rue Mouffetard, about five minutes' walk from the café, and reached by an uncarpeted staircase that smelt faintly of urine. There was a hand basin, a bidet and a two-ring cooker; also a single bed, a chair with frayed arms of red moquette, and a chest of drawers on which were three photographs in ornate silver frames.

The girl started to make coffee, gesturing with her hand at the pictures. Charlie studied them, aware that she was observing him. Two of them featured Elisabeth in family groups, with a man who Charlie guessed was Nicole's father and an old lady, presumably her grandmother. One, though, was a portrait of Elisabeth in her late teens that could have been Nicole now. He glanced at her.

'She was like me wasn't she?' said Nicole.

'You could almost be twins,' he agreed.

'Did you think her pretty?'

'Pretty?' He smiled. 'She was the most attractive woman I'd ever met. Even after an all-night mission, she could look quite stunning. She did so much for us, too. Patient, a great listener. Want to know what I think? she'd say. Usually it was just common sense, but basic. She was about thirty-five then. Years older than any of us. Especially me. I was just a kid.'

She turned with two mugs in her hand. 'A kid like me?' she asked with a bright smile.

'About the same age as you,' he agreed, 'but I was younger in myself, I guess.'

'In yourself?' She wondered what he meant – then shrugged it off. 'You were a boy. Boys are, aren't they? You take the chair.

I'll go over here.' She sat on the bed, with her legs under her, cupping her mug in her hands. 'Please go on,' she said. 'I only just remember her, you know. Vague scenes – like a magic lantern show. Kissing me goodnight before going out to dine with my father. Picnics in the Bois de Boulogne. Vacations at Deauville. Hearing her on the radio sometimes. How had she got in the box? I used to ask. But you knew her well – as a heroine, I mean. She *was* a heroine, wasn't she?'

'She was a heroine all right,' Charlie answered. 'When she arrived we were a bit in awe of her because she was famous. But she was very easy, had us laughing in no time. She was always laughing. Even in action, she'd whisper jokes.'

'She was brave?' The girl's eyes were alight and Charlie sensed her hunger for detail.

'She'd talk of fear,' he went on, 'but she never showed it. She saved my life once.'

'How?' she asked eagerly. 'Tell me about it, monsieur.'

That night was still vivid to him. He and Elisabeth had gone on a simple mission to a village called Saint-Laurent and had run into a unit of Milice, the French political police who worked with the Germans. The Miliciens didn't see Elisabeth, who was passing on orders in a nearby cottage, but they cornered Charlie in some farm buildings. He thought there was a way out between them, but there wasn't. About five men were closing in, taking their time, firing the odd shot to hold him down.

Elisabeth staged a diversion – shooting, then moving position so that it seemed she was one of several. The danger was that there could be other police in the village who would hear the gunfire. But that night they were lucky and the ruse worked. The Miliciens pulled back and Charlie got clear.

He met up with Elisabeth in the forest beyond the village – the Forêt de Côte Belle. 'I do wish you'd take more care, Charlee,' she said in mock rebuke and, embracing him, she kissed him on the mouth. 'Seriously, you had me worried, you know,' she added and kissed him again, more gently, with parted lips. It was the first time she had kissed him like that.

Charlie didn't tell Nicole the last part, but he did speak of the way Elisabeth had always called him Charlee, with the emphasis at the end.

'I think that's a good name, monsieur,' said Nicole.

'Feel free,' Charlie said. 'Use it too.'

She laughed, almost shyly, and shook her head. 'I think not, monsieur.'

'Too soon?'

'Perhaps. And not correct, I think. After all, you're a man of . . .'

Her voice trailed off, leaving the words unspoken – that he was older, more important, merited respect. But he detected an odd note of mockery. 'It's hard, you know,' he went on, 'seeing you as a grown woman. She talked of you often, of course, as a kid of four . . .'

'Maman did?'

'She worried about what would happen to you if she was killed. But she felt a need to fight. She said that you and your grandmother were very close and your father was wealthy, so money wouldn't be a problem.'

'That's amusing,' she said, suddenly bitter. 'That's very amusing, monsieur. You know how he died?'

'I heard something about it.'

'Did you know he'd married again? A young girl – Hortense. Only twenty-two. I always blamed her, but perhaps I was unfair. She liked a good time. What young girl doesn't? But she made him take risks he'd never have taken if he'd still been with my mother. And then . . .' a cynical shrug '. . . well, she liked men – and after the disaster Father wasn't much of a man and there was no good time.'

'You're speaking like your mother – as though you've seen it all. Soon you'll be giving me advice, like she did.'

'I've seen a bit, monsieur,' she said seriously. 'It changed our lives of course – my father's collapse, I mean.'

'You were still living with your grandmother in Annecy?'

She nodded. 'I had to leave school and take a job. In a local café. Then Grandmère died, too. That was a bad business. She left a little money, but not much. Michel said I'd do better in Paris. Michel was the owner of the café. He had friends, he said. So I came to Paris, monsieur.' She gave another wry shrug.

'Does it really have to be "monsieur" all the time?'

She nodded with a little smile. 'Tell me, what do you do? Your profession, I mean.'

'I'm in the shipping business.'

'And you're married, of course, with beautiful young children?'

'Why of course?' he queried.

She giggled. 'You look married, I suppose. What's her name?'

'Philana. I met her through a friend of your mother. Her father has a big shipping business. I joined his company for a while but now I've got my own.'

'So you're rich, monsieur?' she asked, smiling an open challenge. 'You own ships?' Her eyes were wide, but he wasn't sure if she was impressed or laughing at him. There was a worldly air about her, as though she had met rich men before. Also a certain sadness through which the bright humour, so like her mother's, suddenly shone like shafts of sunlight.

'I wouldn't own anything if it hadn't been for Elisabeth. I was pretty ingenuous when we met – wild, too. She taught me to contain the high spirits a little.'

'Tamed you?' the girl mocked. 'That's sad. We should all be a little wild, don't you think, monsieur?'

'Charlie, please,' he said gently. 'I'm the age your mother was then. I called *her* Elisabeth.'

'You were comrades. That's different.'

'I hope you and I are going to be comrades.'

She studied him over the rim of her mug, a smile near. 'And what will your wife say to that?' she taunted softly. 'What will you tell her? "I found this pretty young comrade in the Boulevard Saint-Germain." Is that what you'll say . . . Charlee?' She lobbed his name at him, pronouncing it as her mother had but lingering on it, making the tone sensuous and mocking.

He didn't answer her. 'Well?' she demanded. 'Is that what you'll tell your wife?'

'What happened when you came to Paris?' he asked.

'Let's talk about my mother. Isn't that why you're here?'

'I'm here because I wanted to meet you.'

'That was a surprise for you, I think.' The teasing note had gone from her voice and the pain was naked. Slowly her eyes swept over him in a kind of reappraisal, as if she had just started to see him against the setting of her shabby little room – a man from her mother's glamorous world. She seemed to be noting his clothes – the mohair suit, the hand-made shoes, the silk shirt, the gold cufflinks.

'The links were a gift from your wife?' she queried. 'Last birthday perhaps?'

He nodded and she laughed. 'You see I don't miss much, do I?'

'I'm sorry to be a bit dressed up,' he apologised, 'but I've been out to a rather ritzy dinner. I only heard about you tonight.'

She was impressed. 'You came to find me so soon? I'm flattered, monsieur. Was it a big shock?'

'Why should it be a shock?'

'Why, to find your Elisabeth's daughter in a café, of course. Would Maman have been shocked?'

'She'd have hoped for something more for you, as I do.'

For a second, a look of despair appeared in her eyes. 'I'm sorry to disappoint you,' she said with a child's sulky sharpness.

'You haven't,' he said. 'I'm glad to find you.'

She wasn't reassured. 'Listen, Nicole,' he said, 'your mother changed my life. I'd like to repay her. So would the others who were with us. We're in a position to help – to make things easier for you perhaps, give you a bit more scope to do what you want.'

She was gazing at him, the caution clear in those brown eyes that disturbed him so much. She had heard this kind of talk before and she knew where it led. Not from men who had known her mother, though. Suddenly the bright childish smile illuminated her face again. 'Sorry,' she said, 'if I was a little . . . Well, you know. Some more coffee?' she asked, adding carefully: 'Charlee?'

It was a gesture of peace and he laughed. 'It's not so hard, you see.'

'Well, you said we were comrades, didn't you?' she asserted, leaping from the bed and going over to the cooker. 'Like you were with my mother.' She was filling his cup from a jug as she whispered: 'Even if you won't tell your wife.'

'I didn't say I wouldn't tell my wife.'

She giggled again like a schoolgirl, refilled her own mug and got back on the bed. 'I know a bit about husbands, you know,' she said. 'You'll tell your wife I'm a dull, plain girl you've got to help because of my mother. Isn't that right?'

'Let's leave my wife out of it, Nicole,' he countered gently. 'Truly that's none of your goddamned business, is it?'

'Will you say I looked like my mother? That you sat here alone with me in my room at three o'clock in the morning?'

'May we please come back to the point?' he said.

'The debt to my mother?' The mocking note was back. 'Is that my goddamned business?'

34

'Of course.'

Suddenly she looked vulnerable again. Her moods were mercurial. 'All right, monsieur . . .' she began – then saw his look and relented. 'OK, Charlee,' she said softly, 'what are you going to do for me?'

Charlie glanced round the room. 'Well for starters some money would come in handy, wouldn't it? You'd like an apartment of your own, I expect.'

She stared at him in total disbelief. 'Are you offering to rent an apartment for me?' she demanded at last.

'We won't rent, I don't think. We'll buy so that you've got something behind you.'

'Are you serious, monsieur? It's not a test to see what I'll say?'

He shook his head. 'Then you'll need to furnish it, won't you? Get some clothes too maybe. I'm not sure yet how we'll arrange matters. Some sort of trust fund, I expect.'

Nicole was finding it hard to absorb.

'You'll want to think about a new kind of job,' said Charlie, 'but there's plenty of time for that. So what do you say?'

She shook her head. 'It's hard to believe – except that you knew my mother. I believe that. Your name begins with C. Do any of the others?'

He had to think. 'No, none of them.'

'Well, that settles it then.'

'Settles what?'

'One day I may tell you,' she teased.

He eyed her uncertainly. 'Look,' he said, 'I'm lunching with the others in a few hours. Why don't you join us?'

She was startled. 'Your comrades? Do I have to?' she asked anxiously.

He was surprised. 'Don't you want to? They served with your mother, too. They'd love to meet you.'

'Can't I just talk to you for now . . . Charlee?' She added his name persuasively.

He felt contrite. He had been insensitive. 'Maybe I have taken you a little by storm,' he agreed.

She smiled at him softly. 'You understand, I think.'

'Some of it anyway. After all, you've had a very hard childhood. First the Gestapo. Then – '

'The Gestapo?' she asked in surprise.

'You were taken by the Gestapo, weren't you? When you were small.'

She was looking at him in amazement. 'Whatever made you think that?' she asked.

'We were told,' Charlie answered. 'Perhaps you put it out of your mind. Children do that sometimes with bad experiences.'

She laughed. 'I'd remember that, I can promise you. Who could have told you such a thing?'

'I'm not sure,' he said. 'It probably came in by radio. Or maybe Resistance sources.'

'Well, it wasn't true.' She looked concerned. 'Charlee, do you feel all right?'

It had been a day of surprises, but Nicole's words – or rather what lay behind them – shattered him. 'It's late,' he said, 'I'd better get back to my hotel.'

He got up and she uncurled herself from the bed. 'Am I going to see you again soon?' she asked.

'Tomorrow,' he suggested. 'Today, I should say, since it's almost dawn. What time will you be free?'

'It's my day off, so any time.'

'Then we'll have dinner,' he said. 'I'll collect you at seven.'

She smiled at him. 'Thank you for coming to find me, Charlee,' she said and kissed him gently on the cheek.

It was a fine cold night, but he decided to walk for a while. He needed to think out the repercussions of what she had told him. For if Nicole hadn't been taken by the Gestapo, there was no reason for Elisabeth to have been 'turned' – and that meant he'd killed her for nothing.

As he crossed the river by way of the Ile de la Cité, the sky was lightening to the east beyond the dark towers of Notre Dame. The sense of horror, blunted by shock at first, was enveloping him slowly, chilling him like a dank mist. What in God's name had he done all those years ago? What could he do now to assuage it? He could change nothing. Yet nothing was the same any longer. Suddenly, Charlie felt very scared.

Five

After Charlie told them about the girl, none of them said anything for a few moments. He had arrived late and they had all been there waiting for him at the fish restaurant called Les Ecrevisses near the big market of Les Halles.

The room was hot and crowded, with the hubbub of many voices rising and falling like waves, and a strong aroma of hot fish spiced with sauces.

They already knew that Charlie had found Nicole, because he'd called Sonya earlier that morning, and they were avid to hear about her. What was she like? How had he found her? Did she remember much of her mother?

He answered them as well as he could, while sampling the Fruits de Mer for which the place was famous. But as he told the story, he sensed a subtle change of mood. They were regarding him with a kind of quizzical concern – each one of them, he noted, as he looked at them in turn.

He had realised, of course, that his lone trawl through the cafés of Saint-Germain in the middle of the night might cause surprise; but he related what had happened as factually as he could, describing the girl and what she had told him. Everything, in short. Well, everything except her final revelation. Horrific as it was, that needed more time.

'So we've got to do something, haven't we?' he ended. 'The question is, what?'

He looked around the table, aware that he hadn't convinced them – or, at least, that he had left them with a feeling there was something still unsaid. He felt a need to go on – the mistake they had all been warned to avoid under interrogation. Wait for the questions. 'I mean,' he added, 'you should just see her tacky little room. Jesus, if Elisabeth had seen it, she'd have flipped her lid!'

Duncan, sitting at the head of the table, was studying him closely. He looked older than his age now, greying, his face fleshier.

'Charlie,' he said at last, 'what exactly do you expect of this girl? To speak plainly, do you plan to sleep with her?'

The blunt question took Charlie by surprise. It wasn't good-natured ribbing.

'Perhaps he already did,' Max suggested in his idle, acid way.

'You serious, Duncan?' Charlie asked quietly.

Duncan nodded his big head. 'I speak as a friend, Charlie,' he answered.

'Then you're coming on a bit heavy, aren't you? For Christ's sake, she's only twenty – and looks less.'

'So were you when you slept with Elisabeth,' said Duncan, his eyes serious. 'And you haven't been describing a kid, though you were trying to.'

Charlie was suddenly uncertain. He had had hardly any sleep after the huge shock of the previous night. And Duncan was right. Nicole was no innocent. There had almost certainly been men in her life. She'd had to survive, hadn't she? But it had seemed easier to speak of her as though she were a child.

He looked away for a moment, needing a respite. At the next table a middle-aged man and a young blonde were spooning bouillabaisse into their mouths – clumsily, bits of fish and mussels splashing back into the soup. He was talking too loudly about his Maserati, boring the girl.

'What I mean,' Duncan was saying, 'is that we all know how much Elisabeth meant to you. That was a very big thing for you at a very tender age – all the more so, perhaps, because it ended in tragedy. Do you see what I'm getting at?'

'Not exactly,' he answered, 'but give me time.'

'Well, it's obvious, isn't it?' Leah remarked.

Again, Charlie glanced at each of them in turn. It was obvious to them, too.

'Why haven't you brought her here today?' demanded Max.

'I wanted to,' Charlie answered. 'But she said she'd rather meet you singly.' He could see they didn't believe him. They thought he was keeping her to himself.

'What Duncan means,' said Sonya, 'is that you may be tempted to relive what you had with Elisabeth through Nicole, especially since she looks so like her.'

Charlie was shocked. For a few seconds he stared at her angrily. 'You know, that's quite crazy,' he said. 'Duncan, is that what you're accusing me of?'

'Accusing?' Duncan queried. 'That's rather strong, isn't it? I just want you to see things straight. I'm fond of you, as we all are, and I don't want you messing up your life – certainly not for the wrong reason.'

Charlie shook his head, slightly bewildered. 'Let's get this straight. You're saying I'm haring after some kind of lost dream, right? OK, I was mad about Elisabeth. OK, maybe I still am. So do you really think I'd just use her daughter for a self-indulgent fling?'

'I didn't say that,' Duncan insisted. 'I don't know the girl. I'm sure she's charming. But what we're anxious about is bigger – '

'Bigger?' Charlie cut in. 'How can it be bigger? Haven't I made it clear? The girl's living under dreadful conditions . . . Well, considering who she is.'

'You've made it clear, and we'll deal with it.'

'Buy her off, you mean?' said Charlie.

Duncan gave one of his big, tolerant shrugs. 'Not just with money. We'll help the girl, but just at present it's you we're anxious about.'

'Me?' Charlie demanded. 'You think she doesn't matter? Bit of cash, the odd intro, perhaps a lunch to sort out her problems. You know what these kids are. Oh, sorry,' he added, recalling Duncan's assertion, 'she's not a kid, is she? She's a tart now.'

'I wish you wouldn't put words into my mouth,' said Duncan.

'It's what you meant, isn't it? For Christ's sake, I didn't pick her up in a bar. This is Elisabeth's daughter you're talking about. Just imagine it was one of those boys of yours, Duncan. If Elisabeth hadn't died, Nicole would have had a wonderful life – proper schooling, money, clothes, parties, classy people, a fast car, the choice of boyfriends – and I'm telling you, with her looks the cream of Paris would have been clamouring for her. Whatever career she wanted, she'd have had a great start – like all our kids. And why hasn't she got that? Because *we*, the five of us enjoying this expensive lunch, because *we* held a ballot – and then one of us shot Elisabeth to death.'

It was the first time the truth had ever been spoken aloud – and Charlie felt a certain satisfaction from the shock on all their faces. He lifted his glass and sipped the ice-cold Meursault.

'Charlie,' said Duncan gently, 'we'll see the girl's set up properly. But I must insist on this: Elisabeth died under the heaviest fire we'd ever encountered. You can't know that one of us killed her.'

Charlie gave a short laugh. 'That's the line we've always

kidded ourselves with, isn't it? But I saw her die. I know who killed her.'

'How can you be certain?' Duncan demanded. 'For God's sake, man, metal was coming at us like hail.'

'You want me to lay it out?' challenged Charlie.

But Duncan didn't want that. He shook his head with a sigh. 'There's no point. Even if one of us did kill her – and, as we agreed, that was all of us – we were ordered to. We had no choice, did we?' He saw the way Charlie was looking at him. 'Well, did we, Charlie?'

'No, buddy,' Charlie said, so lightly that Duncan suspected sarcasm. 'We agreed what had to be done. But then, of course, we believed she *had* been turned, didn't we?'

'We believed she could have been,' Sonya corrected, 'with the Gestapo taking Nicole.'

'It was a ghastly dilemma,' said Leah.

'But the order was precise,' said Duncan. 'Charlie, what's the point of all this?'

Charlie hesitated. 'Because there's one thing I haven't told you,' he went on. 'According to Nicole, the Gestapo never took her.'

'What?' exclaimed Sonya in horrified astonishment. 'Are you sure?'

'Positive,' Charlie replied.

'Charlie, there must be some mistake – surely?' Leah put in.

'Oh, there was, Leah. We made it.'

'Perhaps she wasn't telling the truth,' suggested Max.

Charlie shook his head. 'She was telling the truth all right.' He looked around the restaurant, where a dish cost more than Nicole earned in a week, and saw the waiter approaching them. 'Ah,' he declared, the sarcasm unconcealed now, 'here's the Lobster Thermidor!' He leaned back in his chair as the great silver salver of half-lobsters was placed on the serving table beside them, the smell strong of hot brandy and mustard sauce.

Duncan was sitting solidly in his chair, staring at Charlie grimly. 'It still makes no difference, you know,' he said. 'The order was clear.' But it did make a difference. It made a difference to each of them – as Charlie had known it would.

Six

The evening was warmer and the crowds were out on the streets as the cab headed for the Seine. It skirted the Place de la Concorde, running alongside the Jardin de Paris where the chestnuts were still pink with blossom. Ahead to the west, high on the skyline, the sun was setting behind the Arc de Triomphe, and Charlie thought how much he loved Elisabeth's city.

For a moment, the turmoil that had racked him during the last few hours was calmed – like the river, he thought, as they crossed the bridge to the Left Bank. For the surface was like glass. A tug, with barges behind, was cutting ripples in the water, which spread to the banks in undisturbed, developing patterns.

Duncan's question had stayed with him, though. What did he expect of the girl? As they got up to leave the restaurant, Duncan had said to him quietly: 'Watch your step, pal. Remember, it's rough enough being in love with women who are alive,' and they had both laughed, a trifle uneasily.

The cab drew up on the cobbles of the Rue Mouffetard outside the ground floor shop and, as he stepped on to the pavement, he heard her call from above him: 'Monsieur Charlee.' He looked up and saw her waving from the third-floor window of the old building. 'I'm on my way down,' she shouted.

She appeared in the entrance wearing a beige coat. 'Good evening, Monsieur Charlee,' she said with a bright smile.

'So I've a new name now, have I?' he asked as he opened the cab door for her.

'Don't you think it's good?' she said, settling into a corner. 'Friendly, but with respect for a man of . . . well, of importance.' Her eyes were alight with a provocative smile.

'I'm not sure I want to be important.'

Her laugh rang out, disturbing in the memories it stirred. 'We'll see. Try it for size, eh?'

The cab came to a halt at the restaurant where Charlie had booked a table. He had chosen it because it was not too fashionable, for clearly her wardrobe would be limited; so he got a surprise when she took off her coat. Her dress would have knocked their eyes out even at Les Ambassadeurs – in black silk, beautifully cut, with a beaded bodice and a full skirt, costing every cent of a thousand dollars. 'Do you like it?' she asked as they were shown to their table.

'You look wonderful,' he answered.

'But too smart for here, yes?' She giggled. 'I don't care. I wanted you to see me looking like . . . to be a girl you'd be proud to be with.'

'Well, you got what you wanted,' he said. 'You're the belle of the ball.'

'Now you're wondering who bought it for me, aren't you?' She laughed. 'You think it's my rich admirer, yes?'

'Do you have a rich admirer?'

'Of course I've a rich admirer,' she said, watching him with amused brown eyes, so like Elisabeth's. 'You haven't guessed, have you? This was Maman's dress, look!' She took from her bag a press photograph, which she laid triumphantly before him on the table. And there, indeed, was Elisabeth in the dress.

Just for a moment he was breathless, felt the familiar spasm of pain in the stomach. The girl saw at once that she had upset him. 'I thought you'd like it,' she said with slightly hurt surprise. 'Perhaps that I'd be . . . well, the next best thing to her, you know. We do look a bit alike in it, don't we?'

He looked at her as she awaited his response, seeming so fragile, so eager to please, so absurdly young in a dress that was made for a mature woman. 'It's still in fashion isn't it?' she asked anxiously. 'Even though it's old?'

'It surely is,' he agreed. It was, too, being classic in design.

'That's because it was altered by Clothilde. She's my friend who's very clever at such things. Look how she's changed it.' She pointed at her mother in the dress.

Again he examined the picture – taken, he guessed, by a press photographer at a society function. It showed Elisabeth full length against the background of a big room, that was ornate and luxurious. There was a pillar, part of a marble fireplace, elaborately decorated, and people in the background. A man was beside her, but all that could be seen of him was an elbow and his hip.

'You see how Clothilde's dropped the length of the skirt?' said Nicole, standing up so that he could compare her with the picture.

'She's done it well,' said Charlie. 'Would that have been your father beside her?'

She turned the picture towards her. 'No,' she said. 'This man's tall. Father wasn't tall. But the dress suits me, doesn't it? Not too . . . well, too sophisticated for my age? I look chic, yes?'

'You look chic,' he assured her. 'But then you'd look chic in anything – as your mother did.'

She studied him anxiously, sensing he was speaking to please her. 'I wish I'd been older when she died,' she said. 'Then I'd have known her better.' The sadness was bared for a second. 'So you must make up for it, you see,' she added brightly. 'I love to hear you speak of her. When will you be going home to America?'

'In a week or so, I guess.'

She was shocked. 'So soon? I thought we'd have longer.'

'It's later than I planned. I'm staying on to get things settled for you before I go.' He smiled at her. 'But I'll be back. Meanwhile, Sonya's here.'

'Of course, you met them today, didn't you?' she said eagerly. 'Did you tell them about me, that I looked like their Elisabeth?'

'Naturally.'

'Were they worried for you – here in Paris without your wife? I know what they said. Charlee, you must be careful. You know what these Parisienne girls are like. Didn't they say that?'

He shook his head. 'They know I'm happily married.' It sounded priggish. He forced a casual smile. 'I told them how young you are.' After that harrowing lunch he sounded unconvincing. 'We made some plans for you,' he went on rather too briskly. 'You and I must see a lawyer tomorrow. Have you thought at all about what you might like to do now – a new career of some kind?'

She shook her head a trifle glumly. 'Maybe I should go on as I am – for a while, anyway. I've got some friends. Clothilde especially. She works in the café too.'

'And then there's your rich admirer,' he prompted.

'Yes, there's Jean-Paul. You must meet him, but I don't think you'll like him. Perhaps he won't like you either.'

'Then don't introduce us. But I'm sure you should think beyond being a waitress. Doesn't Jean-Paul?'

'We haven't discussed it,' she answered offhandedly.

'There's a great big world out there, you know – as your mother said to me once. That was before she took me in hand.'

Nicole laughed. 'How did she do that?'

'Well, I was pretty raw when I met her, but she figured I'd got potential.'

He thought back to the summer afternoon they had spent lying in the grass on a hill overlooking Saint-Martin, the village they had chosen for their base. Behind them, the mountains formed a high barrier of rock, like a gigantic crust. In the distance facing them was the dark mass of virgin forest.

Elisabeth was lying on her stomach looking at him as he sat beside her. 'You know, Charlee,' she said, 'you underrate yourself. You pretend not to. You take absurd risks trying to convince yourself but you don't need to. You've got the quality, but it's never been tested at home and it's hard to see over the hill. But there's a great big world out there, you know. You can go far, mon chéri.'

'You look lovely lying there,' he said.

Elisabeth ignored the look in his eyes. 'I wouldn't encourage you,' she continued, 'if I wasn't certain. It doesn't help to aim beyond your ability. But I *am* certain, Charlee.'

He stretched out beside her and moved his hand beneath her skirt. Her legs were bare and he stroked the back of her thighs in sweeps that took his hand higher each time, finally reaching between her legs.

'Have you been listening to what I said?' she asked, arching her body slightly to his hand.

'Every word,' he answered; 'about the great big world out there.'

'I mean it,' she said. Then, with a movement that was unhurried, she turned over to face him and began to undo his belt.

'What sort of things did she teach you?' asked Nicole.

'She talked about her life. She told me about books, art, philosophy, politics. Just some of the theories. Enough to discuss them a bit if I had to. Sartre, Freud, Marx. I knew the causes of the First World War. I could trace the revolutionary links to Stalin from eighteenth-century America. She tutored me on what to do in grand company. More important, she taught me about people – especially those with power.'

'What sort of things?' asked Nicole.

'Oh, simple things that were obvious, though they didn't seem it. Never forget, she said: important men never tire of hearing they're important. Beautiful women need constant reminders of their beauty. Truth can be dangerous. If someone asks you to be honest with them, be sure they want an honest answer.'

'Maman said such things?' Nicole asked in disbelief. 'I always thought she was a romantic.'

'She was a romantic all right,' Charlie insisted.

That afternoon on the hill above Saint-Martin came back to him again. 'Will you think of this, Charlee, in twenty years' time?' Elisabeth had asked. 'Making love lazily in the grass. Will you think: What was the name of that girl? The one who wore silk knickers even in the war. Elisabeth, was it?'

'I'll never forget you,' he said urgently. 'I'll never stop loving you.'

'You promise?' She laughed. 'Don't worry, I absolve you from it. I'm going to come in a moment, I think, but slowly please, as we tried the other night.'

Nicole was laughing softly. 'You were a long way away, Monsieur Charlee – with my mother I suspect, so I'll forgive you. Were you very much in love with her?'

The sudden, intimate question took him by surprise. 'We all loved her,' he answered carefully.

'Only *you* came searching for me in the middle of the night – and I doubt if I'll see that kind of look in the eyes of the others when they speak of her. At times you seem terribly sad. You're not going to answer my question, are you?'

'Sometimes you ask too many questions.'

She laughed and put out a hand to him. 'Comrade,' she said, 'let's go to my room for coffee. I've something I want to show you.'

2

In the cab, she slipped her hand through his arm. 'It's odd,' she said. 'I never met you before last night, but I feel very easy with you, as though we'd been friends for years.'

She straightened up suddenly, realising they were in the Boulevard Saint Germain, which cuts straight through the Latin Quarter. 'We'll pass the café,' she exclaimed. 'Why don't we stop. You could meet my friend Clothilde. She's pretty, you know. She'd love to meet you.'

The café was home for her, he realised as he followed her. She walked in as though she owned the place, slipped her coat from her shoulders and performed a half-spin in front of Clothilde so that the skirt of her dress swirled round her legs. 'Good, eh? I've been telling Monsieur Charlee how clever you are,' she said.

She conducted him to the bar at the back and introduced him formally to the *patron*, Monsieur Jacques Dupuy, and his wife, who was busy at the cash till. They responded with courtesy, marked by cautious curiosity. 'You were in the Resistance with Nicole's mother?' said Madame. She was a heavy-breasted woman in her fifties with eyes that were very sharp. Not much escaped her, Charlie guessed. 'So you must have a drink with us.'

The *patron* was a well-built man, bald, with a thin moustache, and ample eyebrows that crowned steel-rimmed glasses like the top of a hedge. 'She's a nice girl,' he volunteered quietly as he poured Charlie a cognac. 'Take care of her, won't you, monsieur? She's had a hard time and there are still problems.'

'Her rich admirer, Jean-Paul?' Charlie asked with a smile.

The *patron* raised his generous eyebrows. 'Is that what she told you? He's not exactly an admirer, you know. She used to work for him. You've heard of Jean-Paul Leblum, I expect.'

'I don't recall the name,' said Charlie.

'You will. He owns a magazine, *La Nouvelle Vie*, and a club. He offers a kind of ersatz philosophy – the key is sexual freedom, promiscuity, experiment, and through this what he calls a release of the soul. Give rein to your desires. Control causes repression. It's dangerous nonsense. Without discipline, there's anarchy. But naturally it has an appeal. Leblum has a big house in the Boulevard Raspail, all-night parties, practises what he preaches, full of young girls.'

'You mean Nicole was one of them?'

The *patron* nodded. 'I wouldn't want my daughter mixed up with him. But he seems to have looked after her when no one else would, I'll say that for him. She was in real trouble. But she's no fool, monsieur, for all her silly talk. She could see where it was leading. Then she got talking to Clothilde on a bus and came back here with her. She'd worked in a café before. She needed time to think.'

'She was fortunate to find you, monsieur,' said Charlie, 'And Madame, of course.'

'I don't know how long she'll stay,' the *patron* went on. 'It's probably a bit dull here after Leblum's crowd. His people often come in to talk to her.'

'To persuade her back?'

He shrugged. 'Perhaps. Also, I think he likes to keep in touch with his girls, make sure they're all right.'

The *patron*'s attention was caught by a man who had just entered the café. 'Talk of the devil,' he said. 'That's one of Jean-Paul's people. I suspect she knew he'd be coming in and wanted to show you off – ammunition, perhaps, if you understand me, monsieur. His name's Thierry Mathieu.'

Mathieu was about thirty, fair with a slim but muscular body, and wore expensive casual clothes. He wended his way between the tables with smooth movements of his hips, a boyish smile on his face. He took in Nicole's dress with an approving look. 'That's delightful, darling.' She flaunted a friendly little curtsey that was marked by challenge. 'Things are going well for you, I see. Jean-Paul will be pleased.' There was no sarcasm. Jean-Paul *would* be pleased, it seemed.

Nicole introduced him to Charlie and he was cordial. 'A great pleasure to meet you, monsieur. You've been looking after our Nikki here?'

'Not *your* Nikki,' she corrected.

'Forgive me,' he said, 'but habit dies hard.' He glanced at Charlie. 'We're very fond of her. May I buy you a drink, monsieur?'

'That's kind of you,' Charlie responded carefully, 'but we only came in to meet the *patron* and Madame.'

'Just five minutes,' Mathieu urged.

Charlie looked enquiringly at Nicole. 'A very quick one,' she agreed.

'You're English, monsieur?' Mathieu asked as they sat down at a table. 'No, American, I'd guess. Do you live in Paris or are you visiting? Visiting, I'd say.'

'Can you tell the difference?' asked Charlie.

Mathieu laughed. 'One gets to know, dealing with people, doesn't one, Nicole?'

'If you say so,' she answered.

'Always careful, this one,' Mathieu said to Charlie with a smile. 'Not one of the giddy kids. Got a head on her shoulders. That's why we miss her. Jean-Paul would like to see you,' he told her.

'So you said last week,' she answered.

'Why don't you bring Monsieur Dawson to the club one night? You're not leaving Paris too soon, I trust, monsieur?'

'I'm not sure of my plans,' Charlie said.

'You'll stay a few days, I'll bet,' he said confidently. 'You direct a company, monsieur?'

'Why ask when you know?' said Charlie.

'Now you're teasing me.' Mathieu's eyes glittered. 'Well, Nicole, do I tell Jean-Paul you'll be coming?'

She shrugged, her reluctance evident. 'Perhaps, if Monsieur Charlee has time.'

Mathieu stood up and shook hands with Charlie. 'It's been a pleasure, monsieur. I look forward to seeing you.' And with a wave at the *patron* he strolled out of the café.

'Jean-Paul's not really my admirer now,' Nicole said as she and Charlie walked back to the Rue Mouffetard.

'I'm relieved to hear that,' said Charlie.

'I've known him a long time, though. He's been good to me at times.'

'At times?'

'Well, not always, but no man's perfect, is he?'

Charlie didn't press her, but Jean-Paul worried him a little. 'What is it you wanted to show me?' he asked.

She laughed and he wished she didn't laugh so like her mother. 'Something that'll interest you,' she said.

3

As she made coffee, she said casually: 'Open the bottom drawer of the chest.'

'What's in there?' he asked cautiously.

'Open it and you'll see won't you?'

He had guessed it concerned Elisabeth, but opening the drawer was a shock. For there, carefully arranged on black velvet, as though in a glass case, were some of Elisabeth's possessions: a silver compact, a cigarette case, three brooches, the red scarf he remembered, a string of pearls, a couple of rings, the beret she'd been wearing when she died, and a blue notebook that he recognised since he had often seen her writing notes in it – for a novel, she said.

It was a strange collection, displayed as it was, suggesting more than pride in a heroine mother. There was a note of homage too.

He glanced at Nicole, as though seeking her permission, and picked up the blue book, thumbing through the pages. Seeing the writing in Elisabeth's hand gave him an odd sensation – as though she was still living. But she hadn't told him the truth. It was a diary.

He was mentioned quite often, always by his initial, which explained Nicole's enquiry of the previous night.

C is learning fast . . . C was in an odd mood today . . . What am I doing with C? He's a baby. Who would ever have believed I'd have a lover of twenty? What do you talk about with a boy of that age – the son of a shop assistant? That's what Hélène and Lucille and my other friends would say. Yet he's bright, and I know I'm good for him, that I'm preparing him. And he only has to look at me and I start to ache for him.

Charlie looked at Nicole. 'You've read this, I presume?'
She nodded, her expression bland.
'So you knew the answer to your question in the restaurant.'
She shook her head. 'It's her diary – not yours.'
He chose another page at random.

Maybe it's because C makes me laugh. I told him that was how to seduce women – make them laugh. Of course he's mad. Yesterday they caught us at a bridge over the Isère. So there we were lying in cover, shooting back and wondering how in hell we were going to get out of it. 'Jesus, it's getting hot,' C said. 'I feel like a swim.' And he just dived into the river with bullets hitting the water all round him. God knows how he wasn't killed.

It took the heat off the rest of us and we were able to cross later under cover of darkness. We found him reading a book. 'Didn't you guys know dinner was at eight?' he asked.

Charlie turned on a few pages.

I couldn't believe it – not even of C. He arrived today on a horse of all things, galloping round and round the cottage. 'Your champion, my lady,' he said reining up in front of me. 'What dragons can I slay to prove my love?'

49

It was no ordinary horse. It had been stolen from the German Commandant in Romans – planned by one of those mad cavalry officers who have escaped here. I didn't know he could even ride. Duncan was furious because of the danger of reprisals. But, as C said, a horse could hardly provoke them more than killing Germans.

Heard from W today. He was in Paris. Made me sad.

Charlie turned to Nicole. 'Who's W?' he asked.

'I don't know,' she answered. 'I thought *you* might.'

He flicked through the pages to the last entry, written the day before Elisabeth died.

I have a premonition that tomorrow may be the last time, though I've felt it before and it wasn't. Would death be so awful? The others feel it too, I think. They're all behaving oddly, seeming to look after me as though I was ninety. C's like I've never seen him before – very loving one moment and totally wrapped up in himself the next.

Charlie remembered that last night. The occasion had proved too much for him. 'First time it's happened to me, isn't it?' he had said to her, trying to make light of it.

'Won't be the last,' she answered. 'Pretend I'm someone else. A chorus girl from the Folies Bergère.'

She was being playful to relax him. Jesus, how could they make jokes? 'I don't want anyone else,' he said urgently and hugged her – which had made it all right. Well, up to a point. The shadow had remained. No flying like the eagles, as she liked to put it. How could they fly? She was doomed – as, in a sense, he was himself.

Nicole was watching him anxiously. 'Perhaps I shouldn't have let you see it,' she said.

'I'm glad you did.'

She poured coffee into two mugs, then turned. 'That same look's back on your face,' she said. 'You really did love her, didn't you?' She looked troubled, clearly needing to assuage his pain. 'Do you think she'd mind if I kissed you?'

'Elisabeth?' he asked surprised. 'I doubt it, but Philana would.'

'Well, we won't tell Philana,' she said firmly. She leaned forward and put her lips to his. It was a gentle kiss of sympathy, of sharing maybe. But he barely responded and she moved back slightly, studying him with concern. 'It's my eyes, isn't it, being so like hers?'

'It is strange,' he agreed.

'Pretend I am her – just for a moment.' She put her mouth to his again, this time with a touch of passion – which for a few seconds struck a matching note in him, seeding the start of desire. Her arms went round his neck.

It disturbed him and he eased her away, holding her by the shoulders.

She looked up at him, not hurt exactly, but wishing he hadn't. 'Let's have that coffee,' he said.

Without a word she passed him a mug, took one herself and sat on the bed with her legs tucked beneath her. 'We're going to be good comrades, aren't we?' she said brightly. 'You're going to show me the great big world out there, change my life.'

'That's right.'

'So you don't feel so guilty. Why do you feel so guilty, Monsieur Charlee?'

'I don't – just indebted to her. Like the others. We'd all like to do something to repay her – me especially, of course. If you'll let us.'

Her face creased into a grin. 'Oh, I'll let you,' she said. 'You're an odd man, though, Monsieur Charlee. You love your wife, don't you?'

'Is that so odd? You must meet men sometimes who love their wives.'

She gave a short, cynical laugh. 'Some say they do. They say they're not looking for other girls. Perhaps they mean it.'

Charlie stood up to go. 'Well, I'm not looking for other girls.'

'What are you looking for?' she asked.

'I told you. To set you up – what your mother would have wanted.'

She giggled. 'Before you met me, I mean. In yourself?'

'I'm not looking for anything.'

'You're not telling the truth again,' she challenged. 'Everyone's looking for something, aren't they?'

'So what are you looking for, Nicole?'

She pondered the question for a moment, allowed a smile to hover. 'Maybe someone like you, Monsieur Charlee,' she replied.

Seven

It was cold as they sat on their horses on Warren Hill – the wide stretch of Newmarket Heath to the north-east of the town. Dawn had broken only half an hour before, and a light mist made a distant string near the Claypit Plantation look like fleeting equine ghosts.

The lads were 'riding work' – coming up the gallop in small groups instead of singly, usually pairs, sometimes three or four. They were keeping the horses on the bridle, not racing, letting them find their own speed. Duncan was commenting on their qualities as they went by. 'The colt I was telling you about will be next,' he told Steve Swinburne.

Always the horses looked small in the distance, and rather indistinct, taking form as they got closer, heads dipping as they galloped, the lads hunched over their necks. 'That's Kestrel, the grey,' said Duncan as the four horses approached, hooves pounding the turf. 'Started twenty lengths behind the others. Look at him now.'

The horses thundered past them, the grey colt way out in front. 'If he goes on like this,' said Duncan, 'he'll stand a chance at Epsom next year. There's just one more pair to come.'

As soon as they came into view, Duncan could see they were going too fast – against his orders. Horses were rarely pressed in training, since it was at high speed that legs got damaged. Then he saw why. Ken, his younger son, was on the offside horse, riding like a maniac as usual. He was only thirteen and shouldn't have been riding at all. Since he had brought down one of their best horses in a stupid display of heroics, Duncan had banned him from anything but the hacks for the time being.

Vincent, the head lad, rode up to them. 'Why is Ken on Brilliant Boy?' demanded Duncan. The rider schedule, usually the horses' own lads, was issued every morning.

'Mr Ken said 'e'd got your permission, Mr Duncan,' said Vincent. ''E told me 'e wanted to show you what the horse could do.'

'Cheeky young bugger,' said Duncan. 'He's not to ride again until I tell you myself. Understood?' He turned to Swinburne. 'The boy's mad, he'll kill himself one of these days – or someone else. His brother Rob's quite different, uses his head, brilliant rider, but guess which one's Annette's little pet?'

Ken rode up, his horse white with sweat. He was beaming as though expecting his father's praise. 'Did you see how she went, Pa?' he asked.

'Do you expect me to be pleased?' Duncan demanded.

A look of shocked disappointment came to the boy's face. 'You'd be pleased if Rob had got that out of the horse,' he said sullenly.

'Rob wouldn't have tried – not against my orders. I'll be seeing you later.' He turned to Swinburne. 'Come on, Steve, let's go and get some breakfast.'

As they rode towards Duncan's big house on the edge of the Heath, he said: 'Glad you could come up. I didn't know you were a racing man till we met at lunch.'

'It's been a great treat,' said Swinburne. 'You've got some fine animals.'

'You mentioned something else,' Duncan went on, riding easily on a loose rein. 'Do you remember telling me about Elisabeth Ferrier's daughter working in a Paris café?'

Swinburne nodded. 'It was just what I'd heard, you know.'

'It was true all right. Charlie Dawson found her. But what the girl told him came as a shock. She said she'd never been taken hostage by the Gestapo.'

Swinburne glanced at him in surprise. 'Was she supposed to have been?'

'Of course,' Duncan said. 'That was the only reason any of us could believe she'd been turned.'

'Turned?' Swinburne asked in astonishment. 'Elisabeth Ferrier?'

Duncan reined in his horse. 'Let's stop for a moment,' he said. 'I don't believe what I'm hearing. Surely you remember the signal about Elisabeth?'

Swinburne shook his head. 'Sorry, you've lost me, old boy. What signal?'

Duncan looked at him aghast. 'The signal ordering her execution.'

'Elisabeth Ferrier?' Swinburne echoed. 'Execution?'

'You can't have forgotten, Steve. For heaven's sake, it must have needed Regional Director approval and God knows who else. Security Section must have checked the evidence.'

Swinburne was confused. 'What *are* you talking about, Duncan? Elisabeth Ferrier died in action.'

A sudden sense of alarm made Duncan cautious. You could never be sure with men like Swinburne. 'You're right, she did,' he said firmly. 'But it doesn't alter the fact: we were ordered to kill her.'

Swinburne was still incredulous. 'God, Steve,' Duncan went on, 'I never thought I'd have to be telling you this. Even for you in London it must have been a hell of a shock. I couldn't believe it either, but I saw Leah transcribe the signal and decode it from my personal cipher. We checked it together – again and again.'

Suddenly, Swinburne understood. 'When was this?' he asked.

'A couple of weeks before D-Day.'

'That explains it. I was away then. In fact I never came back. You know I've got this dicky heart. It started to play up in May. Not surprising. We were working like crazy, sleeping in the office.' He frowned. 'Still, you'd think I'd have heard about a thing like that. I recruited her. She was pulled out from Paris – beginning of '42. I watched her work for two years. She was brilliant.' He paused. 'Lucky you didn't have to obey the order, wasn't it?' Duncan glanced at him. 'Because she was killed in action, I mean,' Swinburne added.

Duncan nodded thoughtfully. 'I suppose,' he said, 'that signal would still be in the files, wouldn't it?'

'Could be,' Swinburne answered. 'They're in a bit of a mess. There have been two fires. They're kept at Reading now. What exactly is on your mind?'

'I'm not sure,' Duncan answered, 'but something bothers me about it. I'd have bet my life Elisabeth couldn't have been turned, wouldn't you, Steve?'

Swinburne nodded. 'Not a chance, I'd have said.'

'Except for her kid,' added Duncan. 'But now we know the kid was never taken.'

For a few minutes they rode on in silence and Duncan thought of the last night of Elisabeth's life. Supper in the cottage in Saint-Martin just before the raid. It had been intolerable. How in the world had they got through it, knowing she was going to die? They had all tried to make it seem normal, deployed all the running jokes, but they weren't funny that night. There was a need to keep talking, anything to fill the silences.

Elisabeth herself was the same – just an octave down from hysteria. 'Do you know how I came into all this?' she said suddenly. 'How I was recruited? You'd expect some bigwig, wouldn't you?' A general at least. Lunch at the Ritz. "Elisabeth, they need you." Even in the Occupation they had lunch at the Ritz. But it wasn't like that. It was a funny little man as bald as a coot. Are coots bald? What is a coot? He was a sports writer. Not even on the staff. Free-lance. They used to cover the small events – just in case something happened. You know – a riot maybe or some great future star, overnight discovery. Oh, but he was funny – small, tubby. He never stopped joking – quick one-line gags. Knew the scandal about everyone in the sports world, all the stuff we couldn't print. Well, I never could resist a laugh, could I, Charlee?'

The look in Charlie's eyes was desolate, but he did his best. 'Give you a giggle, honey, and you're anyone's, aren't you?'

'More than a giggle,' she countered. 'Maybe a belly-shaker. I can't even remember his name – Robert, Roger, something like that – or where I met him. In the lift, I think. I used to see him in the newsroom – or sometimes in a café near the paper. He began to let me know what he was up to and I'd slip him things they would want to know in London. A lot of info came through the office, of course. It was he who fixed for me to be flown out to England. Not much style, I'd say, no trumpets, but it's how I got there.' And there was another of those silences they had tried all evening to avoid.

Then, after dinner, she had taken Duncan aside and asked: 'Will you do me a favour? If anything happens to me, I mean.'

'What a thing to say, Elisabeth,' he replied, feeling the worst kind of bastard.

'Well, it can, can't it? Any time. To any of us. There's a key among my things – in an envelope. It's addressed. Will you take care of it if anything happens . . . and then send it for me, but not until after the war. Keep it safe until then. Will you do that, Duncan?'

'Well, yes if –' he had begun.

She had stopped him with a gesture of her hand. 'Thanks, Duncan. I know I can trust you. You see, it could be a while yet before the war ends, a year or two even – and the key's very important.'

Swinburne turned to him as they rode. 'Tell you what, Duncan. Would you like me to make a few enquiries about that signal? I've stayed in touch with some of the Baker Street chaps.'

Duncan hesitated. 'Yes, Steve,' he said, 'I would.'

They fell silent again. Duncan had much to ponder. When they reached the yard he led the way into the house. They were met by Annette.

'How did it go?' she enquired so brightly that Duncan could see at once that she had been party to young Ken's plan to ride.

'You knew what Ken was going to do, didn't you?' he demanded.

'He did whisper something to me on the way out,' she admitted.

'It doesn't help when you encourage him. He's a little menace.'

'You're so hard on him,' she said. 'He's got spirit, that's all. He just needs guiding.'

'How can I guide him if he disobeys me?' Duncan turned to Swinburne. 'Sorry about all this, Steve. Domestic brawls should be in private, shouldn't they?'

'Hardly a brawl,' countered Annette. 'Just what everyone has sometimes, surely. We've a visitor, Duncan, so we're having breakfast in the dining room.'

Prince Khalid was at the table. He was around forty-five, lean, with strongly sculptured features and an aura of calm about him that, though he never raised his voice, could be chilling when he was angry. 'Ah, Duncan,' he said, 'I hope you'll forgive this sudden arrival. A cancelled meeting in Cambridge, so I thought I'd come over and see you working my horses. Sorry I missed the first lot.'

Duncan welcomed his patron warmly and introduced Swinburne to him. Annette was pouring coffee. 'You may be interested, Highness,' she said, 'that Mr Swinburne knew Elisabeth, too. I've just been telling the Prince, Duncan, about her daughter.'

'A fascinating woman, Elisabeth Ferrier,' said the Prince. 'Her death was so tragic. Did you know her well, Mr Swinburne?'

'Not like Duncan, Your Highness,' Swinburne answered. 'But I recruited her, so I saw a bit of her.'

'You know, Prince,' Annette went on, 'you've never told us

how you came to meet Elisabeth yourself.' She flashed a glance at him that was mildly flirtatious. 'Or is the question indiscreet?'

'Now, Duncan,' he asked lightly, 'would your charming wife ever be indiscreet?'

'It's been known,' Duncan answered, 'I have to tell you.'

'Well, it was all a long time ago,' the Prince said. 'I met her first when she came to interview me in 1935 and we became friends. I was very young then, of course, and got into a bit of trouble. There could have been a serious scandal. She did me a great favour and this was avoided. Does that answer your question, Annette?'

'No, Highness,' she answered.

The Prince laughed. 'Well, you'll have to be satisfied with it.' He turned to Duncan. 'What time will the second lot be going out?' he asked.

2

They were in Nicole's new home. It was in the Rue Saint-Séverin, just off the Boulevard Saint-Michel near the Seine – a top-floor apartment in a building that had been there at the time of the Revolution. There were oak beams in the ceiling, an open fireplace, and a view through leaded windows of the roofs of the Old Quarter.

The final formalities had just been completed and the notary, Monsieur Lombarde, was looking out of the window at the gables and clock tower of the ancient church of Saint-Séverin.

'You'll awake together in the morning to the chimes of the hour,' he said and turned with a beatific smile on his face. 'I envy you. I'm sure you'll both be very happy here.'

'The apartment's for Mademoiselle,' Charlie reminded him. 'You know that, Monsieur Lombarde. You've just drafted the trust deed for the five of us to sign.'

'The arrangements have been admirable,' agreed the notaire with a confidential smile.

Nicole was leaning idly against the wall by the fireplace, with her arms folded. She found the scene, now familiar, extremely funny. Everywhere they had gone in Paris, people had assumed she was his mistress – and everywhere Charlie had made it clear she wasn't, only to be met by the same sceptical response.

'Nicole,' he said, 'will you please explain to Monsieur Lombarde?'

'What would you like me to tell him?' she asked innocently.

'That I shan't be living here, of course.'

She shrugged. 'He won't be living here, Monsieur Lombarde,' she said. But no one would have believed her.

When the lawyer left them, Charlie lit a cigarette and studied her with a weary grin. 'Why do you do this, Nikki?' he asked. 'You *want* people to think we're lovers, don't you?'

She giggled. 'You are funny, Charlee,' she said. 'Most men of your age would be flattered. Anyway, we *are* lovers really, aren't we? We just haven't made love, that's all. But you've put off your return twice for me.'

'That's because I wanted to see you settled. You know that.'

'You watch me – the way I move, the look on my face. I fascinate you – perhaps because I've a look of Maman, but not only that I think. You fascinate me, too, Charlee – for the same reason. I can watch you for hours and wonder about you and Maman. It's a strange feeling but it makes me close to you. I don't mind admitting it, you see.'

'That's because you're young,' he said. 'And sometimes pretty dumb.'

It was two and a half weeks since Charlie had found her, and they had spent part of every day since together. He had taken command of her life, suggesting she arrange leave of absence from the café.

Then he'd conducted her on a search for an apartment, rushing the purchase through, and they had embarked together on a buying spree for furniture, carpets, pictures, clothes.

They had got to know each other well, developing an unusual rapport. She swooped round him like a colourful bird, flirting with him, often outrageously in front of strangers, teasing him, playing mischievous games, growing suddenly angry at some comment she felt was unfair.

She was outspoken, saying whatever came into her mind without thinking, using language he had never heard in a young girl before. 'I'm just a slut, you see,' she would say, and then she would slowly repeat the word that had surprised him, emphasising the consonants. 'Would Maman ever have said such a thing?'

'Not like that,' he would reply, although in certain moods when they were making love she too, had enjoyed an earthy coarseness. 'You're fucking me, Charlee, aren't you?' she would challenge him in English to shock him. 'Say it, Charlee. You can't, can you, not to a woman? It's not what you're used to. You're just an old Puritan really, aren't you? So what is it you're doing, Charlee?' And she would expose him to the same expression of amused challenge that he saw now in her daughter.

'You know what I'd like to do?' said that daughter. 'I'd like us to learn more about her together. To me she's just a faint but lovely memory, an aura of perfume. But even you didn't meet her till she was thirty-five, did you? You know nothing of her in her twenties. Something tremendous could have happened to her then, something that made you love her later. That's when she became famous, isn't it? Oh, do let's do that, Charlee. We could visit her friends and people who worked with her. We could go to the Massif and you could show me the cottage where you all lived – and maybe the place by the railway where she – ' She broke off as she saw his face. 'Well, perhaps that isn't such a good idea, but – '

'No, it isn't a good idea,' he agreed.

She pulled a face like a child, a kind of apology – then replaced it with a sudden winsome smile. He knew that in seconds she would be off on some new tack and he found himself anticipating it with a certain eagerness.

He thought of the shock for her if she ever discovered what had really happened at the railway line. For him, Nikki's revelation had been traumatic. For years, he'd tried to deal with guilt, honing it down with each good reason why Elisabeth had to die. But all of these hinged on the threat to Nikki.

Now, it seemed, Elisabeth need not have died after all. The order in the signal wasn't enough. It was wrong. Orders were often wrong – especially those issued under pressure at so critical a time. But it was hard for Charlie to face the new reality of what he had done – hard for the others too. Duncan had said he would explore it further with Steve Swinburne. For the present, there was nothing Charlie could do – except what he had planned to do anyway. So he had focused his energies on Nikki – and found solace of a kind.

The role he was beginning to play in her life was strange for him – he was the tree round which she flew. He would match her moods, counter her behaviour. When she was down, he would cheer her up; when she was outrageous, he would curb her, usually with quiet ridicule – for she was an odd mixture of a free spirit ('Who cares what they think?') and a performer who needed the applause of the crowd. He became protective, and had asked Sonya about Jean-Paul.

She knew Jean-Paul, she said. Claude had had some dealings with him and they had run the occasional story in the paper. Jean-Paul's magazine, *La Nouvelle Vie*, was built round well-photographed nudes, plus good in-depth interviews by well-known writers. It was a successful formula and the circulation was rising. Jean-Paul was always seen with very young girls. There had been a skirmish with the law, but the charges had been dropped. 'When are you going home, Charlie?' Sonya had asked. 'You're getting in too deep.'

She was right, he knew, as they had all been right at that lunch. Just being with Nicole satisfied something very basic in him. At times, he felt he had been waiting for her ever since that terrible night in 1944 when the Sten gun was vibrating in his hands – as though she were a kind of extension of Elisabeth, preordained, sent to him as part of some divine plan. And that was a disturbing thought for a man who didn't really believe in God, who insisted he was happy with his wife.

This was what surprised and even shocked him – how intense, in only a few days, his enjoyment of her had become. Why didn't she irritate him? She was the sort of girl who would have done before he came to Paris. Maybe I'm getting old before my time, he thought. She's a little minx, but then Elisabeth was probably a bit of a minx until she acquired maturity. Certainly she would have been every bit as bold and cheeky and outrageous.

'You're a minx,' he told Nikki in English.

She glanced at him, not sure if he was teasing. 'What's a minx?' she asked.

'A girl who's no better than she should be,' he answered, though it sounded odd in French. 'A hussy, une petite coquine.'

Her smile was hesitant. 'Do you like minxes, coquines?'

He shrugged. 'So-so.'

'That's not good enough. I shall stop being a minx.'

'Minxes can't help being minxes.'

Suddenly she was serious. 'I don't think you're being kind.'

'Some minxes are OK,' he said, still teasing. 'You're an OK minx.' But she wasn't convinced. 'Would you like to go to Deauville again?' he asked suddenly.

'Deauville?' she said, not understanding.

'You said you went there as a child for vacations. Would you like to go again?'

'That'd be fun,' she answered.

'Do you need to get anything before we leave?'

'You mean . . .' – just seeing the excitement rising in her eyes was absurdly rewarding for him – 'you mean now?'

'Anything wrong with now? You got other plans? I could call for a car.'

It had been a stupid suggestion – made partly because he wanted to please her in a moment of uncertainty and partly because he had suddenly been overwhelmed by a sense of soaring elation that he hadn't known since Elisabeth, a need to do something crazy.

It had been crazy all right. Deauville was two hundred kilo-metres away. They had had to stay the night, which opened to discussion the dark wanting of her that he had tried to keep submerged because it was obviously lethal, with all its guilt and sadness. In truth, this was impossible to conceal. She just had to glance at him with those familiar eyes with the sexuality blatantly exposed. Far less, she only had to get up and move across the room with her skirt swinging from that slim waist – and the spasm of desire in him was sharper than anything he had felt since Elisabeth.

Sometimes, as he looked at her in her rare moments of repose, noting the precise line of her lips, he became immediately erect like a boy of seventeen. He wanted desperately to taste that mouth, knowing where it would lead them; and that was truly a dark tunnel. Even when she left him in the evenings and her lips lightly brushed his cheek in farewell, he often had to fight to stop himself trembling.

However, in Paris he could pretend, even though he didn't fool her. He could play the older man who was not supposed to be disturbed by such demands – the mentor, the friend of her mother. But at the hotel in Deauville he had asked the receptionist for two rooms and the issue was laid out there on the line. 'Two rooms, monsieur?' the girl asked with a glance at Nikki as though she had misheard. And the usual grin had come to Nikki's face. 'That's correct, mademoiselle,' she interposed before he had time to reply. 'He said two rooms,' adding, with a straight face, 'naturally.'

Charlie half expected her to join him during the night, but she didn't, though she knew he had feared it. 'You see?' she declared as he joined her for breakfast in the dining room after a restless night. 'Even we minxes know how to behave when it's expected of us.'

Despite the undertones, the trip had been a huge success from the moment they left Paris. They loved the journey to the coast in the old open Bugatti he had borrowed, and sang together as he drove – French songs, except for one in English that she asked him to teach her. In the morning, after breakfast, they wandered through the town trying to find any familiar landmarks, but she only remembered the beach.

So they strode along the shore below the rows of striped canvas tents that had remained in her memory, leaping sideways when a sudden wave swept higher up the beach than they expected. Once, in a moment of boyish high spirits, he held her so that she couldn't escape and the water lapped her shoes. 'Kiss me,' she said. And he did – on the nose.

They skimmed stones along the surface of the sea, bought ice creams from a vendor and licked them vulgarly with exaggerated movements of their tongues as they walked.

'Why are you laughing?' he asked.

'What would they think if they saw you now, the people who work for you? Would they be shocked at the antics of their boss?' But before he could answer, she pointed at the horizon. 'Is that one of your ships?'

'I'd forgotten I had any,' he said.

They lunched overlooking the water, on oysters and champagne, and then drove back to Paris. By the time they reached Evreux, half way to the city, reaction had set in and his spirits had sagged a little. It had been a bad mistake, he knew. They had been too happy and it could only make things harder for them. Worse, it had been wildly irresponsible, only confirming what Sonya and Duncan had said – that he was trying to recapture what he had had with Elisabeth, to enjoy with a girl who looked so like her that lightness of spirit that lovers can know.

'I don't want the day to end,' she said as they entered the city limits at Auteuil. 'Can we have a drink in your hotel?' They were in the bar when he was left in no doubt that he owned some ships by a call from Terry Johnson, his General Manager. 'When are you coming back, Charlie?' he enquired. 'Things are piling up.'

'In a few days,' said Charlie. 'Can you stall anything that's pressing until then?'

'How about a date? Appointments need to be made.'

'I'll call when I know.'

'That Cunard deal's getting a bit sour. Maybe you could come back through London.'

'Maybe,' said Charlie. 'Sounds a good idea.' As he put down the phone and walked back to the bar he had planned to tell her he was returning home. But he didn't. Well, it would have spoiled the mood, wouldn't it? Anyway he couldn't return for a few days – not until the trust deed was signed and her apartment was ready.

Deauville, with its easy intimacy, marked a change in their relations. Nikki became even bolder. He had revealed more of himself in those two days and it tantalised her. She understood his wanting of her, which she played on skilfully – not overdoing it, for all her provocative talk, using her body and the way she touched him with a subtlety that was beyond her years. But it was his control she found hard to fathom. This was outside her experience and therefore a challenge. Also, of course, *she* wanted *him* – as she was quite happy to admit.

Sex for her was a simple matter. She didn't assess the future, as many women would, or fear the stiring of deep emotions. She knew that sex could be nothing, or quite important, or quite fun. But no one had shown her even a glimpse of the heights.

And that was the difference between them. For she couldn't understand what he meant when he spoke darkly of the emotional minefield that surrounded them. When he tried to explain, she mocked him – about his wife ('I know, I know, you love your wife'), about his age ('You pretend you've become staid and respectable, but I *know* what you've become'), even about her mother ('Remember, I've read the diary').

'Why not just relax, Charlee?' she said. 'All this willpower can't be good for you. You'll come out in spots.'

By the morning they met Monsieur Lombarde in her apartment, she had become quite reckless and he knew he had to stop her. In any case, it was time to go home, to mend the fences with Philana, to attend to his business – and to avoid the inevitable moment when his need for Nikki would overcome all rational argument. He was aware, too, that the only way of doing that was by shocking her – and he knew how.

63

For a few moments, after the notary had left them, he watched her through the smoke of his cigarette. 'Well,' he said at last, 'you've got a new home. Beats your old one, eh?'

She glanced at him strangely, as though sensing, like a wild animal, that things weren't normal. 'I love it,' she said, 'and I don't know how to thank you. At least I do,' she added with that look that made him gasp, 'but you won't let me, will you?'

For a second she held his gaze, openly triumphant, enjoying the power it gave her. Then, with an effort, he broke the contact and walked over to the window, standing looking out at the old cracked tiles on the roof of the church. 'Would that be thanking me?' he asked. 'Would it help you? Now think before you answer.'

'It was only a joke, Charlee.' She joined him at the window, putting an arm through his. 'As you'd say, a gag,' she added, speaking the word in English.

'It's a dangerous gag, Nikki,' he said. 'And you make it too often. You realise that, don't you?'

'Playing with fire?' she teased. 'Because of Maman?' When he didn't answer she added lightly: 'Lucky Maman.'

'All right,' he said, 'say we did make love . . . You'd never know, would you?'

'Know what?' she said, but she knew what. 'You mean if it was her or me you were loving?' she asked carefully, the teasing gone. 'Or rather, how much of it was her?'

She was so mature in some ways, he thought. He felt her tense beside him. 'That's not a nice thing to say, Charlee,' she said after a moment. 'It's a horrid thing to say.'

'Well, would you? Would I?'

'I think you're being beastly,' she retorted, the anger rising. 'All right, you're so honourable, so true to your wife. You know the danger. So why do you put us at such risk? Why haven't you gone home? Why don't you go home today?'

He turned to her. 'That's what I'm going to do, Nikki. I'll book a flight for this week.'

For a moment, as he intended, she was shocked. 'I think that'd be a good idea,' she declared stiffly.

'But it means I must introduce you to Sonya,' he said. 'We can't put it off any longer. Someone has to deal with Monsieur Lombarde.' Always, Nicole had resisted meeting any of the others, fearing perhaps that they would spoil what she had with

Charlie. 'I'm due to meet her at Fouquet's tomorrow afternoon. I think you should join us.'

She was watching him like a desolate child and he knew an intense need to take her in his arms and say he didn't mean it. But he made no move.

She began to cry, fighting it at first in her pride, then conceding. 'I don't want you to go, Charlee,' she said. 'What'll happen to me if you go?'

'Nikki, I've got to go sometime. You've always known that. Both Sonya and Monsieur Lombarde will help you if you need it. The others are only in England. Leah's often in Paris. You and I can talk on the phone. Anyway, I'll be back.'

She was staring at him. 'You said you'd change my life . . .'

'And I've made a start, haven't I?' He took in the apartment with a gesture. 'You need a new job, as we've agreed. Sonya will help with that. You'll see.'

'I'm scared, Monsieur Charlee.' She looked very small suddenly – and absurdly young, a fourteen-year-old with tears streaming slowly down her cheeks. She looked away. 'I don't want to go back to Jean-Paul,' she said carefully.

'You won't do that,' he said.

'How do you know I won't? He'd look after me. He can be kind, as I told you.'

'Don't threaten me, honey. It's not very smart.'

She nodded without looking at him. 'You're so sharp, aren't you? Just watch you don't cut yourself, Charlee. But don't you see? It's going to be hard for me. You come galloping into my life like a knight on a charger – a gift from my mother. And now you're riding off, leaving me stranded.'

'I'm leaving you with lots of people to help you. But it's getting difficult between us. You said I should go home – and you were right. For a bit anyway.'

'So it's all my fault now, is it? It's unkind to twist what I said.'

'Twist?'

'Girls often say things they don't mean. You know that.'

He couldn't help laughing. 'Nikki,' he said gently, 'I must go back to New York. It's not easy for me, but I must. Shall we have dinner tonight?'

She stood a little straighter. 'Thank you,' she said, 'but I'll be busy, I fear.'

He smiled. 'Pity, but you'll come to Fouquet's at four tomorrow, won't you?'

'OK,' she said as though it was unimportant. 'Anything you say.'

3

Duncan sipped his gin and tonic thoughtfully, holding the tumbler against his lips for a second, enjoying the feeling of the ice-cold glass. The Form Book lay open on his lap over the Racing Calendar. Kestrel was entered for the Molecomb Stakes at Goodwood next week and he was wondering whether to run him, checking out the main opposition.

Annette came in. 'Dinner will be ready in ten minutes. What are you going to do about Kestrel?' He glanced up at her and shook his head. She was a pretty woman – hardly changed, it seemed, after fifteen years of marriage and two sons – with dark, curly hair and a small animated face. The clients adored her.

At times he wondered if he would ever have had the strength to go through with the marriage but for Elisabeth. There had been so many impediments: his duty to the family pottery firm, the bitterness his father had felt towards Annette's when their partnership collapsed with talk of fraud, his own passionate need to train horses. Certainly he couldn't have chosen a girl more sure to antagonise his parents.

Elisabeth had just laughed when he confided in her on that winter evening on the Massif. 'Romeo and Juliet?' she mocked. 'Will you want her in twenty years' time when the passion's eased? Well then,' she added when she saw his sure reaction, 'there's your answer. As for your duty, that's to yourself. Fathers have no right to control your life. Train your horses and marry the girl.'

Elisabeth was always so sure about everything. 'It's not easy to break into training,' he started to explain. 'You have to start by – '

'I think you'll manage,' she said confidently. 'I know one or two people who'd be useful. How about Prince Khalid? Didn't he have some good horses before the war?'

'Good?' he echoed. 'Some of the best in the world. Won some top races – the Prix du Jockey Club at Chantilly, the Guineas at Newmarket, the Gold Cup at Ascot.'

Elisabeth had laughed fondly. 'Khalid's a terror. Horses, cars, women, not always in that order. I used to tell him he was a snob. He only married eminent women – Hollywood stars or the British aristocracy. But he took his horses seriously. Go and see him, Duncan, when all this is over. You can give him my love.'

'You know Prince Khalid that well?' Duncan asked incredulously.

'Khalid was always in the news in the thirties,' she answered. 'He could help you. You'll have to convince him, mind you. Do your homework. Know all about every horse he's ever had. As a matter of fact, he owes me a favour.'

Annette was standing looking down at him. 'Well, are you running the horse at York?'

'I haven't decided yet,' Duncan answered.

'You weren't thinking of horses, were you?' she challenged, sitting on the arm of a chair. 'I know who you were thinking of. All right, I'm aware of the theory. We'd never have married but for her – and it's rubbish, Duncan. You always had guts. Our dear fathers could be scary, but they weren't the Gestapo. If she helped I'm grateful – but I've been grateful for fifteen years now and it's long enough.'

The two boys came in. Rob saw the books on his father's lap, and guessed what he'd been doing. 'Have you considered Woodland Star?' he asked.

'He's hardly a match for our colt, is he?' Duncan answered. 'Some of the others now . . .'

'He waltzed six furlongs at Redcar last year. Didn't go out again. Leg trouble.'

'Redcar?' queried his father dubiously.

'All right, it's not Newmarket or Ascot,' Rob agreed, 'but look what he beat.'

Duncan checked in the Form Book and saw what his son meant. Woodland Star had come home a length ahead of a first-class horse who had done well since. 'Good point, Rob. I'd have missed that.' He glanced at Ken and saw the sadness in him. Duncan got on so well with Rob and his knowledge of racing was incredible for a fourteen-year-old.

The telephone rang. 'Answer that for me, will you, Ken?' he asked pleasantly, hoping Ken would take it as gesture of affection, of including him. 'I'll call them back. It's almost time for dinner.'

Duncan's effort failed. 'It's about what I'm good for, isn't it, Pa?' Ken retorted. 'Answering the phone.' Angrily he stalked out

67

of the room, returning almost immediately. 'It's Mr Swinburne. He says could you spare a moment now since he's going out?'

'I happened to be in Reading today,' Swinburne told Duncan, 'so I stopped off at the archives. I wasn't allowed near them, of course, since they're still classified. But I know the archivist and he checked them for me. Took a lot of time over it. There's no sign of that order.'

'Hardly surprising, surely,' Duncan countered. 'You said there'd been chaos – and two fires.'

'That's true, but he told me there's a batch from May 20 for about four days when they were all in numbered sequence. Several hundred . . . all except one, which struck him as strange. Can you remember exactly what date you got that signal?'

'I'll never forget it as long as I live. The night of May 22, just before midnight.'

'That's when a message is missing from the sequence, Duncan.'

For a moment, after Duncan had replaced the phone, he stood silently in the hall, suddenly drained of energy. He found himself thinking of Elisabeth's key – the one she had asked him to keep for her until after the war. He had often wondered about that key, addressed as it was to Dominique someone or other – he couldn't remember the last name. What did it open? Was it connected with the missing signal, with the false news of Nicole's arrest?

With an effort, he joined the family in the dining room. Annette glanced at him. 'I hope you're hungry,' she declared. 'This is a lovely piece of lamb.'

He shook his head as he sat down. 'I don't think I could eat a thing, darling,' he said.

The anger shone in her eyes. 'Elisabeth, I suppose? Oh God, how I wish she'd leave us alone!'

Eight

Charlie was sitting at an outside table at Fouquet's in the spring sunshine. He was early for Sonya but welcomed the time to think. The decision to go home had been hard. Nikki had become a brilliant, dazzling feature of his life and he knew he was going to miss her desperately.

He knew, too, that Philana would sense it. She didn't miss much. She'd play it cool though, just make the usual enquiries about the trip. She'd guess it concerned Elisabeth, that he'd lied to her when he delayed his return because of a supposed deal in Cherbourg. It would be the first time he'd lied to her.

Still, he'd booked a seat on the plane to New York the next day. Sonya would be pleased with him, he thought. He saw her approaching, watched as usual by everyone at the tables she passed. He rose to greet her and she kissed him. 'How goes it?' she enquired with affectionate mockery.

'I'm flying home in the morning.'

'And back again the next day?'

He laughed. 'A bit longer than that. Nikki's joining us shortly, so you can meet her.'

'Now that's a surprise,' she said. 'I thought you were keeping her locked in a cupboard.'

Something was wrong, Charlie knew. The banter was forced. 'What's up, Sonya?'

She sighed. 'New twist to the story, Charlie. Oh, boy, is there a new twist! Duncan called me this morning. He told me Steve Swinburne knew nothing about the execution signal.'

'Swinburne?' Charlie echoed. 'But Swinburne sent it.'

'No he didn't – he'd left Baker Street by then. But he's just checked the archives for us. The files are in a mess, but they're in sequence over four days from May 20 – all except the signal that ordered us to kill Elisabeth.'

'So it's got lost,' said Charlie.

'Why only that one over those four days? Out of hundreds?'

Sonya was watching him. It was worse than Nicole's revelation about the Gestapo. That had still left them with Duncan's basic handhold: they'd been obeying an order. But now there was no sign of one.

'What's Duncan think?' he asked. 'That somebody stole it from the archive?'

'He doesn't know. But one thing he did say was vital. At that lunch, you insisted she didn't die in action . . .'

'There's no doubt.' Their eyes met. 'You know, don't you?'

'I know you think you killed her, Charlie. I've always known. But how can you be certain?'

'I fired on automatic. Almost point blank. I saw her drop.'

'Say the enemy saw her, too. One of the Krauts with a Spandau?'

'Then she'd have gone over backwards or sideways. But she fell forward because I was behind her.'

'Charlie,' Sonya said, 'without an order, it's murder.'

'Murder?' he echoed. 'Jesus, I loved her more than any woman I've ever known.'

'I know,' she said. 'I was there. Remember? Every day, I saw you both. But others don't, and there have been murder charges in the Resistance before – revenge killings mostly. And you're not alone – we're all in it too. So she died in action, Charlie, like everyone thinks she did. OK?'

He hardly seemed to have heard her. 'Why, Sonya?' he asked suddenly. 'Why has the signal disappeared? What possible reason can there be?'

She shrugged. 'We can't ignore the obvious, Charlie. Could someone have wanted her dead – and then removed the evidence?'

He stared at her in horror. 'I need a brandy,' he said, stopping a passing waiter and ordering two cognacs.

'Since Duncan's call, I've been thinking,' Sonya went on. 'What do we actually know about Elisabeth? Even you, who talked to her more than any of us? How much, for example, do you know of her life before the war?'

He thought for a moment. 'Not much,' he agreed. 'Not when you get down to detail.'

'I mean,' she said, 'there are aspects that are odd, aren't there? Such as a star like Romy Lagrange taking Max on as her agent. What did Max know about the profession, for heaven's sake? Such as Ben Jordan backing Leah with barely a moment's thought. Such as the Sheikh putting his horses with Duncan.

Normally, they'd have gone to a top stable – someone like Boyd Rochfort. All right, they were fond of her, as we all were. But there must have been more, mustn't there?'

He shrugged. 'Got a theory?'

'Only the start of one,' she answered. 'Debt. Moral debt. Some enormous favour they were eager to repay.'

'All of them?' Charlie queried. 'How about Claude? I can't see him giving you a job because of duty. And all Marie Cayzer did was ask me to dinner.'

'I'm just feeling around, but let's take those two. Marie's got some odd friends, as you're well aware. Claude knows half the big criminals in Paris. Then there's that key she asked Duncan to send for her. What for? Safe deposit box?'

'Lots of people have things on safe deposit – especially in a war.'

'True . . .' She sipped from her glass. 'But it crossed my mind that if someone did use us to kill her with a signal sent through formal channels – '

'Jesus,' Charlie cut in, 'he'd have had to cut some ice to fix that.'

'Then we might get further,' she went on, 'if we found out more about her. Does that make sense?'

Charlie paused for a few seconds. 'I can't go home now, can I?' he said at last.

'I think it'll plague you if you do.'

'I'll have to use Nicole.'

'Why involve her? She hardly knew her mother.'

'She'd have access that I'd never have. It's natural for a daughter to want to know about her heroine mother, isn't it? And it'd hardly raise any scares where it mattered.'

Sonya looked at him sadly. 'It's like a spider's web – first Elisabeth, now the girl. Think you can keep it under control?'

He glanced at her and smiled. 'It's going to be tough.'

'Then forget it. After all, what's it all matter now? We're talking history, aren't we? Go home to Philana, Charlie. Get on with your life.'

'That your advice?' he asked. She nodded firmly. 'But it's not what I'll do, you reckon?' He grinned at her.

She laughed, reached out a hand and placed it on his. 'Ask me for anything you need, won't you? It could get dangerous, no kidding. Not just emotional disaster. I mean killing . . .' Something had caught her attention over his shoulder. 'You know, Charlie, I think I'm seeing a ghost.'

'Nicole,' he said. 'I told you they looked alike.' But when he twisted in his seat to see her even he got a shock.

For she was wearing exactly what Elisabeth had worn on the day of the ballot – the beret, the red scarf, the black jersey and skirt. She was even smoking from Elisabeth's ivory cigarette holder.

She was standing on the pavement at the edge of the café, looking for them. When she saw Charlie, she took the cigarette holder from her mouth. Holding it high between her fingers, she made her way towards them with an attempt at unhurried elegance that only served to emphasise her youth. It was a new Nikki in yet another rôle – this time a childish, tasteless one.

'Does she realise what she's doing?' asked Sonya. 'What she's wearing?'

Charlie nodded a little grimly. 'She's making a point.' He stood up as Nikki reached the table. She stopped in front of him, displaying the mask of a sweet smile. 'Good afternoon, Monsieur Charlee.'

He introduced her to Sonya. 'Enchantée, madame,' she said with a warmth that was clearly false, taking a seat beside her. 'I've been looking forward so much to meeting you.'

'And this?' asked Charlie with a gesture at her clothes.

She flashed him another artificial smile. 'It's droll, don't you think? Don't you think it's droll, madame?'

'Hardly,' Sonya answered coolly.

'I can see I've disturbed you,' she said. 'Well, I'm disturbed too. That's why I'm wearing these clothes. My mother would know what to do, wouldn't she? Perhaps she'll guide me.'

'Guide you?' echoed Charlie with a puzzled look.

'I'm angry, Monsieur Charlee.'

'With me?'

'Yes, with you – *and* Madame Sonya here.'

Sonya was surprised. 'What can I have done? We've only just met.'

'You don't know?' said Nikki. She inserted her mother's cigarette holder between her teeth and inhaled. 'I find that hard to believe, madame, since your paper is planning to attack my friend.'

'Which friend?' asked Charlie.

'Jean-Paul, of course, as you well know, so don't pretend you don't.'

Charlie couldn't help laughing. 'I promise you, Nikki, it's the first I've heard of it.'

'Or me,' Sonya put in. 'And I can assure you I would have done.'

'Or the prosecution by the police?' Nikki asked. 'How can I believe you, either of you? The inspector was overheard. He mentioned your name, madame. Your reporter's been questioning the girls.' She swung back to Charlie. 'Can you deny you don't approve of Jean-Paul?' she demanded.

'I don't know him,' he answered.

'You know enough. Don't think I didn't hear what the *patron* said to you when you met. And I know you now, Monsieur Charlee. You'll have asked your Madame Sonya to make enquiries. Can you deny that?'

'Naturally – I was concerned about you.'

'Well, I don't want your concern. Not if it means you having my friends arrested, pilloried in the press – charged with forcing young girls to . . . It's all rubbish, Jean-Paul never forced anyone. He's a kind man.'

Sonya leaned forward and put her hand on Nikki's arm. 'Now listen,' she said. 'I'll find out about this when I get back to the office. If there are no grounds, we'll drop it. So will the police. So there's nothing to worry about.'

'Oh, there is, madame,' Nikki said calmly. She was holding herself erect, head high, trying to resume her pose as a sophisticate. 'Truly, Monsieur Charlee, you don't own me. Nor you, madame. I choose my own friends.'

'That's fair,' Sonya agreed. 'You're twenty, aren't you?'

'I must be free to do what I like, see who I please . . .'

'For God's sake, Nikki,' Charlie began. 'You can do what you – '

She turned on him, suddenly furious. 'You don't care what I do, Monsieur Charlee. Don't think I don't know that.'

'Now that's a crazy thing to say, Nikki.'

'Why not speak the truth?' she challenged, tears welling in her eyes. 'It's guilt, that's all. Well, you've paid your debt, haven't you? You can go back to your wife now and say, I've given her clothes and money, and a nice apartment in the Rue Saint Séverin. What more can a girl ask?'

Suddenly, she was on her feet, the would-be sophisticate gone. 'But it's not always easy to settle debts,' she persisted. 'So I give you back your apartment. Here are your precious title deeds.' She flung a packet of papers on to the table. 'Goodbye, Monsieur Charlee. Perhaps we'll meet again sometime. Goodbye, madame.'

She turned and stalked away between the tables of the café into the great avenue of the Champs-Elysées. 'Nikki!' Charlie called out. 'Come back, you dumb idiot!'

She gave no sign of having heard him, just started to run, darting through the people on the crowded pavement – in her mother's clothes, even a little as her mother ran.

2

'Please hold on, monsieur,' said the telephonist. 'I've got New York on the line.' Charlie was standing with the phone in his hand by the window of his bedroom, looking down at the traffic of the Faubourg Saint-Honoré. It was the next day just after lunch.

'Charlie?' It was Philana's voice.

'Hallo, honey,' he said. 'How are you?'

'Fine, but missing you badly.'

'And the kids?'

'They're missing you, too. When are you coming home?'

'I've got new problems, honey. I was booked on a plane today but I've had to cancel. There's more trouble on the Cherbourg deal.' He knew he hadn't deceived her.

'Charlie,' she pleaded in a small voice. 'Come home, please. Father says there is no Cherbourg deal.'

'How can he know a thing like that?'

'You know Father. He knows everything.'

'He doesn't know about this.'

'Please, Charlie darling. I'll forgive you anything, everything.'

'There's nothing to forgive.'

'Then take the plane.'

'I can't, honey. Not for a week or so.'

The line went dead and slowly he put the receiver back on the rest, feeling deeply unhappy.

He hadn't spoken to Nikki since the angry scene the previous

74

day, thinking it wise to give her a breathing space, but he needed to talk to her now. There was no phone yet in her apartment, so he called the café in the Boulevard Saint-Germain. The *patron* said he hadn't seen Nicole for two days. 'Perhaps she'll drop in and see us this evening,' he said.

'If she does, ask her to call me at the hotel, will you?' said Charlie.

For the rest of the afternoon he was in a mood that was strange to him – disturbed and melancholy. He went for a walk, toyed with calling Philana again, wondered even if he should have told her the truth; but Elisabeth was too sensitive an issue. Certainly, if she got any hint of his plan to investigate Elisabeth's death, she would fight it like a tigress – *and* co-opt the power of her father.

So Charlie had done nothing. He was free-wheeling, on a new course, directed by that dark night sixteen years before by the railtrack near Grenoble.

He dined at the hotel – only to be interrupted by a call from Costa Mastorakis in New York. 'How odd you should call, Costa,' said Charlie. 'I was just thinking about you.'

'What are you doing in Paris, Charlie? Why aren't you home?'

'I had to stay on.' Charlie smiled to himself as he imagined the scene in the Mastorakis office. There would be five lines open to Paris with aides calling everyone Costa knew for news of Charlie. The old man would be switching from call to call, cutting in with impatient questions.

'Stay on?' echoed Mastorakis in his strange accented English. 'Why?'

'Business, Costa,' Charlie answered.

'What kind of business?'

'My kind of business. You always said I was a bandit.'

'What's this I hear about a girl?'

'What is it you hear about a girl?'

'Charlie, we're both men of the world. I understand about girls.'

'Oh, I'm aware of that. You're a legend here, Costa, like Speedy Gonzales.'

'You must be discreet, Charlie, or you upset your wife.'

'I wouldn't be upsetting my wife if people would stop reporting nonsense – especially your people.'

'So what's this business you're on to?'

'None of yours, Costa.'

'Don't say things like that, Charlie. I made you and I can break you.'

'You wouldn't do that even if you could, and we both know why. You'll hear about it all in time. Just for now, do me a favour and tell that lovely daughter of yours to stop fretting.'

'So when are you coming home?'

'When I'm ready, Costa.'

By nine o'clock, Nikki hadn't called, so he decided to go to the apartment. She had given him back the deeds, but he guessed she would still be there for a few days.

The Rue Saint-Séverin, lying between the Boulevard Saint-Michel and the Rue Saint-Jacques, the two broad streets that reached south from the Seine, was part of a network of crooked pedestrian alleys arranged round the ancient church – a section of old Paris that had hardly changed in two hundred years. There were small restaurants, clubs, art shops, little delicatessens – and it was always thronged with strolling people in the evenings.

Charlie pushed his way through the crowd to the house where Nikki lived and climbed the old staircase.

She was certainly home. Even two floors below, he could hear the party. He knocked on the door – and the noise grew suddenly louder as she opened it herself, calling out to someone so her head was turned. Then, as she saw him, she just stared in astonishment. They stared at each other, in fact – for the sight of her affected him deeply. She looked quite lovely – in a dress of yellow silk, which they had bought together, with a matching headband – but older somehow, the look of Elisabeth much stronger.

'I thought you'd gone,' she murmured softly. 'You couldn't go.' Her eyes lit up with sudden joy. 'You couldn't leave me, could you?'

'I had business – ' he began.

'Business, pouff,' she declared and threw herself into his arms. He held her to him tightly and she burrowed her head into his shoulder. She looked up at him with a wide, delighted smile. 'I thought I'd lost you, you know. I thought I'd never see you again.'

'I told you I'd come back.'

'You don't think I believed you, do you? You'd be with your wife. She wouldn't let you go. She's no fool, that Philana. It's the third time you couldn't leave me, you know that?'

'Nikki . . .' he began, but she put her fingers to his mouth.

'Don't say it. Business, tankers, Europe – I don't believe a word. Now come in and meet my friends. It's my leaving party. One last fling.'

'The place is still yours. You don't have to leave.'

'Perhaps I don't now,' she said taking him by the hand. 'We'll see. Try it for size, eh?' She led him into the hubbub and smoke of her living room with its oak beams and sloping ceilings. There must have been forty people crammed in there, with far more girls than men. Pretty girls, mostly, but all of a type: small features, like young teenagers, except for their full breasts.

She introduced him to several as she led him through the throng. Julie, Cécile, Marie, Véronique. This is Monsieur Charlee. I thought he'd flown away. Isn't he lovely? They greeted him warmly but impersonally as though she'd bought him off a stall in the Flea Market. She was very easy with them – comrades-in-arms.

Clothilde from the café was at his side offering him a glass of champagne.

'Who are all these people?' he asked her, though he had already guessed.

She shrugged. 'It's hard to cut off your past. Your going unsettled her.'

'They're all from *La Nouvelle Vie*?' he queried. 'Sleep with everybody? Especially Jean-Paul, I presume?'

Clothilde laughed. She was a pleasant girl from the country – no beauty, but amusing. 'It's not as bad as the *patron* makes out. Of course, Jean-Paul's got this theory of personal liberty – like that new magazine in America. *Playboy*, is it? Maybe there's something in it. Why shouldn't a woman make love without guilt? It's 1960, isn't it?'

'To anyone?'

'To anyone she wants. There's a fashion in guilt as there is in anything else.'

'A fashion?' Charlie echoed.

'Ideas about sex vary with the times, don't they? Nikki says Jean-Paul often sleeps with a different girl every night. It intrigues them. Who's he going to choose?'

'Like a Sheikh?'

'Except that they can say no. That's the idea. Freedom. No shackles. But of course it's an honour to be chosen.'

A sudden image of Nikki came to Charlie – and appalled him. 'I suppose . . .' he ventured uncertainly, 'I suppose Nikki was sometimes chosen?'

Clothilde laughed at him. 'Oh, you men,' she said. 'Why not ask her, monsieur?'

He had no chance to reply, for Thierry Mathieu, whom Charlie had met in the café with Nikki, swayed up to them in his graceful way. 'Still visiting us, Monsieur Charlee? Your plans were unsettled. Remember?'

'And what are my plans now,' asked Charlie, 'since you always know so much?'

The youthful smile appeared on Thierry's face. 'That's easy,' he said and pointed at Nikki. She was laughing with her head thrown back. 'She didn't look as happy as that before you arrived, monsieur.'

'You know I'm married, of course.'

'And your wife's awaiting your return,' declared Thierry. 'So are little Rhona and Tim.'

'You know the names of my kids?' queried Charlie, a little alarmed.

'It's my business to know things,' Thierry said with an offhand shrug. He consulted his watch. 'Don't tell Nikki, but there's a surprise for her tonight. Jean-Paul will be arriving at any minute.'

'I suppose that'll please her,' said Charlie.

'Please her?' he echoed, as though they were speaking of the Pope. 'Much much more than that, monsieur. She couldn't bring herself to ask him.'

Charlie was perplexed. 'Tell me,' he said, 'why's he taking so much trouble over Nikki? There are plenty of others to replace her.' His gesture at the girls in the room encompassed all Paris.

'He cares for his girls,' Thierry explained as though addressing the unblessed. 'Feels a duty.'

Even as Thierry was speaking, the entrance bell rang. From across the room, as the door was opened, Nikki let out a delighted scream: 'Jean-Paul!' And all conversation faded.

A man aged about forty, slim and oddly patrician-looking, stood in the entrance. He was dressed totally in black – fedora, trousers, roll-neck jersey, even the jacket loose on his shoulders – except for a broad silver belt at his waist. On either arm were dark-haired girls, aged about eighteen – identical twins, identically dressed in leotards that, like his clothes, were black, relieved only by silver belts.

Nikki moved to the door to greet him. 'What a wonderful surprise,' she said.

'I'm offended,' he declared. 'Isn't that true, girls?' he asked his companions.

'Desolate,' confirmed one.

'Prostrate,' said the other.

'It seems you invited everyone but me,' he went on. 'Still, I persuaded myself you intended to . . .'

Charlie was intrigued – and a little irked. As Jean-Paul entered the room, the guests parted to make way for him. He was offered a chair. The twins sank to the floor on either side. Still hardly anyone spoke. Nikki brought him a glass of champagne and he kissed her fondly on the lips, his hand caressing the side of her face, lightly fingering her ear. 'You look enchanting,' he said. 'No wonder I've been sad without you.'

She smiled affectionately, touched his nose in a movement of tolerant rebuke; and Charlie was disturbed by the familiarity.

Jean-Paul saw him then, leaning against the fireplace trying to look nonchalant. 'You must be Monsieur Charlee,' he said, pronouncing the name as Nikki did.

Charlie shrugged with an attempt at a smile. 'And you, I take it, are Monsieur Jean-Paul.'

'This is an attractive apartment you've bought Nicole,' Jean-Paul declared, idly stroking one of the twins.

'I bought it along with other friends of Nikki's mother,' Charlie corrected him.

'Of course,' Jean-Paul recalled, 'you were a war comrade of Elisabeth Ferrier, weren't you?' He rose in an unhurried movement and strolled over to Charlie, the twins following him like well-trained dogs. 'I knew her, too,' he added, slipping his arm round the waist of a girl next to him. 'Not well, of course. I was a novice reporter on the paper. She was a queen bee by then.'

He raised his hand to fondle the girl's breast. 'Elisabeth did me a great favour,' he went on. 'My first scoop, but dangerous. An important politician. She advised me how to gain consent from that bastard Duclos.'

The girl, beginning to be roused, raised her lips and he met them in a lingering kiss. 'I was very young,' he said, 'as you must have been, monsieur, when you knew her.'

'I was twenty,' said Charlie.

'And fortunate to be so favoured.' He was brushing the girl's nipple through her dress with slow strokes of his fingers. 'And now I hear we're to be attacked by the paper, though why I haven't discovered.' Again, he put his lips to the girl's mouth.

'Your ideas, perhaps?' Charlie suggested with a smile. 'Your influence maybe?'

The girl's eyes were closed as the kissing grew more passionate. She turned her body to him, put her arms round his neck. Jean-Paul eased himself away. 'Chloe, darling,' he asked her, 'do you think my influence is so bad?'

'No, Jean-Paul,' she answered with a giggle, 'but my father might.'

Jean-Paul laughed. 'There's irony there, don't you think?' he said, turning back to Charlie. 'That it's the same paper? In those days I was pointing the gun; now I'm the target.'

'I doubt if they'll pull the trigger,' said Charlie.

'Having second thoughts, are they?' queried Jean-Paul. 'That's wise, I think. I have excellent lawyers. It's been a pleasure to meet you, Monsieur Charlee.' And he moved on to speak to someone else, followed by his twins.

Nikki came up to Charlie. 'What did you think of Jean-Paul?' she asked.

'I think it's time I left.'

'You didn't like him, did you? I warned you.'

'I wouldn't say that. He's got a certain charisma. Can we meet tomorrow? I want to talk to you.'

'We can talk tonight. They'll all be leaving soon. The club gets busy at ten.'

By ten the apartment had emptied, as she'd predicted.

When at last they were alone, she closed the front door and stayed for a few seconds with her back to it, watching Charlie. He was looking out of the window at the roof of the church, which was floodlit at night.

'I thought you'd left Jean-Paul's world behind you,' he said.

'I thought you'd left me behind you,' she countered.

'Before you met me, I mean. That's why you'd gone to work for the *patron*.' He turned to face her and met a sullen stare. 'Now don't look petulant,' he said.

'You've no right to question me,' she burst out. 'You're not my father – or even my lover. Well, not properly . . .' A sudden smile lit up her face. 'Which is a pity, isn't it? But you will be one day.' She moved into the room and started to plump up the cushions of the sofa. 'Perhaps tonight,' she added, glancing at him. He shook his head with a smile. 'I wish I understood,' she said. 'You couldn't leave me and you won't love me.'

He laughed. 'You make it sound so simple.'

'It is simple.'

'Clothilde says the girls wait around to be chosen.'

'They don't exactly wait around.'

'I asked her if you were often chosen.'

A peal of laughter broke from her. 'You're jealous,' she exclaimed joyfully. 'Charlee, you're jealous.'

'Of course I'm not,' he insisted.

'Come and sit here,' she said, patting the sofa beside her. 'I think that's marvellous. You hate the idea of another man having me, don't you? Be honest now. Don't you?'

His shrug, as he joined her on the sofa, was careless. 'It's not my business, is it?'

'It could be. If I said I'd never been in Jean-Paul's bed, would you believe me?'

'I'd find it hard, I think – after tonight. Your friends . . . the open intimacies . . .'

She was sitting in her favourite position, with one leg under her, half facing him. 'They're fond of him. It's hard to explain. He makes them feel protected.'

'Then why did you leave him?'

'Because it wasn't enough, I suppose. Because it was living for now – and now must end, as parties must end. Also, you need to be very young, and no one stays very young, do they? So what happens then? But it's somewhere to run to – like home must be if you have one.'

He was touched by her words and she saw it. 'Oh, Charlee,' she said and put out a delicate hand to touch his face, feeling it with the tips of her fingers. Sitting as she was with one foot on the floor, her thighs were apart beneath the silk skirt, as Charlie was only too aware as she leaned forward and put her mouth to his. The need for her overtook him. For the first time, he didn't ease her away, but savoured her for a few seconds, not exactly kissing her, but moving his lips slowly over hers. Then, taking her by the shoulders, he held her from him, gazing into her eyes. 'No, Nikki,' he said softly.

'You'll stay in Paris now?' she whispered.

'For a few weeks,' he answered.

'You think we can go on like this?'

'We've talked this over, Nikki. Yesterday you got upset.'

'I know, but I've decided to be a brave girl, take the risk.'

He shook his head with a tender smile. 'You don't know the risk.'

'So what happens? We make love. Do you go blind? Do your arms fall off? Or anything else?' She giggled. 'Now that'd be sad, wouldn't it?'

'It's complex. Truly it is. Not only because I'm married.'

'What's complex?' She leaned forward and kissed him on the lips. 'You've changed, you know. Something's different. Does that increase the risk?' she whispered, kissing him again. 'It's not just your wife. It's Maman, but I don't mind you loving her as well. I've thought it out. We'll share you.'

'And you think that tidies up everything nicely?'

She kissed his ear. 'Why does it scare you so much?'

'Because we could set off more than you've even imagined.'

'Like the Atom Bomb?' she asked with a giggle.

'It's not so funny, Nikki. I've seen the mushroom cloud in the desert.'

'Then you can show it to me, Charlee.' With a nimble movement, she lifted her other knee and sat astride his lap, facing him. She kissed him hard, holding his head with her hand, parting her lips, allowing their tongues to meet. 'Let it happen, Charlee,' she whispered. 'It's going to anyway.' It seemed beyond him now. He put his arms round her waist and drew her to him, began to explore her body, just touching her through the silk of her dress – her breasts, her nipples, her buttocks, her neck, her ears. He slipped both hands beneath her skirt, feeling the smooth soft skin of her legs on either side of him, her knees, her calves, her toes. He ran his palms up the underside of her thighs and she lifted herself slightly so that he could slide his fingers into the wet softness between them. He kissed her, moving his mouth over her face, revelling in the smell of her skin, the taste of her lips.

She began to unbuckle his belt when, quite suddenly, a picture flooded his mind like a vision. He was back near the railtrack on that cloudy night, the detail so vivid it dominated all other thoughts – including his desire, though this stayed with him in some side-sector of his mind, so that through it all he remained oddly aware of the girl.

He could just make out Elisabeth ahead of him – the narrow

waist, the outline of her hair below the beret, the way she moved with smooth, small steps like a dancer. The sudden revealing shaft of moonlight, offering them up to the waiting Spandaus. The *ba-ba-ba-ba* as they opened up, the red lines of tracer bullets feeling for them just as the first of the mortar shells exploded, close on the left. The Sten shaking in his hands – the old nightmare. Even the way she fell was graceful, as though rehearsed. Sweat was streaming down his face. He was looking into Elisabeth's anxious eyes, but in fact they were Nikki's.

'What's the matter?' she asked.

'It's no good,' he said. It was now that he was sweating, he realised, now in 1960, not just in memory. 'I should never have let it start. I'm sorry, Nikki.'

She grinned like a teenager. 'That'll teach me to rush things, won't it, to be a racy Paris lady?' She kissed him on the forehead and got off his lap. 'It was Maman, wasn't it?' He nodded and she added: 'She's going to make it hard, I can see. Not strange, I suppose. We're two rivals, even if one of us is dead. Not that she is dead. I'll get some coffee.'

From within the kitchen doorway she said: 'Charlee, I was telling the truth just now. I've never been in Jean-Paul's bed. Do you believe me now?'

'Other beds?'

'Of course.'

'Rich customers of the club?'

'Once it was a member. Not a very rich one. But the others were from outside – and before, of course.'

'Before?'

'Before the club.'

'Were there many before?'

'A few. That was a bad time, Charlee.'

'A few,' he repeated, more to himself than to her. He'd always known, but he'd never really faced it. 'Been around, haven't you,' he said quietly, 'for a girl of twenty.'

'You never thought me innocent, did you?' She approached him with two mugs of coffee. 'Sometimes I think I am.' She sat beside him, both hands round the mug. 'When did you decide to cancel your flight?'

'Yesterday.'

'After our meeting at Fouquet's?'

'You were very foolish.'

'Can't always be sensible, can I? I'm only twenty as you said. It worked, didn't it?'

'I'd decided before then. That's what I wanted to talk to you about. I'd like to do what you suggested the other day – learn more about your mother, go and see some of her friends, people she worked with.'

'What's changed your mind?' she asked. 'You hated the idea.'

'I was afraid it'd touch raw nerves. I was right. Look what just happened. But maybe I need to face up to her, break the spell. Can't be possessed for ever, can I? Not fair, is it? On Philana, I mean.'

He said it with purpose, knowing it would hurt her, and she winced. 'Or you,' he added.

'Oh, I don't matter, do I?' she said softly. 'No rights. No kids. You're on loan, aren't you? But I think Philana can manage. Philana's clever.'

She took his hand for a moment. Then abruptly her mood changed. The happy grin returned. 'Oh, that'd be fun, wouldn't it, Charlee?'

'Fun?' he queried. 'It may not all be fun. She may have enemies, too.'

'Enemies?' she echoed. 'Maman?'

'Most people have enemies, Nikki. Especially if they're important people. And then they're important enemies.'

Nine

Three days later, Claude Duclos leaned against the frame of his french windows and surveyed his city. A cigar was held between the fingers of his left hand, which hung at his side, the smoke rising in a narrow spiral up his body.

'Elisabeth?' he mused aloud. 'The first time I saw Elisabeth, she was twenty and you couldn't miss her. She wore a scarlet dress and a little hat with a spotted veil. Her hair was bobbed and curved forward to a point on each side of her face. It was jet black like yours, Nicole, and she was ravishing. It was 1930, just after the Great Crash. The world was collapsing, but life went on and we were at the opening of a new store called Bonheur . . .'

He turned towards them, a man who was now in his late fifties, the passing years etched deep, Charlie reflected, like the rings on the trunks of trees. He'd lived well and his face had become a trifle fleshy; the early swell of a paunch was starting to show. But the sense of energy was still there.

Charlie had never felt easy with Claude. From the moment Elisabeth had first mentioned him, he'd known that acute jealousy of the young, and its traces remained. Even if she hadn't been his mistress, Duclos had played Svengali, shaping her career, tailoring her talents.

For Nikki, he was awesome. She had never met a man with such power, which he deployed quite openly, enjoying it like a game. Charlie hadn't wanted to face her with him so early, but Duclos was a key figure in Elisabeth's life, an obvious starting point.

Charlie had planned his investigation like a detective, starting with a long meeting with Sonya and Duncan, who was in France to watch his colt, Kestrel, run at Chantilly. He had spoken briefly to Leah and Max on the phone, arranging to see them later in London. Systematically, he, Sonya and Duncan had listed everyone they could think of who had known Elisabeth – and who they hoped would provide information and also leads to others. They mapped out areas of her life, considering how they could gain entry into each: her childhood, her work, her marriage, lovers, friends. Charlie spent hours talking to Nikki about people her grandmother or her father had spoken about, studied the diary for clues.

In essence, the problem was the same as that confronting the police in the case of any murdered woman. What was the motive? Jealousy? A *crime passionnel*? Money? Blackmail? None seemed very likely in this case, yet the killing had been elaborately arranged, as Charlie in his bitter anger never forgot. So the plan was to explore Elisabeth's life, sector by sector. Somewhere a motive must emerge. Meanwhile everyone was a suspect – even Claude Duclos.

Nikki, of course, was bait and Duclos rose to it. Practised old ham that he was, he put her at her ease in no time. 'I knew Elisabeth when she was about your age. You could almost be her. It's quite disturbing.' His broad warm smile embraced her as he added: 'I wonder if you've got her talent.' With Duclos, there was always challenge. 'Or her style,' he added cruelly.

'Her style, monsieur?' Nikki countered. 'Perhaps I've other qualities of her that – ' She broke off.

Duclos detected the sharpness. 'You're a survivor, I'd say,' he said. 'She was a survivor.'

She looked at him, wide-eyed like a child. How could he say such a thing? 'She didn't survive, did she?' she reminded him.

'That's true,' he agreed. 'Perhaps even survivors can only survive so often. There could be a lesson there.'

Now, as he spoke of his first meeting with Elisabeth, he paused, studying the girl with obvious pleasure as he inhaled from his cigar, the end glowing red. 'I can still see her vividly,' he recalled. 'The cigarette in the long ivory holder, the lipstick bright red like blood, the way she stood, as though challenging the world.'

'I strolled over to her. "You're the most striking woman I've seen in years," I said, "so, if I may please ask, who are you?"

'She looked at me as though I was too bold for her liking. "I'm still finding out," she answered. "It takes some people years, I'm told. Do you know who you are?"

'"I know my name," I replied.

'"That's no answer," she said.

'"It's a start," I countered. "Always build on what you know, as we advise our reporters."'

He held the cigar away from him. 'You see, Nicole, how

clever we thought we were with the repartee. I was only seven years older than her, but I was arrogant and I controlled a newspaper. She was very young, but already married and ambitious, of course, which gave her a veneer of confidence.'

Sonya was witnessing a scene that had long since become familiar. She had known he would be attracted to Nicole even without Elisabeth. There had been so many young girls now. Twice she had left the paper, and with it his inner circle, but she had missed the vibrancy, the colour, that surrounded him, and each time she had returned.

He was continuing with the story in his urbane, dramatic way. 'That day at Bonheur, I had a problem,' he said. 'Henri Aragon, the owner of the store, needed publicity in my paper and I needed his advertising. But, as usual for that kind of party, there was no story – as I told her.

'"Are you sure?" Elisabeth demanded.

'"You think there is?" I asked. "Paris has another store. Hold the front page."

'She laughed. She had this ringing, musical laugh that I loved to hear. "Surely problems should be defined," she said.

'"I've just defined mine. No story."

'"Why not go further, monsieur. Define what would make a story, something happening, something you'd want to print?"

'"It's academic, isn't it?" I said, dismissing it casually.

'"Say it wasn't," she pressed. "Say I made something happen for you, would you give me a job on your paper?"

'She was joking, of course. Newspaperwomen in those days were pretty tough. I couldn't see a pretty girl like Elisabeth in the office. "Why in the world would you want to work for a newspaper?" I asked.

'She gave a cool shrug. "I like being at the centre of things. I know I'd be good at it."

'"All right," I said, "what are you going to make happen for me?"

'" Do we have a deal?" she insisted. "A job in return for a story if you print it?"

'She sounded serious, but I sensed she'd outsmarted me. I seemed to have lost the higher ground – to a kid of twenty. But I went along with her terms and asked what she had in mind.

'"I'm going to change my dress in the Buyers' cloakroom,"

she said simply, "put on a mask and hold up the girl on the till in the Jewellery Department, which is immediately adjacent."

'"Divine," I mocked. "What are you going to do then?"

'"Why, return to the cloakroom, change back into this dress I'm wearing and rejoin you here for a glass of champagne. By then, the alarm bells will be ringing and the police will have been called . . ."

'"And almost certainly someone will have seen you going into the cloakroom," I added.

'"A woman in yellow who'll disappear," she insisted. "Remember the gun. I doubt if they'll follow. I'll be seen coming out of the cloakroom in this scarlet dress, I grant you that, but I'd hardly be suspected. My husband arranged the bank loan for the store."

'By now, I wasn't sure of her again. If it was a game, it was well thought through. "You might be asked about a lady with a mask," I pressed.

'"Of course," she agreed, "but I wouldn't have seen anyone from a cubicle would I? Perhaps, I might hazard, she escaped through the window."

'"And flew away like a bird?" I noted.

'"Maybe there was an accomplice on the roof with a rope. Of course, once you've printed the story, everything will be returned to Monsieur Aragon – and both of you will be delighted, won't you?" And she allowed the smoke from her cigarette to escape slowly from her lips, so that her face was partly concealed, but I could see she was laughing.

'I still didn't quite believe her. People had set up stunts like this before – but never actually committed the crime. "You still don't think I'm serious?" she asked. "Look!" And she opened her handbag, holding it so I could see inside. And there was a gun, a Smith & Wesson 38, and a black mask. "I was told you'd be here today," she said, "so I came prepared."

'"And the other dress?" I said.

'"In the cloakroom – in a valise, which is how I'll take out the stolen cash and goods. It's with my coat."

'"And if you're stopped going out?" I asked.

'"Stopped?" she said. "When I'm with my husband, the store's banker?"

'"Will you tell him?" I asked.

'She laughed again. "Pierre? Good heavens no. He'd be horrified. Well, now I'll start things moving, monsieur." And she began walking towards the stairs – I can still see her now, with her quick, elegant movements, the skirt swinging from her hips.

'She was already half way down to the lower floor when I got to the staircase. "Madame," I called out, leaning over the banisters, "we've gone far enough."

'She looked up at me scornfully. "You mean you don't want me to do it?" she asked. "Well aren't you a scaredy cat, Claude Duclos!"

'"It could go wrong and I can't risk that. My Fashion Editor will cover it. Not as exciting, I admit."

'"And our deal, monsieur?"

'"Oh, you have a job with me all right," I assured her.'

Duclos moved from his position by the window and perched on the back of a sofa. 'Well you knew her, Charlie. Do you think she was kidding me?'

Charlie shook his head. 'I doubt it. "Never bluff, Charlie," she used to say. "Not unless you're prepared to go through with it."'

'There *was* a valise in the cloakroom,' Duclos said, 'and a second dress. I made her show me that, at least. I think she'd have gone ahead. She was often just as outrageous – she brought in stories that would have eluded anyone else. At times it got her into trouble.'

'And then, monsieur? When you gave her the job?' asked Nikki, adding with a shy smile, 'This pretty girl you couldn't see in the office?'

'She used her looks quite shamelessly. She'd use anything.' He smiled. 'I started her on local stories here in Paris. They were exciting times. We were near to revolution. She was best at high drama – very personal and intimate. That's why she found her real métier in radio. We'd sent her on several foreign assignments when her big chance came from RTF radio. They posted her to Berlin as resident correspondent. It was 1933 and Hitler had just gained power. I'll never forget her report of the Night of the Long Knives. It made her, turned her into a national name.'

He began to prowl round the room. 'It's odd to talk about her after so long. Who else have you met of her friends?'

'None, monsieur.'

'None?' he asked in surprise.

'She was only four when Elisabeth died,' Charlie reminded him.

Duclos gave a sympathetic nod. 'That's sad. You should take her to see some others. Let's think now.' He ruminated, his brows heavy. 'She had hundreds, of course. Not all real friends maybe. Hélène Prevost was closest to her, I suppose. She was her producer at RTF, used to handle her reports. Another was Lucille Levallier. They'd known each other as children. You know the Levalliers, don't you, Sonya?'

His eyes were on her, that sudden sharp glance she knew so well. 'Hardly,' she answered. 'I interviewed René Levallier, but I never met *her.*'

Duclos nodded, his gaze uncertain. She wondered if he had any notion of what had happened with René, if he'd sensed that something was missing in the copy. She doubted it, but she could see that even now his antennae were ranging, still tuned, searching.

'Remind me of that story,' he said. 'Wasn't Levallier's name linked to that black market scandal – with the Allied forces in Frankfurt?'

'There were rumours,' she answered. 'It was his job to investigate such matters. But there was no question he was clean.' She met his eyes boldly.

'How can you be so certain?' he asked.

'Because I checked, Claude. I talked to everyone who could know.'

What would he have done, she wondered, if he'd known that she'd concealed the scandal? René had explained away the corruption – with lots of very French gesticulation, talk of younger days, the war, you name it, *and* that mesmeric charm. My God, she had asked herself, what would Elisabeth have thought? She was a professional from her toes to her fingertips, but she was human in that department – might even have done the same. Just once is OK, she'd have said with a laugh.

What Sonya hadn't known until now, though, was that Lucille Levallier had been so close to Elisabeth. René had never told her this. Almost certainly, she was the Lucille of the diary.

'Women seem to find Levallier attractive,' Duclos remarked, still watching her.

'He is,' she agreed. You bastard, she thought, how far are you going to press this?

'You found him attractive?' he asked lightly, but before she had time to answer him he went on to Nikki. 'I'll call Lucille for you. Then you'd better drop her a line. She's a bit of a *grande dame* now. Unspeakably rich. You ought to see Marie Cayzer, too. Get Charlie to take you to New York. She worked for the *Tribune*, saw a lot of Elisabeth in Berlin. But you know Marie, don't you, Charlie?' The question was pointed, since it was through Marie that he'd met the Mastorakis, with all the benefits that had flowed from that evening. 'No one better than Charlie to get you to Marie,' he mocked.

He turned abruptly to Nikki. 'I've got something to show you, though I've wondered if I should. Even Sonya's never seen it. Still, you're grown up now, aren't you? Come with me.'

He led the way to his bedroom and opened the door. 'There,' he said, 'what do you make of that?' Arranged on a chair lit by a spotlight was a painting of Elisabeth. Charlie felt the familiar spasm in the pit of his stomach, and for a few seconds neither of the others could speak either.

For the picture depicted her nude, in a simple but unusual pose – on her knees, sitting on her heels, with her head raised as though she were looking up at someone. What affected them was the way the artist had caught in her face and in the positioning of her body a great depth of emotion. Challenge, passion, anger, sadness, it was all there – the private portrayal of a woman in love, as though unobserved, with all the conflicts bared, the fears, the elation, the need.

Charlie had seen that look on her face often enough. As a twenty-year-old, he'd believed it was reserved for him alone, that she'd never looked at another man quite like that. But this picture had been painted before they even met. Now, at thirty-six, he was appalled. Nikki slipped her hand into his, as though sensing what he was feeling. She tightened her fingers, then let go.

Sonya broke the silence. 'Where on earth did you find that?' she asked at last.

'In her apartment – just after she escaped to London to join the SOE. She sent a message to me to get something for her. The odd part was that the painting was on a chair, just as it is now, with the frame dusty – as though she'd taken it from some cupboard for a last look at the past. The Gestapo would have slashed it to pieces, or worse . . . so I took it with me. Then I forgot about it. I only came across it the other day – in the villa at Menton, stacked with others in the loft, under the dust of years.'

Nikki hadn't spoken. She was still just staring at the picture. 'Was I right to show it to you?' Duclos asked her.

'Oh yes,' she answered, unable to tear away her gaze. 'I'm glad I've seen it.'

'Good,' he said. He walked through the bedroom door to the apartment entrance, dismissing them. 'I've enjoyed meeting you, Nicole. Come and talk to me again soon and' – he gestured with a smile at Sonya and Charlie – 'leave these two behind.'

It was as they were leaving that she turned back. 'One last thing, monsieur,' she said. 'Did Maman have a friend called W?'

'W?' he asked with a puzzled look that Sonya recognised. She'd seen it before when he needed time to think.

'I have a few letters she wrote,' said Nikki. 'She speaks of someone called W. I thought you might know.'

Duclos pondered for a moment – then shook his head.

'Are you positive, Claude?' asked Sonya.

He directed a sharp glance at her. 'Yes, positive,' he said, turning back to Nikki. 'Your mother was quite a dark horse, you know. That's why she was so interesting.'

Ten

Leah was scanning the restaurant anxiously as she waited for Marie Cayzer. Repeatedly she glanced at the entrance, fearing she would see Hugo. Trader Vic's at the Plaza was fashionable. Monty of AMC had said it was his favourite spot in New York for lunch – that and the Twenty-One – which was why she'd been about to suggest somewhere else when Marie rang off. My God, I should have been at Franco's ten minutes ago!

Having an affair must be like this, Leah thought as she looked around her – wondering all the time if you'll see friends, trying to check where your husband will be.

One thing was certain, though: if Hugo saw her with Marie Cayzer, he'd be furious. Elisabeth was forbidden territory – and, after the previous night, they were in trouble enough. What puzzled Leah was that the American development, which they were in New York to finalise, would at least treble the size of their business; and Hugo had been the architect of it, just as he'd engineered their whole progress from the day she'd first met him with his father. But he resented her central rôle as designer, the name the public knew. Only that week he'd given an interview to *Women's Wear Daily* in which he barely mentioned her, speaking of 'my plans', even suggesting he was the source of most of her ideas.

'What am I supposed to be?' she had demanded when she read it the previous evening. 'Some kind of glorified seamstress?'

It had turned into one of those furious quarrels that happened so often now, but this had been more searing than most. Dawn Chambers had been at the party they'd gone to. Leah admired Dawn, who was probably the closest rival she had, also making young offbeat clothes. But she didn't enjoy Hugo fawning over Dawn or talking in the cab on the way back to the hotel about how relaxed she was, how she seemed to work without the neurotic tantrums displayed by so many designers. Quite a figure, too, he remarked, meaning she wasn't skinny like Leah.

'You poor darling,' Leah sympathised. 'How can you bear

living with a woman who's so emaciated and lives on her nerves – especially when you have to give her all her ideas?'

It had been stupid of her. She should just have ignored it. As it was, he'd been able to play the tolerant consort. 'Sweetheart,' he said. 'You mustn't take it personally. You've got a lovely little body. Haven't I said so hundreds of times?' And he kissed her gently – but on the cheek, not the lips.

Later, in bed, he started to fondle her breasts and she said she was a bit tired.

'I want you,' he said. 'Badly.'

'In the morning, darling,' she pleaded.

'We'll take it very easy.'

'I'm dead tired. It's been one hell of a day.' Dawn had got him going, she thought. Why in God's name should she act as a substitute when she was on her knees?

His hands were on her as he tried to add stimulus to his request – and failed. 'Just try it, darling,' he said.

'All right,' she sighed. 'Stick it in.'

It was a graceless response. The games people play, the pattern of marriage. Certainly she should have co-operated a little, might even have quite enjoyed it once they got started. It wouldn't have hurt to pretend, at least, as God knew she often had; but why the hell should she? Especially after the business with Dawn. So she just lay there, almost falling asleep, until he stopped. 'Thanks,' he said bitterly.

It had been a restless night for them both. She woke early, and as he stirred she put out a hand as a way of saying sorry and it would be better now if he wanted it, but his humiliation had lingered. 'Time's getting on,' he said briskly. 'We'd better get up.'

Their partnership had been a long one, supported by a marriage that was now eight years old. Though nothing had been said, both realised that day that a peace was vital, and it had been made – of a sort. It was fragile. The smallest thing could break it, spark another quarrel – such as seeing her lunching with a friend of Elisabeth's without telling him.

She had tried to avoid this meeting with Marie Cayzer and was reluctant when Charlie phoned and asked her to contact her. 'It was an age ago,' she said wearily.

Shocked, he exclaimed: 'This is Elisabeth we're talking about.

You loved her, remember? She was quite a help, too, wasn't she?'

'Don't make a meal of it, Charlie,' she said. She knew what she owed Elisabeth. There were plenty of girls with a talent for design who had got nowhere very much.

'You were exploited to kill her, Leah. You were used, honey. Never forget that.'

'There's no chance of that,' she said. There certainly wasn't, nor of forgetting that night in the Vercors. Sometimes she wished there was.

'You're going to be in New York. Just call Marie and say it was my idea you got together. Talk about their life together in Berlin. Who did they meet, go about with, become close to? Somewhere Elisabeth made an enemy who went to a lot of trouble to see that she was killed. Maybe she met him in Berlin, maybe damaged his career with something she wrote. We need to know who, and why, and how he could get a signal sent from Home Station.

Leah became aware that a woman was standing in front of her with a bright smile on her face. She was about fifty, as Elisabeth would have been, grey-haired, with alert attractive eyes. 'You must be Leah,' she said as the restaurant manager drew out the table for her to take her seat. 'I'm Marie. I've been looking forward to this meeting so much. You must have known Elisabeth almost as well as I did, but she was very young, of course, when we first met. That glorious age when anything's possible – in a place, too, where anything could happen.'

She ordered a martini and asked: 'Well, how's Charlie and what's all this he's up to in Paris?'

'Doesn't he have business there?' Leah queried vaguely.

'Business, my eye,' Marie scoffed. 'Costa Mastorakis tells me that he's found Elisabeth's daughter, been to see some of her friends. Is it true she looks just like her mother?'

'Charlie says they're pretty similar,' Leah agreed.

'Of course, Costa's so dramatic. It wouldn't surprise me if he's having Charlie tailed by detectives. Philana, poor lamb, is out of her mind, but stoic. A lot of girls would be rushing to their attorneys, wouldn't they? But not her. She just wants Charlie back. Costa says it was OK Charlie carrying a torch for Elisabeth, because she was dead, but a daughter who looks like her is a very different ballgame. He's got a point, hasn't he?'

'Philana shouldn't worry too much,' Leah assured her. 'The girl's only twenty and Charlie's never been one for playing around.'

'No,' said Marie doubtfully, 'but if this kid's anything like Mama, I wouldn't let my husband within a mile of her, I can tell you. If I still had one, that is. Actually, I remember her being born. The war had just started. I sent over some baby clothes, which were already scarce in Europe.'

She smiled fondly. 'Elisabeth was crazy, you know. We both were, which I suppose is why we got on. Know how I met her? In a riot, no kidding. Well, that's not quite true. I saw her first at a reception at Ambassador Dodd's but we didn't talk. He was our man in Berlin, which, in '33, was a very odd place – a cross between Al Capone's Chicago and Dodge City. Hitler had just taken power. Brownshirt Stormtroopers were staging fights all over town. Every night you heard the sound of shooting. Sometimes you saw it.

'Elisabeth was dining in a restaurant called Romanisches. In the old days it'd been a place for writers and intellectuals, but it wasn't healthy for most writers to be too visible just then, so business had dropped off. We were OK because they were courting the foreign press. As I walked in, I recognised her from the reception and waved, and she waved back. She was sitting with this guy near a group of Brownshirts, but she hadn't been there long enough to sense the signs of trouble. By then, I could smell it a mile away – but it was already too late to get her out.

'The Brownshirts' table went over with a great crash and the party started. Their target was another group they reckoned were Communists. Elisabeth and her escort were in no-man's-land. In seconds there were bottles flying, followed by a charge and vicious fighting. One man was actually hurled through the plate-glass window and lay in the street with blood pouring from a cut in his neck.

'Elisabeth was struck on the head by a bottle as she tried to get out of the line of fire. It knocked her out cold, made a bit of a mess of her with broken glass. I dragged her into the manager's office, forced some brandy between her lips and mopped up her face. She was lucky. The damage wasn't as serious as it looked, and she came to as I held her – but kept her eyes closed, trying to figure out where she was before admitting she was conscious.

"It's OK," I said. She opened her eyes and grinned. "Why's it so dull around here?" she asked. "Nothing ever seems to happen."'

I had an apartment in Voss Strasse and I took her back there and made her scrambled eggs. There was a spare room, so she spent the night there. Next morning the bruises had come out, so she stayed a few more days – and kind of never left. We had a lot of fun. Parties. Dancing to an old Victriola. Receptions at the embassies – especially ours. All sorts of people. The Foreign Press Corps, of course. People like Knickerbocker and William Shirer of Hearst and Norman Ebbutt of the London *Times*. Also diplomats. Even Nazis. That's how we got a lot of the inside dope. One or two army officers, too. They didn't get on with the Party men, of course. In Germany, officers had always been a special class. They dismissed Hitler as an upstart – for a while. There wasn't much of an army anyway under the Treaty of Versailles – at least not officially. There was the Black Militia – a kind of civilian National Guard that was pretending not to be. Elisabeth did a story on it, slipping out of the country to broadcast it uncensored – and only just escaped being expelled when she got back.

'Putzi Hanfstaengl, Hitler's old buddy who was in charge of us, hauled her before Goebbels, but she could be so persuasive with those expressive eyes of hers. She was blaming the Allies for Versailles, she insisted. Hadn't it been disgracefully harsh on Germany? And wasn't that what Dr Goebbels felt, too? She'd broken the story of illegal military training, but what could they do?

'Those months were the calm before the storm. We had access to everybody – even the party leaders. You'd see them sometimes drinking lager in the Adlon. They tried to stop us reporting the attacks on the Jews without being too heavy-handed. They needn't have worried. At home no one believed us anyway. The stories were always toned down when they ran them. Weren't we being a bit sensational? we'd be asked in the cables.

'They sure were funny times. Sometimes in the summer we'd go out to the woods at Wannsee on picnic parties. Often they included Putzi and Rolf Diels, the head of the Secret Police. Diels was a bit sinister in his black SS uniform. Jumpy as a cat, too, swore Goering was having him watched. In the Party everyone was spying on everyone.'

'You went on picnics with the SS?' asked Leah incredulously.

Marie laughed. 'Hard to believe, isn't it? Remember, it was early days. Germany was in a terrible state and Hitler had a lot of support in England, America, France. OK, there were aspects that shocked us a lot – but you had to balance these against the achievements. Our job was to get news. Putzi and Rolf were sources. They were often at Embassy parties. Putzi even went to Harvard.'

Marie realised Leah was not convinced. 'Honey,' she went on, 'you should have seen those rallies. Gawd, were they impressive! That year, Elisabeth was with me at Nuremberg. We were with thirty thousand people in the Luitpold Hall. Darling, you've got to believe me. It was *pure* theatre, like High Mass in a cathedral, like Wagner. As Hitler approached outside, the band stopped playing and that huge throng fell silent. Then came the Baden-weiler March, and he appeared at the back of the hall, moving slowly down the long centre aisle with the other Nazi leaders as everyone went wild – "Sieg Heil! Sieg Heil! Sieg Heil!" Arms out in the Nazi salute, eyes ecstatic.

'The orchestra switched to Beethoven. Great Klieg lights lit the stage where Hitler'd taken his seat among his party officials. Behind them hung the 'Blood Flag' that had been carried in the failed Munich Putsch of '23, flanked by hundreds of hanging Nazi standards. There was a roll call of the Nazi martyrs who'd died that day – then speeches by Hess and others before Hitler rose himself.

'Say what you like, he was mesmeric. They said there was no sex in his life, but the sex in watching him on the platform was overwhelming as he screamed about the great future of Germany, about her being the last bulwark against Communism. It wasn't just what he said. He'd got those intense blue eyes, that darted about the audience as he spoke – unwavering for a second when they were focused in your direction, kind of transmitting to you all that raving emotion that he was building all the time to a great crescendo. It's hard to understand if you weren't there – or to convey the excitement he could provoke. All round, the women would be crying, eyes rolling, gone completely like women get at black evangelists' meetings. I was crying too, kid. Somehow it got to me and I wasn't even German. Phew, baby, what didn't happen to me that night?

'It was the hope he offered, I think. Hope can be very moving. *And* the hypnotic way he offered it – the chance for the Germans to climb out from the degradation that they'd endured, the picture he . . .' She broke off, realising that Leah was staring at the entrance. 'Seen someone you know?' she asked.

'Only my husband,' said Leah quietly. 'Coming in with Dawn Chambers.'

'Oh, they're villains, aren't they?' Marie sympathised. 'The bloody lot of them. That was what Elisabeth called them – though it was affectionate, as if she understood and forgave. Would it help if we changed places?'

Leah shook her head. 'I don't think he'll see me if I'm careful.' They were in a booth at the side of the restaurant. She tried to make light of it. 'Probably just ran into her in the street. But Dawn's the opposition, of course, so I hope he's discreet. Funny this should happen when I'm with you. I only met Hugo because of Elisabeth. She'd done this favour to a man called Ben Jordan – '

'Ben Jordan!' exclaimed Marie. 'That was some favour. Gawd, she ran close to the wind with that one. That must be the kid. Did you say Hugo? Of course. He was ten at the time.'

'You knew about it, then? Ben would never speak about it.'

'That's not strange. He was minutes off death. We were the outside world, so we had muscle – as everyone knew in Berlin. Jews often turned up at our homes begging for help. Sometimes we weakened – especially before the Purge.

'With Ben the problem was his wife. They were splitting up and the fight was over Hugo. That lady was right out of her tiny mind. Times were extra-sensitive. Something was clearly going to happen. If you'd got sense as a Berliner, you played it very easy. The SS were knocking on doors a lot more in the night. OK, she hated Ben, but this was breaking rules. She told them he'd once been a Commie. Jesus, this guy was a financier – respectable family. But as a kid, like lots of kids, he'd been caught by the Marxist ideal. But he'd long got over it. One word from her, though, and he was in Prinz Albertstrasse before you could say pass the butter. That was the Gestapo HQ in the centre of town. Sometimes, as you went by, you could hear the screams.

'That was a bad night. We liked Ben. He was often in the apartment. Well, we pulled every string we had – and between us we had powerful friends, you understand. We got him out. Then Elisabeth saw him across the frontier with little Hugo – in person, just in case there was any trouble.' Marie consulted her watch. 'Gawd, look at the time. How long are you staying in New York? Come to cocktails Friday. At five. Bring Hugo with you if you're still speaking. You will be, I'm sure.' She gave Leah a reassuring smile. 'Want to get out without him seeing you? I'll screen you as we leave.'

As they left the restaurant, Leah glanced behind her to see if Hugo had seen her, but he was too engrossed by Dawn.

They walked through the foyer of the hotel. 'Tell me,' asked Leah. 'If Ben was actually taken by the Gestapo, how could Elisabeth possibly have got him released?'

Marie displayed an enigmatic smile. 'There were ways, baby. We'll talk some more. Meanwhile . . . Well, is it quite healthy what Charlie's doing? I mean taking that girl through Mama's past? Raking over ashes that maybe still smoulder a bit. After all, Elisabeth was a great lady, but she sure as hell was no saint.'

'The girl's got a bit of an obsession about her mother, I gather,' Leah explained. 'Not surprising really. Charlie says she's found a letter of Elisabeth's, keeps mentioning someone as W. Any idea who that might be?'

'W?' said Marie. She eyed Leah curiously. 'You know, you've got to tell Charlie to slow this down. I mean, we must have known some guys whose names started with W, but I don't know that I can think of anyone special. But Jesus, honey, you're talking thirty years ago. Why doesn't Charlie get on with his business, buy tankers, come back to his wife? This isn't doing him any good – or the kid. Go back and call him now.'

She smiled suddenly. 'See you Friday, darling,' she said, and stepped into the big Lincoln that was waiting. There was a wave of her hand as it swept away from the hotel into Central Park South.

Eleven

Conrad Blake was alarmed by Charlie's sudden question. For a few seconds he stared at him – then carefully laid his knife and fork on the plate. 'I don't think that's something you should ask,' he said.

'Why ever not?' asked Charlie.

'Official Secrets Act,' Blake answered.

'Conrad,' said Charlie, 'the war's been over for years.'

'Those signals are still classified as secret. To protect the codes.'

'Secret from us?' exclaimed Charlie with mounting impatience. 'God damn it, Conrad, the signal was sent to us.'

'To Duncan,' Blake insisted stolidly. 'Eyes only for Head of Circuit. His own personal code. So I assume, at least – for a signal like that.'

'OK then, tell Duncan.'

As Duncan drove Charlie from Heathrow Airport to the Thames-side town of Marlow, he had warned him that Conrad Blake might need careful handling. Swinburne had had trouble persuading him to meet them at all. 'He's always been a bit of a loner,' Duncan said. 'But as Section Signals Officer, he'd have seen every message that was sent out from Home Station before it was put into cipher.'

'So he's got to be able to help, hasn't he?' Charlie responded. 'We sure as hell could use a break. We've got nowhere so far. We know how she joined the paper, we have a graphic picture of her life in Berlin – but not the faintest sign that anyone might have wanted to kill her.'

'You're too impatient, Charlie. Something will emerge, you'll see.'

Now, in his frustration at Blake, Charlie looked out of the window of the restaurant in an effort to restrain his anger. The scene was peaceful. Across the water, spanned by a suspension bridge, was the town, with its old church and ancient terraced cottages. On its outskirts were big houses with sweeping lawns.

It was June but the day was overcast. Swans hovered near the landing stage in the hope of pickings from the hotel guests.

He thought of Nikki. She had mistrusted the whole trip, didn't believe he had business in London. It was like talking to Philana. 'Why do you think I'm going?' he'd asked, chancing his arm a little since any hint of that signal, or what had followed, would have horrified her.

She ignored his question. 'How do I know you'll return? You might take a plane home from London as you meant to do from Paris.'

'Well, I didn't, did I?'

'Because you couldn't leave me. It might be easier from London.'

'Afraid the English Channel might break your spell?' he teased.

'Weaken it,' she corrected, watching him anxiously. 'You wouldn't go, would you, not without saying goodbye?'

Lunch had been a slow affair. Duncan and Swinburne had rambled on about the people at SOE's Baker Street HQ before moving subtly to the matter of the system – the way signals were issued by Section Officers, progressed through the Signals Officer before being teleprinted in cipher to a village in Buckinghamshire for transmission to France. But when, at last, Blake realised they were talking about an actual signal, and a dramatic one at that, he began having trouble with a memory that had been pretty detailed through the prawn cocktail and the Sole Meunière and the best part of a bottle of Saumur.

It was then that Charlie, exasperated, had intervened. 'Conrad,' he said bluntly, 'do you remember any signal before D-Day ordering an execution?'

The directness had shocked Blake, who had run for cover with all the talk of secrets and 'eyes only for Head of Circuit'.

'OK,' Charlie repeated, 'tell Duncan. He was Head of Circuit wasn't he?'

'We're not asking you to recall the text,' added Duncan. 'Do you remember such a signal at all?'

'I've seen a few of that nature,' Blake agreed cautiously. 'Occasionally.'

'Just before D-Day,' Charlie pressed. 'The order concerned a woman. Surely you'd remember a woman?'

It was between Blake and Charlie. The others were mere onlookers.

'Why ask me?' said Blake. 'If you received it, you know it was sent.'

'We're interested in why it was sent,' Charlie told him, 'and who by.'

'The Section Officer,' said Blake. 'Signals were always originated by Section Officers.'

'So you do remember it?'

'I didn't say that. I said the Section Officer might answer your questions.'

'We don't know the Section Officer,' said Swinburne. 'I was in hospital by then.'

They waited for Blake to suggest a name, but he didn't. 'Have you any notion of the pressure on us at that time?' he asked quietly. 'The traffic was enormous – at least a hundred and fifty messages a day.'

'OK,' Charlie conceded, 'you were working your guts out, but do you remember the signal?'

Again there was silence, the bland gaze. 'I don't know,' Blake said at last. 'I don't know what I remember. That time's all a haze. If my mind clears, I'll contact Swinburne.' He stood up. 'Now, if you'll excuse me . . .'

2

That night, Charlie went to bed early in his room at the Dorchester. He had dined alone, which always dampened his spirits.

Duncan had planned to spend the evening with him but had been called back to Newmarket by a frantic Annette. Young Ken had been arrested. She said it was just a kid's prank with a friend, but the police didn't see it that way – a dare in Sam Armstrong's yard, involving the favourite for the Derby, the most valuable horse in England.

'They're being ridiculous,' she'd insisted. 'You know what boys are.'

'I know what Ken is,' Duncan retorted. 'A bloody young fool. What in heaven's name do I say to Sam?'

'It's what you say to the police that's important,' Annette said. 'Sometimes I think you get things topsy-turvy about that boy.'

'Me? What's he got to do before you get at least a little shocked? Assassinate the Queen?'

'You'll leave at once, won't you?' she said.

After his lone dinner, in an attempt to ward off a mood of melancholy, Charlie called Nikki in Paris.

'How is your business?' she mocked.

'Not good.'

'There *is* no business,' she challenged. 'What do you take me for, Charlee? I think you've a beautiful girl there . . . whose mother you didn't know.'

'I wish I was in Paris,' he assured her. 'I'll be back tomorrow.'

He called Philana but she was out, and Mona, who looked after the children, answered the phone. Her tone was cool, accusing. 'Tell her I called,' said Charlie.

'Yes, Mr Dawson.'

'Can I talk to the children?' he asked. But they too were out. In New York it was late afternoon. 'Tell them I'm missing them, will you?'

'They'll be pleased to hear that.' The voice was colourless, as though he were an unknown caller.

'And give Mrs Dawson my love, will you, Mona?'

'If that's your wish, Mr Dawson.'

He sighed and called his office. 'Well, if it isn't the boss of our great enterprise,' said Terry, his general manager. 'Where are you, Charlie? I called Paris and they said you'd checked out. We were just about to contact Interpol.'

'I'm in London.'

'Seeing Cunard, yes?'

'Not yet, Terry. I'll try to see them in the morning.'

'Try? You mean you're in London and you haven't called them?'

'I've been busy, Terry.'

'Don't want to impose, Charlie, but you haven't retired by any chance?'

'I'll see you soon.'

'You said that last time. How soon is soon?'

'I'll call you, Terry. Maybe later this week.' He rang off, feeling oddly remote from the business. Somehow it didn't seem to matter much, not compared with Elisabeth. All the same, he thought, maybe he should fly home for a few days.

It was past eleven when his phone rang. 'Mr Dawson?' It was a woman's voice. 'Sorry to ring you so late, but I've just been dining with Conrad Blake. He told me about your lunch today, and I thought perhaps we might have a talk. You see, I was a cipher clerk at Baker Street. My name's Thelma Hardy.'

For a moment, he could hardly believe his ears. 'I can't wait to meet you, Miss Hardy. When do you suggest?'

'*Mrs* Hardy,' she corrected. 'Well, that's the problem. I'm going to Scotland in the morning, but we could meet for half an hour now. If it's convenient. I'm downstairs in the lobby.'

'Give me five minutes,' said Charlie, 'and I'll join you.'

Nikki's challenge was given substance. Thelma Hardy was beautiful all right – in her mid-thirties, dark, with large slightly slanting eyes that gave her an Asian look. A tailored black suit revealed a fine figure.

She got up from a chair in the lobby as he stepped out of the lift and held out her hand with a smile. 'Hope I didn't wake you,' she said.

He suggested a drink and they walked into the bar. 'I hear you've been grilling poor Conrad,' she said. 'Though I suspect you didn't get very far. He thinks the war's still on. Did he answer all your questions with just his name and number?'

'More or less.' Charlie asked what she'd like and ordered a couple of Scotches from the barman.

'Conrad was my boss as Signals Officer,' she said, 'but you might do better with me. Let's start with this. I knew Elisabeth – and I'll never forget that signal if I live to be a hundred.'

He had several seconds of soaring hope. 'I can hardly believe this, Mrs Hardy. You remember it? You mean you actually saw it?'

'I certainly did – I put it into cipher. We didn't send messages like that every day – especially about a woman I knew. You see, I'd met her once or twice because Frank Charlwood was my boyfriend.'

'Who's Frank Charlwood?' asked Charlie.

'You don't know that?' she said, surprised. 'He was the Section Officer who issued the signal.' Charlie found it hard to control his elation. 'Frank was on duty when the information came in,' she added.

'Information?' queried Charlie. 'You mean about her daughter and the Gestapo?'

'I never heard about that. My God, poor child. What happened to her?'

'Nothing. The report was wrong.'

'Thank heavens. No, I mean the information that started everything.'

The anxiety that had lifted seconds before was back. 'You mean there was more?' he asked. She nodded. 'Suggesting she'd been turned?'

She paused, watching him in puzzled surprise. 'Didn't you know that either?'

'No . . . well, I suppose we thought that Nikki . . . You see, we'd never have believed anything else and . . .' He broke off. The truth was he'd never thought it through. For Charlie, as for the others, Nikki's arrest had always been the sole basis for any suspicions of Elisabeth. 'Sorry, Mrs Hardy,' he said. 'Go on please.'

'Are you sure you want me to?'

'Quite sure.'

She hesitated, then shrugged. 'Frank was at the meetings,' she said. 'To decide what action should be taken. I couldn't believe it when he told me. He found it hard himself. We'd both got to know her when she was in England for training. Well, you probably know about that, don't you?'

Charlie lifted his glass, drank deep and put it back on the table firmly. 'Why not assume I don't know anything, Mrs Hardy.'

'Thelma, I think, don't you? Charles, is it?'

'Charlie,' he corrected. 'I saw her every day for months. We talked a lot, but who tells anyone everything?'

She was still doubtful as she sipped her whisky. 'OK,' she said cautiously. 'Well, after the Germans took Paris, she gave up broadcasting because of the censors and went back to her old paper.'

'*France Aujourd'hui.*'

'On the management side – not as a writer. She had come into contact with one of our Paris circuits, used to slip them intelligence that came through the office. Then one night she saw the SS loading a train with Jews for transportation. She'd heard it went on, of course, but seeing it . . . Well, that was the crunch. The circuit signalled us that she'd asked to work in the field and she was flown out by Lysander. Everyone was knocked out by her, even the women, including me. At the time she seemed a great catch to F Section.'

'Seemed?' he queried.

Thelma shrugged. 'Depends who you believe. We had to fight

for her since de Gaulle demanded her for the BCRA. After all she was a French national – with a famous voice, what's more, though she proved she could disguise it. But she knew us and wanted to stay, so we managed to hang on to her. She passed security vetting with flying colours. In the field, she was brilliant.'

'I can vouch for that,' Charlie said.

'Before she joined you, of course, she'd been caught up in the Prosper disaster, when the Gestapo got so many. It was a miracle she escaped. Section sent her to the Vercors to rest up since the Massif was so remote. But she wasn't supposed to stay. There was a notion in Baker Street that even two women together in the field were bound to quarrel, let alone three, but events began to move so fast.'

Charlie smiled. 'That's really English, isn't it? What they learn in the classy boarding schools. The girls got along fine. We were a close team. As for Elisabeth, everyone loved her.'

'Especially you.' Thelma studied him for a second. 'It still shows.'

Charlie's shrug was sad. 'Maybe.'

'It must have been awful for you. The signal, I mean. It was awful for us, but there was no doubt about the evidence.'

'What evidence?'

'Suddenly everything gelled. Started with a message from Butler, head of Pianoplayer. That was the biggest of the Paris circuits, you'll recall. It warned of strong evidence that Elisabeth was a double agent. Some of it was inconclusive: a couple of drops she'd known about in Paris when people had been arrested. But some of it was hard: contacts with the enemy viewed by more than one witness.'

'Contacts with the enemy?' Charlie echoed. 'That's nonsense for a start.'

She shrugged. 'She spent hours in a hotel bedroom with a German general.'

Charlie could hardly contain himself. 'It's impossible – so impossible it's laughable. When was this supposed to have happened? Who was the general?'

'We never knew who he was, but there were two occasions, one reported, one confirmed. There was even a photo of them, taken in daylight, but the agents had to be careful and you could only see her clearly, not him – not his face, that is, but his insignia of rank were visible. Add to that a bank account in a false name showing funds credited in Germany and drawn in Annecy. Well, that's where Elisabeth's mother lived with Nikki, wasn't it?'

'You mean they thought she was being paid by the other side? Thelma, this can't be true. It's a story.'

'Perhaps. I couldn't believe it either. But the physical evidence was pretty hot. It convinced them at Baker Street. It convinced Security Section, which is to say MI5. It convinced Frank . . .' She broke off, understanding what he was feeling. 'Remember it was only two weeks before D-Day. No one was taking chances then. There'd been too many traitors, proven or suspected – Prosper, Archimbaud, Déricourt. The photo and the bank evidence were flown out.'

'It was rigged – must have been. Elisabeth just couldn't have been a traitor. I knew her very well. Jesus, they can do anything with photos.'

'Who'd rig it, Charlie?' she asked. 'And why?'

'That's just what I'm trying to find out. Tell me just one thing, Thelma. Why did you call me tonight?'

She hesitated. 'I was never happy about it. I've always had doubts. Mainly because the evidence was just too strong. I mean, if you were going to fabricate a case against someone, you'd make it strong, wouldn't you? And I just couldn't see Elisabeth as a double agent. Then Conrad told me what happened today, how angry you got when he stalled. I guessed something of what you were doing and wanted to help. I wish you could talk to Frank. He was the one who was there.'

'I'd like to. Are you still in touch with him?'

She shook her head. 'He used to surface occasionally before I was married. He's an actor. Last I heard he was working with a small travelling company in Cairo.'

She studied him. 'It's been a great shock for you, hasn't it?'

'You've changed everything. We were chasing a missing signal, thought the system had been penetrated somehow. Now it's obvious that someone fed in rigged evidence. So the signal itself doesn't matter any more.'

'It's still missing, isn't it?' she said.

'You think that's significant? Why, for God's sake?'

'It could have stirred the water, enough for things to be looked at again. The signal was written, hard evidence. Not just memories. Well, it's obvious that someone wanted it lost, isn't it? Conrad saw it in the archive a couple of years back.'

'You don't mean it!' exclaimed Charlie. 'The close bastard!'

'He's careful. You scared the life out of him when you said it'd gone.' She stood up. 'Let me know if I can help any more. Here's my address.' She took a card from her bag and handed it to him. 'Where can I contact you if I hear anything?'

'The Bristol in Paris.'

'Another thing struck me as odd,' she said. 'I saw the answering signal, that she was killed in action. Was that true?'

'Yeah,' said Charlie.

'So she wasn't executed?'

Charlie was tempted to admit the truth, but resisted it. 'We were ambushed. Never seen such heavy fire,' he said.

She studied him for a moment. 'You're a lousy liar, Charlie,' she said, 'but it's been good to meet you.' And she walked out of the bar.

3

'No more calls, Sally,' Max said as Charlie walked into his office near Leicester Square the next morning. 'Not while our important visitor's here.' He put down the phone. 'Well, Charlie,' he said, with the nearest expression he had to a smile, 'isn't this a pleasure?' He leaned back behind his big desk, his cigar between his teeth. 'You're not looking so good, you know. You eating plenty of carrots?'

'A bad night,' said Charlie, 'that's all.'

'I get bad nights, too,' Max volunteered. 'Got myself a partner. Hotshot agent from Hollywood. Take us into the big time. International movies. That was the deal. Have MCA shaking in their boots. Well, maybe Ollie will, but the way he carries on you'd think he was the Emperor Augustus. Biggest mouth I ever heard. Thinks the English haven't progressed since Trafalgar. Never stops trying to make Sally.'

'I get the idea you don't like him,' said Charlie.

'Too right. But he's got a big deal going through. He pulls that off, it'll be worth it all. Now is this a social call or you got something on your mind?'

'I'm hoping you can help,' Charlie said. 'I want to find an actor called Frank Charlwood.'

'That shouldn't be hard. Probably in *Spotlight*.' He pulled toward him the actors' directory and started thumbing through it. 'Is it a secret why you want him?'

'Not from you, Max. He was an SOE Section Officer – he sent the signal about Elisabeth.'

Max glanced up at him, seeming unmoved as always. 'Progress, eh?'

'Too soon to tell.'

Max found the right page. 'This is the guy. Flemmings is his agent.' He picked up the phone. 'Sally, call Flemmings, will you, and ask what a guy called Frank Charlwood's doing. And bring us some coffee, darling.'

He replaced the receiver. 'Great girl that. I'm a lucky guy. How are things with that kid of Elisabeth's?'

'I'll be bringing her to see you. She's met Sonya now.'

'What's Sonya think?'

'They've got real chummy.'

'And Elisabeth's buddies?'

'The gun's still jammed. Loads I didn't know, but nothing tangible. Yet there's got to be a clue somewhere in her past.'

'You ought to talk to Romy at La Galère. She and Elisabeth were pretty close – Berlin in the thirties. Maybe she could give you a new line.'

'You've got to know her well, Max, haven't you?'

'Of course. She gave me my first break.'

'Did you ever ask her why?'

'Why?' Max echoed. 'I made a deep impression, Charlie.'

'Nothing to do with Elisabeth?'

'Of course it was. Elisabeth told me to call her.'

'That all? I mean friends do their best to help. They don't hand over their careers to kids with no form. How old were you? Twenty-four?'

Max observed him with his big impassive eyes. 'You're looking for a debt, aren't you? Something big from the past. Well, why not ask her yourself? Join us down there in a couple of weeks. I'm giving Sally a treat. Isn't that right, darling?' he asked as she entered the room.

'Isn't what right?' She set a coffee tray on a table beside his desk.

'That I'm giving you a treat. Taking you to the Côte d'Azur. I just suggested Charlie should come down, too – with Nicole. She a looker like her mother, Charlie?'

'Yeah,' said Charlie. 'See the photos of Elisabeth at twenty. Could be the same girl.'

'That's another reason to meet. Who knows, eh? She might have some talent. That bastard been putting his hand up your skirt again?' he asked Sally.

'Milk and sugar, Charlie?' she asked.

'Black, please, Sally.'

'Only one man allowed to do that, eh, Sal?' said Max, running his hand up the inside of her leg as she poured the coffee.

'Stop it, Max. Not in front of the crowd.'

'Charlie's not the crowd. Charlie's a pal from way back. Got anything yet on that Charlwood character?'

'He left the agency about six months ago,' she said. 'They've got an address. Said they'll forward anything we want.'

When she had left the room, Charlie said: 'Let me ask you a question, Max. If I gave you proof, could you believe that Elisabeth truly was a traitor?'

Max stared at him. 'Now we know they didn't take the kid?' Charlie nodded. Max shook his head. 'Not a chance, Charlie. Why? You got some reason to ask that?'

'Enough to make Baker Street issue the order.'

'Set up, eh? Have you put that question to Sonya?'

'I called her this morning. Her reply was the same as yours. And mine. And Duncan's. I haven't asked Leah yet since it's still early in New York.' He stood up. 'I'll let you have that letter for Flemmings.'

Twelve

After the conference, Sonya walked into her room and sat quite still at her desk for a few seconds. Jeanne, her secretary, put a cup of coffee in front of her.

Sonya nodded thanks, picked up the cup and held it with both hands in front of her lips without drinking. How serious, she pondered, was her position? It wasn't the fact that Duclos was sleeping with young Linette Deneuve. She was used to that. Always before, though, he'd made clear her own special status on the paper, how much he valued her advice.

The *Nouvelle Vie* story seemed different. Linette was keen on it, sensing it had all the elements that could make a journalist's name in 1960. Teenagers being exploited. Private orgies. A magazine that urged sexual freedom; a club where the serving girls wore revealing costumes, cut high at the thigh.

The first Sonya had heard about the project was from Nikki at Fouquet's – and she'd found this disturbing. She guessed Linette was working on it and asked her. 'That's right,' the girl said, her gaze unwavering. 'Looks promising.' She'd taken the story quite a way without it being raised at conference – clearly one of Duclos's special briefs, but he usually talked these over with Sonya. This time he hadn't said a word.

Sonya had opposed it, as he'd known she would, but not *because* of Nikki. It was wrong for the paper – risky stuff with a fragile basis. Nothing she'd heard about the *Nouvelle Vie* business gave scope for the morals or prostitution charges Linette was aiming for.

That day, three weeks after Nikki had told her, the project had at last been considered at conference. No, Linette had conceded, none of the girls she'd met had slept with men for money, and most had liked Jean-Paul. 'But they live in a world where there's no sexual restraint,' declared this bright, pretty brunette with the uplift bra. 'If you want to do it, then go ahead; take a different lover every night if that's your fancy.'

'Which might shock some people,' Sonya said, 'but it's a view Leblum expresses openly in his magazine.'

'Exactly,' Linette replied, as though this proved her point. 'The Sûreté are considering charges.'

'If they proceed,' said Sonya, 'then it's a different matter.'

'What if I can get proof that Leblum has seduced a girl under age?' Linette challenged.

'Then come back to us,' Sonya answered.

'No,' Duclos cut in. 'Come back to *me*, Linette.' He was glaring at Sonya. 'I don't think we need a prosecution before we run a major story.'

'Not if it's founded on fact, not rumour,' Sonya retorted. 'You've always insisted we're not that sort of paper.'

She saw the anger in him. 'I hope, Sonya, you're not reminding me what sort of paper I direct?'

She hardly knew how to answer. The rules had changed, it seemed. 'I'm putting my view,' she answered. 'Isn't that the purpose of the editorial conference?'

'That girl, Nicole Ferrier . . .' He was speaking very softly. 'Didn't she work for Leblum for a while?'

'I think we should leave Nicole out of this,' said Sonya, 'considering who her mother was.'

'Linette should meet her,' he went on as though he hadn't heard. 'Put them in touch.' It was an order. He wasn't discussing it. He looked round the table. 'Thank you, everybody. Linette, I want to talk to you in my office.' And without even a glance at Sonya, he left the room.

Jeanne came in again. 'Have I come back too soon?' she asked. 'There are one or two things . . .' Sonya nodded with a resigned smile. 'Madame Hélène Prévost called. She's back in Paris and free for lunch tomorrow. You asked for the Levallier file from the library.' She laid it down on the desk. 'The other calls were . . .'

Sonya hardly heard her. She opened the file. The top clipping displayed a picture of René and Lucille Levallier at a gala dinner. He was in tails, looking as usual as though he'd come out of a bandbox. She was in an elaborate ballgown that had Balenciaga written all over it. Sonya had seen it before, as she'd seen the whole file. There was nothing new. She stood up to leave. She was due to meet Charlie. 'Tomorrow,' she said to Jeanne.

As Sonya walked along the corridor, Linette caught up with her. 'How do I contact this Ferrier kid?' she asked.

'You don't,' said Sonya. 'Not until I say you can.'

Linette flushed at the sharp tone. 'But Monsieur Duclos said . . .' she began.

'I know what Monsieur Duclos said,' Sonya retorted. 'Or didn't you notice I was there?'

As she walked along the Rue de Richelieu she wondered if she'd be leaving the paper again, this time maybe for ever. She was always being approached by the opposition. Only last week she'd had two offers: a column in *France Soir* at double the salary; and the editor's chair of a big magazine. Either way, it seemed that Claude might no longer care, which saddened her. She had followed in Elisabeth's footsteps, both in French journalism and in Duclos's life. The connection had always pleased her, as though she was carrying on a kind of trust. Even now, she wondered sometimes how Elisabeth would handle a story. How would she handle Duclos in this situation? More skilfully than she had, Sonya guessed.

She thought again of Charlie's call the previous day from London. He was clearly shaken by what Thelma Hardy had told him, but he had insisted that his belief in Elisabeth was unchanged. Sonya knew he must have wondered, though. Always, when faced with evidence, it made you wonder, no matter how well you knew someone. Happened every day in a newspaper. Wives who couldn't believe their husbands were killers. Mothers who knew their sons weren't crooks.

But they always knew it was possible. With everyone it's possible. Even Elisabeth? She had her secrets, but who hadn't? No, Sonya said to herself firmly, not Elisabeth. Not a traitor. Not without Nikki at risk.

As she reached the Boulevard de la Madeleine and headed towards the Brasserie Joséphine, she could see that Nikki was with Charlie. She'd taken to the girl, enjoyed her infectious high spirits, the easy laughter.

Sonya's relations with her, like Charlie's were a reverse of what she'd known with Elisabeth. Now Sonya was the experienced woman, advising the young girl, reproaching her sharply when she needed it. One look from Sonya would be enough – by contrast to Charlie, who handled her as though she were a spirited mare, cajoling her out of her dark moods in a ritual that

Sonya knew was a shameless put-on. Nikki didn't mind Sonya seeing through her. It made them sexual comrades. Sonya disapproved of Nikki's designs on Charlie, but she would guide her sometimes. 'Stop teasing him about his wife, you silly girl. You're just making him feel guilty.'

Nikki would openly demand her help. 'Tell him now, Sonya,' she would say. 'He won't be able to resist me for ever, will he? Not unless he enters a monastery?' She burst into a peal of laughter. 'Good morning, Brother Charlee,' she said reverently, arms folded monk-like in front of her. 'Time for vespers, Brother Charlee?'

Meeting often, they had become a team of three that was comfortable, Sonya slotting naturally into their easy partnership. Nikki, of course, was still ignorant of the real purpose of the investigation, believing they were merely engaged in a review of her mother's life that she herself had proposed.

That evening, Nikki was sitting with her back to her and, as she reached them, Sonya put her hands over the girl's eyes.

'Have you brought it?' asked Nikki.

'Of course.' Sonya sat down, reached in her bag for the file and laid it open on the table. 'There you are,' she said, 'Lucille Levallier, your hostess at lunch tomorrow.'

Nikki leaned forward to study the photograph. 'She looks a bit formidable.'

'She is,' said Sonya. 'Go back in the cuttings and you'll see the progress. Ten years ago they were entertaining exiled royalty and fashion editors. Now it's heads of state and presidents of such international corporations as IBM.'

'I hope none are there tomorrow,' said Nikki.

'I doubt it. She'll want to give you time. People love talking about their past, and your Maman is a bright note in anyone's past.'

Nikki glanced at her with a smile. 'That's a nice thing to say, you know.'

'What was that story Claude was talking about?' asked Charlie.

'Corruption scandal – but René wasn't involved.' The lie came smoothly. Not even to Charlie would she ever admit what had happened with René. 'Interesting man, though.'

'That interesting?' queried Charlie with a smile.

'Look, Charlee,' cried a delighted Nikki. 'She's gone red.'

'Rubbish, Nikki.' Sonya aimed a friendly slap at her. 'René's come a long way. Going to be Assistant Director at the Ministry of the Interior, I hear. That's a big job.'

Nikki left them for a moment, chasing after someone she'd just seen passing by. Sonya sensed his despair. 'The London trip must have upset you,' she said.

'It's made me more determined,' Charlie answered. 'If only I could find just one lead. I bet it's in Berlin.'

'You'd still be back to why.'

'She was a great journalist, could have made enemies. She took big risks – that much we know from Leah. She even fooled Goebbels, kidding him that knocking stories were in the Nazi interest.'

'She could certainly be persuasive.'

'You can't go on fooling people, and we're not talking of Father Christmas, for Christ's sake. She pulled Ben Jordan out from the Gestapo and got him across the border with Hugo, and who ever heard of anyone doing that? But we've got no names yet, no motives, nothing to bite on. Marie was worried about what we were doing with Nikki. Thought she might be shocked by what her mother got up to.'

'You'd need a thousand volts to shock Nikki,' commented Sonya with affection. 'Charlie, it was never going to be easy. You're learning a lot. My God, you picked up something in London, didn't you? Also, Lucille Levallier may help tomorrow. They saw a lot of each other as kids. Why not tell Nikki to take that picture of Elisabeth with her – the one in the dress that Nikki wore. With only half her escort showing. Lucille will know who he is if anyone does.'

2

Sonya's guess had been right. They were the only guests at lunch, but Charlie was surprised that René Levallier had taken time off to be there as well. 'Couldn't miss this,' he'd said as he kissed Nikki's hand. 'My curiosity exceeded any affairs of state.'

He was too tailored for Charlie, yet he could see that Nikki was taken with him – a handsome man with an effortless easy manner, friendly blue eyes, manicured nails.

Lucille Levallier was observing Charlie with a cool detached gaze. 'Elisabeth spoke much of you,' she said. 'She found you remarkable, considering your youth and . . . well, your background, I suppose . . . Now, I understand you're a millionaire, with a fleet of tankers, so her judgment was sound wasn't it?'

The Levalliers seemed a good combination – in an ideal environment. Their home was a mansion on Avenue Foch and everything in it was perfect, and rather conservative, from the Meissen china on the table to the servants in their black coats and the Fragonards on the wall.

She herself, like most of Elisabeth's friends, was around fifty, but she looked older, rather drawn, with the skin tight over prominent bones. Oddly, behind the controlled façade, were an easy humour and a talent for vivid description.

She was obviously struck by Nikki, who had been warned to look demure. 'Sometimes,' Sonya had mocked, 'we have to do things that are quite against our nature.'

It didn't seem that hard for Nikki, thought Charlie. She looked delightful – in a simple blue frock with her hair brushed loose and only a touch of lipstick. 'You're a bit different to your mother at your age, I'd say,' Madame Levallier declared. 'She was always out to make a bit of a clang, as she put it, wasn't she, René?'

'She clanged beautifully,' he said with a smile.

So can her daughter when she feels like it, thought Charlie, meeting Nikki's defiant gaze with a wink.

Nikki turned back to Lucille. 'You'd known Maman for many years, madame?'

'Since we were children,' she answered. 'Our fathers were always close friends, which was strange. My father was very solid, bored my mother to death, but he was clever and did well, whereas Henri . . . Did you know your grandfather? No, you couldn't have, of course. Well, he was a funny little fellow with a drooping moustache and wide, expectant eyes. Marvellous company – a fund of stories, scandal. But it was all froth, I fear. The slightest setback and he was in trouble.

'He was a dealer. One of those men who are always about to make a fortune. My old friend, he'd say to my father, this idea's a winner. Can't think why no one's thought of it before. I can, my father would reply. He'd never lend him money, because he knew that debtors didn't visit you, but he invested in his crazy schemes, knowing this would bring him back.

'Always they were on the move – Paris, Lyon, London, even New York at one stage. That's how Elisabeth got her languages. In English she was fluent, and not too bad in German and Italian. Sometimes the creditors came for the furniture and Henri would send out Elisabeth to ask for time to pay. She'd get it, too. She was brilliant at handling people.'

René turned to Charlie. 'I hear you're married to Philana Mastorakis,' he said pleasantly. 'I know her father well. He has interests in French dockyards. In fact, I was talking to him only yesterday on the phone. I said you were coming to lunch. He's concerned.'

'Concerned?' queried Charlie.

'She's a charming girl,' René said with a gesture at Nikki. 'A young Elisabeth. Can't be easy for you, given the past.'

It was the casual tone, the smile of sympathy, that put Charlie on his guard. 'She's very different to her mother,' he replied. 'I've changed, too, over the years – as you'd expect.'

'Doubtless you've grown wiser.' The smile was polished. 'It'd be easier if you were Greek, I suspect. Could he put pressure on you if he was disposed to?'

Charlie laughed. 'Mastorakis would never do that. It's not how he'd play it.'

'I wouldn't be too sure. Would it be wise to go home? For a short time at least, to put minds at rest. I mean, she's attractive, lively, young. It's bound to raise questions, isn't it?' It was clever. So inoffensive.

'I feel a duty to her,' said Charlie. 'We all do – all of us who were with Elisabeth. She's got no family now and her life's been pretty tough. She'd met none of her mother's friends and to approach them by herself was daunting.'

'So you're her escort.' Again the smile, understanding, man-to-man, not quite mocking.

'I'm one of them. Sonya Mason goes with her sometimes. You know Sonya, I believe?'

'She interviewed me. A delightful lady – and a fine writer. Please give her my regards.'

'The others too are doing what they can. Elisabeth was a great help to all of us. We're deeply in her debt, you realise?'

'Naturally,' Levallier agreed. But he didn't, Charlie knew, and he was aware that René was still studying him.

Nikki was talking to Lucille. 'And my father?' she asked. 'You knew my father, madame?'

'Pierre?' said Lucille. 'Oh yes, I knew him well. Pierre was a decent man but he was outshone by his brothers, so they didn't let him do much in the bank. They had a summer house near ours at Deauville, which is how he met Elisabeth. She was staying with us. She was always good with shy people. She saw them as a challenge. Pierre hoped that with her help he could square up to his brothers.

'Of course, Pierre, with his wealth, seemed the answer to all Henri's prayers – so there was a lot of pressure on her at home. She adored her father, always wanted to please him, didn't she, René?'

'And she succeeded,' he agreed with a smile.

'It was a disaster,' she went on. 'Probably Pierre should never have married a sparkler like Elisabeth. He married again, I believe, after she died. A young girl, I recall. Did you know her, Nicole?'

'Yes, madame,' she answered. 'She was a sparkler, too.'

Lucille noted the tone. 'Poor Pierre, he didn't have much luck with women.'

'What went wrong with Elisabeth?' asked Charlie.

Lucille shrugged. 'She wasn't wife material. She tried, I think, but it wasn't enough for her, and before Pierre could turn round she was working for Duclos. Pierre tried to forbid it – the only time I've seen him stand up to her. They were staying with us for the weekend. She didn't argue, just said: "I need to, Pierre. You'll be proud of me. You'll see."' Lucille rose from her chair. 'We'll have coffee in the drawing room, I think.'

They followed her into the big pillared room with its large windows that overlooked the trees of the Avenue Foch. The butler placed a tray beside her.

'And when you both grew up, madame?' ventured Nikki as Lucille poured the coffee.

'We didn't meet so often. She was always flying off to foreign capitals. But she wrote to me a lot. We kept each other up to date.'

'I have a press cutting,' Nikki continued, reaching into her bag. She produced the picture of Elisabeth in the black silk dress. 'Would you have any idea who her escort might be?'

Lucille put down the coffee pot and peered at the photograph through her spectacles. 'It was obviously taken at a formal function,' she remarked as she studied it. 'Yes, of course, I know who that is.'

René bent to look at the picture, resting his hand on her shoulder. 'I don't think you do, my dear,' he said. 'I know who you think it is, but you're mistaken, I assure you. You thought it was Michel, didn't you?'

Charlie was watching them carefully. He saw her involuntary response: 'No, René, surely it – ' and the way she checked herself in mid-sentence, alerted by the pressure of his hand. 'Of course. You're quite right. It's hard to tell without a face.' She handed the picture back to Nikki. 'Sorry, Nicole, we're not much help, are we?'

'I remember the dress, I think,' said René, taking a cup of coffee to the mantelpiece. 'Just before the war. She looked marvellous in it – as you can see. Where did the picture come from?'

'I've got a few of her things,' Nikki told him. 'Not many, I'm afraid. I've even got that dress,' – glancing at Charlie – 'though it's a bit too sophisticated for me, I think.'

'Perhaps,' said René. 'What else of your mother's do you have? Letters, I suppose?' The question was so smoothly put that Charlie almost missed it.

'Hardly any,' she answered, 'which is a pity. There's a – '

'A beret,' Charlie put in, guessing she'd been about to mention the diary. 'And a cigarette case, a powder compact . . .'

'One or two pictures from when she was young,' she added, taking the hint from Charlie.

'Now let's think how we can help you,' said René, standing in front of the fireplace stirring his coffee. 'Who should we send them to, my dear?'

'I expect Claude's introduced them to Elisabeth's closest friends,' Lucille replied.

'Did he suggest you called on Dominique Saint-Jean?' asked René. 'She was Elisabeth's lawyer. Her father was her executor, but he's dead now.'

Charlie was suddenly alert. Elisabeth had asked Duncan to send the safe deposit key to a Dominique. René's eyes were on him. 'Elisabeth mentioned her to you perhaps?' he queried.

'Oh yes,' said Charlie. 'At least, I recall her speaking of a woman lawyer.'

'Lucille will give you her number.'

It was time to leave. The Levalliers accompanied them to the entrance – the elegant powerful couple in their Second Empire mansion. While a servant called a cab, René assured Charlie that he was at his service. 'Bear in mind what I said about Mastorakis,' he said.

'What I don't understand,' said Nikki in the cab as they headed up the Avenue Foch, 'is what they're all holding back – and why? That photo. She knew, didn't she?'

'I thought so,' Charlie agreed.

'Even Claude Duclos was careful,' Nikki said. 'I'm sure he knows more than he told us about that painting – *and* about Maman. After all, he knew her for years. Marie Cayzer was the same, by the sound of it.'

She slipped her arm through Charlie's and snuggled up to him. 'Sometimes I feel you're holding back too. Do *you* know the secret, Charlee?'

He shook his head. 'No, honey.' He smiled at her. 'But if there is one, I'll do my best to find out.'

Thirteen

What am I doing here? thought Leah, as she took the elevator to
Marie Cayzer's lavish duplex on East 65th. She hadn't planned to
attend her party, nor mentioned it to Hugo, since she'd have had
to explain how she knew Marie. But something had drawn her.
The old aura of Elisabeth, perhaps? The memory that remained
so vivid?

Maybe, too, it was an uneasy sense that she'd let Charlie down
by not pressing Marie enough. 'Jesus, honey,' he had exclaimed
when Leah called him, 'she must have made enemies in Berlin.
She was a journalist, for Christ's sake.' She had tried to explain.
He knew Marie. It wasn't easy to get a word in. 'Try again,
honey. Tell her you've got to know.'

'But not *why*?'

'Of course not why. What are you thinking of, Leah?'

So there she was, once more like a wife with a secret lover,
hoping she wouldn't meet anyone who would tell her husband.
And who was it who had the lover? Well, maybe he didn't. Hugo
had told her about his lunch with Dawn without any prompting,
said he'd run into her outside the AMC offices. Perhaps that was
the way it really had been. Certainly he had not made any more
insistent demands of her. No energy maybe – they were working
their butts off. Usually before, though, he'd had the energy.
Oddly, she felt sad about that.

Marie's face lit up when she saw her. 'Darling,' she cried, 'I
knew you'd come. No Hugo?'

'I didn't tell him.'

Marie put a finger to her lips. 'Not a word. But there's
someone else you should caution.' And Leah saw Hugo's father.

They fell into each other's arms. 'I've got a secret,' she said.
'Hugo doesn't know I'm here.'

'All right.' Ben Jordan smiled at her.

'It's to do with Elisabeth.'

'The old group?' he asked, understanding at once. 'Well, he
doesn't own you.'

'Mr Jordan, if I'm not mistaken?' The voice was heavily marked by a foreign accent. Leah turned to see a man in his sixties – tall, grey-haired, somewhat stern, holding himself erect.

'My God,' said Ben, 'this takes me back.'

'Not too happily, I suspect.'

The stranger turned to Leah, and Ben introduced him: 'Carl von Eysebeck, who was a young captain when I knew him in Berlin in the thirties.'

'Only a colonel even now,' he said with a smile, 'though I'm long retired, of course.'

'Strangely, Colonel,' said Ben, 'we were just talking of Elisabeth Ferrier.'

Cold eyes focused on Leah. 'You were acquainted with Mrs Ferrier?'

'In the war,' Leah replied.

'When Elisabeth lived with Marie in Berlin,' Ben explained to her, 'the Colonel was among their visitors.'

'Only occasionally,' added von Eysebeck. 'I heard she was killed.'

'It was a great tragedy,' Ben said.

'For you perhaps,' declared the German. 'But it would be wrong for me to pretend. She was a good friend, I concede, but a ruthless enemy.'

Leah's interest was aroused at once. 'She was your enemy, Colonel?' she asked.

He nodded sadly. 'She ruined my career. I'm the only member of my family for three generations who hasn't reached the rank of general through a line regiment.'

'And you blame Elisabeth?' queried Leah.

'Without question. My own fault, though. I was a foolish young officer and she exploited the folly. I'm sure she regretted it.'

'Why was that?'

'I've said enough, I think.' His tone was oddly wistful.

'Do you live in New York?' Leah asked.

'Not all the time, but I'm often here.'

'Leah,' said Marie, appearing at her side, 'here's someone you know. Remember Philana?'

Leah found herself facing Charlie's slim dark wife. There was a hesitant, almost haunted smile on her face, as though she feared what she was going to hear. Leah guessed that Philana had been reluctant to meet her, but Marie, in her robust way, had forced her to cross the room. 'Hallo, Leah,' she said.

'It's been a long time,' Leah answered, remembering the reunion when Philana had come with Charlie – and had felt so obviously an outsider, as all their partners did, as Hugo did.

'Have you seen Charlie recently?' Philana asked.

'Not since the last meeting. When was it now? April?'

'And the girl?' she asked softly. 'Have you met the girl – Elisabeth's daughter?'

'No,' said Leah, 'but . . .' She broke off, guessing how hard it must be for Philana to expose such fears to a woman she barely knew.

'Charlie still hasn't mentioned her to me, you know,' Philana went on. 'I heard it from my father. What's this about an apartment?'

'That's all of us,' Leah assured her hastily. 'We're all paying for it – and doing our best to help her.'

'Lucky girl. Is she in love with Charlie?'

'I shouldn't think so,' said Leah. 'To a twenty-year-old, a man's as old as God at thirty-five, isn't he?'

Philana gave a pained smile. 'It happens, though, doesn't it? And what about a young girl to a thirty-five-year-old man? That's an older story still.'

'If I said it wasn't the girl,' said Leah, 'but something else that's obsessing him, would it help?'

She saw the hope rise in Philana's eyes. 'Is it to do with Elisabeth?' Leah nodded and the hope faded. 'Then thanks, but I doubt if it would. Not much.'

Leah didn't get a chance to call Charlie until the next day. 'I may have got something for you,' she said. 'A German officer who knew Elisabeth in Berlin. Colonel von Eysebeck. Believes she ruined his career. Said he was sure she came to regret it.'

'But that's great!' Charlie exclaimed. 'What happened?'

'He wouldn't say, but I'll try to get more out of Marie. Oh, and Charlie . . . I saw Philana last night. She's pretty cut up.'

'I know,' Charlie said, 'but what do I do?'

'Write to her, tell her you love her, call her, for heaven's sake.'

'She rings off every time. Asks if I'm coming home and then the line goes dead. What did you tell her?'

'What an upright fellow you were, so she needn't worry. She

asked if Elisabeth was involved. I couldn't say she wasn't, could
I?'

'I suppose not. Thanks for trying anyway.'

2

'Saturday was a beautiful day in Berlin . . .' Elisabeth's voice,
coming through the crackling of the old recording, affected
Charlie more even than her photographs.

Many of us went out to the lakes of the Wannsee. The road
was busy – people on cycles with children in the sidecars,
walkers in *Lederhosen* with knapsacks on their shoulders,
motorcyclists in goggles. One group of hikers was singing –
boys and girls in their teens, eyes shining, haunting joyous
voices that faded behind us in that summer countryside.

They were happy hours beside that still lake water, the air
scented by the pines, and as we drove home in our open Ford
Roadster, we even sang ourselves.

What a contrast we found in the city. The crowds that
always thronged Tiergartenstrasse on Saturday nights in
summer were absent. On every corner were army trucks,
machine guns manned.

There were troops and police – the SS in their black
uniforms, the blues on their motorcycles, the State Police in
green. But there were no Stormtroopers, no Brownshirts – and
this was strange, my friends, because it was the Brownshirts
who thrust Hitler to power, who have paraded the streets,
persecuted Jews, fought the Communists.

This night will be remembered. In Munich the Brownshirt
leaders were to hold a secret meeting. It never happened. By
4 a.m. Hitler's plane had landed.

Rumours abound of Ernst Röhm, the Brownshirts' chief and
Hitler's old friend. A chance to commit suicide, a gunning
down? We don't know yet. But we do know that hundreds
have died in Berlin and Munich, thousands throughout the
nation.

In one savage strike, Hitler has switched his support to the
Wehrmacht, the regular Army. Today it is small, limited by
the Treaty of Versailles, but, friends, the question we must ask
is: How long will it be small . . .?

Charlie turned off the machine, unable to speak for a moment.
He looked at Nikki and Sonya. They didn't say anything either;

both were deeply moved. For Sonya, it had been an eerie experience, as though Elisabeth were still alive; for Nikki, the first time she'd ever heard her mother's voice, warped though it had been by static.

It was the only one of her broadcasts they had listened to. But just reading the transcripts of others devastated Charlie. For through her words, the question plagued him: Could this woman possibly have been a traitor? Could she have been in touch with the enemy when he knew her, adored her? Could all that talk of loving France, of the ideals of democracy, have been lies? Could the passion she so often voiced, the need in her eyes so clearly depicted in Duclos's painting, have been contrived? Could she have looked like that at a German general, as Thelma had reported?

Charlie's need for proof that Elisabeth was framed had grown desperate. He'd pestered Max by phone. The letter to Frank Charlwood had produced no reply, but the search for him obsessed Charlie. Something suspect must have surfaced in those meetings at Baker Street – a flaw in the evidence, possibly not even recorded – that would give him the one clue that'd open up the whole investigation.

He had tried to trace others who were present at those critical meetings, but some had died. Others had maintained the wall of silence he'd encountered with Conrad Blake. Charlwood, who'd been in charge of the case, seemed crucial. Couldn't Max talk to someone at Flemmings, Charlie demanded? Couldn't he pursue some other avenue to find the actor?

'Easy, Charlie,' Max said. 'We're doing our best. Everyone I meet I ask: Do you know Frank Charlwood? Sometime, someone will say yes, he's playing the Royal at Windsor, or that's the guy that Tony's cast at Elstree. Are you joining us at La Galère to meet Romy? With the kid?'

The idea was attractive. Previously, Charlie had hesitated because he thought they wouldn't have time. But now he felt checked at every point. His enquiries had revealed nothing significant about Colonel von Eysebeck. The lawyer, Dominique Saint-Jean, was away. Sonya, after her lunch with Hélène Prévost, had warned that, though friendly, she'd been oddly cautious – reluctant to meet Nikki for lunch, saying she'd join them in the Radio France library if she had a moment.

Her reticence had seemed almost churlish, but as the three of them sat there in silence Hélène Prévost came in and Charlie had liked her at once. She was a pleasant, easy woman of about fifty-five who at thirty must have been most striking. She was still slim and contained, with iron-grey hair and a quiet, confident voice. She'd been assessing news for years. The human condition, valued in seconds. What could it carry? A sixty-second spot? Who had died? How many? Who cares? Better cut it to thirty. But if she was tough, it wasn't obvious.

'So this is Nicole,' she said after greeting Charlie. She took a seat near her. 'Well, I'd have guessed it. Your mother and I were great friends – and I still miss her badly. It was my job to handle her broadcasts. It wasn't always easy. Often, when she was away from Berlin, there were no studios, so she'd report live over a phone. Sometimes she'd be cut off by the censors. Not often, because she'd studied the way they thought and French is a subtle language.

'Of course, she was well placed with Marie Cayzer. Marie had Nazi friends, high up in the Party – one in particular. So she had a strong power base that Elisabeth used. Elisabeth had her own contacts, too. She could always get to the Party leaders when she wanted to. That's often how she got her scoops.' She glanced at Charlie. 'Do you feel all right, Mr Dawson?'

'Fine,' he answered casually, but in truth he was in shock. For every word conformed with Thelma's graphic picture, as seen from Baker Street. A power base among the Nazi leaders, for Christ's sake!

Hélène studied him with the hint of a smile. She's doing it deliberately, thought Sonya, wondering if she'd guessed more of their real purpose than she'd revealed at lunch. Nikki, always sensitive to Charlie's reactions, was alarmed by the effect on him.

'Today, that sounds pretty disturbing,' remarked Sonya. 'The idea of Elisabeth with an inside track to the Nazi leaders. Yet at the time no one would have thought anything of it, would they? It was routine for any foreign journalist.'

'That's true,' Hélène agreed, 'as I've had to say quite often in her defence.'

'Defence, madame?' echoed Nikki.

'Why, yes, Nicole,' she explained, sympathy in her tone. 'For others wondered, too, especially as we got closer to war. Her reports were highly critical. She took incredible chances, like leaving the country to file uncensored, yet they never expelled her. Why not? They expelled others – like Tebutt of the London *Times* – but not Elisabeth. Even after she left the Berlin posting, they let her return often as a roving correspondent. Why didn't they refuse her a visa? It was a fair question, wasn't it? It even came up in a treason trial in Paris after the war.'

'A treason trial?' asked Nikki with a startled look. 'I don't understand, madame.'

'Only as a side issue,' Hélène added, 'so there's no need to look so alarmed. In support of some legal argument. But Elisabeth's contacts in Berlin did seem a bit too good. Some people even saw them as sinister – which was nonsense, of course. Why, on one occasion she had to escape across the border with the SS screaming for her.'

'I've never heard that,' said Charlie.

'It was much later – '38 maybe – and Marie smoothed it out for her, as usual, but it was getting harder. By then, Marie was deeply entrenched with the Nazis. She'd been totally caught by the Nazi myth, the resurgence of the new Germany. What's more she'd married Meisinger, one of the men who funded Hitler.'

'Good heavens!' exclaimed Charlie. 'Is that really true?'

Hélène nodded with a smile. 'She kept quiet about it later in America. It wasn't hard. She'd never stopped working for the *Tribune*, so she was better known by her by-line anyway. And her husband had died before America joined the Allies.'

'They were still friends, though?' asked Sonya. 'Despite that?'

'Oh yes. Elisabeth always stayed with her when she was in Berlin. She was fascinated by powerful men and Marie was very cosy with them. For me, Marie was always a problem. I warned Elisabeth early on that she was too close to her. People judge you by your friends. But she wouldn't listen. The way I talked, she'd argue, anyone would think we were at war with Germany. And of course Marie helped her get some wonderful stories – but she was tainted, and when it became obvious we *would* be at war there was a backlash.'

'Backlash?' said Charlie cautiously.

'It was subtle. Typically French – unstated, but there. She left RTF after the Occupation, stopped writing. Even that seemed suspicious in some quarters. Why didn't she escape to Britain and go on broadcasting to France from the BBC?'

'She joined the Resistance, for Christ's sake,' Charlie cut in. 'What more did they want?'

'To deploy her power, her reputation. That's what they wanted. Her words could damage the Germans far more than any weapons – but in a manner that would have been very public, which the Germans would never forgive. Add that Marie was her friend, her . . . buddy?' She used the slang word with a tentative smile. 'It may not have been known in New York, but it hadn't been forgotten in Paris. But, when the chips were down, Elisabeth's loyalties could never be challenged.'

Charlie stared at her, suspicious of his sudden excitement. 'I'm sure of that,' he said, 'but how can you be so certain, madame?'

'What a question!' exclaimed Nikki. 'How can you ask a question like that?'

He put his hand on hers to check her. 'Well, madame?'

The look on Hélène's face showed that she'd guessed his fears. 'Because she was Jewish,' she answered simply.

'Jewish?' echoed Nikki, amazed. 'Maman wasn't Jewish.'

'As defined by the Nazis she was. Her grandmother was Jewish. Your great-grandmother. Didn't you know that, Nikki?'

'No, madame, I didn't.'

'Not that it would have made any difference to what she did. In fact, I remember the night she decided to join the Resistance. She came to my apartment. She was very pale. "Know what I've just seen?" she said. The transporting of Jews was always kept quiet. Everyone knew about it, but you didn't see it going on. That night she had by chance – she'd had to go to an office that overlooked the railway sidings. "The kids," she said, "I can't get over the kids." It was worse than anything she'd seen in Berlin – and she'd seen plenty there, but not *en masse*. She needed revenge, a basic instinct. "With a gun, Hélène," she said. "I need to use a gun – not a bloody microphone."'

3

It was a fine day, and after leaving Hélène the three of them walked back to the Hôtel Bristol. Little was said. Each of them needed time to think, for her words had changed much.

As they strolled along the Cours la Reine beside the river, Charlie slipped his hand into Nikki's. He knew how hard it must be for her. For Sonya and himself, Hélène's disclosures had brought relief, though they also made him uneasy. It was

unpleasant to think of Elisabeth mixing with the Nazi leaders –
even if her job had demanded it.

For Nikki, though, it was worse. There weren't many ikons in
her life, and her mother had been unquestioned as a heroine since
Nikki was a child of four. Now she was aware that there were
shadows across her name. She returned the pressure of Charlie's
hand, glanced up at him, and tried to smile, though it was a poor
effort.

When they reached his suite in the hotel, Charlie ordered a
bottle of champagne to be sent up. When he offered Nikki a
glass, she shook her head. She was perched on a seat over a
radiator beneath the window, with one knee clasped by both
hands, fingers entwined, looking down into the street. She was
pensive and withdrawn. 'Go on,' he said, 'have a sip. Good for
you.'

She took the glass to please him. He put a comforting hand on
her shoulder for a second, then went into the bedroom to change.

After a few moments, she asked Sonya: 'Have you heard those
things before, what Madame Prévost was saying about Maman?'

'Yes,' said Sonya.

'Why didn't you tell me?'

'Because I didn't believe it. Nor does Hélène. You heard what
she said.'

'Didn't you suspect it might be true?'

'Not really.'

'Didn't Charlee?'

'Didn't Charlie what?' He appeared in the doorway still tying
his tie.

'Ever suspect Maman.'

'Good Lord no.' He turned back into the bedroom.

'Not even when you thought I'd been taken by the Gestapo?'
she called after him.

'Oh, Nikki, do stop this,' said Sonya. 'Quite a few people
were turned – some of them highly trusted. We knew it was
possible, especially if her daughter was in enemy hands. But you
weren't, were you?'

'Did you know about her life in Berlin?'

'Of course. Berlin was the hottest capital in Europe. It was full
of foreign correspondents in the thirties.'

Nikki was quiet for a moment. 'You know what I think,

Sonya? I think you know much more about Maman than you've told me.'

Sonya was about to reply when the telephone rang. 'Answer that, somebody,' Charlie called out. Nikki was nearest, so she picked up the receiver.

'Is Monsieur Dawson there, please?' asked a woman in English. 'Thelma Hardy here.'

Charlie came into the room and Nikki held out the phone to him, her eyes dark. 'Thelma Hardy,' she said.

'Good heavens!' he exclaimed. 'Hallo, Thelma. This is a surprise.'

'I've got some news for you,' she said. 'I've found Frank. He's in a play in Manchester, but he's going abroad at the end of the week. He's willing to see you. Suggested Thursday morning about eleven.'

Charlie was holding the phone close to his ear but he wasn't sure if Nikki could hear her. 'I'll come over tomorrow,' he said.

'I've checked,' said Thelma. 'There's a plane at five in the afternoon, your time. BEA. I could get to Manchester to meet it. I'd better be present, I think, knowing Frank.'

'That's a great idea, Thelma.'

'You realise he's . . . how can I put it? Well, a bit nervous. The background's delicate.'

'I understand,' said Charlie.

'I'll book you into the Midland. By then I'll have finalised things. See you at the airport.'

He replaced the receiver and met Nikki's gaze. 'And who's Thelma Hardy?' she asked accusingly.

'I met her when I was in London. Her father's a big wheel in shipping,' he lied.

'Like Costa Mastorakis?'

'They know each other. There's a friend of hers who's got a couple of freighters he needs to offload. Quite new ones made in Norway. We could use them. He's been abroad but she promised to call me when he returned. He's only back for a few days.'

Nikki was studying him sceptically. 'She sounded pretty,' she said. 'I think I'll come with you this time.'

'No, Nikki. Not on business. I'll only be gone a couple of days.'

'I could be your secretary. How old's this Thelma?'

He sighed. 'Ever so old. Like me.'

She got up, looking at him coolly. 'I don't believe one word,' she said. 'I've been a fool, haven't I? I believed all that stuff about your wife, and all the time it was Thelma in England.'

'Now you're being absurd. I've met her once for a quick drink. Sonya, tell her to stop being an idiot while I finish dressing.'

He went back into the bedroom. 'Goodbye Charlee,' Nikki called out. 'I'm going now.'

He reappeared in the doorway. 'Where are you off to?' he demanded.

'It's not your concern is it?'

'Now listen – ' he began.

'Goodbye, Charlee,' she repeated. 'Perhaps I'll see you when you come back.' And she walked out of the room, slamming the door behind her.

Sonya smiled at him and he shook his head. 'Doesn't miss much, does she?' she said. 'I thought your story held up well.'

'I wish I could tell her the whole thing,' he answered, 'but we just can't let her know about the signal. It'd lead to all sorts of questions, wouldn't it?'

'Yes,' she agreed, 'it certainly would.'

Fourteen

Rain slashed the windows of the DC-14 as it descended into the weather, streaking back in lines of water that merged, forming opaque squares on the panes. The aircraft touched down on the runway, and for a moment Charlie's high expectant mood was dulled by the grim view on that dark, wet day. But what did he expect? Manchester was famous for it, wasn't it?

Even before the plane had taxied to a halt, his spirits had revived. Thelma had warned him that the meeting with Frank next day wouldn't be easy; but Swinburne had been far more confident. He had known Frank well and, because he had agreed to see Charlie, was sure he would co-operate. Since Frank had been at all the meetings that had led to the decision to kill Elisabeth, he would be able to suggest new avenues they could pursue.

Swinburne had booked into the Midland too, and would be dining with Thelma and Charlie. Duncan planned to be there, as well, though this would depend on his son Ken's appearance before the magistrates. He was still hoping the police would drop the case, but the sheer value of the horse – in a town that was the centre of British racing – had caused great alarm. Meeting Frank was so important that Duncan had asked for the hearing to be put back.

The plan was that Charlie would start off by talking to Frank with only Thelma present – then ask if the others could join them. They had both been key figures in the Elisabeth case – Duncan as the Head of Circuit who had been sent the order; Swinburne who had recruited her.

Thelma was waiting for Charlie in the airport building. She greeted him with a wan smile and kissed him on the cheek as though she'd known him years – an old friend in deep trouble. 'Hope you didn't have to put off anything too vital,' she said as they walked to her car.

'Nothing could be as vital as this,' Charlie responded carefully. She said nothing further and the silence was strained as they got into the car. As she started the ignition, Charlie asked: 'What's wrong?'

'Bad news, Charlie,' she answered. 'I hardly dare tell you, but Frank's changed his mind.'

'Jesus!' Charlie exclaimed. 'Why?'

'I'm not sure,' she said as she drove out of the carpark. 'There was a message waiting at the hotel. We had a bit of a talk at the theatre. By that time you'd left Paris, so I couldn't warn you.'

'Did he give any reason?'

'Not really. Just said he'd thought about it. He's leaving the cast of the play, too. He wouldn't even tell me why he was doing that – "Personal reasons, darling," he said – but he was in a very odd mood. So I'm afraid I've got you over here for nothing.'

'It's not nothing.' Charlie smiled at her. 'At least we can all have a good dinner together.'

Duncan and Swinburne were in the bar when they got to the hotel. Thelma knew Swinburne from their days at Baker Street and they embraced as old colleagues. Being in his forties suited him, Thelma noted, with his dark hair just touched with grey and his prominent jaw.

'The news ain't good, fellers,' Charlie said as he ordered drinks and told them what had happened.

'He always was an odd chap,' Swinburne remarked, 'but this sounds pretty strange.'

'Do you think someone leaned on him?' asked Duncan.

'It's possible,' said Swinburne. 'Did he talk about Elisabeth at all when you saw him?' he asked Thelma.

'Oh yes,' she answered, 'I made him do that. He's quite convinced of her guilt.'

'That figures,' said Charlie. 'He issued the order that she was to die. Not pleasant. Middle-of-the-night stuff. So he's got to believe it was right.'

'He did ask me one question that I couldn't answer,' she went on. 'How did you hear that Nikki had been taken by the Gestapo? Did it come in from Allied HQ in Algiers?'

'No,' said Duncan, 'not by signal. Locally, I imagine.'

'The child was supposed to be a hostage, wasn't she? So the Gestapo must have got in touch. How? Didn't anyone ask Elisabeth, Duncan?'

'I don't remember.'

Thelma took a sip from her drink. 'Do you know what Frank thinks? That she made up the whole story.'

'Made it up?' Charlie echoed.

'He reckons she'd heard Pianoplayer had got the evidence. So she gave you a reason to sympathise, and perhaps disobey the order when it came in, or at least delay events.'

'That's impossible,' Duncan retorted. 'If it was true, she could have run for cover. There was a bloody German barracks in Grenoble.'

'That would have committed her to the Germans,' Thelma persisted. 'With the Allies winning the war, about to invade Europe. Elisabeth believed she could talk her way out of anything, didn't she? And let's face it, she was among friends.'

'It's absurd,' Charlie insisted. 'She'd never have taken that risk. I told you: she couldn't possibly have been turned.'

'Frank would say he'd heard that before.'

'About a woman with Jewish blood?' asked Charlie.

For a moment there was silence. 'I never heard that,' said Swinburne. 'Are you sure, Charlie?'

'Positive.'

Thelma sighed with relief. 'I wish I'd known that. Might have helped with Frank.'

'I doubt it,' said Charlie. 'Did you get in any questions about the sources?'

'I asked about Butler. He was the Head of Circuit, but he died in a riding accident about five years ago.'

'Anyone else?'

'Well, it's odd. Just after I kissed him goodbye, I asked Frank if he knew how Butler had got the evidence, and he said no, but as we reached the door he seemed to have second thoughts. "I can think of someone who might know," he said. "Roger Briedon. Member of Pianoplayer from very early days. Knew Elisabeth when she still worked for the paper. Even fixed her flight to London."'

'That sounds interesting,' said Duncan.

'Any idea where we might find him?' Charlie asked.

She shook her head. 'Just that Briedon was French and was living in Paris then.' She smiled an apology. 'Not much, is it?'

'No,' Charlie agreed, 'but it sure as hell isn't nothing. You've been nursing it, haven't you?'

She winked at him. 'Paris is a big city.'

They got up to go into dinner. 'How are things with young Ken?' Charlie asked Duncan as they entered the restaurant.

'I managed to get the hearing put back,' he answered, 'but they won't drop the charges.'

Swinburne was very quiet after they had ordered. 'Roger Briedon,' he said at last, more to himself than to the others. 'Roger Briedon, damn it,' he repeated, sipping his wine reflectively. A sudden smile came to his face. 'I remember now. The Goetz trial. Goetz was in the Paris Gestapo that was investigated by the War Crimes Commission. I helped ferret out some of the evidence. Roger Briedon had been in contact with them, no question. They were going to prosecute him, I recall, but for some reason they didn't proceed.'

'A friend in high places?' queried Duncan.

'I just can't remember,' said Swinburne.

Charlie was elated. 'If you're right, Steve, it means that the decision to execute Elisabeth was made on evidence supplied by a proven traitor.'

'Not quite,' cautioned Thelma. 'Frank only said that Briedon could know the source.'

'Maybe that was code,' Charlie suggested. 'And Frank wanted to tell you something.' He paused. 'I'm sure it was code.'

2

As Duncan drove along the Cambridge Road towards Newmarket the next day, the sun was setting behind the high woods that backed the Egerton stud. Shafts of light, striking between the trees, made light green pools in the paddocks where a couple of mares still grazed. It was a beautiful moment, just before dusk, and Duncan would have savoured every detail had he not been so preoccupied with Ken. How much was his own fault as his father? What could he do that would help the boy?

It was the same question he asked about his horses. Each was different. You had to find the key to them, what made them work best. Ken's problem was one of temperament, as it was with the thoroughbreds. He was talented and keen, but he needed to be out there all the time at the front – in every aspect of his life. He thought only in extremes. He couldn't just be high-spirited, he had to be dangerous. Duncan wished he had some of

Rob's quiet judgment, but then, he conceded, Rob could use a bit of Ken's push.

He came to the head of the High Street, passed the Jockey Club which controlled all flat racing in Britain, and as he reached the junction by the ancient clock tower at the foot of the town he headed off west up the Fordham Road. He could soon see his home, with its Victorian gables and walls that were thick with creeper, and he knew the deep sense of pleasure that always came to him as he turned into the driveway. Over to his left, as he came to a halt, was the yard with its eighty loose boxes. The horses had all been locked up for the night, but, as he got out of the car he detected the familiar sounds of movement. For a few seconds, he just stood still, enjoying them before walking to the house. For the thousandth time he wished Elisabeth could see what she'd enabled him to start.

He opened the front door and called out as usual to Annette that he was home. There was no answer and he assumed she hadn't heard him – but she had. As he entered the living room she was sitting facing him, cold anger evident in every inch of her. 'So the master has returned at last,' she said acidly.

The two boys were in the room with her – and also Jack Warren, another trainer, who had only had a yard in Newmarket for a couple of years. Jack was about thirty – a onetime steeplechase rider, with a quiet, easy-going personality that had made him popular in the town.

He had become very friendly with Annette in the past few months and Duncan had heard the rumours – the kind that were always rife in racing circles; but when he had urged her to take extra care to counter the gossip, she denied it hotly. 'He's a nice young chap,' she told him, 'trying to build up a stable. No sheikhs in *his* life with debts to Elisabeth.' Annette could really put the needle in when she was roused. 'My God, I'm ten years older than him,' she added as though that proved her innocence.

Jack had got to his feet as Duncan walked in. So had the two boys. No one was behaving naturally. 'You look as though you could use a drink,' Jack said. 'Been a long day, I expect.'

'If he doesn't need one now, he will by the time I'm through,' said Annette.

'Would you like me to play barman?' asked Jack.

'Thanks,' Duncan answered. 'Scotch, please. What's going on?' he asked.

'Oh, nothing much,' said Annette with airy sarcasm. 'Apart from the minor matter of your son in court.'

'In court?' echoed Duncan. 'The hearing was postponed.'

'Someone got their wires crossed. Don't ask me who – the court, the police, the lawyer, even you maybe. Perhaps you didn't bother to check.'

'I was assured everything was agreed,' Duncan insisted.

She shrugged. 'All I know is that your son was there on trial answering his accusers. I can't tell you what a help Jack's been. A tower of strength. Don't know what we'd have done without him.'

'You're making far too much of it,' Jack said, holding out to Duncan the drink he'd made for him. 'All I did was come with you to court.'

'When you had a colt running at Windsor,' she added, 'going for a mile for the first time. The magistrate thought you were the boy's father.'

'Only because I spoke up for him. The whole thing got out of proportion. Sam's horse didn't even get out of his box, thank God. But he could have done, no question. It was bloody silly, wasn't it, Ken?'

'Yes, Jack, I realise that now. It was great of you to say what you did.'

'And where was his real father?' Annette asked accusingly. 'In Manchester indulging his mania about Elisabeth. How long has she been dead now? Sixteen years, is it? Did you get any further?'

'Yes, a little,' Duncan answered.

'Well, I hope it was worth it.'

Duncan turned to Jack. 'Thanks for helping out. It was good of you,' he said, adding with a smile: 'How did the colt do?'

'Came second, but going on strongly. Didn't need me there at all.'

'Sorry not to have been with you, Ken,' Duncan said.

'That's all right, Dad. You weren't to know. It wasn't too bad. Just probation.'

Annette was glowering: everyone was being too nice to him. 'You know what Jack's suggested?' she said. 'That maybe Ken could join him as apprentice trainer – when he's old enough. Isn't that a wonderful idea?'

Duncan was surprised. Warren's yard was still small. And if Ken was going to work in another stable, there were others he'd have chosen first. Still, it was a generous offer. 'That's a kind thought, Jack,' Duncan told him. 'Might be a fine idea. We'll see how he's shaping in a couple of years.'

'He's got a good touch,' said Jack. 'Gets 'em reaching out. Pity he's too big to make a jockey.'

'At least,' Annette put in, 'Elisabeth can hardly interfere with that.' Then some instinct made her correct herself. 'Maybe I shouldn't be too sure. I've learned the hard way: never underestimate Elisabeth.'

3

Leah stared at the sketch pad with distaste. What had seemed a good idea looked totally uninteresting in the sketch. She rubbed out the shoulder line, lifted it, drew in a collar hoping that this might make it more dramatic, but it didn't.

Outside, the London sky darkened. It was going to rain – a summer storm which would match her mood. She flung down the pencil and wandered out into the workroom, noisy with the chatter of the girls. Like monkeys, Leah thought ungenerously – and felt she was being unfair, for they were a good bunch.

Even the garments they were making seemed drab and old-fashioned. I feel as though I just designed the crinoline, she thought. 'Tighter, darling,' she said to one girl. 'You'll lose the line otherwise. Sandra,' she told another, 'that seam's not straight.'

She wandered upstairs to the showroom. Hugo was with Monica, the manageress, talking to a customer. Leah recognised her – a buyer for quite a big store – and knew she should join them, but she didn't feel up to it. Hugo caught sight of her in the doorway as she turned away. He excused himself and followed her into the passage. 'What's the matter, darling?' he asked.

'I don't know,' she said irritably, going back down the stairs. 'Everything I do is rubbish.'

'Nonsense,' he said, following her. He closed the door of her office behind them. 'Let's have a look at it.' He studied the sketch. 'What's wrong with that? Have you thought about colours yet?'

'What the hell do the colours matter?' She rarely swore, even that mildly, and he recognised the problem – the inherent fear of most creative people that they'll never get another idea.

'Don't panic now,' he said. 'Analyse it. What are you trying to do? Talk theme.'

'I can't. I don't know. I thought I knew, but I don't. It's all tired, almost pre-war, for heaven's sake. It's time for something completely new, young and above all dramatic – something like Dior's "New Look" ten years ago.'

Hugo laughed and kissed her. 'That all?' he queried, for nothing in the fashion world had ever caused such a sensation. 'Tell you what. Go home, take a long bath. Then we'll go out to dinner and talk it through.'

They didn't go far – Alonso's in the King's Road. It was like a club, as indeed the King's Road had become. They knew the diners at three other tables at least – and waved, resisting offers to join them.

They ordered avocados, a new delicacy for London restaurants, steaks and a bottle of wine. 'Now shoot,' said Hugo.

She smiled at him affectionately. 'What would I do without you?'

'Find some other sucker, I expect,' he answered with a grin. 'And don't you dare say it.'

'Say what?' she asked, though she knew.

'Say what we owe to Elisabeth. Never say that again.'

Leah smiled at his vehemence. 'Tell me,' she enquired with care, 'can you actually remember the night she saw you across the German frontier?'

'How did you know about that?' he asked, suddenly angry.

It had slipped out. She couldn't say Marie Cayser had told her, since she had never told Hugo she'd met her.

'Ben told me,' she said, making a mental note to warn him. 'In New York.'

'He never speaks of it,' Hugo persisted. 'Not even to me.'

'He did to me. Well, can you remember it?'

'Of course I can. Have you any idea what it's like for a child to be with adults who are petrified? I was ten – old enough to know exactly what was happening. Father had lost two stone since his arrest by the Gestapo. There were still bruises on his face. He was certain they'd turn us back at the border. Even Elisabeth wasn't sure. That's why she came with us. She was far too chatty – and even as a kid I knew why. They held us for two hours, making phone calls, checking the suitcases down to the linings.

That's when I grew up. I was twenty when at last they lifted the barrier – with the body of a kid of ten.

'She took us to the first town, where we could get a bus, then drove back to the frontier. She waved from the car as she went – and as soon as she'd gone Father started to sob, shoulders heaving, tears streaming down his face.'

'Why have you never told me?' asked Leah.

'It was the most terrible night of my life. I don't ever want to speak of it again.'

Leah looked perplexed. 'But she saved Ben's life. Probably yours, too. Don't you feel grateful?'

'Yes,' he admitted, 'but after twenty-five years I've reached the end of it. I don't want her in my life any more. And there's something odd about the way you all speak of her. It's almost as though she's not dead.' He smiled brightly – a rather awful artificial smile. 'Aren't we here to talk about your work – about what's going to grab them because it's so new and dramatic. Like Dior in the forties. So shoot, baby doll.'

Leah laughed. 'Well, I'm close, I think. These are new times, darling – but the fashions aren't. Not yet. Everything's changing. The theatre, books, films. Youth has become big business. The kids are reaching for things their parents never knew, shaping their own culture. They've got money to spend, a sense of freedom. They've got new idols – not Clark Gable but heroes they can recognise like poor James Dean and Marlon Brando. New dancing to new music.

'And take this new pill. Think what it'll mean for a girl to *know* she won't get pregnant. The clothes they wear should reflect this, and I suddenly know how – by going back to the twenties when there was the same sort of mood, though for different reasons.'

'You mean short skirts?' said Hugo, catching her excitement.

'Of course. Oh, it's so good that you understand. But shorter than then, Hugo. Very short. Skirts made for dancing, for easy movement . . .'

'For sex?' he asked with a smile.

'Yes, maybe sex, too,' she agreed. 'And different materials. Cheap ones. Even canvas or plastic. But dare I do a whole collection?'

'Phew,' he said. 'You're talking revolution, aren't you? But start designing. Maybe you should just run four or five short numbers first time round. The press would love it.'

She reached out and clasped his hands with both of hers. 'You're such a help, darling. Really. I mean it.' She noticed the odd sadness in his face. 'What's the matter?'

He hesitated. 'You think I'm a help?'

'A fantastic help. What is this, darling?'

'Well . . . maybe you'll think I'm being a bit of an ass but . . . well, I'd like it if you'd say so a bit more.'

Leah feigned surprise. 'I've just said it. I've just gone overboard, haven't I?'

'I mean to others.'

'I'll tell the whole world, darling,' she exclaimed. 'But I thought the whole world knew. Why, we'd have gone bankrupt in two minutes without you, everyone knows that. You're the managing director. And I'm always telling people how much I need you.'

'As support, but I'm more than that, aren't I? Oh, let's forget it. I'm being a bloody fool. I know — let's celebrate. We've just been making history, do you realise that?'

'I've still got to do the designs,' she said cautiously.

'They'll be wonderful designs,' he declared confidently. 'We'll talk them through — together, bounce the ideas between us.'

He turned to summon the waiter to order champagne, and Leah had an odd feeling as the excitement began to drain from her. Just then she caught sight of Dawn Chambers at a corner table.

Dawn waved, then got up and walked over to them. 'Well what's this?' she queried. 'Dining *à deux* as if you'd just got married?'

'Great business decisions,' Hugo said, though Leah wondered why he needed to explain.

'The price of success, I presume?' Dawn remarked as the champagne arrived.

'Success to come, perhaps. A moment of wild optimism. Sit down and have a glass with us.'

'Sweetie, I can't. I got customers — and the draggiest. But I need to talk to you about something, Hugo. Boring charity business. So call me, will you, sweetie?'

As soon as she'd left them Hugo held up his glass to Leah. 'To very short skirts.'

She lifted her own in response. 'To wild optimism,' she said, adding: 'Sweetie.'

4

The moment she walked into the conference room, Sonya knew it was High Noon. She was a little late and the others were all there at the table, including Linette Deneuve, with her little high-pointed breasts and a look of excited confidence.

Sonya could tell from Duclos, too. She'd seen him often enough at such times – always calm, leaning back, hands on the table, fingers clasped. It just saddened her that for the first time she was playing the wrong rôle in the scene.

'The *Nouvelle Vie* story,' he said. 'Linette's got something to report.'

Linette looked boldly at Sonya. 'I've got what you wanted,' she said. 'Facts, not rumour. A girl under age, who's willing to testify. She's been in bed often with Jean-Paul Leblum, at times with other girls.'

'How old is she?' asked Sonya.

'Just sixteen, but it's been going on for a year.'

'Are the Sûreté bringing charges?'

'They've interviewed the girl.'

It still didn't smell right to Sonya, but she knew she was prejudiced. Not that there was much wrong with Linette: she was just another ambitious young girl reporter. Sonya even felt a degree of sympathy for her.

'Why haven't you put Linette in touch with Nikki Ferrier?' Duclos asked suddenly.

'I didn't think it appropriate for Elisabeth's daughter.'

'It was an instruction.' He was watching her coolly. It was as though there'd never been anything between them.

'Elisabeth's outside your instructions,' Sonya declared.

'Just who is this Elisabeth?' enquired Linette.

'Good question,' replied Sonya. 'Someone you should check out. Look her up in the files. She was important here once – both to the paper and to our esteemed editor-in-chief – like me. So maybe you should take note. She wouldn't have wanted Nikki exploited in a somewhat dubious scandal.'

'Would you say that if it was your daughter who'd been seduced?' Duclos demanded. 'I want the kid's phone number, please.'

She stared at him. 'You'll have to find it for yourself. I'm leaving the paper.'

A patronising smile. 'Again?'

'For good this time. I've been offered a column by *France Soir*.' She stood up. 'Watch him, Linette. This story'll backfire or I'm a Dutchman, and guess who'll get blamed.'

Linette laughed confidently – and Sonya knew what she was thinking. She'd deal with any blaming in bed. She could deal with anything with Duclos in bed. That's what she was thinking.

As Sonya walked into her office, Jeanne said that Charlie was on the line. 'Sonya,' he said, 'I can't find Nikki. She's not at the apartment. I've tried the café but Clothilde couldn't help.'

'How about the club? She always runs to Jean-Paul when she's in trouble.'

'She's hardly in trouble, is she?'

'Every time you say you're leaving the country she thinks she's in trouble. And this time she reckons there's competition.'

'She's a real dumbo. I suppose I'll have to go there tonight. Any chance of you coming too?'

She smiled to herself. 'I'm free enough. In fact, it'd suit me. Let's go paint the town red, Charlie.'

That early in the club the music was muted. Later it would get louder, hotter, with some jazz numbers, rock 'n' roll – but not too much. Control was the key. And quality. The girls looked sexy in costumes that were revealing but chic. The decor theme of satyrs coupling with nymphs was explicit but well-drawn. The furnishing was designed for comfort with fine sensuous fabrics like velvets and silks.

The ambience was stimulating and friendly without being demanding. A chap could feel at home there – and rather dashing.

Several of the girls recognised Charlie from the party and waved. 'Anyone would think you were a regular here,' teased Sonya.

Thierry came over and sat with them. 'To what do we owe this honour?' he enquired. 'As if I didn't know. I don't think she'll come with you.'

'She will,' countered Charlie. 'Ask her to get ready, will you?'

'Masterful, eh?' Thierry asked with a smile.

'Just tell her what I say.'

A few minutes later, Nikki appeared in the doorway. She was

in the club costume that showed every curve of her body – and standing as she was, looking at him, with one knee slightly bent, she looked such a cliché that he laughed – Marlene Dietrich in *The Blue Angel*. But oh, how he wanted her at that moment – and she knew it. The childish grin of triumph lit up her face and she strolled towards them, overplaying the vamp – deliberately, which was the point. She was mocking herself – and them. But there was a cutting edge.

'How was your Thelma?' she asked.

'She's not my Thelma,' Charlie insisted. 'She's happily married.'

'Just like you. Did you buy your freighters?'

'We're still negotiating.'

'You're lying again, Charlee. There aren't any freighters. Sonya, does he tell you lies, too?'

'Sit down,' said Sonya. 'There's something I want to ask you.'

'I'm not giving interviews,' Nikki said, perching on a velvet-covered stool. 'Your paper's got it in for Jean-Paul.'

'It's not my paper any longer,' Sonya explained. 'I resigned today. But the reporter, Linette, says she's made contact with an under-age girl. You've heard about it, I expect?'

'Heard about it?' she echoed, leaning forward. 'It's Véronique. Do you know how much they've offered her?'

'I know the kind of figure. Is it true?'

'It's disgraceful. We're all furious. She's having second thoughts, of course.'

'But is it true?' Sonya repeated.

Nikki nodded reluctantly. 'Well, she *is* sixteen and Jean-Paul had her when she was younger if that's what you mean. One of his favourites for Fiesta nights.'

'Fiesta nights?'

'That's what he calls them.'

'You mean orgies?' asked Sonya. 'Several girls at once?'

Nikki shrugged agreement.

'And you never took part?' demanded Charlie in disbelief. 'You told me you'd never slept with him.'

She flashed him a sad, provocative smile. 'What do you want me to say? Yes, I was there. Yes,' she taunted in her accented English, 'he fucked me every night, at every Fiesta. Why should I lie to you?' she resumed in French. 'I wouldn't be ashamed of giving myself to Jean-Paul. It's just that I haven't. You see, he loves girls, in all their aspects, not just one side. And they love him because he makes them feel good about themselves – which is why we're going to fight the paper. And the Sûreté. And the courts.'

'How are you going to do that,' asked Sonya, her interest caught, 'if Véronique was under age?'

'Because she told him she was eighteen – and she looked it. She told us the same thing. So, ten of us are going to sign a statement saying that Jean-Paul never knew. He does his best to avoid this, you know. The girls have to bring a letter from a responsible adult. Véronique's was forged. Will that help, do you think?'

'I think it might,' Sonya replied. 'In fact, the competition could well take it up. The loyalty of the girls would make a good story.'

'The problem is that Véronique signed something, so it may not be so easy.'

'Depends,' said Sonya, 'but I suspect the guns are spiked.'

Charlie stood up. 'It's time we were going. Do you want to get changed, Nikki, or are you coming as you are?'

'I'm staying, Charlee.'

'I don't hear you, Nikki, though sometimes I wonder why I take so much trouble.'

'Because you love me?'

'Maybe,' he agreed. 'A little.'

'Or because you still love my mother?'

He didn't answer – just took her by the hand and walked towards the entrance. 'No, Charlee,' she complained as she tried to keep up with him on her high heels. 'I've signed with the club, Charlee.' But he took no notice.

In the reception area, Thierry approached him, smiling. 'I don't think you should take her against her will, Monsieur Dawson.'

'Then I should call the police,' said Charlie.

Thierry laughed. 'Touché,' he said. 'Perhaps a cab would be more to the point.'

Nikki sat between Charlie and Sonya in the back seat of the cab and looked from one to the other. 'Am I under arrest?' she asked as it started moving.

'Not yet,' said Charlie, 'so long as you behave yourself. We're off to La Galère tomorrow. That's near Cannes.'

'Really?' she said. 'Well, aren't you full of surprises?'

'We'll be meeting Max there – and Romy Lagrange, the actress.

You'd like a few days in the sun with the famous, wouldn't you? Or have you got something better to do?'

She looked at him quizzically, the lights of Paris illuminating her face in flashes, then slipped her arm through his. 'I might find time,' she said, 'among my heavy list of appointments. What would you do if I refused, Charlee?'

'Abduct you.'

'I thought you had.'

'In the cause of your mother, remember? We're engaged in a project.'

'The man of iron. Except when your Thelma calls and you're off to England like a greyhound.'

'That's business.'

'Of course, the freighters. Is he a man of iron with you, Sonya?'

'I'm not a wayward young girl,' Sonya answered.

'Is that what I am? Wayward?'

'Very wayward,' Charlie confirmed.

She smiled at him. 'That's the minx in me, I suppose. All minxes are wayward.'

Fifteen

Nikki looked away from Max's steady gaze, finding it discon-
certing. Men eyed her every day, but Max's interest, though
penetrating, was different and oddly impersonal. Ever since they
arrived, she had been conscious of him watching her, sitting back
on his chair on the terrace with his straw hat pulled forward to
shade his eyes.

They had travelled from Paris by train and been met that
morning at Cannes station by Romy's chauffeur, who drove
them to her idyllic villa at La Galère, set among pines above the
sea.

They had clambered down steps cut in the rock to bathe from
her private jetty in water that was so clear that, fathoms down,
the fish were easily visible as they nosed lazily along the bottom.
But even there, splashing water at Charlie, she was aware of Max
watching her with a kind of total concentration like a camera. As
she climbed back up the steps to change her wet costume, she
knew he had been recording every movement of her body.

It was midday now and hot on Romy's terrace, despite the
light wind flicking at the awning. The strong sweet scent of wild
herbs, the monotonous buzz of the cicadas, the profusion of
mauve bougainvillea that emblazoned one wall induced a heady
sense of peace. Across the small bay, a black yacht had just come
into view off the purple cliffs of the Pointe d'Esquillon. The sun
glinted off the sea, in a thousand reflections.

Nikki had avoided Max, sitting as far away as she could and
keeping her head turned away from him, but she knew he was
still observing her.

At last he spoke in the deep voice that was like a growl. 'Ever
been tested?'

'Tested?' she asked, forced to face him.

'He's going to make you a star,' said Sally. It wasn't a taunt.
She wasn't even talking to Nikki. It was between herself and
Max.

Nikki shook her head in answer and he seemed surprised.

'Camera would love you,' he rasped. Does he ever smile? she wondered. 'As it would have loved your mother. I told her.'

Strangely, Nikki was irritated by the comparison. Always before she'd been flattered. 'What did my mother say?' she asked idly.

'Laughed at the idea,' Max answered.

'That you could make her a star?' queried Sally. 'Some people just have no faith.'

'She already was famous,' Max said. 'And I was in no position then to make anyone a star.'

'You made me a star,' said Romy walking on to the terrace.

'You were already, Romy darling.'

'Well, you made me a bigger one.'

She settled herself on a long swing chair, sitting casually with one leg, tanned knee bent, on the cushion beside her – a lovely woman in her late thirties, with curly dark hair and eyes that sparkled in a face that was as classic as an ancient Grecian head.

'Maybe I should laugh at the idea like my mother,' said Nikki.

'Maybe you should,' said Charlie.

'You suggested it,' she challenged, 'the night we met.'

'You weren't keen,' he answered. 'You've got to be keen to become a star. Isn't that right, Romy?'

'It has its price,' she said, 'like everything. Sometimes I wonder if it's worth it.'

Nikki was pleased by Charlie's negative reaction; she liked him being possessive. 'Perhaps I'd be keen if I tried it,' she said, preening slightly, turning her head to show her profile.

'You'd be one of hundreds,' said Sally. 'I've heard him say it often. He even said it once to me.'

'This one's exceptional,' Max insisted quietly. 'She glows.'

'Thanks,' said Sally, her pain apparent.

'Don't push me, Sal. I say things I don't mean when you push me.'

'Stop it, you two,' Romy said. 'You scratch at each other like a couple of cats.'

Nikki found Sally hard to fathom. She was quite a pretty girl – lithe and fair with the look of a schoolgirl, though that wasn't how she talked to Max. Everything she said to him was barbed, as though she resented him, yet she was affectionate too, touching him often, her eyes oddly soft sometimes as she watched him.

'Nikki hasn't got time to do a screen test at present,' Charlie remarked lazily.

'What's keeping her so busy?' asked Max.

'That's a dumb question if ever I heard one. You know why she's busy, why we're here. Not knowing your mother is like not knowing yourself. She can test later if she wants to.' He knew that one screen test would lead to another. Then there'd be meetings, phone calls, scripts.

Nikki was watching Charlie as he argued with Max, lying back on a recliner, a glass of wine beside him; and a mood of elation slowly enveloped her. He doesn't want me to test, she thought. Not any more. He wouldn't want me to be a star, because you share a star with half the world. The thought delighted her, because just lately she'd begun to feel jealous about him – absurdly excessively jealous – and it disturbed her.

It had started with Thelma. The uneasiness had been there before, but she hadn't been conscious of it. However, that day in his hotel suite when Thelma had telephoned it had surfaced with alarming force. She had known she was being petty and unreasonable, but somehow the notion of a woman with a voice like that calling him from England offended every instinct in her. And while he was away she had been tormented by thoughts of Thelma, conjuring up a sensuous blonde doing sensuous things. Since his return, it had got worse. She found herself resenting any woman he talked to or even thought of – including her own mother, which shocked her, since Elisabeth had been so important a bond between them.

The knowledge that Elisabeth and Charlie had been lovers had never been visual – until Thelma appeared on the scene, with the unwelcome fantasies she inspired. Then a strange thing happened. Elisabeth began to replace Thelma in Nikki's imagination, taking on physical form so that she would wake sometimes in the night, appalled by vivid pictures of her mother with Charlie, in intimate sexual detail.

Thelma had only been a threat, but there was no scope for doubt about Elisabeth. Elisabeth had known him, enjoyed him – only had to look at him, as she'd written in her diary, to start aching for him. And her aching had been answered, hadn't it?

Now, as Nikki watched, Charlie stretched lazily on the recliner and raised one knee, the movement seeming to involve his whole body; and a sudden vision filled her mind of a woman straddled across him – as she herself had been on that abortive occasion in the apartment.

It wasn't a clear image, more a feeling of easy rhythmic movement in the midday heat, a shadowy impression of parted legs that barely reached the ground, of breasts taking fuller form as she leaned forward to kiss him, all blurred as though she were viewing it through gauze – except for the eyes as the woman turned to look at her. They were her mother's eyes, quite clear, her own eyes. For a few seconds the image was vivid and tactile, as dreams can be – of strong, haired male thighs, a rough male face, firm male hands gripping female hips – and it aroused in Nikki a sense of angry, empty resentment. At that moment she hated her mother – and it shocked her because it was ridiculous, because Elisabeth had been a heroine to her for years, because she wanted so desperately to be like her, because she was dead for heaven's sake. What was happening? she wondered. What was changing? Had she gone crazy?

She shook her head to rid her mind of the disturbing vision and turned back to Charlie, who was lying looking deeply contented in the shade. The image of him with Elisabeth had drained her earlier sense of pleasure, and a sudden fury surged through her. How could he be so calm? She wanted to hit him, hurt him. Her fists clenched so tightly that her nails dug into her palms.

With an effort she controlled herself and stood up. She strolled over to Max and stood in front of him in her tight shorts and the sleeveless cotton shirt that revealed the outline of her nipples. 'You really think I should test?' she asked him.

He looked back at her, lazy desire unconcealed in his red-rimmed eyes just visible below the brim of his hat. 'I told you, didn't I? The camera'd love you. Everyone'd love you. No wonder Charlie's kept you out of sight.'

She smiled at him and ran her tongue over her lips. 'Are you sure I shouldn't test, Charlie?' she asked without taking her eyes off Max.

'Sure I'm sure. For the moment. In a few weeks you can test if you still want to,' Charlie said idly. 'So why not sit down, Nikki, and stop acting like a tart. You'll give Max a heart attack.'

'Now he's giving me orders,' she said to Max. 'You heard that? You've got no right to give me orders, Charlee.'

'Just sit down,' said Charlie. 'Please.'

'Don't mind me,' Sally remarked, standing up. 'Save a lot of trouble if he got a heart attack. I'm going for a walk in the woods. I feel like the clean smell of pine.'

'Don't let Sally bother you,' said Max as they watched her walk off the terrace. 'She gets like this sometimes.'

'So would I,' Romy remarked, 'if you treated me like you treat her. What are you going to do about her, Max?'

'Do?' he queried. 'Why, nothing, Romy.'

'Isn't that colour crazy?' Nikki said suddenly, wandering past Max to the bougainvillea on the wall. 'Have you ever seen a purple as lovely as this?' She made much of smelling the rich blooms. It was what actors call business, because she didn't know what else to do, feeling as she did a little silly. Then she strolled back to Charlie and picked up his glass, sipping from it in a movement that was intimate. 'Was I being a minx?' she asked softly.

'A real minx,' he answered. 'Go on like this and you'll win the minx prize of the year.' He smiled at her and swung his legs off the recliner, sitting upright so that there was room for her beside him. 'Look at that,' he said pointing out to sea. 'Isn't she beautiful?' The black yacht they'd seen earlier had almost crossed the bay now, leaning from the wind, her sails close-hauled. Soon she'd be hidden by the Pointe de la Galère.

'Know who that belongs to?' remarked Romy. 'Prince Khalid. I'd know it anywhere with those lines and the schooner rig. I wonder if he'll call? He usually does when he's down here.'

'You're well acquainted with him?' asked Charlie.

She smiled. 'I've known him for years. Since Berlin in '37 when I met Elisabeth. We've shared a few scrapes, I can tell you.'

Nikki felt Charlie's body tense beside her. He'd become alert. No one else would have noticed, but she knew him well now. Unhurriedly, he took a sip of wine. 'Has Max told you about our old pal Duncan? He trains the Prince's horses.'

Romy's smile was enigmatic, provocative. 'Have you, Max?'

Max surveyed her without expression as he often did. 'The horse won. You backed it. Last year. Duncan's tip-off.' He spoke fast, without change of tone or pitch.

She replied, copying his voice: 'Of course. Forgot. A thousand dollars. Very nice.'

Charlie laughed at her response. 'The Prince,' he said, 'told Duncan that Elisabeth saved him from a scandal.'

Romy looked at him, her eyes wide and mocking. 'Now surprise me, Charlie. Khalid's lived with scandal all his life. He thrives on it.'

'This was exceptional, I think,' Charlie went on quietly. 'It was why the Prince gave him some horses to train. Because of Elisabeth. It was a wonderful chance for him to get started.' He paused before adding: 'Like the chance you gave Max.'

She stared at him indignantly, as though he'd been indelicate. 'Max darling, I didn't know Charlie was going to interrogate me or I mightn't have asked him to lunch.'

'I'm sorry if I've offended you,' Charlie said.

'Charlie was deeply in love with my mother,' explained Nikki by way of apology.

Romy laughed. 'I know he was. As she was with him, I gather. And at a casual glance, I'd guess it runs in the family.'

'You're mistaken, madame. I'm not in love with Charlee. He's in love with his wife.'

'Very proper, too.' Romy laughed and took off her sunglasses. 'Nikki, I'd like you to call me Romy, as the others do.' She stood up in a graceful movement and took the bottle of wine from the ice bucket. She was wearing a light-blue skirt and a straw hat with a large brim.

As he watched her, Charlie thought how familiar she seemed. That was the trouble with stars. You'd seen them so often you felt you knew them – *and* so many of their expressions: anger, laughter, shock, despair and the whole range of subtle variations in between. Talk about glowing – as Max had said, the inner quality. Romy glowed, as if there were a great big sun inside her. 'How did you meet Elisabeth?' Charlie ventured as she refilled his glass.

'At it again already, Charlie?' Romy asked with a quizzical smile.

'Please. It's important.'

'How can it be important? To whom? Not to Elisabeth, that's certain.'

'It's important to Nikki. Everything about her's important to Nikki. Elisabeth must surely have done you a big favour, too.'

'Because of Max? I liked Max. He made me laugh. I'd never have given him my business if he hadn't made me laugh.'

'All the same it was a gamble, wasn't it?' Charlie insisted.

'An act of total madness,' Max agreed.

'Charlie, Elisabeth was a good friend. The world's a lesser place without her,' Romy said.

'Are you saying she never did you a favour?'

'Of course she did. That's what friends do.'

'A very big favour?'

She hesitated, gazing at him, cool and unblinking, for a few seconds as she'd gazed at Mr Rochester in *Jane Eyre*. 'I know what you're angling for,' she said. 'It's crossed your mind, Detective Charlie, that Khalid's scandal could be mine.'

'And was it?'

'What if I said it was a secret? Khalid wouldn't tell your friend, would he?'

'Secrets come out eventually – especially secrets about famous people.'

'How do I know I can trust you?'

'You don't, but we all loved Elisabeth. Max has your confidence. Elisabeth was Nikki's mother – and Elisabeth lies at the centre of it all, doesn't she? That's what the Prince said, but how in hell could she save a man as famous as he was?'

Romy smiled. 'She really fascinates you, doesn't she?'

'I find it hard sometimes. When I hear people talk of her, she doesn't seem like the woman I knew, the woman who changed my life, the woman I loved, for Christ's sake – and maybe still do in a way.' He saw Romy glance at Nikki and detect the fleeting wince of pain. 'I mean,' Charlie went on, 'how did she get that sort of power in a place like Nazi Germany? More than that – in the world. Khalid in a scandal would have made headlines anywhere.' He paused, but when Romy didn't speak he added: 'We'll find the answer, of course, if we go on asking the question. In time we'll find it.'

She studied him intently for a few seconds. 'I don't want you to go on asking the question, Charlie. Some day you might ask it of the wrong person.'

'There's a wrong person, then?'

'There could be. But what interests me is why you need to know.'

'I told you, Romy. Nikki – '

'*You* need to know, Charlie. It's not just Nikki.'

'All right, I need to know, too.'

'You won't tell me why?'

'I told you why.'

She shook her head in disbelief. 'You didn't, Charlie.' She moved over to Max, pouring wine into his glass. 'Someone else asked me once, you know – way back in the thirties. Called on me without warning. I even remember his name – Captain von Eysebeck.'

'Von Eysebeck!' Charlie exclaimed. 'Leah ran into him in New York only two weeks ago. Leah was one of our group.'

She glanced at him in surprise, then controlled it and looked away. 'I wondered what had happened to him,' she said quietly.

'Calls himself Colonel,' Charlie went on, 'though he's retired. Supply Corps and ashamed of it. Well, it *is* surprising for a "von". Said he knew Elisabeth. Wasn't friendly. Did you tell *him* the answer?'

She shook her head. 'He knew it. He wanted to use it.'

'Use it?' queried Charlie, adding carefully: 'Leah said Elisabeth broke him, despite his Junker family. The only one who hadn't made General in three generations, he told her.'

'That's right. Elisabeth did.'

'She broke a Prussian aristocrat on line to become a general? Jesus, Romy, what was she – a female Machiavelli? Are you surprised I want to know?'

Again she gazed at him with the same serious expression that she'd exposed to Cary Grant in *The Promise*. 'Say I do tell you something about it,' she said at last, 'will you stop asking the question? I mean of anyone else.'

He shrugged. 'There'll be no need then, will there?'

'Is that a promise?'

'You have my word.'

'Does that go for you two as well?' She looked in turn at Max and Nikki, the bottle poised in her hand – then she replaced it in the bucket. She turned, her expression softening. 'It was centuries ago, another world, but it'd still cause trouble. I was twenty-one at the time and I'd been married for two unhappy years to an Austrian politician named Count Otto Werner. Otto was in Berlin on long-term assignment, connected with the Anschluss, the merging of Austria with Germany. At first he'd hoped I'd give up my acting career, but then he found it gave him a certain cachet among his friends.

'I met Khalid on a movie set. I had a small part in a film that Erich von Stroheim was directing. Erich was pretty old by then, but he and Khalid had known each other for years and got along well. From the start it was a very powerful thing between us. You know – the old story of a look across a crowded room. Well, it was true with us. Khalid was in his late twenties and had a terrible reputation for women – and almost everything else, too: horses, the tables, fast cars, stunts in airplanes. He was crazy but delightful – the despair of his father, who'd sent him to Berlin on a special mission, a kind of last chance to display at least some sense of duty.

'The family was immensely rich, of course, and very powerful. Khalid's father was impressed by Hitler's progress with the Third Reich. So the Nazi officials had been ordered to treat him well – and they tried, but they weren't very subtle. They saw anyone who wasn't totally white as a peasant, even though Khalid was a graduate from Oxford.

'Khalid only had a smattering of German but he knew they were laughing at him and he got his own back easily enough – by sleeping with their wives. It was the talk of the town, but it didn't bother me. I was positive that what we had transcended everything, that it would last for ever.

'Khalid thought so too, I think. He asked me to marry him – and I would have done, even though by then he'd been married twice, to say nothing of hundreds of affairs, so he wasn't exactly a good bet. My divorce would have been horrific, of course. Otto would have fought every inch of the way if only to save his career – but as it turned out the issue never arose. Instead, we faced something far more serious.'

She wandered over to Nikki and stood for a moment, looking down at her with a smile. 'You do remind me of your mother, you know. You'll watch it, won't you? Don't get too involved with this feller here. I bet he's been saying that, too. You married, Charlie?'

He nodded with a grin.

'I wouldn't be in your shoes,' she said to him. 'Not after Elisabeth, not with Nikki here as a replica. Must give you a funny feeling sometimes.'

'It does,' Charlie agreed.

'Gives me a funny feeling, too,' rasped Max from the other side of the terrace.

'Elisabeth was cool-headed,' Romy went on. 'Always in control. Never panicked. Of course she was older than you, Nikki, when all this happened – twenty-five maybe. By then, she and I were pretty friendly. We'd met several times at diplomatic parties and she'd seen me in a play at the Deutches Theater and come backstage afterwards. But she knew Khalid much better. They'd met in various places – Paris, London, New York. When she saw him in Berlin they fell on each other like long-lost friends.'

'But what happened that was so serious?' asked Charlie.

'Don't rush me, Charlie,' Romy responded. 'This isn't easy for me.' She sat with her back to the sea on a low wall that fronted the terrace, her face shaded by her big hat. 'In 1937 we were due in Nuremberg as usual for the Party Rally. That year, though, Otto was under great pressure. The Anschluss was getting close and he was delayed in Berlin. I was to go straight from Paris, where I'd been staying. So for a couple of days I'd be in the hotel without him. Elisabeth was there too, covering the event for Radio France, and also her friend Marie from the *New York Tribune*.

'And so was Khalid. For us, it was a wonderful chance to spend all night together – and oh, did I yearn for that! We often met in the afternoon but nights were hard for us to arrange. He was too well known, so hotels were dangerous. But at Nuremberg we had a perfect cover.

'On the first evening, we had dinner with Elisabeth and Marie and later I joined him in his room. But I'd underestimated Otto. I suppose he'd heard the rumours, knew Khalid's reputation. He arrived during the night, quite late – around one or two o'clock, I think. And when he found I wasn't in my room, he went to Khalid's, which was just across the corridor.

'Khalid wouldn't let him in at first, but Otto was in full cry. Nothing would persuade him to go away that night. There was no escape, no point in hiding in cupboards. So at last Khalid opened the door and there we were, *in flagrante* as they say. There was a fight. Otto was a big man, fancied himself as a boxer, but Khalid was a judo black belt.

'I remember sitting up, still in bed, with my arms clutched round my knees, watching this nightmare that was going on in front of me, hoping to God I'd wake up. Then Khalid did one of those judo flips and sent Otto flying – and as he fell he hit his head on the wash basin and lay there on the floor in a heap, totally still.

'For a few seconds, I remember, neither of us could speak. Khalid was out of breath and panting, and I was shocked. There was a very light knock on the door – and a whispered "Elisabeth here." '

'She had the room next door and she'd heard them fighting. She took it all in at a glance – the fact that was Otto was surely dying and the repercussions that not even Khalid had yet begun to think about. Austria, Germany, the Party, the British since India was in the Empire. It was horrendous, but already her mind was fixed on essentials. Appearances were the most important thing, she said. Facts could be dealt with.

'First, the body had to be moved to my room. It was only across the corridor but we took a lot of care that nobody saw us. There isn't much blood with a head wound like that, and what there was could easily be washed off Khalid's basin. Of course, a little blood had to be found on my basin, for that was the story Elisabeth concocted. He fell in my room. It was late, dark. My husband hadn't turned on the light because he didn't want to wake me up.'

'And the police bought that?' Charlie asked in astonishment.

'The police?' echoed Romy with a smile. 'Charlie, this was a senior Nazi – Austrian, but a Nazi. Detectives wouldn't be analysing hair samples on the carpet. It was a question of appearances, as Elisabeth said. And she dealt with them brilliantly: I've never met another woman who would have done what she did. Khalid must spend the rest of the night with her, she said. The maid would see them in bed together when she brought up breakfast – catch them still asleep. And Khalid would give her a huge tip to keep quiet.'

'You mean,' said Nikki, 'that my mother was Prince Khalid's alibi?'

Romy nodded. 'If he'd spent the night with Elisabeth, Otto could hardly have caught me in bed with him in his room, could he? It was totally believable, despite any forensic evidence, and that was what mattered. Khalid was known for his success with women. As for your mother, well she had to watch her reputation. In those days any woman did, though she had her admirers, of course. She was very attractive. Discretion was vital, so what she did for us was noble. No other word's adequate and neither of us will ever forget it. You see, Otto died three days later in hospital. He'd never regained consciousness.

'Soon after, Khalid left Germany which suggests some hints were dropped at diplomatic level. Sadruddin, his younger brother, was sent to Berlin to take his place and it was all swept under the carpet.'

'Until Captain von Eysebeck paid you a visit,' Max suggested.

'Ah yes,' Romy countered. 'The Captain knew the body had been moved – and realised why. How, I never knew. Maybe someone saw us despite the care we took. Maybe he got friendly with one of the detectives and there was a clue we'd overlooked. He was in money trouble, but I knew that blackmail would be an endless path so I screamed for help. Elisabeth could have stopped him stone cold dead in the market. She and Marie had immense power in both the Army and the Party, but even then there was talk of plots against Hitler. Things could change. She wasn't taking risks.

'Luckily for us, the Captain had a skeleton in his own closet: corruption – sweeteners for Army contracts. He was up to his neck in it. Just a few enquiries and she had him begging for mercy – but she wouldn't grant him any. He had to be discredited, she insisted. Then it would always be her word against his – and under any law she'd outrank him. I'd never seen her being ruthless before. We were driving to Munich, I recall and she said: "Sometimes, Romy, there are things you must do, like soldiers must kill in war. And what I must do is pick up a phone and that'll be it."

'"And he'll be disgraced?" I said. Oddly, I felt sorry for him.

'"I expect so," she agreed, "but his family's got influence. It won't be too bad for him." Then she said a very strange thing: "You know, Romy, it's not just what it seems. In fact, I'm involved too. I know the captain well. I have to do this for my sake as well as yours."

'"I couldn't think what she meant and I pressed her, but she gave that mischievous grin of hers – a bit like yours, Nikki – and said: "I'll tell you sometime, perhaps. Just for now, it's best you don't know" – and of course I never found out.'

Romy smiled and placed her hands on her thighs as a gesture that the story was over. 'Don't you forget your promise, Charlie. No more questions – not to anyone. You've all promised. Right, who's ready for lunch?'

Everyone stood up except Nikki, who remained sitting, her back rigid, staring in front of her, so deep in thought she didn't seem to realise what was happening around her. 'Come on,

Nikki,' Romy said with a smile. 'Aren't you hungry? We've got some delicious lobsters.'

'Tell me, madame – ' she began.

'Romy.'

'What would have happened, Romy, if my mother hadn't intervened?'

'It would have been very serious. Khalid would have been guilty of manslaughter. I'd have been involved, too – as an accessory, or even a conspirator. Because of Otto and the Party, it would have gone to Hitler for decision – and no one ever knew how he'd react. Almost certainly, as Charlie said, there would have been a world-wide scandal.'

'And my mother prevented all that?' said Nikki.

Romy nodded. 'You can see why we'll always be in her debt, can't you?'

'By lying, though.' Nikki was still sitting on the recliner, looking suddenly like an angry child. 'She did it by lying, didn't she?'

'This was Nazi Germany, Nikki,' Romy reminded her gently.

'You mean she wouldn't have helped you cover it up if it'd happened in France or England or America?'

Romy smiled. 'Yes, she'd have helped us anywhere. She was a friend. Friends often face conflicts. Talk to Charlie – he'll explain.'

Nikki seemed unimpressed. 'I already have,' she said, looking at him. 'Truth can be dangerous. That's what Maman said to you, isn't it? That's what you told me just after we met – one of the gems she taught you.'

Charlie held out his hand to her and pulled her gently to her feet. 'Truth would have been lethal for Romy, wouldn't it? But it's not black and white, darling. Truth was important to Elisabeth, but as she said, it can get grey at the edges.'

Nikki smiled at him suddenly. 'That's the first time you've ever called me darling.'

'Slip of the tongue,' he said with an affectionate smile, and she aimed a blow at him with her fist.

'Next time, I'll do it hard,' she warned, laughing.

Sally rejoined them as they all strolled across the terrace to where the table had been set in the shade of a tree. Then the butler called Romy to the phone. She wasn't away long. 'Didn't I say Khalid would ring?' she declared. 'We're all invited to lunch on the yacht – the day after tomorrow. There's going to be a writer there who wants to do Khalid's life story, a kind of Playboy of the Western World. Khalid hasn't agreed to anything yet, but thought he should listen to what he had to say. Not that anything about Germany's likely to come up. Khalid had never been there before – and never went again. Hardly surprising, is it?'

2

Sonya awoke to see René standing naked at the window, looking down into the street through the crack in the curtains. He had a good body, even though he was around fifty now, no paunch, full firm shoulders, tight muscular buttocks. He turned back to her and she noticed that even after a night in bed his hair was barely ruffled. Maybe he had run a comb through it, but she doubted it. He was just well co-ordinated. Everything fell into its rightful position when he moved, as it does with animals.

'What were you looking for?' she asked.

'Just natural caution,' he said and turned, displaying the brilliant smile that had touched her so acutely when she had first interviewed him in his huge pillared office on the Quai d'Orsay – René Levallier, Assistant Regional Director of the Ministry of the Interior. 'Never too sure what Lucille will do when she goes away,' he added.

'You mean she might be having you followed?'

'It's possible.'

'I thought you got on so well.'

'We do, but she's aware of the human frailties, likes to know what's going on. At this moment I don't want her stirring the pond. It's an important time.'

'The new job? This is France, René, not America. No one would give it a thought if they knew you had a mistress.'

He got back into bed beside her. 'That's true, but I don't want speculation – of any kind. No one would think de Gaulle had a mistress, would they? That's how it should be.' He put his arm round her shoulders and gently fondled her breast while he was talking. 'If the appointment's confirmed, I'll be one of the most powerful men in France. The influence that flows from that office is enormous, much of it very subtle, all nuances.'

'I'll never see you then, will I?' Her tone was good-natured. It wasn't a challenge.

'Of course you will. And just think what a wonderful source of news I'll be.'

She kissed him. 'Baloney,' she said softly. 'Do you realise we haven't met for two months?'

'How can you say a thing like that? I rang you constantly. It's been a crucial time.'

'I know. I understand, too.' She ran her hands over his body. His skin was amazingly smooth. 'Will it get any better with more power?' she asked. 'I mean seeing you.'

'Of course. The heat'll be off.'

She felt him harden to the touch of her ranging fingers. 'What, more activity?' she queried.

He smiled at her. 'We haven't time, darling,' he said. 'I've got to lunch with Costa Mastorakis.'

'That's just an excuse,' she said. 'The truth is you can't perform. We've worn him out.'

'That's right,' he agreed with a smile. That's what she liked about him: no male posturing. 'Last evening, middle of the night, this morning already. At fifty you have to recognise your limitations.'

'You're the best lover I've ever known.'

'Better than Duclos?'

He didn't really care, she knew. It was just a light aside. Lovers were all different anyway. She said: 'I was younger then, a different woman. Why are you seeing Mastorakis?'

'In theory, about a dockyard scheme, but I suspect the real reason is your friend Charlie and young Nikki.'

'What's he expect you to do about that? It's his own family.'

'He has faith in my persuasive powers, but I've tried them and they didn't work. Charlie probably told you.'

'He said you thought Mastorakis might turn nasty.'

'He could, too. I wouldn't cross Mastorakis, not where his daughter's concerned. What's Charlie doing all this for anyway? Just for the kid?'

'Don't shrug her off like that. You said she was delightful.'

'She is, but there's more to it, isn't there? I understand him going for her, Elisabeth all over again, but he doesn't strike me as a fool. Why doesn't he go home and keep his wife happy and come back to Paris often?'

'Like you would?' she challenged.

He was leaning on one elbow watching her closely, and he let his smile spread slowly across his face. 'Probably,' he agreed.

'It's more complex for Charlie,' she said. 'There's never been an Elisabeth in your life. She changed all ours, but his drastically.'

His eyes were still on her. 'You make him sound like Cinderella.'

'It was a bit like that.'

'So you're telling me fairy stories. What's the truth, Sonya?' The question was suddenly sharp.

'I'm not "darling" any more?' she queried. 'Nor any of those lovely things you said while we were making love?'

'Of course you are. I'm just intrigued because I think you know more than you're telling me.'

'I've told you all I know.' She faced him out, the challenge lasting only for an instant. He kissed her lightly on the lips, got out of bed and put on the bathrobe she'd given him. What was it about him, she wondered, that attracted her? Usually she didn't like highly-groomed men.

'It just doesn't make sense,' he said. 'I like things to make sense.'

As he went into the bathroom she lay back and pondered the fact that she had kept the truth from him. She'd experienced no doubts, no conflict. The Elisabeth bond, the unsworn oath that went with it, was stronger than the feelings she might have for any lover. Perhaps that should tell her something. What was she doing with her life? Always her lovers had wives – or didn't want wives, like Duclos. It was time she settled down, got married, had a baby while there was still time.

Even if her emotional life was a mess, she was probably one of the most envied women in France – famous, with a fan mail of thousands of letters a week, her articles read avidly throughout the nation, even argued about occasionally in the Chambre des Députés.

Yet Duclos had made no effort to stop her leaving the paper. The impact on him of that Linette had astonished her. It wasn't like him. Of course he was getting older, the age when men made fools of themselves, but he wasn't that stupid. The worst part was that she missed him. Even after their affair had ended he remained a permanent feature in her life – someone she could go to, who took her to lunch if she was unhappy, shared her successes.

She had hoped he would call, but he didn't. Once, she'd had cause to ring the paper, and wondered if word would get back to him – not that she really expected it to. That had been a lucky break in the search for Roger Briedon. She had telephoned London, Washington, and various Resistance contacts in France, without even the smell of a lead. Then suddenly she remembered an evening when Elisabeth had talked about him in the Vercors. Not by name, but about a man who was her early contact in the SOE. A small-time freelance journalist who had done odd jobs for the paper. Sporting events – racing, cycling, football. Nothing major like the Tour de France, just small occasions that had to be covered in case something happened. Elisabeth had found him amusing. A funny little man, she'd said, totally bald, with an endless fund of scandalous stories.

Sonya couldn't think why she hadn't made the connection before. Frank Charlwood had told Thelma Hardy that her early contact with the SOE, with Pianoplayer, was Roger Briedon – and it fitted. As a sporting journalist, he would have good reason to travel, which would be useful as a member of an SOE circuit. He had to be the man Elisabeth had talked about.

Sonya had grabbed the phone, called the Accounts Department of the paper and asked for an old clerk named Bruner. 'Monsieur Bruner,' she said, 'will you do me a huge favour and cast your mind back a few years? Did we ever use a freelance for the sports page named Roger Briedon?'

There was an agonising pause as the old man thought back. 'Hold on a moment, madame,' he said. 'Sounds familiar, but there are so many, of course. I'll just check back in the indexes.' About a minute passed before she heard the phone picked up again. 'Yes, madame, we did. Actually, I remember him now. He often came into the office. Wasn't there some hint of scandal?'

'That's true,' Sonya agreed.

'Talk, probably. There was so much talk just then, wasn't there, madame? Can't have been too serious, for we seem to have gone on using him. Last time was five years ago.'

'Five years?' she echoed exultantly. Five years gave her a chance. It wasn't like fifteen. 'Have you got an address, Monsieur Bruner?' she asked.

'Of course, madame. And a phone number.'

The address was a small street off the Rue de Mauberge, a dilapidated area near the Gare du Nord, and in view of the background she decided to phone rather than make a sudden visit which might scare him. So she had called, pretending to be working on a story of an old champion cyclist whom Briedon must have known. And, to her surprise, since life was seldom this easy, Briedon still lived there and answered the phone himself.

He agreed to meet her – but not at home. He suggested a bar in the Boulevard de Magenta, about five minutes away. At two o'clock on Friday if that would suit her. She put the phone down gently, hardly daring to believe she'd found him. Her plan was to maintain the fiction, to check out the cyclist before the meeting so she could talk about him. This would give her a chance to assess Briedon, discover something of the pattern of his life. That night, she had called Charlie at his hotel in La Napoule, but Nikki had been with him in the room; even so, he had managed to get across his agreement with her proposal.

It was Friday today as she lay in bed waiting for René Levallier to emerge from the bathroom, and she was looking forward to the meeting at two o'clock with the kind of excited anticipation she hadn't enjoyed since her first scoop. This wasn't just reporting. She was investigating a murder.

The phone rang and she answered it. It was Duclos. 'Sonya? Claude here,' he said.

'I do know your voice, Claude,' she answered.

'I expect you're angry with me.'

'Disappointed more than angry.'

'I behaved badly. There, I admit it.' It was a familiar tactic. 'I think I thought you were challenging my authority.'

'That's not against the law.'

'In my office it is. What are you doing for lunch today?'

'Busy, I fear.'

'I expected as much. Thought I'd try, though. Something I wanted to talk to you about – as well as making my apologies.'

'Another time, Claude.'

'Next week maybe.'

'Maybe.'

'Old Bruner told me you called him.' She'd been mistaken: Bruner was pretty low down the scale in the Accounts Department, but the news had still got to the Lord Almighty.

'He did?'

'Did you manage to get in touch with Briedon?'

'Yes, as a matter of fact. Bruner was a great help.'

'Sport is strange territory for you, isn't it?'

'I'm branching out. No limits on my new assignment. Look, Claude, it's lovely to talk to you but I've got someone here. Just tell me: how's the *Nouvelle Vie* story coming along?'

'We had to kill it. I should have listened to you, shouldn't I?'

'Is Linette very upset?'

'A bit. All right, if you must know, she resigned over it, though I hope she'll reconsider.'

'The same old Claude.'

He laughed. 'The same old spots on the same old leopard. Well, are you going to lunch with me next week?'

'Why? You've found out what you wanted to know, haven't you?'

'I miss you. You're part of my life. So what do you say?'

'I'll think about it. Goodbye, Claude.'

She replaced the receiver and saw René standing looking at her from the foot of the bed. 'Claude Duclos?' he queried. 'What did he want?'

'He'd got wind of a story I'm on to.'

'Did you tell him?'

'A bit – to whet his appetite. I did him a favour even speaking to him.' The lies slip out quite easily once you start, she thought. And why was she lying? Would Elisabeth have lied? There was a certain irony there, since she was lying for Elisabeth. Or was she?

3

The bar was crowded, mostly with working men, some unshaven without ties or collars, many with berets. There was a counter of aluminium and bakelite, with a glass case of sandwich baguettes that didn't look too fresh. The air was thick with cigarette smoke.

It was what Sonya had expected. There were bars like this all over Paris. She had dressed simply in a jersey and skirt, a bag slung from her shoulder. As instructed she enquired at the counter for Monsieur Briedon and was directed to a corner table where three men were sitting.

As she pushed her way through the throng towards them, they saw her and two of them stood up to leave. At once she knew there was something wrong, for the man who remained at the table had a full head of dark hair, combed back. He was about forty-five, thin, with a sallow, skeletal face. If asked to guess his profession she'd have said he worked in a nightclub. He was observing her with serious, cautious eyes – very different from the amusing little bald man who'd told Elisabeth all those scandalous stories.

'Monsieur Briedon?' she asked and he nodded. There was a cigarette between his lips but he took it from his mouth now, using his thumb and forefinger, and gestured towards a chair.

'Monsieur *Roger* Briedon?' she asked as she sat down.

'That's my brother. I'm François Briedon.' He held himself very still, watching her.

'We didn't speak on the phone?'

'No. You spoke to my brother, but he couldn't come. I knew Emile Dillon, too. What did you want to know?' Emile Dillon was the cyclist she was supposed to be writing about. She realised what was happening. The Briedons were doing what she had hoped to do – taking a preliminary look.

'What writers always need,' she said, answering his question. 'Personal details. Anecdotes. Colour. Things that make a person come alive to the reader. You need someone who knew the man well for that. Roger knew Dillon well, didn't he?'

'Pretty well,' he answered, the cigarette back between his lips.

'Perhaps I could make another date to see Roger.'

'He's not in Paris at the moment.'

'Will he be returning soon?'

'I'm not sure.' He removed the cigarette. 'Perhaps I can answer your questions. I know quite a lot about Emile. Many times I saw him race. I've heard Roger speak of him often.' He was looking at her evenly, determined.

'I don't think you quite understand,' she said. 'Did you know Dillon's wife?'

'I never met her.'

'You see what I mean,' she said.

'I'm not sure Roger knew his wife.'

'Oh, I think so.'

'I thought this was about his racing,' he said.

'It's about the man – how he trained, prepared, how he lived, the women in his life, the friends, the rivals. It's about racing, too. The techniques, the tricks he used. Overtaking, maybe. Corners. Pacing. Can you help me with all that?'

She saw doubt in him then and realised she was winning. 'I don't know the tricks,' he replied.

'It's better I speak to Roger then, isn't it? Do you live with him?'

He nodded.

'Is he married?' she asked.

'He was, but they're not together any longer. We both live with my mother. She's quite old now, of course.'

'Does Roger's wife live in Paris?'

'I believe so, but I'm not sure where.'

'Don't you ever see her?'

'She comes to the apartment occasionally when she needs to talk about the children. There are two of them.'

She waited for him to go on, giving him rope, but he fell silent, sensing, she guessed, that already he'd said too much. 'This isn't helping you with Emile, is it?' he asked.

She nodded agreement. 'Perhaps you'd ask Roger to call me when he gets back.' She fumbled in her bag for a card and handed it to him. 'That's the office. If I'm out, he can always leave a message with my secretary.' She stood up. 'By the way, where did you say he'd gone?'

'I didn't.'

'Is it a secret?'

He shook his head. 'No. It's just that he didn't tell me. He goes away a lot.'

'What does he do?'

'This and that. I'll give him your message when he returns. It may be a while.'

She hesitated, wanting more, but he just gazed at her, the cigarette hanging from his lips, the smoke rising in a straight line in front of his face. There was no obvious hostility, no expression really. 'Thanks,' she said at last and shouldered her way out of the bar.

It was on Monday, when she was in the *France Soir* office writing her column, that Jeanne came in. Jeanne had moved with her from Duclos's paper. 'There's a Madame Briedon in Reception enquiring if you'll see her.'

Sonya glanced up at her with surprise. 'Madame Roger Briedon?'

'She didn't say. Do you want me to ask?'

'No. I'll see her at once.' Any Madame Briedon could be helpful.

In fact, it was Roger's wife – not his mother. She was a small woman of about forty – like a little bird, all tight skin and sharp bone. 'I heard you were enquiring for my husband,' she said.

'I hoped to see him,' Sonya agreed. 'We want to do a story on Emile Dillon, the cyclist. Well, you probably know that.'

'My mother-in-law told me,' Madame Briedon said. 'I saw her yesterday evening and she said you'd met François. Is it an important story?'

Sonya shrugged. 'All stories are important. Why do you ask?'

'Tracing Roger could be expensive.'

It seemed an odd thing to say. 'Tracing?' she asked. 'What do you mean?'

'He's left the country. Didn't François tell you?'

'He didn't say he'd left the country. He said he was away. I was surprised, since I only made the date to see him earlier in the week.'

'It was very sudden, very odd. I didn't hear until last night.'

'Have you any idea where he's gone?'

'America. New York probably. He's got a cousin who lives there. He may be using a false name.'

Sonya looked at this little woman who had been speaking quite calmly, as though what she had said was unexceptional. 'I gather you don't have an address?' she asked.

Madame Briedon looked down at her hands, that were clasped on her lap – rather tightly, the only sign of stress. 'No.'

'You think he's emigrated?'

'Perhaps. I think he's gone for some time.'

'Has he made financial provision for you? I hear you have two children.'

'Not really. It's always been up and down with him. At times, he's generous. At others, it's been difficult. Especially lately. It worries me he's gone without arranging anything. His mother, too. She's old now, of course, but she's been on my side – well, more on the children's, I suppose – but she's always thought he should have treated me better.'

'Let me get this straight,' said Sonya. 'You're hoping we may help you trace him in New York. That's why you've come to see me.'

The woman gave a little shrug, birdlike. 'I couldn't possibly do it on my own.'

'You realise it'd be hard for him to get into America? You need

169

a visa even to visit. Certainly you're not allowed to work there, except under rigid conditions.'

Madame Briedon almost smiled, then shook her head as though Sonya was being naïve. 'I don't think that'll be too much of a problem. Roger has friends. Did you know he worked for the Resistance in the war?'

The question took Sonya by surprise after the Emile Dillon cover and she almost admitted she knew, but stifled the impulse. 'No,' she said. 'No, I didn't.'

'He was an informer, too, for the Germans. A bit of one. They discovered what he was doing and agreed not to arrest him if he'd help them sometimes. They knew about me and the children, of course, and warned that something could happen to us if he didn't co-operate. After the war, there were going to be charges of collaboration, but they never came to anything. As I said, he's got friends.'

'Any idea what name he might be using?' Sonya asked.

Madame Briedon hesitated, thinking. 'I know one he's used before. His cover name in the war was Jean and he liked it, so he adapted it. He needed an English alias for some scheme of his so he called himself Johnson. Jean is John, isn't it?'

'He speaks English, then?'

'Yes, but he could never pass himself off as English. He didn't have to meet anyone as Mr Johnson – just receive letters.'

'And how about his cousin in New York?'

'His name is Alan Soisson. His mother is Roger's aunt. I don't know where he lives.'

'What does he do?'

'I don't know that either. I might be able to find out more,' she ventured, 'from his mother or François. Sometimes I see a man he's done business with in the past.'

Sonya hesitated, considering what she'd just been told. 'Are you sure he left at such short notice? Without plans?'

'That's what his mother told me. Something came up, she said.'

Sonya stood up. 'Tell me where I can contact you, Madame Briedon,' she said, 'and I'll see what our New York bureau can suggest.'

After she had left, Sonya sat at her desk doodling with a pencil, pondering the strange story. Then a disturbing thought came to her. One man knew she'd asked old Monsieur Bruner in the

Accounts Office of *Aujourd'hui* for Briedon's address. Duclos. Why should the clerk report such a trifle to him? Orders? Could Duclos have guessed Charlie's real purpose in exploring Elisabeth's life? Did Briedon know too much? Certainly Duclos had been sceptical about Sonya writing a cyclist story. Was it he who wanted Briedon out of the country? Could he have contacted him on Friday morning after talking to her, and told him to send François in his place and leave before Sonya had got any further?

Certainly he could have arranged it – visas, false names, the lot. But it was a ludicrous notion. Why should he go to so much trouble? And that question raised the unthinkable. Could it be Duclos who'd wanted Elisabeth dead? It was absurd, but Duclos could be absurd. In a minor way, he had been about young Linette. But this really was absurd. And even if there was any basis, the old question still persisted: Why? What could possibly have been the motive?

Jeanne, with her sense of timing, came in with a cup of coffee. As Sonya grasped for it, Jeanne saw her doodling and said: 'Drawing pictures? We are in a bad way, aren't we?'

4

The big black yacht slowed as it approached the Ile de Sainte Marguerite, passed the old fort with its wooden jetty and entered the small deserted bay at the far end of the island. There was no sound except for the light wind in the sheets and the soft hiss of the water under the hull – until the anchor was released with a noisy rattle of the chain. The yacht heaved to, before starting to swing slowly on the cable. It was midday and there were no clouds. The sun was hot and the bay was quiet.

On the big afterdeck, under the awning, about ten people lounged on chairs. A steward was serving drinks. Near the stern rail, two girls were stretched out in the sun, lying on their stomachs with shoulder straps off. Khalid, wearing shorts, the black hair thick on his torso, was nursing a John Collins and watching Nikki beside him with the evident pleasure of a man who loves women. 'Romy,' he said without moving his eyes from the girl, 'you never warned me about Nicole.'

'I wanted to see your face when you saw her,' Romy countered.

Khalid turned to the writer James Maitland. 'It's strange for me, Mr Maitland. This beautiful young girl looks very like her mother, whom I knew well in the thirties. So she brings back memories for me. You don't mind my saying that, I hope?' he added to her.

'No,' she answered with a shy smile. 'Not so long as you don't think of me as second-hand.'

The Prince laughed. 'Sharp like she was, eh? Never fear, you have your own special qualities, as she did. Elisabeth Ferrier was a much-respected journalist,' he told the writer.

'Oh I know that,' said the young man.

'You do?' Khalid asked in surprise. 'You must've been a child when she died.'

'I know a lot about her,' said Maitland. He was about thirty-five, with fine fair hair, a rather long face and a small blond moustache. Watching him, Charlie thought he didn't look tough enough to write exposés of powerful men. Clearly, even in the shade of the canvas awning, he found the heat oppressive; a single rivulet of sweat trickled down one side of his face. 'After all,' Maitland added, 'Elisabeth Ferrier's part of your story, Prince Khalid.'

'She was a friend,' Khalid agreed, 'but hardly part of my story.'

'A woman friend.'

Khalid laughed. 'If you're going to include all my women friends it'll be a long book. Tell me more, though. What sort of thing do you have in mind?'

'You've lived through troubled times, Prince. You've pushed life to the limits. You've raced – steeplechasers, cars, planes. You've known famous women, married two film stars, survived scandals.'

'It'd make a great movie,' said Max.

'Certainly would,' agreed Sally. 'Maybe you should buy the rights yourself, Max. That's what Ollie would do.'

'I know, I know. That new partner of mine – why, he can walk on the water. Christ, what must he be like in bed?'

'Want me to tell you?' she mocked. 'My, it's a hot day, isn't it?'

The Prince was considering what Maitland had said. 'Shouldn't you be writing of my young brother Sadruddin?' he asked. 'Look what he's done for my country. You've heard the rumours.'

'That you might be passed over in his favour by your father? I don't doubt his qualities, but you're far better copy. You've contributed to society, too. Look what you've done for racing, some of the horses you've bred.'

The Prince laughed. 'Yes, we've made an impact there, I grant you, but even that I owe to my trainer, Duncan Stewart. He was a war comrade of Elisabeth's, you know – *and* of these two.' He gestured at Charlie and Max. 'Came to me after the war, hadn't got one horse in his stable. For Elisabeth's sake, I gave him six – and he did wonders, so he's got them all now. This year he's got a real champion coming up, too, still a two-year-old . . .' He smiled with pleasure at the thought. 'But I'm straying from the point, aren't I? Your book now . . .' He stroked his face thoughtfully. 'I don't know, Mr Maitland. Some of it sounds pretty delicate. Why should I help you?'

The writer leaned forward earnestly. 'You have two choices, Prince. You can co-operate, which will make it a far better book; I'll take up as little of your time as possible, or you can refuse to help, in which case I'll have to manage without you.'

'How can you do that?'

'By talking to your friends, your enemies, your wives, your lady friends, people who've known you – or know about you.'

'My friends wouldn't talk to you if I asked them not to. Even my ex-wives would be reluctant.'

'Others would talk. Some already have.'

'And what control would I retain?'

'You're welcome to read the manuscript.'

'And if I asked you to omit something or to make changes?'

'Then that would depend.'

'On what?'

'On whether or not it was the truth, Prince. I'll correct anything that's inaccurate.'

Khalid sipped his drink, watching the writer with his dark eyes. 'There's truth in all our lives, Mr Maitland, that we may not wish to be displayed before the world.'

The writer smiled. 'They call them warts, Prince. And this type of book is called "warts and all". After all, you've never tried to keep out of the newspapers, have you?'

'That's not easy, you know. You can't call up the editor of a big newspaper and say "please don't print that story".'

'There are ways of containing it a little, Prince. Your love affairs have hardly been discreet – the best restaurants, the fashionable resorts. The huge winnings in the casinos. The occasional fight in front of the cameras.'

'I suppose I was a little hot-blooded when I was younger,' Khalid agreed. 'There, Nicole,' he added, putting his hand on her knee, 'now I've reached the age of wisdom, you don't need to worry about me, do you?'

'Who's worrying?' she laughed, with a provocative glance at Charlie.

'The Prince was joking, Nikki,' said Charlie. 'With respect, sir, I'd guess there's plenty of hot blood left.'

Khalid smiled at him. 'Am I trespassing, Mr Dawson? Is she yours? I wouldn't want to . . .'

'His?' exclaimed Nikki indignantly. 'He's married.'

'So am I,' said the Prince with a laugh. He stroked her knee. 'Are you too warm? If you wished, we could move further offshore where there might be more breeze.'

'I'm very happy here,' she answered.

'Then I'm very happy, too,' said the Prince. He signalled to the steward to attend to her glass and turned back to the writer. 'You were saying, Mr Maitland, before I was distracted by this lovely girl and such disturbing memories . . . Your book is to be warts and all – which you think I deserve for the follies of my youth.'

'Not follies, Prince,' Maitland protested. 'You're a big person-ality. It's the way you're made.'

'I prefer the word "follies" to "warts". It has more style, don't you think? I'm not inclined to help you expose all my follies, Mr Maitland. But you're pointing a gun at my head, aren't you?'

'I'd hardly say that.' For the first time the writer seemed unsure, the sweat even more prominent on his face.

'Weren't you threatening me, Mr Maitland? Co-operate or else?' His tone had become sharp, but his hand was still stroking Nikki's knee, sweeping higher up her thigh. Charlie wished she would check him before matters slid out of her control. She saw his concern – and winked. 'Didn't you offer me two choices?' Khalid demanded.

'Everyone has the same two choices, Prince, when faced with a biography. But we can talk about detail. I accept that there may be follies you'd prefer me not to print.'

'So you'd give me a measure of control?'

'To a degree, perhaps.'

'I thought that degree hung on the truth.'

The Prince was glaring now, though you'd never know it from the idle movement of his hand. The writer was meeting his eye, trying to challenge him, though Charlie could see it needed courage.

'The truth can be arguable,' Maitland answered.

'You mean,' Nikki suddenly put in, to Charlie's horror, 'that it can be grey at the edges.' She was quoting Elisabeth's words but the ice was thin enough. Oh God, he thought, she was in that mood, was she?

'Correct,' Maitland said. 'Especially the truth of some of the Prince's follies.'

'Such as?' queried Jassim.

'Well, the car crash in Paris in 1954, for example.'

'That went before the courts.'

'The morals charge in Los Angeles over Moira Dean.'

'Even that was cleared.'

The writer raised his eyebrows sceptically. Rich men had ways of arranging such clearances. Then, meeting the Prince's gaze, he added: 'Nuremberg 1937.'

The silence then was total. For a few seconds no one even breathed. On Nikki's thigh the Prince's hand tautened and Charlie could see he was hurting her. She looked at Charlie again, with appeal not challenge, and he cautioned her with a shake of his head. Please, he thought, don't speak now.

He saw the Prince relax his hand and take it from her knee, ostensibly to remove his sun-glasses. 'I'm not sure what you mean, Mr Maitland,' he said. 'What about Nuremberg?'

'You were there in 1937?'

'Yes, I think so. Was it '37?' He gave a shrug as though it was of no importance.

'At the same time as the Countess whom I admire so much as Romy Lagrange. You were there too, weren't you, madame?'

'Many people were,' answered Romy, 'as you'd expect at a Party Rally. Nikki's mother was there, too.'

'Ah yes,' said Maitland. 'And so was your husband, wasn't he? In fact, that's where you became a widow, I believe. That must have been hard for a young wife who'd only been married two years.'

'At the time it was dreadful,' agreed Romy, the actress. 'But it was all long ago.'

'What is the point you're making, Mr Maitland?' asked the Prince. 'I thought we were speaking of *my* follies.'

'You mean because your name was not mentioned?'

'Of course. So it could hardly have a place in your book, could it?'

'We're not speaking only of follies that were reported, Prince,' Maitland said, 'otherwise I could write the book from press cuttings. But there are two versions of what happened in Nuremberg. We spoke of the truth – and this is a case where I could be . . . well, helpful, shall we say, without conflict with my integrity as a writer. Of course, one of the versions would make the book a run-away best-seller, wouldn't it?'

Jesus, thought Charlie, how can he say that to one of the wealthiest men in the world? It took guts, though, he'd say that for him.

Khalid had frozen, controlled anger in his eyes. 'I think, Mr Maitland,' he said after a moment, 'that you're trying to blackmail me. But I don't deal with blackmailers.' He turned to the steward. 'Fetch the Captain!' he ordered.

'Prince, I must – ' Maitland began.

'Please keep quiet, Mr Maitland,' the Prince cut in. 'I have nothing further to say to you.' In the silence that followed he returned his hand to Nikki's knee, as though seeking comfort. She placed her own hand over his, allowed him to caress her lightly beneath it with his fingers. Then gently she removed it from her leg and kissed him on the cheek. For once Charlie was impressed, for she did it very deftly, giving comfort, allowing the intimacy, then ending it without offence to a man who was used to having any woman he wanted.

'Captain,' ordered the Prince as soon as he appeared, 'Mr Maitland will not be staying for lunch. Kindly have him taken at once in the launch to the jetty at Sainte Marguerite where he can pick up the ferry to Cannes.'

'Prince Khalid,' said Maitland, 'I'm sorry to have angered you. I think you misunderstood, but I do ask you to consider what you're doing.'

'Captain,' demanded Khalid, 'kindly carry out your orders.'

The steward returned with a telephone. 'Mr Duncan Stewart is calling from Kentucky, Your Highness.'

Khalid was cool, Charlie thought admiringly as he watched him pick up the phone with a smile of pleasure. 'Duncan, how are you? We've just been talking about you. I've got your old friends Charlie and Max on board here – and Elisabeth's beautiful daughter. What are you doing in Kentucky? The sales aren't on.'

'Special private one. Thomas Foster. Five hundred horses. There are two yearling colts I think you should buy. One's by Ribo; the other's by Crepello. Dams are good. Conformation perfect, but they won't go cheap,' Duncan said.

'Be specific.'

'Quarter of a million maybe.'

'Buy them. Want to talk to your pals?'

'A quick word with Charlie.'

The Prince held out the phone to him and Charlie took it. 'Something you ought to know,' said Duncan. 'Swinburne called me last night. Thelma's been on to him in a dreadful state.'

'Why? What's happened?' Charlie asked.

'She was shopping in a supermarket and one of her kids disappeared – a little boy. Apparently it happens often. They wander off up the wrong aisle. He was gone an hour and she was frantic. But he was OK. They found him in the carpark.'

'That's a relief,' said Charlie.

'The point is she got a phone call. She was told if she talked to you again the kid would be gone for a lot longer.'

'I can't believe this, Duncan.'

'Try calling her. She won't speak to you.'

'Will you call her for me then? Tell her how sorry I am and thanks for her help.'

'I doubt if she'll talk to me. She's taking no chances. So take care yourself, Charlie.'

'Sure.'

'I mean it. Oh, and wish Max well for me – and Sally, of course.'

5

It was while lying on his bed in his room at the hotel, when Nikki was changing in hers, that Charlie was at last able to speak to Dominique Saint-Jean – Elisabeth's lawyer and the woman to whom Duncan had sent Elisabeth's key. She had been back in the office for a few days now from vacation but always he'd been checked by a secretary. Even now, she hadn't been friendly.

'I'm speaking for Elisabeth Ferrier's daughter,' said Charlie. 'I understand from René Levallier that you were her mother's lawyer.'

'And her friend,' she said. 'And you . . . Mr Dawson, was it? Are you in the profession?'

'No, but I was with Madame Ferrier during the war – when she died, in fact.'

'Ah yes,' said Madame Saint-Jean. 'I think I remember now. Well, I don't know how I can help you, but I'd like to meet Nicole. I tried to find her at one stage, but she'd left Annecy by then and no one seemed to know where she'd gone. I'm afraid I can't see you till Friday at the earliest. Say 11.30.'

Almost as soon as he put the phone down, Sonya called. 'I think I've blown it,' she told him. 'Roger Briedon left this week for New York, where he's living under an assumed name. His brother met me instead.'

'You mean he fled because you made a date to see him?'

'I think it's possible. I've asked our New York office for ideas about finding him. He's got a cousin there he's bound to contact, but I've no address. Also, Mastorakis has arrived in Paris, breathing fire. You're going to have to go home, you know – if only for a while.'

'OK, I'll think about it. We'll be in Paris Friday. Only don't let anyone tell Mastorakis – not yet anyway.'

After they'd finished talking, Charlie lay back on the bed for a moment. He ought to call home even though he knew what the reception would be. Reluctantly, he asked the hotel operator to get him the number.

Philana answered. 'Charlie?' she said.

'I'll be back next week,' he told her quickly to deflect recriminations.

'What's your flight number, Charlie?' she enquired.

'It's not booked yet.'

'So nothing's changed. Call me when you've booked it. Better still, call me from the airport.'

'Now listen, darling – '

She cut in: 'Goodbye, Charlie.'

Once again, he listened to the monotonous tone of a disconnected line. He called his office in New York. 'Don't tell me, let me guess,' said Terry Johnson. 'You're the founder of the firm. The guy whose picture's on the wall in a wing collar.'

'You're such a wit, Terry. I'm lying here dying laughing.'

'Lying where, if it's not indelicate to ask?'

'In a hotel in La Napoule. That's near Cannes.'

'I wish it was Marseilles. At least they make ships there.'

'I'll be back next week.'

'I can start making dates for you?'

'Not before Friday. I'll see you then.'

'Seeing is believing.'

'I'll be there. Goodbye, Terry.'

'Where? New York?' asked Nikki. She had come into the room while he was speaking and was standing with her back to the door, looking serious.

'I just got an idea,' said Charlie.

'Where will you be? New York?' she repeated, refusing to be diverted.

'We're going to see your mother's lawyer in Paris on Friday.'

'Where did you say? New York?' she persisted.

'And I thought we'd spend a couple of days in the Vercors on the way. We'll hire a car and drive and . . .'

The change in her was dramatic, her expression of delighted surprise lighting up her whole face. 'The Vercors? Did you say the Vercors?'

'We'll go and see the cottage we used as a base – '

'I don't believe you.'

'Some of the villages, too. We'll walk in the forest and – '

'Oh, Charlee!' she exclaimed. 'That'd be wonderful.' And she threw herself on to the bed beside him and kissed him on the lips – lightly, affectionately, not with passion. 'Don't think I've forgotten, though,' she added.

'Forgotten what?'

'That you're going to New York next week. No . . .' She put her finger over his mouth. 'Don't say it! You've got a business to run, a wife to placate, children to sweep up in your arms and tell: "Look, Daddy's home." I'm not going to think about it, though. I'm just going to enjoy you. And then while you're away . . .' She paused, watching him with her gamine smile. 'Well, maybe the Prince will be in Paris.' He smacked her hard on the bottom. 'See,' she challenged in triumph, 'you care.'

'You think I don't care? Was that why you were making up to Max, why you were leading the Prince on?'

'I mean really care,' she answered, pausing before adding: 'Like you cared for my mother.'

Her bluntness took him a little aback. Then he smiled and shook his head. 'What am I going to do with you? I care. Can't you leave it at that?'

'No,' she said, but not unhappily, 'I can't leave it at that. I won't leave it at that.'

6

The sense of alarm came slowly to Leah as Dawn chattered on. Gradually, her words began to acquire a meaning beyond what she was saying.

The party had been thrown by *Elégance*, a new fashion magazine, in a big apartment in the Rue de Sèvres, which was the home of many of the quality dress shops. The timing was right – early August, when people had their antennae tuned to the rumours coming out of the big houses; but before the big buyers had arrived from the States.

Most of the younger London designers had flown over for the occasion – including Dawn. 'Fortune has smiled on you, sweetie,' she told Leah. 'Hugo's such a darling, isn't he? And talented, too. I only wish Jack would take the same kind of interest – and display a quarter of Hugo's flair.' Jack, Leah knew, was a stockbroker.

'It's a bit different,' Leah protested. 'Hugo's in the business with me. Jack's in another kind of job.'

'But that's just what I mean,' Dawn agreed. 'It must be so rewarding. He's got such a feel for the market, hasn't he? Well, you know that better than I do, but I've never met a man who could pick up those subtle shifts in the public mood like Hugo can.'

Leah laughed, hoping her anxiety didn't show. 'What *has* he been saying?' she asked as lightly as she could.

'Well, we were having a drink after the charity meeting the other evening,' said Dawn, 'and I can't remember if he said it or I did, but we agreed that it really is a new world we're living in, isn't it? Everything's changing so fast. Theatre, films, books. New music, new dancing, new idols – men like Dean and Brando. A pill to stop getting pregnant. I mean the kids are shaping their own culture. We ought to be catering for them, but we're not, are we?'

'Is that what my brilliant husband said?' Leah asked after listening in horror to what she'd told Hugo herself at Alonso's.

'Well, not in those exact words, of course.'

'And how did he propose we should cater for them?'

Dawn noted her tone and glanced at her. 'He didn't, sweetie, but I suppose that if you're going to talk about freedom and movement, you're not talking of three-quarter-length skirts, are you? And that's what we're both wearing.'

'So what are you planning?'

'Sweetie! How can you? It's a business secret, isn't it?' And with a wave, she drifted away across the room, leaving Leah wondering what Hugo had done. For that evening at Alonso's, they had made their new plan. They were going to present a limited collection in mid-September, before the main London showings in October, and though most of the designs would be traditional there would be a block towards the end of seven or eight outfits, all with short skirts.

In the cab after the party, Leah remarked: 'Dawn was telling me about your cosy little talk after the charity meeting.'

'She's a bright girl,' Hugo said with a confident smile.

'She thinks you're bright, too. I wish I was as sure as she is.'

He looked at her, surprised. 'What am I supposed to have done now?'

'Can you remember what you said to her?'

'Sure.' The memory was vivid, for their feelings for each other had come to a kind of climax that night. They had recognised the mutual attraction, whereas before they had always skated round it.

Dawn had been looking marvellous in a new dress in vivid pink, with a deep plunging neckline. The charity meeting had gone on for ever and, as they left it, she suggested they went home for a drink to her flat in Elm Park Gardens. 'Jack's out of town,' she said as she filled the glasses. 'Liverpool, I think. Looking over a big company. So the cat's away.' And as she handed him a gin and tonic, their fingers touched. 'Dare I sit next to you?' she asked.

'It's a risk,' he warned.

'I always was a gambler,' she countered. She sat beside him, one leg crossed over the other, so that her toe was almost touching him. 'You know what I like about you and me?' she said. 'It's not just the sex thing. We've been honest about that. We've admitted it like adults and we know we just mustn't let it happen. It's the rapport that I enjoy. I love talking to you. I mean, Jack's a sweetie, but he really doesn't know a zip from a hemline. But you understand what's going on in a woman's mind when she's buying clothes. You're so creative, Hugo.'

'Do you really mean that?' he said.

'Of course I mean it, darling. Believe me.' She put her hand on his knee for emphasis and realised what she'd done. 'Sorry,' she said. 'Shouldn't do that. Doesn't make it easier, does it?' She leaned away from him for a moment and smiled at him over the rim of her glass. 'I wonder sometimes if Leah realises what she's got.'

'Oh, I think she appreciates my help,' he said, 'marginal though it is.'

'Now, sweetie, there's nothing marginal about you. I can tell by what you've said to me. You discuss ideas with her, make suggestions, talk through the trends. I know you do. Here and now in 1960 is a case in point. I mean, it's fifteen years since the war, so where do we go now? It's a fascinating time. Fashion could follow so many routes, couldn't it?'

'Why, that's just what I was saying the other day,' Hugo exclaimed.

He warmed to the theme first explored at Alonso's and as he did so she leaned forward again, touching his knee once more, her eyes excited. 'That's incredible, sweetie. I knew you were going to say exactly that. You think the clothes should be like the twenties, too. That's what you were thinking, isn't it?'

'Well . . .' he began.

'You think the skirts should be up here, don't you?' She leaped up and drew her skirt above her knees. 'Like this?'

'That's the idea,' he said doubtfully.

'Or higher?' she queried, showing more of her thighs. 'Higher still?' She pulled the skirt up to her stocking-tops. 'No, that's too high isn't it?' But again she got her answer just by looking at him. 'Maybe not,' she added more certainly. 'It sure is sexy, isn't it? Too sexy?' She sat down close beside him. Then she kissed him briefly and took her lips away, smiling. 'Sorry, I couldn't help it.'

'Nor can I,' he responded, wrapping her in his arms and kissing her hard.

'Oh God, darling,' she whispered, her lips apart, her hand on the side of his face. 'I've wanted this so long.'

'So have I,' he said, fondling her breast within the open

neckline. 'I need you so badly.' He moved his hand to her bare thigh above her stockings – which is when she checked him with her own. 'Give me a moment, darling,' she said. 'Let's think about this. Why don't I get you another drink?'

He came over to her as she poured the drinks. 'Dawn,' he said, putting his arms round her from behind, 'you know I'm crazy about you.'

'I am, too, darling,' she assured him, 'but we've got to talk this thing through. So be a good boy and sit down for a moment. Say we let it happen, how would you feel when you went home to Leah? How would I feel when I saw Jack tomorrow? Would you tell her?'

'No, I couldn't. It'd upset her dreadfully.'

'I'd feel awful,' she said. 'I'd be afraid that Jack would sense it. Wouldn't Leah guess?'

'I don't know. I just know I want you very badly.'

'Well, let's go on talking for the moment and simmer down a bit.' She sat down gingerly beside him, not touching him. 'Now, how short do you think these skirts should be?'

'Well?' queried Leah in the cab in Paris. 'What did you say to her? Did you say I was thinking of short skirts?'

'Of course I didn't talk of our plans.'

'Did you mention short skirts at all?'

'Only as a possible trend.'

'Oh, Hugo, what am I going to do with you?'

'Why? What's the matter?' he asked.

'She was trying to find out from you what I was doing – and I suspect she did. What I don't know is whether she was just trying to faze me this evening, or whether she's in serious competition.'

'The more of you who do it, the bigger chance you've got of the fashion taking off,' he said.

'That's not the point, Hugo. If you're going to discuss my ideas with other designers, I really think you ought to ask me first.'

'Ours,' he corrected.

'Sorry?'

'*Our* ideas,' he said.

Sixteen

'My God!' Nikki whispered as they drove round another bend of the twisting road that had been tunnelled through the mountain. For it bordered a narrow gorge – a dark, deep crevice in the Massif – that at this point suddenly opened out so that the rock face of the Grands Goulets on the far side soared sheer and wide for thousands of feet. 'My God,' she repeated as they passed under a series of natural arches, hewn from the limestone, 'it's creepy.'

They were almost the first words she had spoken that morning. In fact, there had been a shadow over their mood ever since they had left the coast the previous day in the Renault Charlie had hired. She had tried a joke: 'What, no Bugatti like we had at Deauville? Don't I rank any more?'

'This is better for the mountains,' Charlie answered.

She had given him a weak smile and they drove much of the way north in silence. Occasionally, he pointed out something of interest in the Provençal landscape – a big château on a hill, Mont-Sainte-Victoire, which Cézanne had painted so often, the spire of the cathedral of Saint-Sauveur at Aix – but she seemed unimpressed.

At Avignon, he had left the Autoroute and driven into the town to show her the famous bridge, now partly collapsed. In desperation, as they rejoined the motorway, he started softly to sing 'Sur le Pont d'Avignon . . .' but his voice faded as he realised it was having no effect.

He knew why. He would be going home next week, a prospect that had always scared her. The investigation into Elisabeth's life was nearly over – for Nikki at least. Dominique Saint-Jean was the last of her mother's friends they'd arranged to see. Even the visit to the Vercors Plateau had a finality about it. He hadn't been back for ten years. Certainly, he wouldn't have risked it much earlier. He'd only proposed it now because he knew that the haunting memory of Elisabeth was something he must come to terms with – whatever the truth that lay behind the execution signal.

They had stayed the night in Valence – in separate rooms as always – but this time Nikki had made no point of it. That morning, they had risen early, for although the Vercors was not far away Charlie knew how long it would take to ascend the narrow tortuous roads on to the Massif.

It was a sunny morning as they crossed the Rhône and left the town, though a light haze cast a thin veil over the broad flat expanse of farms and vineyards. At last he said: 'Well, there it is – the Vercors,' and she'd seen the gaunt white cliffs, thousands of feet high, gradually emerging into focus. They rose straight and majestic from the plain, as they might from a distant island, reaching away into the obscurity of the mist – vast gaunt ramparts forming a high, seemingly endless skyline.

She was speechless. How could that be the setting for a love that had marked his life for so long? she wondered. War was a different matter. That massif was suited to war, to death. The Vercors was impressive, but from the west it wasn't beautiful or romantic. Those cliffs were gloomy, monotonous, even threatening.

Her spirits sank even lower as they passed through Saint-Nazaire and turned off into the foothills. At first, the approach was unexceptional, but at the village of Pont-en-Royans they crossed the Vernaison River, and the climb into the gorge began in earnest. Her depression deepened as they drove between cliffs that at points almost touched overhead, so that even on that brilliant day it was so dark that Charlie needed the Renault's lights and the sky was a distant strip of blue above them. This sombre mood was no part of her earlier sadness, she was certain. Its roots lay in the place.

They were in a tunnel, one of the longer ones. They emerged briefly, still hemmed in by the looming sides of the gorge, climbing the road on the edge of a precipice, and went straight into another tunnel.

She began to feel a need to escape. They were inside a mountain and it seemed to be closing in on her. A temptation to leap out of the car – an urge to run, to scream – began to overwhelm her. She made a huge effort to control herself, knowing she was being absurd. She'd been in tunnels before – why should this be different? Sweat began to stream down her face. Her hands, already clasped on her lap, were clenched so tight that they hurt.

Charlie seemed to sense something of what she was feeling. He put a comforting hand over hers. 'We'll be through any second,' he said. It wasn't a second, more like a minute, though it seemed to Nikki like an hour. At last they rounded a bend, and suddenly they were going out through the tunnel entrance into the glare of a blazing sun.

They passed between a few houses and then they were in country that was open and undulating, and the grass was a rich green and leaves were thick on the trees. There were fenced fields with black-and-white cattle that looked fat and contented, and they might have been driving through Surrey or Connecticut. The contrast, the sheer relief after the oppression of the approach, was so dramatic that it touched some emotional chord within her. Suddenly, tears began pouring down her cheeks.

'Why am I crying?' she exclaimed. 'Why in the world am I crying?'

Charlie laughed. 'You've heard too much about the place – much of it deeply personal, some of it very tragic.'

'It's not what I imagined. I didn't expect it to be pretty. I've heard of forests and mountains.'

'Plenty of those, too. France's largest virgin forest, for a start. As for mountains, look around. We're in a kind of crater, high above the surrounding country – a huge one, thirty miles long, twenty miles wide. Pretty hard for the Germans to get up here – and plenty of warning. Easy for people to get back after raids on the plain. Like an old Western. Cowboy country really.'

'But the Germans came, didn't they?'

'Occasionally, and always in force. Then everyone would disappear into the forests – except for the villagers, the girls and the old people.'

'You make it sound as though it was nothing.'

'Oh no, it was terrible eventually. But that wasn't until much later after the Allies had landed. The Germans still controlled the south, and the Vercors became a legend. They came in by air then – a real attack and – ' He broke off, for he didn't want to talk about the massacre. They weren't there for that. 'That was long after Elisabeth, of course,' he added.

They were silent for a few seconds, then elation surged

suddenly through her tears. 'You know, I'm happy, Charlie. Suddenly I'm wonderfully happy. Are you happy?'

'Sure I'm happy.'

'Not too many memories?'

'Give me time. I only just got here.'

'Can you feel her?'

'Feel her?' he echoed.

'Maman. Can you feel her around you? This is where it all happened, isn't it? I mean, you must have gone along this road with her often like we're doing now?'

'Sometimes,' he agreed.

'It's an odd sensation, you know . . . after what you've told me, what I've read in the diary. I must get used to it, though. We're going to lots of places you went to with her, aren't we?'

'Well that was the idea. Maybe it wasn't such a good one.'

'Regretting it already?' she asked lightly, but watching him.

He shook his head with a grin. 'I needed to come back – and it's right for you, too – so that you can kind of pay your respects.'

'Know what I'd like to do first?' she said. 'Could we have a picnic? It's a perfect day for it, isn't it?'

'Sure. We can pick up a bottle of wine and something to eat in one of the villages.'

'You used to have picnics with Maman, didn't you? On a hill near Saint-Martin. Didn't you say that?'

He hesitated, wondering if this was so wise. 'Yeah we did,' he agreed. 'We had a lot of time on our hands, but there were emergencies, of course. We had to be in easy reach so that they could send for us.'

They stood on the hill where he had been so often with Elisabeth. There was shade from a small group of pines, and they had bought a bottle of wine and some bread and salami and fruit. Behind them, the mountains formed a high ridge of bare rock. In the far distance was the dark virgin mass of the Forêt de Lente. Below them, they could just see the little town of Saint-Martin that had once been base for him. 'Nothing's changed,' he said, 'except for the TV aerials.'

'And Elisabeth is dead,' she added, so firmly that he glanced at her. She was standing very erect, carrying a package of the food they had bought, wrapped in brown paper. She held her head high in a way that had a note of defiance as she surveyed the terrain – like a general planning an attack. She felt him looking at her as he drew the cork from the bottle – and met his smile with a shy laugh that had a touch of shame, as though he had caught her unawares. 'Is this the exact spot you came with Maman?' she asked. He nodded. 'Always?'

'It's a good place.'

'Where did she usually sit? No, don't tell me. I want to see if I can guess.' She shut her eyes to concentrate. 'I reckon she sat to the right of you.' She opened her eyes, smiling. 'That's true, isn't it?'

'I don't think we chose anywhere special. When you go on a picnic you don't say "Look you sit there and I'll sit here." What's it matter?'

'Because,' she said, kneeling on the grass to his right, 'I want to sit where she usually sat. Can you remember any time she didn't sit on your right, Charlee?'

He thought for a moment. 'No,' he said reluctantly, 'not now you come to mention it. What's this all about, Nikki?' he asked, though he had guessed the answer.

'So you can face up to her. Remember what you said? "Couldn't be possessed for ever." Those were your words. Isn't that why we're here, to break spells?'

'I don't think we should work at it, just take it easy a bit.'

'I am taking it easy.' She unwrapped the food as he filled two glasses with wine, then she sat back on her heels. 'This is how she sat in Duclos's painting,' she said. 'How's this for the look on her face?' She tried to imitate Elisabeth's expression in the picture, narrowing her eyelids and parting her lips. It was so far from the artist's subtlety that she looked absurd, obscene, as she knew. She was playing – but he wasn't. It shocked him, like seeing a cruel cartoon. 'No good?' she enquired with a giggle.

'I said take it easy,' he insisted.

Her shoulders moved in a casual shrug. 'I'm taking it easy, having a joke. You're the one that's not taking it easy.' She saw his glance of anger. 'I know,' she went on, 'it's like laughing in church, isn't it? Sainte Elisabeth. Perhaps we should light a candle. Can I have some wine?' She was in a mood he hadn't seen before – just below hysteria, mocking, bitter, half-teasing.

He sat down beside her, passed her a glass. 'I don't think this is the best way – to challenge her memory.'

'Don't you?' she asked with an artificial brightness. 'It's a new way. We need a new way. It's no challenge. Charlee, if we can't sit on a hill where you sat with her – and take it easy, and kid around, as you'd say – then we're always going to be in trouble, aren't we?'

She was lounging on the grass, leaning on her elbow, idly swilling the wine around in her glass – exactly as Elisabeth had done so often – and she was watching him with the teasing smile she'd inherited. It was very strange, almost as though she was sensing what Elisabeth had done.

Just looking at her lying there provoked a stab of desire in Charlie, but it was a confused response. He knew her very well now – and his wanting of her had grown harder for him. But the memory of Elisabeth – in that familiar place – was very vivid. He could see her, hear her – the way she would throw back her head with that musical laugh; the look of gentle reproach when he got jealous ('No questions, Charlee. I'm not sixteen. There must be a past'); the knowing half-smile when she was aroused, the firm guidance ('You're getting skilled in the art, Charlee. You make music, Charlee, just play the notes. The trebles, Charlee, the trebles . . .').

Nikki interupted his musing. 'You're thinking of her, aren't you?' she said.

'Be surprising if I wasn't, wouldn't it?'

'Oh yes,' she agreed, 'if we're to face her. She really is dead, isn't she, Charlee?'

'That's a funny thing to say.' For a moment, he wondered again what she would do if he told her the truth about her mother's death.

'Not so funny,' she answered. 'Shall I tell you a secret? I've been a bit jealous just lately – of Maman, I mean.'

'That's crazy.'

'It's crazy all right. I've been having bad dreams about her. With you. You know – doing things together.'

'What sort of things?'

'Oh, don't be dense, Charlee. You know what I mean. It's a bit scary. In the dark of the night it didn't seem she was so dead. I even had a daydream, which was awful. On Romy's terrace. Maman was making love to you, Charlee, and she looked at me. I could see her eyes as clearly as you can see mine now. Can you believe that, Charlee?'

'It's garbage, Nikki.'

'It's not. I've got to face up to her – more maybe than just pay my respects. What was she really like, Charlee – my heroine mother? I need to see her, too – as you did. How was she at your picnics? Like this?' She exaggerated the way she was lounging on her elbow. 'Or like this?' She sat up and put her arms round her knees. 'Or sitting elegantly like this?' And she sat stiffly upright, her legs folded back beside her under her skirt, as though she were about to serve tea in dainty china cups. 'Well?'

He shrugged. 'Like all of them, Nikki.'

Nikki was watching him, lying back again on her elbow. 'Did she have a mole on her left breast?' She giggled at the look on his face. 'Were her teeth uneven? Did she have a bit of a tum? She was getting on a bit, wasn't she?'

'Why don't we just eat the salami and enjoy the scenery?'

'Because we're facing her, Charlee. What did you talk about, when she wasn't instructing you on life? Did you talk about the future, about after the war, about me? Perhaps you'd have been my stepfather. Isn't that a funny idea, Charlee?'

He wished he could stop the words pouring out of her. She was high – for the wrong reasons.

'Did you make love here?' she asked suddenly.

'That's enough, Nikki,' he said quietly.

'Well, did you?'

'It's none of your business.'

'I bet you did. How did you do it, Charlee? Would she be lying here, looking at the view, on her stomach like this . . .' She rolled over on to her front, resting her chin on her clasped hands. 'The wine's made her feel good and the sun's hot – '

'Nikki, you've got to stop this,' he said. 'It's tasteless.'

'And she's telling you all those things that you said made such a difference to your life,' she went on, 'and her skirt's ridden a bit high just like mine has, as they do if you move around and maybe want them to. And you're twenty, Charlee, in your prime and mad about her, so you can't keep your hands off her.' She turned her head and grinned at him. 'Not old and stuffy like you are now.' She saw his face and giggled. 'Well, you're married, aren't you, and powerful, and a father . . . But at twenty, there's no guilt, nothing to stop you. So what do you do? You lie down beside her – it's very easy between you, for you've been lovers a while – and you put your hand – '

'Please, Nikki!' ordered Charlie.

She gave him an angry smile. 'Am I upsetting you?'

'Of course you are.' He was disturbed by the accuracy of the picture she was drawing. Not that it wasn't predictable. What would happen at a picnic there between lovers?

Nikki turned over on to her back and gazed at him with serious eyes. 'Isn't that part of the treatment, to upset you?'

'Not like this. You're playing a stupid game. Now sit up and let's have lunch.'

It *had* upset him – which she had intended, but not quite in the way she'd thought. She sat up, almost meekly. She put out a hand to him across the paraphernalia of the picnic and he took it, returning the pressure. 'Sorry,' she said.

'OK,' he answered.

2

Charlie parked the Renault in the small main square of Saint-Martin near the doors of the Mairie. It was a hot dusty afternoon and there weren't many people about. 'They used to have parades here sometimes,' he said. 'Put on quite a show. There were some cavalry officers who'd escaped to carry on fighting – the 11th Cuirassiers, formed by Louis XIV. They'd brought their horses with them and full uniforms, swords, the regiment's battle standard. Jesus, this was in the middle of a war with the Germans on the plain down there. We had some local Alpine troops, too. Even the Maquisards wore hats and ties at these times and the blessings were conducted by a fighting priest with grenades in his belt.'

'Did he ever kill anyone?' It was a listless question. She had no interest in the answer – in anything, it seemed.

'I expect so,' Charlie answered. 'And that little hotel over there was where the council used to run the plateau with the help of glasses of pastis.' He pointed to a small white building, with walls of cracked stucco and the words 'Hôtel Breyton' that had been painted a long time ago. 'Madame Breyton was a tough lady who ran the place like a school. She lost two sons, but then lots of people did.' Nikki nodded with an effort at sympathy but didn't comment.

The girl's voluble high spirits had drained from her after their picnic. It was a strange day for them both. They walked to a cottage at the edge of the village without saying much. It was like the others – terraced, with wooden shutters over the windows, paint peeling because of the sun, spikes on the roof to control the snow in winter. 'This is the place,' Charlie said as he knocked.

'Where you all lived?'

'And where the orders came in by radio.'

The old lady who opened the door eyed him curiously; her wrinkled face broke into a smile. 'I remember you,' she said. 'Monsieur Charles, isn't it?' She looked at Nikki. 'Why do I recognise you? You must have been a baby then.'

'I'd guess you're thinking of her mother, madame,' said Charlie. 'Remember Madame Elisabeth?'

The old lady gave a little cry. 'Of course. Oh, that was so sad, wasn't it? Like so much that happened here.'

'I was hoping you wouldn't mind if I showed Nicole the cottage. I've talked of it so much.'

She shrugged permission with a doubtful smile. 'You should have written, given me time to clean up a little, tidy things.'

Charlie grinned. 'I bet it's tidier than it was, madame.'

They went upstairs first, to the bedrooms. 'Leah used to transmit the signals from that room there,' he said.

Nikki looked oddly uninterested. 'Where did you sleep?' she asked. 'With Maman, I mean. Did the others mind?'

He observed her for a second, realising the direction of her thoughts. 'People didn't have their own rooms, even their own beds. It was changing all the time. To start with, there was just Duncan, Leah and Max. Then I was sent in by the OSS. Then Sonya came. Elisabeth arrived later. Sometimes people would be away on missions. Sometimes we were joined by others. There were no special arrangements. Usually the girls would be in one room and the men in another, but not always. Sometimes somebody would sleep downstairs.'

'But you slept with Maman here?'

'Nikki, this isn't necessary.'

'Did you?'

'There's a tiny single room. We went there sometimes.'

'Show me.'

'This isn't ending spells, you know.'

'Please show me,' she said sharply.

He shrugged, crossed the small passage and opened the door to what the old lady clearly used as a store. There were wooden chests of drawers, cupboards, suitcases, dusty parcels tied with string, even a rusty bicycle; but beneath it all, barely visible, there *was* a bed – the bed that at times he'd shared with Elisabeth.

Nikki was staring at it. 'So it happened there,' she said bitterly, 'those mad nights of passion.'

'Hardly that.'

She glared at him. 'Are you telling me there was no passion?'

'Of course not. But you're demeaning it, making it banal. Things happen at times like that. There's no routine. We weren't married, living in the suburbs, making history Saturday nights. You can't get away from it, Nikki – I loved Elisabeth very much.'

'Oh, I know that. You still do.' Her tone was hostile.

'That used to be a bond between us,' he said gently; 'why we got on so well. What's happened, Nikki?'

'I told you, up there on the hill. She's giving me bad dreams.'

'Nikki,' he said and moved to take her in his arms – a gesture of affection, of sympathy. But she twisted away.

'Don't touch me, please!' she demanded.

'OK,' he said and, turning, led the way downstairs to the room they'd all lived in, where the ballot had been held. There was no sign of the old lady. Perhaps she had thought they would like to be alone there, to mourn a little.

He looked round the room, furnished now for an old lady's life with armchairs and antimacassars, a polished oak table, a bookcase – used for mementoes rather than books. The curtains were the same, though – rust-coloured in heavy fabric, hanging to the floor. There'd been a fire then, of course. Almost more than anything else, he remembered the flickering of the flames, and the shadows, moving and surreal, they'd cast on the wall.

Now, in high summer, the fire was unlit, but it was laid ready, with newspaper and kindling, and there were a few logs on the hearth. In a few weeks, the nights would be getting cold.

It was hard for him, standing there again – far harder than he'd found Nikki's reaction upstairs. He'd understood that. To come back with Nikki had always been seamed with danger – more obvious to him than to her. But it was here, between these walls, that Elisabeth's destiny had been decided – or rather its fulfilment; here that the plan of someone he didn't know, for reasons he didn't know, had been formalised; here that he'd been chosen as the killer of the woman he adored.

Nikki was looking at him strangely. She had spent a lot of time with him, watched so many of his reactions – but she had never seen him looking as he did at that moment. She shivered. 'There's something I don't like about this place,' she said. 'It's cold – like it was cold when Grandmère died.'

'It does feel cold,' he agreed and they went out into the hot afternoon sun.

The mood of the day didn't change. He drove her to the east side of the Massif by way of the Gorges de la Bourne – which was another huge crevice eroded in the limestone, with tunnels and natural arches and roadside cliffs, and even a bridge that had replaced the one he'd seen the Maquis destroy. But it wasn't as huge or as magnificent as the Grands Goulets that had so affected her that morning.

They drove on through the town of Villard, the largest on the plateau, and after a few minutes began to descend by way of a steep, twisting mountain road. Just above the village of Saint-Nizier, Charlie braked and turned off to the small national cemetery where Elisabeth was buried. It had been chosen as a site for heroes. The east side of the Vercors was not at this point as dramatic as the west. They were in the easiest of all the eight passes to the Massif, which only gave access to the lower plateau, but the view was superb of the immense valley three thousand feet below them – the valley through which Napoleon had passed with his army on the surprise march on Paris after his escape from Elba.

The city of Grenoble lay exposed, seeming strangely compact, bordered as it was by two rivers, the Isère that flowed north to join the Rhône, and the Drac that ran south – set against the distant mountain ranges of the Chartreuse and Belledonne. Above them at the cemetery loomed the Moucherotte with the strange three-fingered obelisk that they called the 'Three Virgins'.

'They hung the Tricolour from that,' Charlie said, 'in full view of the German barracks down there.' She gave no answer – just the hint of a nod to show she had heard.

They stood by Elisabeth's grave. The sun was lower, almost touching the higher peaks in the west.

'I don't feel anything,' said Nikki. 'I'm paying my respects, aren't I – so why don't I feel anything, Charlee?'

'You didn't know her very well.'

'Do you feel anything, Charlee?'

He never had, not even on earlier visits, and it had surprised him, too. 'I feel more when I think of her alive,' he said.

She turned away from the grave, looking down on the city. A train was approaching from the north on the line that ran parallel to the river. Already there were a few lights on in the carriages. 'Is that the track you were trying to blow up when she died?'

'Yes,' he answered, 'but it was a bit further north past Egrève. You can't quite see it from here.'

'Would you feel anything if we went back there?'

'I went there ten years ago – just to see how it was in daylight. I found it very harrowing.'

They walked to the car in silence and he drove up the mountain road.

'How did you change from comrades to lovers?' she asked suddenly.

'Do you need to know every detail?' he asked softly. 'Does it help?'

'A bit.' She wasn't looking at him – just watching the road ahead through the windscreen. 'It's often a difficult moment, the change. For anyone.'

'I told you about how she saved my life, how she drew the fire of the Milice when they had me trapped. Well, after that, when we met at the rendezvous in the woods, she kissed me. It was relief that I was alive, but it was a lover's kiss.'

She was silent for a moment. 'Did you ever see her kill anyone?'

'Of course.'

'Why of course?'

'Well, that's what we had to do sometimes.'

'What did she do when she killed someone – let out a cry of triumph? Whoops, "I've got one!" Was it like that? Like hunting deer?'

'Of course it wasn't. Nikki, I don't know what's got into you today or rather, I do. We should never have come.'

'Well, how was it?' she persisted. 'I want to know, Charlee.'

'It was a lot of things. We were usually scared, wondering how the hell we were going to get out. And pleased if the objective was achieved. And a bit sick – mostly they were ordinary soldiers who were dying.'

'Did killing make you sexy – when you got back, I mean? The

reaction. Did you desperately need to have her, after seeing her kill?'

He stopped the car beside the road and looked at her. 'That's an incredible thing to say, Nikki!'

'Well, did you?'

'We were on our knees, dead tired. We'd been up all night. You've seen how long it takes to get down from the Massif.'

She looked at him with an expression that was strangely blank. 'People can be half dead and they can still make love,' she said, 'if the need is there.'

'How do you know so much about it?' he asked. He could never think of her past without a trace of bitterness, unfair though it was.

'It's what I've heard from the girls. Did you ever make love together after she'd killed?'

He hesitated.

'Please,' she said. 'I want to know her.'

'Yes,' he said reluctantly.

'Do you think the man who killed her made love afterwards?'

That was the most awful question she'd ever asked him, because he knew the answer. 'I don't suppose he knew,' he lied. 'Lots of them were firing.'

'If he'd seen her fall maybe *he* cried out: "Whoops I've got one!".'

'Please, Nikki, no more,' he said. Behind them, a horn blared as a bus emerged from a bend, and the road was too narrow for a vehicle that size to overtake. Charlie put the Renault into gear and drove on.

3

They stayed the night in La Chapelle, which Nikki said gave her an odd feeling. 'A lot of people died here,' he told her. 'The owner of this hotel was sat in a red-hot frying pan to make him talk.'

'How terrible,' she said. 'I've always thought of the Vercors as a romantic place, a perfect setting for your great affair.'

'The scenery takes some beating, doesn't it?'

'Yes,' she agreed with dull sarcasm, 'the scenery is very pleasant.'

They were having dinner in a pretty dining room with floral curtains and candles on the tables. There weren't many other diners. The weather was too hot for walking, which was the reason most people came to the plateau in summer.

'Your wife knew about Elisabeth, of course?' she asked suddenly.

'From the moment I met her. We were partners at a dinner party in New York given by Marie Cayzer. We talked about her during dinner – what she'd done, how she'd died.'

'And your Philana picked up the real truth on the jungle drums?' He nodded, wishing she would stop. 'I suppose,' Nikki went on, 'she thought she could live with that. After all, Elisabeth was dead, and she could give you roots, couldn't she? That's what she reckoned. She wasn't to know you wouldn't get over it, but she learned, didn't she?'

'Just leave it,' he said. 'We had to kill people. I'm married. Those are facts.'

She looked at him, a little hurt, and he felt that awful spasm in his stomach. 'I suppose I want to know you better,' she said simply. '*And* my mother. And even your wife. Everyone around you. Sonya says I shouldn't talk about your wife because it makes you feel guilty. Does it?'

He looked at her evenly. 'I don't have anything to feel guilty about, do I?'

'Like a tortured priest?' she queried, forcing a laugh. 'That's not you, Charlee. And you've plenty to feel guilty about. You committed adultery, didn't you? Or didn't my mother mention she was married?'

'It had been over between them for a long time.'

'So that made it all right, did it? Does your wife know about me?'

'Oh yes. She met Leah a few weeks back and asked about you. Her father had heard. He's got many sources in Paris.'

'And she hasn't come over? If I'd been her, I'd have chased you, you know. I'd have wanted to see a girl who looked like the woman who'd been so important to you.'

'She doesn't have to chase me. Her father's just hit Paris with a shotgun. He's Greek, as I've told you. The Greeks are funny about their women.'

'So that's why you're going back. You're scared.'

He laughed and shook his head. 'I'm not scared of Mastorakis – we know each other too well. You know why I must go. You listed the reasons at La Napoule and told me I mustn't speak of them.'

She was silent for a moment, just looking at him with all her pain visible. Then she said: 'Tell me, will you think of me back in New York?'

'Of course.' It was what men always said. Better than just 'yes'.

'Will I haunt you? There you'll be at breakfast with your wife and the children, and you'll be reading the paper and your wife will say "More coffee, darling?" and the children will be talking about the kids at school and what the teacher said yesterday. Will you wonder what I'm doing?'

'Of course.'

'*Will* you, Charlee? Will you think of the expressions on my face, the eyes like my mother's, the laughter we've shared, the way I disturb you, the touching . . .' She put a hand over his, knowing she had good hands, as he'd told her, with long slim fingers. 'Will you think of that? And if you say "of course" I'll kill you.'

'I'll think of all those things,' he said. 'Very often. And more. I'll think of you in the café in the Boulevard de la Madeleine, among the crowds of Saint-Séverin, in the surf at Deauville.'

She smiled. 'I'd say that was haunting.'

'Perhaps,' he agreed.

'Like Elisabeth's haunting?'

He sighed. 'Do we have to come back to Elisabeth every time? You're different women. I've changed since I was twenty.'

For a second, her gaze was tremulous, like a fawn's, sensing danger. 'We're only here because of Elisabeth,' she said. 'I won't haunt you like she does, will I? Not when you're back there with your wife?'

'Please, darling . . .' he began, trying to contain his impatience.

'That's clever,' she snapped. 'Throwing in a "darling".'

'How do I convince you that it's different? It'll always be different because it has to be different with different people, even if they *are* mother and daughter.'

She was observing him coolly. 'I want to haunt you like she haunts you.'

'That's impossible because she's dead.'

'In New York I'll be dead to you.'

'Now that's absurd, and you know it. I'll talk to you often on the phone. I'll come over sometimes. I'll write.'

'And will you tell your wife when you do?' He shut his eyes, not knowing what more to say. 'I don't think you care much, Charlee. I was wrong: I don't think you're tortured. I don't think I'm much more than a bit of fun to you. And I need to be more than fun. I couldn't eat another thing, so I'll go to bed.'

He opened his eyes and watched her walking away through the dining room. He decided not to follow her immediately – to give her time to cry. He apologised to the waiter, explaining that Mademoiselle was not feeling too well, but he couldn't eat much himself.

At last he went up the stairs to her room and knocked on the door. There was no answer, so he tried to open it, but it was locked. He knocked again. 'Nikki!' he called out. 'Let me in for a moment.'

'I'm trying to sleep,' she said.

'Wouldn't it be better to talk about it?'

'We've said it all.'

'Let me in,' he said again.

'No,' she answered, 'I'm tired. Goodnight, Charlee.'

He went to his own room, but he couldn't sleep. Nikki kept coming into his mind. What existed between them was strange and underwent subtle changes. In a way, it had become less explosive, less physically demanding, except for moments when she looked at him in certain ways, when she revealed herself, the inch that made all the difference – the inside of a thigh, the swelling of a breast. It was always deliberate, he knew. She needed to keep the flame between them burning brightly. But they knew each other now, shared a growing understanding that had evolved through daily contact. When she talked about the laughing, she had touched a chord, for that was what he'd miss, the lightness of spirit that he knew would often draw him back to Paris.

It was the strange resentment of her mother that was new, that had provoked the compulsive need for intimate detail she'd displayed all day. She saw it as campaigning – a way, she hoped, of stripping the colour from his memories, underlining the fact that Elisabeth was dead. She didn't seem to think of her as quite dead, nor alive for that matter, but as a rival female force that could still exercise a lingering power. Then it had begun to obsess her – which happens if you play dangerous games. Well, he had brought her to Elisabeth's terrain. And where would it all lead now? Where was there to go?

He turned over in bed for the fiftieth time, then decided to read for a while; but he couldn't concentrate, so he turned off the light and made an effort once more to drift from the conscious state, using all the tricks he knew, like relaxing his body part by part, thinking of blackness, trying to sink himself lower into the bed.

But he was still fully awake two hours later when his door opened and Nikki stood in her white silk nightgown with the dim light of the corridor behind her. It surprised him, for they had now spent many nights in hotels and she had never come to him.

'Charlee,' she whispered.

'Hallo,' he said.

'You're awake. I'm cold, Charlee. This place is cold. So many people dying, I suppose. Can I just lie with you for a while? We don't have to try to do anything, just lie together. So you won't have to worry about Maman getting in the way. Or your wife. We can pretend you're my brother.'

She looked so wan, so like a child, as she stood in the doorway that he couldn't help laughing. The dangers were obvious, but he'd got used to them now – as troops got used to distant gunfire, or climbers to the fear of falling. He could hardly send her away – not that he'd have been able to. 'Come on then,' he said.

She closed the door and he heard the faint rustle of her nightgown as she moved towards him – and the sap rose in him sharply, as it had to, considering the wanting of her that was always latent in him. And he thought that it must be one of the most exciting things a man can know – a girl approaching his bed in the dark.

As she got into his bed and lay in his arms, she was shivering – but it wasn't sexual trembling. She really was cold. She hugged him with her arms around his neck, and he could feel every tiny part of her naked body through the flimsy nightgown – her nipples, the point of her hipbones below the narrow waist, the pit of her navel in the firm curve of her stomach, the hairs on her pelvis, the contours of her thighs. But she held herself straight, no parting of knees, no subtle relaxing against him. Her cheeks were pressed to his on the pillow but she didn't kiss him. She must have felt the pattern of his body, too, as he could feel hers.

He was hard, of course, but she didn't mention it. She wasn't there for teasing; she needed the security of him, as if he was an old oak, he thought. She was hugging him at shoulder level, but barely touching lower down.

'Why couldn't you sleep?' she whispered, her lips close to his ear.

'I don't know,' he answered. 'A lot on my mind, I suppose.'

'Were you thinking of me?'

'I'm always thinking of you.'

'I'm serious. Were you?'

'We'd just had a quarrel. I never like you to be unhappy.'

'Or were you thinking of Maman? I'm not complaining this time, I promise.'

'She came into my mind too.'

'Have we broken her spell over us?'

'I don't know.'

'How will you ever know?'

'I'm not even sure about that.' It was a banal answer, but they were speaking of different things – she of loving, he of killing.

'One day we'll make love,' she whispered, 'and then you'll know. Not tonight, but one day. When you come back to Paris maybe – if you've missed me.'

'I'll have missed you.'

She relaxed her body and snuggled within his arms. 'Remember what you said all those weeks ago? How if we made love I'd never know if it was her or me you were loving?'

'Yes.'

'Then we risked it because I said I'd share you with her . . .'

'You could never really figure out what I was fussing about.'

'. . . And it was a weak moment when you weren't being a noble husband,' she went on in a whisper. 'But it was Maman who upset things that night, wasn't it? Not your wife.'

'What are we talking about it for?' he asked softly.

'Because it's interesting. You should have seen yourself, you know. It was like you were waking from a nightmare. Your face was wet with sweat. What was in your mind that night, Charlee?'

'More questions . . .'

'What was it that night, Charlee?'

'Do we have to go on with this?' he asked. One of his hands lay on her waist, and he could feel her hipbone through the silk. He was tempted to fondle her, to move his hand under her bottom and pull her to him. She knew it, too, and, though his hand was still, she put hers on his to stay it.

'Why won't you tell me, Charlee? Is it a secret? You were sweating. We were on the point of making love. Some girls would have been upset, I can tell you.'

'I know. You were very good about it. I said so.'

'Was it a sudden vivid memory?'

'I don't want to talk about it.'

She kissed him then – just lightly. 'I feel much better, you know. I'm glad I came to you. Of course . . .' She hesitated, unsure how he'd receive what she was going to say, moving her body slightly. 'If we did make love tonight, and it was all right . . . well, you'd know sooner about the spell, wouldn't you? You could go back to New York a free man. I can think of someone who might even be pleased.'

He laughed. 'That's minx talk if ever I heard it. You're incorrigible, Nikki. OK, you want to make love . . .'

'Don't you?' She put her hand on him. 'My God,' she exclaimed. 'You couldn't want to more than that.'

'I want to. I always want to. But we don't have to pretend we're doing any favours. And that someone you're talking about wouldn't be a bit pleased. She'd hate your guts. She'd probably hate mine.'

'How is it with her? Do you get the sweats with her, the bad thoughts with her?'

'No.' He wished she hadn't talked of Philana. It seemed like revealing a confidence.

'But she's still married to a haunted man, isn't she?' Nikki whispered. 'We don't have to, Charlee. It was only an idea. I know you'd like to stay faithful to her – except that I'm not just any woman, am I? I'm part of Elisabeth, who's always been with her. Or is that being a minx again?'

She heard him laugh. 'It's a little devious and you don't have to give me any excuses. I can think up my own,' she said.

She caressed the side of his face with the back of her fingers. Again she kissed him lightly. 'I want to try again, Charlee – very quietly, very gently, in the dark. I want you to know me, every part of me, so that you remember in New York.'

'It could happen again – what happened before.'

Her mouth was on his lips and she spoke without moving them away. 'So it happens again. We'll fight it, Charlee.'

202

With the movement of one hand, she undid the sash of her nightgown so that it fell away from her, and she laid her naked body against his. 'Let's take our time, Charlee,' she said.

It *was* quiet and gentle. They explored each other's bodies – and their own, for they often found each other's hands and travelled them together – and to feel his gentle touching beneath her own fingers was a delicate delight.

At one moment, she moved one hand firmly over his whole body from his calves to his face, unhurriedly, lingering where she wished. 'Oh, I've wanted to do that so often,' she said.

And as she arched her body to his touch, his lips, she seemed feline. 'You take pleasure like a cat,' he whispered.

'Must be good to be a cat,' she answered.

In their movements, the slow intertwining of limbs, the caressing, the kissing, there was no conscious decision to enter her; neither said: 'Well, we've taken our time, haven't we?' Nor did they position themselves in any deliberate way for the union. It was just that there he was inside her and he heard the joy in her little breathy laugh. 'Is it as good as you expected?' she whispered.

'I couldn't have expected this,' he answered.

'Now you're joking.'

'Only partly.'

'It's dangerous to joke about such things.'

'You have a lovely body.'

'Didn't Elisabeth have a lovely body?'

'Pretty good. Perhaps you should be thankful: it's in the genes.'

'Would you know if it was her or me here in the dark – I mean if she was alive?'

'Darling, this isn't the way to make love – not even gently and slowly in the dark.'

'I need to know, Charlee. Who are you loving? How can you know? How can *I* know? That's what you said. Am I Elisabeth?'

He knew it was a deliberate challenge – and brave, given the background. 'No,' he said, 'you're Nikki all right.' Then a strange thing happened. His thoughts flew back. He was with Elisabeth in the forest on a fine day, shafts of sunlight slanting through gaps in the cover of old pines. Elisabeth liked to make love on the ground – the smell of bark, of earth – 'nearer to God' she called it.

Like her daughter she was mercurial, but that day she was also restless and violent. 'Hurt me,' she said. 'Hurt me, damn you!'

None of those chic suggestions she offered as a woman of experience, no sophisticated guidance, no exploring. Not this time. 'Just hurt me, Charlee. Drive into me hard. More than that, for God's sake! Split me in two! Divide me! Your teeth, Charlee. Bite me! Harder than that, Charlee! It's hurting . . . It's hurting, Charlee . . . Harder . . . harder . . . harder . . .' Then she screamed in climax – a loud piercing shriek that seemed barely human as it echoed through the forest. And at once her body convulsed in a sudden fit of shaking, sweat mingling with tears as it poured down her face.

'Charlee . . . Charlee.' He heard Nikki's voice as though it came from far off. The vivid memory had totally filled his mind. He woke as if from a dream to find himself lying on top of her, realised that his face was as wet with sweat as Elisabeth's had been then. 'Stay inside me, Charlee,' Nikki pleaded. 'Whatever's going on in that head of yours, stay inside me. Then it'll be all right.' She was gripping his buttocks, holding him so tight to her that her nails were hurting him. His thoughts had been so powerfully diverted that he had softened within her, though she'd known it before he did.

'It was Maman, wasn't it?' said Nikki.

'Afraid so.'

'It'll be OK,' she said, then let out a cry: 'Please, Maman, let him go . . .' It was a desolate cry to the gods. 'Let me have him, Maman.' She kissed him gently with slightly open lips, still holding him tightly within her. 'Just love me a little, Charlee. Enjoy me. Smell me. Taste me.'

And he did. He kissed her ears, her neck, her breasts. He stroked her shoulders, her back, her hips, her thighs – and he began to harden and, after a moment, she relaxed the iron grip that she'd locked on him and he could sense her joy – such joy that she came to climax first, gloriously, whispering: 'Thank you, thank you, thank you,' though whether it was him or her mother she was thanking he was unable to tell. Certainly, she too had sweat pouring down her face.

A few moments later, they were lying, with that wonderful sense of fulfilment that sex can induce when it's right. Dawn was breaking and through a crack in the curtains they could see the lightening sky. The clock of the village church began to strike, dull echoless clangs.

'Have we broken that spell?' she asked.

'We've done something,' he answered.

'It's odd, you know, when I think that before I met you in April, she was like a goddess to me. I worshipped her memory.'

'I'm sorry if I've stopped that. It's good to worship somebody. She was a great lady.'

'She certainly had her faults though, didn't she?'

'Every great man in history has had his faults – *and* every great woman.'

She turned towards him, with her head on his shoulder. 'Will it be hard for you when you face your wife?'

'A bit,' he admitted, 'but I'm grown up. Lots of things are hard.'

'It's not as though I want all of you – just a part. Do you have to tell her?'

'We'll see.'

'I don't want you to tell her. It'll upset her terribly. And make everything harder.'

'You know it all, don't you?'

Her hand was wandering down his body and she felt his arousal. 'Since we've done it once,' she said, 'it wouldn't make much difference if we did it again, would it?'

He laughed and took her in his arms. 'You're a minx.'

'Yes,' she agreed, 'but a nice minx, a loving minx, and – even though I say it myself – after tonight, quite a clever minx.'

Seventeen

Dominique Saint-Jean sat behind a large white modern desk and surveyed them both with tired grey eyes that, if not exactly hostile, were cautious. She was an odd-looking woman, with blonde hair which she wore straight in a pageboy style, and a face that was heavily wrinkled so that she looked older than she probably was, judging by most of Elisabeth's friends.

She had gone through the courtesies, quickly and sharply. 'Now,' she said, placing her elbows on her desk and clasping her fingers, 'what can I do for you?'

Charlie was surprised by the abrupt question. 'Well, naturally, madame,' he began, 'Nicole wanted to meet you. As for the five of us who were with her in the Vercors . . . there are aspects of her life that puzzle us . . .'

'Such as?' she snapped.

'Such as the key she gave to Duncan Stewart to send to you after the war.'

'Is there a problem?'

'We'd be interested to know what it would unlock.'

She looked puzzled. 'What in the world has that to do with you, Mr Dawson?'

'We were very close. It could well be of concern to us.'

'And if I were to tell you that it was not?'

'Then I'd wonder how you could know. I grant that we may have no legal right to ask such questions, but I'd say that Nicole, as her only child, most certainly has. It could involve property.'

Madame Saint-Jean had barely moved, just watched him as he spoke, with eyes that hardly blinked. 'You told me you were not her representative,' she said.

'If you wish, I can assume the role.'

The lawyer glanced enquiringly at Nikki and the girl confirmed it with a vigorous nod. The Vercors had changed much between them, added an extra dimension, and given her a radiance, obvious even to outsiders. 'She appears to trust you, Monsieur Dawson. Mind you, I could question whether your influence on a young girl is excessive . . .' – a sudden smile came to that walnut face – 'but I won't.'

'I'm grateful, madame.' He sat back in his chair. 'The key was small,' he went on, 'which would suggest some kind of locker or deposit box. Is that correct?'

'Possibly,' answered the lawyer. 'That wouldn't be unusual – especially during the Occupation.'

She offered nothing more. 'It's sixteen years since Elisabeth died,' Charlie went on. 'Is there still a reason for keeping information from her daughter?'

'I haven't kept anything from her yet.' She studied him with a look of amusement. 'To be frank, you're placing me in some difficulty, Monsieur Dawson. This isn't a property issue in the normal sense, as you seem to think. Anything of that sort was dealt with after Elisabeth's death, though there was little to dispose of. Elisabeth had always been a big spender. What *was* in the locker at the Gare du Nord was a small suitcase, containing various items but mainly letters. I'd long held a note from Elisabeth to be opened only if she died. This instructed me to return the letters in person, and privately, to the writer of them. I haven't been able to do so.'

'After sixteen years, madame?'

'I couldn't trace him.'

'Was there no address on the letters?'

'No, Monsieur Dawson. And naturally they're signed only by a first name or just an initial.'

'Naturally?' queried Charlie.

'Because they were love letters, Charlee,' Nikki put in, 'from a man who was married. Then, if they fell into the wrong hands, there would be no indication of who they were from.'

Madame Saint-Jean smiled at her worldliness. 'You're your mother's daughter, I see. I trust there've been no married men in your life.'

'Only one, madame,' she answered with a glance at Charlie, 'and he hasn't written me a letter yet.'

The lawyer sighed with a slight smile. 'It's not a good idea for a young girl. It really isn't.'

'Oh, Monsieur Dawson would agree with that completely, madame. He took a lot of persuading.'

'Nikki,' he said, 'you really mustn't say things like that.'

'She's got some of her mother's wit, I'm glad to see,' said the lawyer. 'So I've answered your question about the key, haven't I? Private letters.' The smile was back.

'They could contain vital information,' Charlie said, knowing she was playing with him.

'Of what nature? As you say, she's long dead.'

Charlie paused. 'Inconsistencies, you could say. Tell me, madame, about your instructions. Does the time that has passed make no difference?'

'It could.'

'He may be dead.'

'I do not think he's dead. I think he doesn't wish to be contacted.'

'You mean the police are looking for him?'

'In theory. Not with much zeal, I suspect.'

'Jesus,' he said quietly, 'that's hardly Elisabeth's scene, is it?'

She smiled again. 'Charlie, anything was Elisabeth's scene. Surely I don't have to tell you that.' She'd lapsed so effortlessly into the personal from her previous formality – far more significant in Paris than it would be in New York – that Charlie had hardly noticed.

'Doesn't Nicole have some rights to the letters under French law – as an only daughter, I mean?'

'Possibly. May I ask please: did Elisabeth ever speak to you of anyone who might have been – how shall I put it? – important in her life?'

'Occasionally,' Charlie said. 'Claude Duclos cropped up often.'

'Ah yes – Duclos. You've seen Duclos, I believe?'

'I've known him a long time.'

'Elisabeth never mentioned anyone else, who might be more – well, controversial than Duclos?'

'He seemed pretty controversial to me.'

'But acceptable,' she said firmly. 'I gather she didn't. Now, Charlie, I'm going to be frank. I wasn't Elisabeth's *notaire*. I was her friend, and it was in that capacity that the key was sent to me. That frees me professionally, but makes the personal decision harder. The letters will make neither of you happy, but truth, I've found, tends to come out. So I'm prepared to hand them over. First, though I'll just tell you the basics . . .'

She stood up from her white desk and looked out of her window on to the Rue de l'Université. Her figure was still trim, though her shoulders were a trifle broad, like a man's. 'In the spring of 1933, when she was in Berlin for Radio France, she met a young captain. His name was Wolf . . .'

'The W!' they both said in unison.

She glanced back at them. 'He often signed his name as W,' she agreed. 'The Army was still restricted by the Treaty of Versailles to 96,000 men and 4,000 officers, but Hitler had just gained power and in the next six years it was to become the most powerful force in Europe. Wolf came of a well-known Army family and he was a member of the General Staff. He was close to most of the leading figures: Beck, Brauchitsch, even poor Blomberg.

'He was a man of talent, honour, courage and, from a career point of view, he was the right age in the right place at the right time. But he fell madly in love with Elisabeth on sight – as she did with him. Which was a pity, since he was married and so was she. Even that early, her marriage was a shambles, and a Catholic shambles at that. Wolf was about ten years older, already had a daughter. Their affair went on for a long time, survived many obstacles, and it wasn't their fault there was a war.'

She returned to her desk and sat down. 'You'll know his name well enough – General Karl Wolfgang Heinegg.'

'Good God!' exclaimed Charlie in amazement.

'Who was he?' asked Nikki. 'Why are you so surprised?'

'I knew it would be a shock,' said the lawyer before turning to Nikki. 'He commanded the 34th Panzer Division,' she explained, 'though that won't mean much to you either.'

'He was famous, Nikki,' added Charlie. 'Almost legendary as a Wehrmacht tank commander. Always worked closely with Rommel. But it's impossible to believe he was Elisabeth's lover for so long. She never once mentioned him – not even the early days, not even obliquely. Of course, it would have been hard to take: we had friends dying, sometimes suffering worse. Still, she'd talk at times of Germans she'd met in Berlin, when we were on our own usually, often laughing at herself for the mistakes she made. "Know how to pick 'em, don't I," she'd say. But Jesus, Heinegg.'

'He was no mistake, Charlie,' said Madame Saint-Jean. 'He was far too important . . . as indeed were you,' she added quickly. 'You just played different roles for her at different times. I should tell you that Wolf was also charged with war crimes,' she went on. 'Much later, of course – after Elisabeth's death. And quite wrongly. He was still a colonel when the incident occurred, instigated by the SS, and was away from his regiment at the time. He was with Rommel, in fact, as recorded in the Headquarters log. But justice was pretty rough in those early post-war days and he was taking no chances. He disappeared – to South America, like many of the real guilty men.

'He's returned to Europe, I believe. I've heard of business dealings – black market, sales of army surplus. Not savoury, but not too serious. Half the Allied armies were doing the same, but not on such a scale, of course. I found his family and left messages for him, but he's never responded, so I've closed the file.'

She smiled and gave a shrug. 'That's the background. And here are the letters.' She leaned down to pick up a small attaché case by her feet and placed it on the desk – then pushed a document towards them. 'I want you both to sign for it, please, though it places on record that I am handing the property of the late Elisabeth Ferrier to her daughter. His wife's address is inside the case, but you won't find her very co-operative – especially if you mention Elisabeth.'

She stood up as they signed, and held out her hand to each in turn. 'Good luck to you both – and take care.'

As soon as they got down to the street, Charlie said: 'I feel a bit punch-drunk.'

'So do I,' said Nikki, clutching his arm. 'A German general! Who'd have thought such a thing of Maman?'

'And what a general! Even the Allied press kind of liked him – he was brilliant at sudden strikes. And let's face it: he was just a captain when she met him.'

She looked at him wonderingly. 'Aren't you jealous?'

He nodded. 'Yeah, but nothing, I guess, to what I will be when I've seen the letters.'

'Do you have to? I'll tell you anything you need to know.'

He laughed. 'I have to.' He kissed her on the forehead. 'Tell you what. We'll call Sonya and have a good lunch. After that we'll go back to your apartment and face the truth.'

2

I am walking in a daze. I've collided with people in the street, walked into lamp posts, even fallen headlong. I'm aware that life will never be the same for me again, that what I've known so far has been limited as for someone who is blind, or crippled, or even mentally retarded.

Otto has suggested I apply for immediate leave on medical grounds related to my sanity. I told you of my colleague Major Otto Grolmann, but you weren't listening to what I said. I hardly heard what *you* said. The music of your voice was enough, filling my whole mind with a wonder at its beauty, at the perfect match it provides to the way you look. I can still see every detail of you – your hair coming as it does to those two points on your cheeks, the softness of your skin, the shape of your lips, those wonderful brown eyes. I can hear you speaking now – the lilt, the range, the laugh that's always there just waiting to surface.

Von Eysebeck has been taunting me. Worse, he told the General that I'm the captain who's not there today, since I've shown no sign of hearing anything he's said. I spoke of von Eysebeck last night – my cross, my enemy even. But you won't remember that either.

So you see already you've put my career at risk, and if I'm court-martialled tomorrow, it'll have been worth every second. Last night I told you my whole life story, which you didn't hear. Within minutes of our meeting, I was sharing with you my most intimate thoughts. I told you I loved you – and thank God you didn't laugh. I'll always remember your response, for it's pinned up in my mind in a frame like one of those truisms in needlepoint that people have on walls . . .

Charlie was forced to stop reading for a moment, shock making his mouth dry, his heart beat faster. She'd shared this kind of emotion with another man *for years*? Yet, in all those nights Charlie had spent with her, all those picnics, journeys when she had talked of Duclos and other men she called her friends, when she had told him about her mother and Nikki and that crazy father and poor Pierre, who should never have been her husband, and even about Marie and Berlin at this very time, she had never once mentioned Wolf, never hinted that there had been someone in her life of such long-lasting and overwhelming importance.

Charlie shook his head in disbelief, and became aware that Nikki was looking at him with a pain in her eyes that almost matched his own. She pursed her lips in a kiss of sympathy.

The three of them were sitting on the floor around the open attaché case, reading the letters, which were written in French.

He forced a smile, mouthed a silent kiss in response to hers, before looking down at the page again.

The scene that Wolf had drawn was vivid and highly detailed, every word they had spoken seemingly repeated on the pages, every expression noted. It was at a reception at the AA – as the Auswärtiges Amt, the Foreign Ministry, was known – and it was in that great room with its pillars and chandeliers that he'd confessed to his sudden obsession for her.

'I don't believe it,' Elisabeth had said.

'That I've fallen in love so fast?'

'No, idiot – that *we've* fallen in love so fast. I'm a reporter, for God's sake. Love at first sight is for magazine stories, not real life – surely you knew that?'

'I'm real,' he said.

'I don't believe it. I don't believe any of it.'

'Let's go out to dinner. You'll believe the food. You can taste food, even touch it.'

She was smiling at him, her long cigarette holder between her teeth. 'Let me just find Marie and tell her we're going,' she said. 'Have you met Marie Cayzer of the *New York Herald Tribune*?'

'I don't think so.'

'Well, now's your chance. We share an apartment on Voss Strasse.' She was standing on her toes to see if she could spot Marie in the throng. 'Ah, there she is – surrounded by men as usual, all giving her wonderful front page stories.'

She took his hand and led the way. 'Marie darling,' she said, 'you haven't met this wonderful captain. He speaks French like a dream – spent years in Paris as a boy. We've fallen in love but we don't believe it, so we're going out to dinner to find solid reality.'

Marie looked at her in amazement. 'Captain, what have you done to her? This isn't the Elisabeth I live with . . . Oh my God . . .' She was looking over Elisabeth's shoulder. 'If you want some solid reality, honey, just turn around. I didn't know *he* was coming.'

The two of them turned, still holding hands – and sure enough, there was Hitler. Elisabeth hoped desperately that he wouldn't come over to her or send an emissary, as he'd done at times, though normally she'd have grabbed the chance of a story. 'Please talk to someone else,' she murmured.

'I'm not leaving your side for an instant,' Wolf said in a shocked voice.

'I meant the Führer, stupid,' she told him.

Hitler started talking animatedly to a man near him and she sighed with relief. 'Can we go then?' Wolf whispered.

'I think so. I'll get my wrap . . .'

The writing on the notepaper was neat, slanting forwards with exaggerated loops on such letters as Gs and Bs:

. . . I'm over thirty but I've never known an evening such as that. I told you I had a wife, and you just shrugged and said you were married too as though it was unimportant. That's the cruelty of it, isn't it? Everything else seems dwarfed by contrast – marriages, promises, careers, even honour. And even now, as you read this, I can see you laughing: not at my words – oh God, I hope you'll agree with my words – but at the condition of Man, the follies, God's joke as you put it, the Divine Comedy . . .

Again, Charlie had to stop reading. This had touched a chord, for it was something she had often said to him, to them all. 'Remember her talking of God's joke?' he asked Sonya.

She smiled. 'She always made God sound like an old gentleman about to wink.' She was sitting with her legs doubled under her – as usual looking elegant and carefully arranged as though she were about to be photographed. 'Time for stiff upper lips, Charlie,' she reminded him. It was what they'd often said in action just before the shooting started – usually teasing Duncan, who could get pompously heroic at such times.

Nikki picked up the nuances in this exchange between comrades, even felt a pang of jealousy. She met his eyes, then returned to the letter in her hand:

How can I put what I feel into words? I've possessed you and it's as if I've never known another woman. I've always thought, despite what is said, that making love was a pretty equal business, but deep in our natures it's a giving and a taking. Not always, of course. A woman can take; a woman can use. With a woman of spirit and independence as you are, the gift is greater. But last night you had a need to give that was beyond the most extreme desire, a need that in quality was spiritual, even sacred, so that there was a merging of a kind I've never known before, of our bodies, our minds, our very souls . . .

Nikki was moved and strangely shamed by the intimacy, as though she were viewing a sexual embrace. This was her mother he was writing of, yet Wolf's words provided an echo. He was striving to describe an emotion that was so basic that layer after layer had been scraped away to reveal it. She understood, for she had felt a trace of something similar herself in the Vercors.

She wondered how long they had waited before consummating so powerful a love, but the letter was merely dated 'Sunday, 14th'.

'Is there a date on your letter?' she asked Charlie. 'The one of their meeting.'

'Wednesday, 18th.'

'No month?'

'Why do you ask?'

'No reason really. Just wondered.' The delay could have been just four days or many weeks, though the latter seemed unlikely.

'Show me the letter,' said Charlie.

'I don't think so. You shouldn't read this.'

'Nikki, let me have it.'

'I should do as he says,' said Sonya. 'He's in too deep already.'

'I couldn't. I just couldn't.'

'Nikki . . .'

'Listen to this,' Sonya said, as she turned the pages of a long letter, skimming the words. 'It's their first quarrel – and crucial.' She wasn't just diverting the others. She was fascinated because the row was over the kind of issue she'd faced herself over René. 'It's written just after Hitler marched into the Saar. That was '34, wasn't it? The year of the purge and the broadcast that made her famous, but that hasn't happened yet. When did they meet?'

'The spring of '33,' said Charlie. 'Hitler took power in January.'

'So they've known each other a year – and they've been found out.'

'By his wife?' Charlie queried.

'I don't think so, but certainly by the Army. Incidentally, that's now 300,000 men.'

'Jesus, that means it trebled in twelve months. Hitler didn't lose any time in tearing up the Treaty of Versailles, did he?'

'Wolf's a major now,' Sonya said, her eyes running swiftly over the words. She read aloud:

I'm still reeling from last night. Never have I known such desolation as I felt when you left. I watched you from the window hoping you'd look up, but you didn't. Your anger was in your stride. I'd recognise you anywhere, you know, even if you were hooded, just from the way you move. I phoned, but of course you weren't answering.

I know what your career means to you, as mine does to me. So let me just recap that terrible day so that we can see the issue clearly – from my summons by the General. He is relaxed, sitting back in his chair, smoking a cigar. 'Sit down, Wolf,' he says. 'Make yourself comfortable.' But he is looking at me strangely, studying me. 'Rehmer will be joining us shortly.' That means trouble, for Rehmer is senior SS.

The General leans forward to tip the ash from his cigar. 'You know, Wolf, you have a great future. I've seen officers come and I've seen them go. Sometimes they flare brightly and the flame goes out. Sometimes they are slow burners, getting brighter all the time – as you are. I'd put money on you, Wolf. You'll probably become a great commander – tanks, I'd guess. You have nerve, panache, quick but cautious thinking. It'll happen, mark my words, as long as . . . Well, just don't cross the Party, Wolf.'

When Rehmer arrives, he isn't alone. Von Eysebeck is with him trying to look stern. Rehmer is businesslike but informal. He sits on the edge of the General's desk. He is thin and balding, and his grey skeletal face seems to match the black SS tunic with its death's head insignia. 'So, Major,' he says, 'you've captured the affections of the beautiful Elisabeth Ferrier.'

My heart stops because policy on contacts with foreign journalists changes every day. I say nothing, just wait for him to go on, with an awful feeling of dread. 'You are, of course, married,' he continues, 'with a delightful young daughter, I'm told, with blue eyes and fair hair. Not that you need be concerned about the Party's discretion, of course – nor shall I urge you to end the liaison.'

My relief is immense – and so obvious that he laughs – but I realise it's premature. For why are we both there? 'However,' Rehmer goes on, 'I know you'll be eager to serve the Führer' – which is unnerving, because he's well aware of what the Army thinks of Hitler. 'And you should be proud that you can.'

'You should indeed,' puts in von Eysebeck. 'I'm sure he is, Colonel.'

'I speak of your influence with Madame Ferrier,' says

Rehmer. 'You could surely change her perspective of the great task to which the Führer has addressed himself.'

'You mean – ' I begin.

He cuts in: 'Does she show you transcripts of her broadcasts?'

'Sometimes,' I answer.

'Then you'll know how critical she is. She doesn't understand our problems – with the Jews, the treaty, the Communists . . . the role of the Stormtroopers, the changes in our laws that the foreign press make so much of . . . Need I go on? I'm assured that you're a great patriot, that your talents as a soldier presage a brilliant career. So you'll guide her, won't you, Major?'

I protest, speak of your independence, explain how stubborn you can be. 'Nothing I can do, Colonel,' I tell him, 'will prevent her from reporting the truth as she sees it.'

Rehmer stands up and puts on his gloves. 'You must persuade her, Major. You must explain that the road is hard, that it demands measures that we might not choose if we had more time . . .' He breaks off, a glacial smile on his face. 'Who could explain this better than you, Major, after a night of ecstasy?'

'And if I can't persuade her?' I ask.

'You will, Major, for the sake of your family, your career, your duty – to say nothing of hers. It can hardly help her if we demand her withdrawal. You see it's in her interest, too.'

Only hours later we meet as usual, but you know there is something troubling me, and the ecstasy is shadowed by Rehmer's coarse reference. I toy with keeping it to myself but we don't have unshared secrets, do we? So, as we lie in each other's arms, I tell you – saying at once that I expect you to ignore Rehmer's threats. Your reaction is dramatic. You're out of bed in a second, standing there naked like an angry Roman goddess. 'You don't mean that,' you say accusingly. 'You're warning me off, aren't you?'

'What have I just said?' I insist. 'I told Rehmer. You'll always write what you choose.'

'Oh yes,' you agree sarcastically. 'And have them deny you promotion? Do you think I could write freely under those conditions? The whole notion's absurd.'

'You must write what you believe, darling,' I tell you, 'whatever the cost. I insist on that.' By now, you've begun to dress hurriedly. 'What more can I say?' I ask.

'I don't know,' you snap back. 'It's your country, your Führer, your Jews. That bastard knew what he was doing.

And don't lie there pretending it'd have no effect on my work. You knew damn well what effect it'd have.'

That's a terrible thing to say – and it certainly isn't true. 'Hadn't they just been telling you what a famous general you were going to be?' you challenge. 'Hadn't they praised your skill with tanks? And we all know how important tanks will be next time, don't we?'

You realise what you've said. You manage a sad smile. You've got your dress on by now, straightening it, doing up the hooks. 'Face it, my darling,' you go on. 'Our affair's over, destroyed by our careers.'

'It'll never be over for me,' I tell you.

'Maybe not, but East is East and West is West. It was great while it lasted . . .' Then suddenly all the harshness leaves you. 'I've never known anything like this, and doubt if I ever will again . . . But that's life, isn't it?' The edge is back in your tone. 'I love you,' you say softly and you're gone.

Sonya looked up at Charlie. 'She could be pretty tough for a young woman, couldn't she? That's why she was good. Remember, this is ten years before we knew her.'

'What else does he say?'

'The usual stuff. Doesn't accept it's life. Sure they can figure out something.'

Nikki had picked out another letter from the case. 'It was all show anyway,' she said. 'She called his office first thing next morning. She adores him, she says. He's everything that makes her life worthwhile. She's in the café on the corner of Wilhelmstrasse. Can he slip out for a second?

'She shows him the report she's just written. She wants him to check some facts for her.' She looked up with a giggle. 'Isn't she awful? What's more it's the toughest story she's ever done. He says it'll never get past the censors. Maybe, she says, but at least it'll show Rehmer he can't gag her. After all, what can they do to him? she asks. He doesn't know, he says. Tell his wife perhaps. Stop the promotion he's been promised. "I'll bet you they don't," she says. "You're too valuable. They're rushing to build an army and they surely need any officer who's got the panache to become a brilliant tank commander. I think we should draw their fire."'

'It worked,' Nikki went on, turning the page. 'Rehmer made noises but did nothing. They went out to dinner to celebrate. Von Eysebeck was at another table. He came over. "You're a brave man, Heinegg," he said and turned to Elisabeth. "You've made him take a big risk. I hope you don't come to regret it – either of you." '

Sonya was leaning over the case, picking up letters at random. 'It's a scary feeling, isn't it?' she said. 'Looking into someone else's life, set against the grand march of history. He writes so vividly – he was wasted in the Army.'

'He wasn't,' countered Charlie. 'At one moment in the desert war they were afraid his tanks would reach Alexandria.'

'His wife's found out now,' said Sonya, reading swiftly. 'The Germans have occupied the Rhineland.'

'That makes it 1936,' added Charlie. 'They've known each other three years.'

'He's in big trouble, though he's now a colonel, commanding a tank regiment, as predicted. Our old friend von Eysebeck's given the game away – and not just the affair. He really did have it in for him, didn't he? Elisabeth and Wolf have been found together in the Black Forest in a village inn – by his wife and the Gestapo. He's been ordered back to Berlin and Elisabeth goes with him. She's based in Paris now, a roving reporter, but obviously visits Germany often. The letters are being sent by hand now to avoid the censors. Oh no, they've discovered she's got Jewish blood and . . . Oh God, poor Wolf . . .'

Sonya began to read aloud once more:

Rehmer again, the day you left, this time in his office. Well, he's more important now, sees Himmler every week. His usual charming self. 'What are we going to do about you, Colonel? I'm told you're the best tank commander we've got – yet reports of your love affair are constantly on my desk.'

'Why, General?' I ask. 'I grant my situation may merit disapproval, perhaps, but it's not that rare – especially in the Army. Madame Ferrier and I have always been discreet. And, if I may say so, the intrusion in the Black Forest was disgraceful.'

Rehmer stands up. He likes to walk about, shrugs an apology of a sort. 'It's not the fact, Colonel. It's *who*. A woman of prominence, with power to harm us.'

'Why do you keep renewing her visa?'

'She's a special case, Colonel, as you're aware. Her friend Marie is married to Meisinger, who is close to the Führer, who anyway is intrigued by your Elisabeth – not what she writes, of course, but as a woman. And with the Olympic Games here this year, how would it look if we banned her? It's easier now she's based in Paris, of course, but this new information . . .' I obviously look puzzled. 'That she's Jewish, Colonel,' he says. 'Well, presumably you knew . . .'

But of course I didn't, darling, did I? Why didn't you tell me about your grandmother? Surely you didn't think I'd care? Rehmer, too, is much surprised at my ignorance before he delivers his bombshell. 'Even your daughter, Ingrid, knew, Colonel,' he says. 'It was she who reported the fact – much to her credit, I might add.'

I cannot tell you how hard that was, my darling – even though I know the kids are urged to inform on their parents at school: the Party must come before everything. And I know von Eysebeck told her mother the whole story in front of her, so she ran to school screaming with pain and anger at her father's terrible behaviour. I'll never forgive him. My latest promotion seems to have infuriated him, but, imagine going to all that trouble to check out your family. Truly, this absurd vendetta must be stopped.

Sonya looked up. 'And Elisabeth stopped it, didn't she? The next year at Nuremberg after the business with Romy and the Prince.' She looked back at the page. 'That was a bad day for Wolf. As if his daughter wasn't enough! It was his friend Otto who told the Gestapo where they were in the Black Forest. Lost his nerve, though Wolf understood this. They were following up von Eysebeck's tip-off. It hurt, though, for he and Otto had been cadets together. But there's worse to come.' She read out:

Rehmer stops striding about and faces me. 'We are tolerant, Colonel, but there are limits – especially for a senior officer, expected to go far. But not a Jewess, Colonel. That's over the line. I've an order for you from the Führer himself. This affair is to end at once.'

I don't have to describe to you the effect on me of those stark words. You know me so well. For a moment, I'm lost. Wild thoughts flash through my mind – to resign, leave Germany, divorce, go to America with you . . . if you'd come, though we've been through this so often, only to step back always from the abyss. But I know we need time to think, darling, so I decide to agree; but it's an order I can never obey. You'll say I did the only thing I could. You may even suggest that we do try to end it, as ordered, but I must tell you that I'll never stop loving you, and I cannot for one second accept the thought that I'll never again hold you in my arms. But clearly we must act with great caution now. This letter, of course, is coming to you by hand.

'Think of that!' said Nikki. 'A direct order from Hitler. Maman certainly ranked.' She was lying on the floor on her stomach, moving one leg idly with the heel in the air, as she scanned a letter she'd taken from the case. 'They disobeyed it, of course,' she added, then gave a laugh. 'They used false names, met secretly when she was in Germany. She even wore a wig. And they still didn't fool the SS.'

'"This is 1939," she told them. He's a general now, in Prague with his tanks, which is where things come to a head. Maman's there, too, covering the story of the German entry into the city. They spend the night together – as the SS know. He's summoned before his Commander-in-Chief in Berlin to explain himself. Oh my God, Himmler's present, too, as well as Rehmer. But again he gets away with it.' She read from the letter:

'They know there's going to be a war, so there isn't much point in their taking serious action since we're going to be parted anyway – especially since my division is the finest in the Wehrmacht.

Perhaps it was the threat of war that made it the most wonderful of so many wonderful times that we've made love – the fact that once the fighting starts we may not meet for years, that we'll be on different sides. Or maybe it was because for the first time we were hoping our love would result as nature intended, that – as you said – you'd have something of me that was living.

You know, I can still see that beatific smile on your face as at last we relaxed and you rolled over on to your back. 'The act of creation,' you whispered. 'It was incredible. What shall we call him?'

'You're so sure?' I asked. 'Already?'

'Positive. I know it's impossible to be positive, but I am.'

'It may be a her . . .'

It was only then that the implication of the words began to dawn on her. Charlie had been amazed by the slowness of her reaction. He'd already glanced at Sonya, who was as tense as he was. Nikki lay quite still for a few seconds. 'What month did the Germans enter Prague, Charlee?' she asked softly.

'I think it was March – around then. Listen, Nikki . . .'

'I was born in December.' She remained motionless. 'Oh my God,' she said and sat up. 'He's my father, isn't he? My father was a Nazi general . . .'

'Well, not necessarily,' said Charlie. 'Pierre was around still . . .'

'Not in that way, was he?'

'And Wolf wasn't a Nazi,' said Sonya. 'It's obvious . . .'

'He was with the Nazis, wasn't he?' countered Nikki. 'Rehmer was a Nazi. I'm German, aren't I? Ferrier isn't even my name. Oh my God,' she said again – and tears suddenly began streaming down her cheeks.

Charlie went to her. 'Darling, listen to me . . .'

'No,' she said, 'I'm all right. Just let me get used to it. It's hard, that's all. Oh my God . . .' She broke down, sobbing suddenly, then she leaped to her feet and rushed out of the room.

Charlie started to follow her, but Sonya stopped him. 'Leave her for a moment. She'd rather be alone.' The war had only been over for fifteen years. Nikki had grown up with stories of Nazi brutality in the Occupation, of French girls having their heads shaved because they'd befriended German soldiers, of a mother she'd hardly known because of a German bullet.

Sonya held out her hand to him. 'We should have guessed, I suppose,' she said. 'Been a rough day hasn't it, Charlie?'

'A bit hard to take in,' he agreed. 'It was odd, though. After a while today, I got to like him, to be intrigued. It was as if we were pals with the same enemies. I understood so much of what he did. Well, we've got a lot in common, haven't we? And you know something, Sonya? He could know a hell of a lot we don't – like who might have been exposed if Elisabeth had stayed alive, and why. Even if he doesn't, he might have ways of finding out. He's got dubious friends now.'

'You don't give up, do you?' she said with a smile. 'He won't be easy to track down.'

'Someone's got to know where he is. He must have business associates. Maybe people he's crossed. There's his wife. She might let something slip.'

'If he ever goes home. By the way, Madame Briedon called on me again this morning – Roger's wife. Apparently, Alan Soissons is an electrician – that's Briedon's cousin in New York, remember? She was certain Roger would contact him. There are a lot of electricians in New York, of course . . .'

'Narrows the field a bit, though,' Charlie agreed.

'I cabled my friend in the New York bureau. He might get a lead. Meanwhile she gave me this so we'd know Roger if we saw him.' She took a snapshot from her bag and passed it to him. 'The picture's of them both – about five years ago. Briedon's on the right.'

Charlie studied the photo. It showed two men in bathing trunks on a beach, both in their forties. Briedon was short and bald, with a paunch bulging over the belt line. Soissons was taller and well-built. They were laughing and Soissons had his arm round Briedon's shoulders.

Charlie was aware that he was looking at the man who'd passed the facts to London that had condemned Elisabeth to death. The idea of her being pictured in Paris with a German general didn't seem so absurd now.

Sonya guessed what was in his mind. 'There was a camera waiting for them. How did Briedon know they were meeting – or where? Someone must have tipped him off.'

'Briedon was collaborating by then, wasn't he? A double agent – isn't that what his wife said?'

'You mean Wolf might have told the Gestapo he was meeting Elisabeth?' she asked incredulously.

Charlie shook his head. 'No, that's impossible. But Briedon must know the answer. God, it's important I find him.'

'And someone else thinks it's vital you don't – someone who knew I was due to meet him. So take care.'

Charlie gave no sign he'd heard the warning. 'It's so bloody frustrating. We're still no nearer to knowing who needed her to die – or why.'

'I'm sure Duclos is involved,' said Sonya, 'even if he didn't organise it. He knew I'd arranged to meet Briedon.'

'But where's the motive?' he asked.

'With Duclos, there are always wheels within wheels, debts to be honoured or called, interests to be protected. Claude knows more than he's told us, I'm positive.'

'That goes for all of them. Marie, the Levalliers, Hélène

Prévost, even Romy – they were all close friends. None have mentioned Wolf. Why's it all so secret?' Charlie felt suddenly tired. He sighed. 'What about Nikki? There's going to be a gap in her life when I go. She'll need a bit of help – a job maybe.'

'It'll be tough for her,' she agreed. 'How's it all going to end, Charlie?'

'I don't know. How do these things normally end?'

'Normally?' she echoed. 'Marriages break up or the girls realise there's no future or they settle for what they've got or the fellow gets too guilty or the affair just runs out of steam. That's normal, isn't it? This time . . . Well, you can't end it, can you, darling? You need her as bait to bring Wolf in – the long-lost daughter.'

'You make it sound venal. Surely they'll both want that?'

'Of course. It'll be an act of charity.'

Her friendly sarcasm irritated him. 'Sonya, Wolf's a key figure – a German general, for Christ's sake. Are you saying I should forget he exists?'

She laughed. 'No, Charlie. So you've got a beauty of an excuse to go on seeing Nikki, haven't you? It's just that all around the water's getting deeper.' She reached out and touched his hand. 'OK, I'll see what I can do to keep her busy for a while.'

Nikki came back into the room. She'd been crying and her eyelids were swollen, but she'd done her best to remove the traces of her tears, and put on some lipstick. 'Sorry about that,' she said.

'It was a big shock for you,' said Charlie. 'And for me. It'll be strange meeting him, won't it?'

'Meeting him?' She looked at him, amazed.

'Well, a girl ought to get to know her own father. I want to meet him, too.'

'But how?' she asked. 'Madame Saint-Jean couldn't trace him.'

'Maybe we'll try harder than Madame Saint-Jean.'

Her expression changed. 'So you won't be going home next week?'

He shook his head. 'No, I must go – but I'll be back. Then we'll go to Germany.'

Anxiety was in her eyes. 'When will you be back?'

'As soon as I can sort things out over there.'

She gave a sad little shrug. 'Charlee, it's all talk, isn't it? Philana won't let you come back – not now she knows about me. She's no fool, Charlee.'

She was right. Philana would put up a fight. 'I can't stay in New York for ever,' he answered. 'She knows that. People in my business are always going someplace.'

'He'll be back,' Sonya assured her.

'I promise,' said Charlie.

'And then you'll find my father?' she asked uncertainly.

'I'll find him,' said Charlie. 'You can bet your last dollar I'll find him.'

3

The few days before he left were hard for them. Most of the time she was quiet and reflective, resigned to his going, but the anger would suddenly flare up. 'You won't come back, Charlee. You'll phone and say you're sorry. Been held up, you'll say. Talk about contracts that need closing. Maybe we should end it now, pretend it's over – like Maman told Wolf. It was great while it lasted.'

'That didn't work – they were back together the next morning,' he said a trifle ruefully.

Immediately, she felt contrite. 'Sorry, Charlee, I shouldn't have said that.

'What's it matter? It was long before I knew her.'

'Who are you fooling, Charlee? Of course it matters. Everything matters. Elisabeth was long before I knew *you*, but I still resent her. I even resent Philana. I try not to, but I can't help it. What's going to happen to us?' she asked, the fear back in her eyes.

He hesitated. 'I don't know. I suppose you'll meet someone else in time – younger, unmarried.'

'He couldn't be like you,' she said, then, suddenly accusing: 'Wouldn't you mind?'

'Of course I'd mind. How can you ask a question like that? I'd miss you desperately; but it's a price I'd have to pay. He could offer you more than I can.'

'You wouldn't mind all that much, though, would you?' she said. 'I mean, you'd be back with your Philana and I'd be a memory, a fling – Paris in the spring. Sometimes, Charlee, you can be very cruel.' And she'd hurried out of the restaurant before he could answer.

It was a pattern that was repeated, though such moods never lasted for long. She would call him at the hotel or, if he followed her to the apartment, let him in, greeting him warmly. He knew, of course, what lay at the heart of it, as married men always know, though she never uttered the dread word – until at last she couldn't stop herself. 'Didn't Elisabeth ever question what'd happen between you – eventually, I mean?'

'We lived for the present. They were dangerous times. Also she happened to be married.'

'There's such a thing as divorce,' she said quietly.

The word had been uttered and Charlie paused for a second. 'They were both Catholics. Pierre would never have agreed.'

'But you're not a Catholic, are you, Charlee?'

'No,' he answered. He let the silence hang in the air, meeting her eyes blandly.

'I know,' she said, 'it's not easy. Not with the children. Not unless you have terrible fights with your wife. And you don't, do you?' He shook his head, guessing what would follow. 'Or if your love for another woman is so strong that . . . What if Elisabeth had lived, Charlee?'

'I've told you,' he said. 'You ask too many questions.'

'You'd have left her for Elisabeth,' she whispered.

So often, Elisabeth cast a shadow over them but, during that short period, Nikki seemed to have a great need for self-inflicted wounds. She knew he had to shop for his children, for his wife. He agreed to her helping him choose toys, but even that had disturbed her deeply. She became tearfully wistful, asking him to describe Rhona. 'Is she fair or dark. What'll she say when she gets this doll? Will she throw her arms round your neck and say what a wonderful daddy you are? Will you have time to help Tim play with the train – or will you be too busy with your ships? I wish I knew them both. Can I meet them sometime – or would that be forbidden?'

He sighed, wondering how to explain that it wouldn't exactly be forbidden. It just wouldn't be the greatest idea in the world.

'I know,' she said, 'your other life.'

Certainly, he didn't want Nikki with him when he was buying Philana's present, as she knew, but she guessed where he would be. She walked into Cartiers just as he was studying a sapphire ring. 'She likes sapphires, does she?' Nikki enquired. 'They can't match her eyes. She's Greek; Greeks are dark aren't they?'

'She has blue eyes,' he answered patiently. 'It's unusual, as you say. And a ring doesn't *have* to match them, does it?'

'No, but it's good when it does. What finger will she wear it on?' she asked, adding quickly: 'Does she have good hands? As good as mine?' She gave a hurt little laugh. 'I'm embarrassing you, aren't I – being a minx? Well, even the best minxes step out of line sometimes.' She turned and walked out of the shop and, though she kept her face averted, he could see she was crying.

They talked often of Wolf. She wondered about *his* marriage, too. How could he and his wife stay together when his passion for Elisabeth was so demanding? No apology for Charlie's feelings this time. 'His career, I suppose,' she said glumly. 'No divorce permitted for generals. Just mistresses – so long as they weren't Jewish. But how could his wife bear it? What do you think he'll be like, Charlee?'

'Fine-looking man, I'd guess, though he'll be in his sixties by now. I'm sure you'll be proud of him.'

Charlie checked out of the hotel the day before his departure and spent the last night in her apartment. He gave her a present of a diamond clasp. 'It doesn't match my eyes,' she said, 'but it's lovely.'

'It matches your eyes when they're flashing,' he countered and she laughed. She cooked a meal and they made love and she clung to him afterwards, keeping him within her. 'I want you to stay part of me,' she whispered, 'as long as possible.' There was a note of desperation in their embraces, no jokes. Later, in the night, they made love again and she cried as she came. 'Why should I cry?' she whispered, wetting his cheeks with her tears. 'You're just going away for a while. Then we'll make wonderful love again, won't we?'

'That's right,' he said.

But by the time he awoke in the morning, she had left the apartment. There was a note on her dressing table: 'I hate goodbyes. Come back soon. I love you.'

Sonya had offered to drive him to the airport. It was as they were in the main concourse that he looked up and saw Nikki on the higher floor, leaning over the rail. She didn't wave – just looked at him without smiling. 'Watch my things, will you?' he asked Sonya and hurried through the crowd to the stairs. But when he got to the head of them, Nikki had gone. He searched for her, but there was no sign of her.

He heard his flight called. 'Did you see Nikki up there?' he asked Sonya when he returned to her.

'No,' she said.

'I must have imagined it,' he answered. But he knew he hadn't.

Eighteen

'For God's sake, why can't you tell me?' demanded Philana with a sudden fury he'd never seen in her before.

He was still in bed and she'd swung back from the dressing table, naked beneath the open négligé except for lace-fringed pants and stockings. 'I've tried,' she said. 'I've done my best to pick up as we were, but you're a stranger. You're not here half the time. You've got to share it with me, Charlie.'

'Share what?'

'Whatever happened in France, of course. Then maybe we can live with it, put it behind us or . . . well, at least show me what I've got to handle.'

The outburst took him by surprise. She'd been cleaning her face with cream, still on her feet as though she was in a hurry, leaning towards the mirror. There had been no warning. They'd been talking idly about plans for next summer. Should they go to her father's place at Newport or join friends in Europe? The next second she'd become a different woman.

He understood why. He'd been back three days now and she'd been behaving as though everything between them was normal. Just another business trip. She welcomed him warmly at the airport, hugging him to her, delighted, it seemed, to have him home. There were no accusations, no sign even of the tough line she had taken about the flight number in the phone calls. She was thrilled with the sapphire, which truly did match her eyes – as the children had been with their presents, acting out the scene that Nikki had foreseen in every bitter detail.

But they were like characters in a play – in familiar roles. He was glad, for it gave him time to think, and he had much to think about. The Wolf revelations and the lead to Roger Briedon – coming as they did after the flight of Frank Charlwood and the threats to Thelma Hardy – had induced in him a sense of deep foreboding. He knew he was getting closer now to solving the mystery of Elisabeth – which had to carry its dangers. Maybe I'd better get a gun, he thought.

Even without this, he would have feared the return to Philana – in particular the sex, wondering if Nikki would inhibit him, invade his thoughts with her taunting. In the plane, his unease about this had grown. He knew men who were often unfaithful to their wives, boasted about the girls they had. 'Boy, was she wild in the sack!' But he'd never even been tempted before Nikki. It wasn't the way he wanted to live.

In fact, his sexual anxiety had seemed groundless. The moment he saw Philana again he thought what an attractive woman she was. In bed Nikki was there in his mind, but not usually until afterwards, and then it was her laughter that was most vivid to him. She haunted him, no question about that. The high spirits, the teasing, the moments of sadness, even the fits of childish jealousy. He was tempted to phone her every day just to hear her voice, her laughter. But oddly, he felt no guilt. The two women were in different compartments of his mind. Sometimes he wondered if the transition shouldn't be harder. 'See,' he could hear Elisabeth mocking, 'you're just an old Puritan really.'

Philana had never mentioned his long absence and he was starting to think she'd decided to ignore it. That morning they had seemed to be in harmony. They'd even made love – so her sudden rage, her accusation that he was a stranger, came as a shock. 'Was I being a stranger just now?' he asked.

'Oh, that was just sex,' she answered. 'Men think everything comes down to sex.' She moved towards him, cream still on her fingers, and stood by the bed, the unfastened négligé revealing her bare suspendered thighs and full hard-pointed breasts.

Almost instinctively, he reached out to touch her – but she backed away angrily. 'Don't do that!'

'What's the matter?' he asked.

'I should be asking that,' she answered. 'I hoped you'd talk about it. I suppose it's the girl, isn't it? All right, I've seen Mother live with hundreds of Father's girls, but you never seemed like that. I was enough for you. But you went to Paris for a week, Charlie, and how long did you stay away? Months. And you haven't given me one reason. Well, have you?'

'No,' he agreed. 'I'd have preferred not to talk about it.'

'Did you think we could go on like we have been?' she demanded.

Charlie thought how striking she looked standing there, flaunting her body, those blue eyes wide and indignant. It was rare for her. Usually she was so calm, so collected. 'I figured we were kind of taking it easy,' he said, 'getting to know each other again.'

'You thought I'd accepted it.'

He shrugged. 'Not exactly. I knew how hard it was for you.'

'Too hard, Charlie. I've tried, but I'm not my mother. I've spent too long in America, I suppose.' She sat on the bed, well out of his reach, her palms held upwards because of the cream. 'I hear she looks like Elisabeth. Is that true?'

'Like she probably was at her age,' Charlie agreed.

'Did it become a big thing?'

'She's a kid,' he answered, hoping he wouldn't have to lie. 'I'm old enough to be her father.'

'Charlie, you're saying she's a pretty young girl, aren't you?'

He shrugged. 'Sure. She's a cute kid,' he added, feeling a pang of disloyalty to Nikki.

She was studying him. 'I need to know, Charlie. Leah told me there was nothing between you and the girl, but Father says she was just covering for you.'

'Oh, Costa thinks everyone's in bed together,' said Charlie.

'Leah said it concerned Elisabeth.' The anger seemed to have drained from her – but not the anxiety. 'How can that possibly be true? How long is it now since she died? Sixteen years?'

He got out of bed and picked up his dressing gown from the floor. 'I'll tell you sometime, honey. I can't for the moment. Just don't worry, OK?'

It wasn't OK, but what could she actually do? She paused, started back to the dressing table, then turned again. 'Just tell me this, Charlie. Is it still going on? With the girl, I mean.'

'It's not to do with the girl – not really. She's only involved on the fringe.'

An anxious look crossed her face. 'I'd almost prefer the girl. No, that's not true,' she corrected herself hastily. 'Not Elisabeth's daughter. But this sounds more dangerous.'

'It's OK, honey, I promise.'

'Why can't you tell me?'

'I've told you too much already.' He had, too, he thought as he went into the bathroom, because he wanted to avoid lying to her. What he'd done, in fact, was to divert her – and worry her. And it had gained him nothing; for as soon as she thought about it, she would realise exactly what he'd done. As Nikki had said so often, Philana was no fool.

2

Charlie stood looking out of the window of his office at the massive columns of the Chase Manhattan Plaza. He savoured the noise of the city – a police siren a few blocks up, the blare of horns. He watched the people hurrying along the sidewalk on Nassau Street, the men with coats off, the girls in sleeveless blouses or cotton dresses. It was a hot day, in the nineties. In a nearby office, a radio commentator was giving a rundown of the ball game that afternoon. This was New York in high summer and he loved it. My town, he thought. He'd been born there, raised there – not too far away off Second Avenue, near Mr Weinberger's drugstore, where his father still worked.

New York was home – the city he left often but always returned to with a sense of great comfort. This time, though, too much was occupying him – Wolf, Nikki, Duclos, Briedon, the whole Elisabeth circus. By contrast, the business of the office – the meetings, the deals, the contracts – seemed remote. It was as though he were a visitor to his own company.

He wasn't alone in feeling this way. Terry Johnson came in – a slight man with a lively, mobile face. 'Just can't get used to your being back, Charlie,' he said. He was teasing, but dead-pan. 'Know who's been running this business? An empty chair . . . your chair . . . I used to talk to it, no kidding, take it the problems. I'd say: "Chair, what do you figure Charlie would say about this can of worms?" And it'd tell me. "They got all this corn in the silos," it'd say. Not out loud of course, but I knew what it was thinking. There's got to be a market. Asia probably. Some guy's got to ship it there. Soya beans were harder because . . .'

The phone rang. Charlie picked it up. 'Mr Mastorakis is calling,' said Lena, his secretary. 'I said I thought I'd seen you go out but wasn't sure.' She was a bright girl, but there was no point in putting it off.

'Charlie,' boomed his father-in-law. 'Lunch today. Cancel any plans. It's vital I see you. Twenty-One at 12.30.'

'OK, Costa.'

'The big white chief?' queried Terry. 'He offered me a job while you were away. I thought of taking it.'

'I should wait until I'm in charge.'

'You'll be in Europe chasing tail.'

'Don't push it too far, Terry.'

Terry knew he had. His face assumed the look of a funeral director – hushed respect but no feeling. 'Sorry, boss. Elisabeth's daughter's not tail, is she?'

'Too right,' said Charlie in quiet anger. 'She wasn't what kept me either.' Charlie had met Terry during his sea training on the Mastorakis ships. They'd fought their way together out of trouble in a Bombay nightspot, Charlie using tricks he'd learned in the SOE, Terry deploying the instincts of a natural fighter. It had been the start of a close friendship and Terry had helped him set up the company when he went solo.

'So what kept you, Massa?' he asked. 'Or will I be flogged for asking?'

'Sit down, Terry,' said Charlie, 'and drop the clever talk for a moment.' Terry flopped into a chair, one leg hooked casually over the arm. 'I've never kept a secret from you, pal,' Charlie went on, 'but this time I've got to. I don't want you involved. For your own good – and the firm's. I'll tell you when I can.'

'Sounds pretty serious.'

'I haven't told her ladyship either. Nor anyone. Don't worry, I've made my will.'

Terry shrugged, bony shoulders arched. He was hurt. 'So I go on running the business? Me and the chair?'

'You've done pretty well, I notice, but I'll be around. Just not all the time.'

Terry nodded. 'OK. Whatever you say. There's an oil deal we could pick up, Charlie. Not all that big – but the contacts are good. Japan where they import more crude than any country in the world. A merchant. Not among the biggest but the deal could open doors. We ought to do it but I got no tanker space. Can I charter?'

The phone rang again. Charlie picked up the receiver. 'Paris,' he said.

Terry got to his feet with an easy movement. 'Seriously, I didn't mean it when I called her tail.'

'I'll tell her you're sorry.'

'See you then.'

But it wasn't Nikki. 'Charlie,' said Sonya's voice, 'we've got a break. The New York bureau have got Alan Soissons's address.

Fifty-two, West 95th, between Amsterdam and Columbus. And Charlie, take care now. You're not playing cowboys and indians.'

3

Sonya had just put down the phone after talking to Charlie in New York when René called. 'Success!' he declared. 'The appointment's confirmed. How about celebrating tonight?'

'Delighted, René. Its wonderful news. When shall I see you?'

'At seven. Too soon? I can't wait any longer.' It was tight, but in Paris it was the end of the day. She had checked the proofs of the column, cut a couple of inches as they'd asked. There was time – and she was flattered he'd called her so urgently.

An hour and a half later, Sonya surveyed the floor from the bed and smiled. There were clothes lying everywhere – stockings, one still attached to her suspender belt. Bra. His jacket in a crumpled heap. Odd shoes, hers with their high heels lying on their sides. Her skirt hanging from a chair arm like a windless flag. A blouse, with a button torn off.

It was how sex should be sometimes, she thought. Just occasionally. Urgent, demanding. He'd flung her on to the bed, taking her at once. It wasn't like René. Normally, he was a cool, meticulous lover who used his fingertips, his lips, with a delicate precision.

He'd arrived with champagne and roses – and a new ardour. 'The aphrodisiac of power,' he'd teased. They'd never finished the second glass. He'd kissed her, just touched her breast, and the violent mutual need had suddenly flared in them.

He stirred beside her. 'Did the earth move?' he enquired. 'Or was it the Métro? Time for more champagne, I think.' It was a smooth remark, more suited to the man who never had a hair out of place than to the demanding lover of minutes before, but it pleased her.

He got out of bed and went into the sitting room, returning with the two glasses. 'I've been hearing things about your friend Charlie. The Sûreté say he's on some kind of investigation, using young Nicole as bait. He's ruffled some feathers in England.'

'How did you hear that? I thought you were above all that sort of thing now.'

'I made a few enquiries when they came to lunch. After all, we knew Elisabeth – and we heard the rumours at the time, of course.'

'What rumours?'

'About the company she'd been keeping. You know about Wolf Heinegg, I expect?'

'Elisabeth's German.'

'It's a delicate business. It was delicate then. Elisabeth never took enough care. Today Wolf's a wanted man. He's got a big operation in very dubious territory.'

René's a fine one to talk, thought Sonya, after the Frankfurt scandal. But that was way back. Maybe now, in his new position, he'd become respectable.

'There are links to Marie Cayzer,' René went on. 'Nazi money's suspected. Lots of it. Your Charlie's probing something he doesn't understand. Maybe you should warn him. I don't want to hear that he's been found in the Seine.'

'Is he in that much danger?'

'Well . . .' He hesitated and sipped his champagne. 'Has he ever mentioned a man called Roger Briedon to you?'

'Briedon?' she queried. She was astonished at herself. Why didn't she just answer the question? Again, the bond with Elisabeth was more important than her lover – the unsworn oath that she shouldn't tell anyone what Charlie was doing. 'Why do you ask?' she said.

René was watching her. 'Because he's disappeared, because Charlie was enquiring about him. That came in from England, too.'

'Did you ever meet Wolf?' she asked.

'Oh yes, we knew him well. He came to Paris sometimes. Elisabeth wasn't made for secret liaisons. She didn't care if the world found out. It caused a lot of trouble. We met him in Berlin, too. We were there for the games in '36. Oddly, when we had lunch Nicole brought a photograph – of Elisabeth at a reception in a black dress. That was taken at that time. Wolf was beside her but partly hidden by the edge.'

'I saw the picture. Charlie said you didn't know who the man was.'

'That seemed wise in front of Nicole. Where would it have stopped? The Sûreté are raising Wolf's priority. To find him, I mean. I don't want Charlie mixed up with anything we uncover.'

'Aren't you making a bit too much of this?' she asked.

'Depends. What exactly is he doing?'

She forced herself to look at him, just as she had when he'd asked a similar question before. 'What he said, I think – refinding Elisabeth with her daughter. Perhaps you're looking for more than is there.'

He hesitated, studying her. 'I hope so,' he said, 'but I doubt it.'

4

Mastorakis was waiting for Charlie at the Twenty-One, his great bulk hunched forward, elbows on the table as he nursed a martini. He watched Charlie carefully as he approached, a mixture of amused enquiry and admonishment in the dark eyes under the forest of brows – a kind of men-amongst-men look. Oh God, thought Charlie, he's still woman-mad, even at seventy. It was the girl in the plot that intrigued him. That was what was urgent.

'Home is the traveller,' Mastorakis boomed. 'Champagne?'

'Just a glass of wine with the food,' Charlie answered.

'You call that celebrating?' queried Mastorakis.

'Who's celebrating?' asked Charlie. 'I've got a lot of catching up to do, need a clear head. Terry's looking for tanker space to Japan. Got any free?'

'Better than that,' declared his father-in-law. 'I've got a tanker for you. I don't want more tankers. I hate tankers. Only took it because it was a bargain. Half a million. Twenty-eight thousand tons. *Pacific Star*'s the name and it's yours, my boy, for what I paid. Lying at Hoboken. I'll tell them Terry'll be in touch to fix things up. And I'm celebrating even if you're not. Champagne,' he told the waiter. 'Now just what have you been up to all this time?'

'A few little problems.'

'With the girl?' Mastorakis asked with a shrewd look.

'No – not with the girl.'

'But there is a girl, isn't there?'

'Costa, the whole world doesn't have to revolve round girls.'

That amused him. The deep laugh started way down in his stomach, shaking his whole body. 'Arguable, Charlie, arguable.' He grew serious again. 'I don't like the sound of it. I was in Paris last week.'

'So I heard.'

'I'm told it's to do with that Elisabeth Ferrier. That true?'

'I'll tell you when I can.'

'What's wrong with now?'

'I'm not quite ready.'

The waiter uncorked the champagne and filled two glasses.

Charlie demurred but the old man wouldn't hear of it. 'A few sips to keep me company.' He lifted his glass to his lips. 'When will you be ready?'

'Soon.'

'It's thoughtless, Charlie. I hear about you from all these people – René Levallier, Prince Khalid, Claude Duclos. How do you think I feel being in total ignorance? You're part of my family.'

'What do any of them know that's such a big deal?'

'The girl, that's what they know. A picture, they say. Just like her mother. And you tell me there's nothing there.'

'I could hardly tell you if there was, could I? I'm married to your daughter, for Christ's sake.'

The old man nodded. 'I suppose it'd lack taste. I like that, Charlie. Don't know where you got it. After all, you were dragged up – didn't go to Yale, did you? And I believe you. I don't think your problem is the girl. Talking of that Elisabeth, I saw Marie last night at dinner. Did you know she married Meisinger?'

'Yes.'

'How did you know? I've known her for years and I didn't know.'

'I heard in Paris this trip.'

'Well, maybe you don't know everything,' Mastorakis went on. 'She controls big investments in Europe. Did you hear that in Paris?'

'No, but she's a rich widow. Rich widows have investments.'

'I don't mean just her own money – I'm talking many millions. Guess where the rest comes from.'

'South America.'

Mastorakis looked disappointed, rebuffed even. 'How did you get so clever?' he growled.

'That wasn't hard. She was close to the Nazi hierarchy.'

'Well, you're right,' he said reluctantly. 'The old story of Nazi gold, shipped there before the war ended. Charlie, you don't seem surprised.'

'Oh I am – not at the source of funds, but that they let her control anything sizeable.'

'She had to prove she could, I'm told. I'm sure she has to consult. But Marie's shrewd – and no one would suspect the extent of her control, so she'd be good cover, wouldn't she? And it makes sense. There's scope in the new Europe.' He looked at

Charlie for a second. 'Is this secret business of yours connected with Marie?'

'I don't think so,' Charlie answered, though what Mastorakis had just told him had set him thinking. 'I better get back,' he said. 'Been good to see you. You're looking well, you old bugger.'

'Don't rush off,' said Mastorakis, placing a restraining arm on his. 'Marie and Elisabeth were close, weren't they?'

Charlie shrugged. 'They shared an apartment in Berlin.'

The old man's canny smile appeared. 'Charlie, this is all smoke, isn't it? Now tell me the truth about the girl.'

'She's a good kid, as your friends told you. Now you must excuse me, Costa.' He stood up.

'I hear you've given her an apartment.'

'I've contributed – with all the others. The least we could do, considering what we owe her mother.'

'What did her mother do to make the debt so great?'

'Led me to you, Costa,' Charlie answered with a grin.

5

Charlie sat in a bar on the corner of Columbus Avenue and 91st Street, suspecting gloomily that he'd mishandled his first move towards meeting Roger Briedon. He had given it much thought, planned to ring Soissons rather than calling cold at the door, chose the time of 6 p.m. because it was then that most men would be home from work. The bar was neutral ground.

He'd called from a phone in the bar and been answered by a male voice with a French accent.

'Mr Soissons?' he said.

'Who wants him?'

'My name is Dawson.'

'Give me your number and I'll ask him to call you back.'

Charlie hesitated. Was he actually talking to Soissons, who was being cautious, or was it someone who maybe shared the apartment? Could it even be Roger? 'Well, it's not Mr Soissons I really want to speak to,' Charlie went on carefully. 'I'm trying to trace a friend of his – his cousin, in fact.'

'Who would that be?'

The tone was more wary, and at once Charlie wondered if he'd been wise to show his cards so soon. But he was in too deep by then, so he went on: 'I'm not sure about the name. It could be

Johnson,' he ventured, using the alias Roger's wife had told Sonya, 'but more likely it'd be Briedon. Roger Briedon.'

There was a pause, then: 'What's your business with him?'

'I'd like a short talk about something of mutual interest.'

'Such as?'

'I'd rather not say on the phone. I'm in a bar close by, so if he's around . . .'

'He's not around.'

'That's too bad because it's important. Wouldn't take more than five or ten minutes. I haven't got long myself. Got a date – with a friend in US Immigration and – '

'What kind of remark is that? Mr Briedon certainly wouldn't want to talk to you after a remark like that. Not even if he was here.'

'Tell him Monsieur Claude Duclos suggested I called.'

'Who's he?'

'Is that Mr Soissons speaking?' Charlie asked, though he suspected he knew who was speaking.

'No. Mr Soissons is away.'

'Well, Mr Briedon certainly knows Monsieur Duclos.'

'Sorry, mister, but you've wasted your time. If I see Mr Briedon I'll tell him you called. Want to leave your number?'

'I'm out so much it's better if I call again.'

'OK – though there's not much point. I'll tell him if I see him . . .'

'I must get in touch with him urgently, you understand,' Charlie said, fearing the man would hang up – sure that Briedon was there even if he wasn't speaking to him. 'It's important for him as well as for me. Monsieur Duclos wants me to see him. I'm in a bar on the corner of Columbus and 91st.'

'Look, I told you it isn't possible.' The tone was harder, impatient.

'I'll wait here half an hour.'

'There's no point.'

'All the same I'll wait. Monsieur Duclos would want me to wait.'

Charlie rang off, making sure he was the first to do so. Then he returned to his table, where he'd left a half-finished glass of Budweiser. It was touch and go. Maybe Briedon would turn up, maybe he wouldn't. But Charlie reckoned he'd think about it because of Duclos. Perhaps he'd call Duclos to check Charlie out.

What would Duclos tell him to do? Probably duck the meeting, but you never knew with Duclos.

Charlie looked again at the photo of Briedon with Soissons that Sonya had given him, so that if he did turn up there would be no mistake. He went over to the bar and ordered another Budweiser. The time passed slowly. When half an hour had gone by and Briedon hadn't shown, the prospect began to look dim. Maybe he hadn't been in the apartment after all, despite the signs. But Charlie was pretty sure he had been there. He considered calling again, perhaps trying a more open threat, suggesting his life was in danger. It seemed too melodramatic. So he sat in the bar, wondering how much longer he should give him, thinking another call couldn't do any harm, even if he didn't make threats.

Then, just as he was checking his change for the phone, Briedon walked into the bar. Charlie recognised him at once and signalled to him with a movement of his hand. This was the funny little bald man Elisabeth had told Sonya about, the freelance stringer with the scandalous stories of the sporting world. Only it was sixteen years on now and times had been hard and they'd left their mark. What hair he had left was white and his face was deeply furrowed. He was heavier than the photo suggested – what women might call cuddly – and he walked with an odd rolling motion.

He was scared, the fear evident in his eyes as he quickly took in the few people in the bar, in the way he paused when he saw Charlie. But he put on a good front. 'What's all this about then?' he demanded.

'I'll tell you,' said Charlie. 'Want a drink? Scotch?'

He nodded and Charlie went to the bar with Briedon watching him closely. Charlie put the Scotch in front of him and Briedon sipped it. 'I haven't seen Claude Duclos in years,' he said. 'Even then, I hardly knew him. I dealt with the sports editor.'

'Duclos knows *you*, I can assure you.'

Briedon shook his head. 'I just called him, but he wouldn't talk to me. In conference, the girl said. I doubt if he even remembers. What is it you want with me, monsieur?'

'The truth,' Charlie answered. 'Don't worry, I'm no threat.'

'Everyone's a threat,' said Briedon. 'Who are you? A detective?'

'Not exactly. I worked with the SOE in the war – like you. You were in the Pianoplayer circuit, right?' Briedon shrugged a kind of assent. 'You recruited Elisabeth Ferrier in 1940, right?'

Another shrug, though more reluctant. 'And reported to London in 1944 that she was in contact with the enemy, right?'

Briedon didn't respond for a second, his eyes on Charlie. 'Why do you want to know?'

'I was in the Vercors – with Elisabeth. I'm interested in your source for that information.'

'Why – after all this time?'

'We were friends. So were you, I gather. She spoke of you a lot.'

'Of me?' he queried. He laughed in disbelief. 'I was a pretty small fish.'

'She found you amusing.'

Briedon's expression softened with the memory. 'We shared a few stories.'

'You liked her?'

'Everyone liked her.'

'So it must have upset you, sending that report to London. You must have known what'd happen.'

'I knew what'd happen if I didn't.' The look in his eyes had hardened. 'There was no doubt about Elisabeth Ferrier, monsieur.'

Charlie paused to sip his Budweiser, watching him. Things could go wrong now, but he'd have to go in heavier if he was going to get anywhere. 'You were working for both sides by then, weren't you?'

Briedon was shocked by the blunt statement, and for a second Charlie thought he was going to leave. 'You seem to know a lot,' Briedon said.

'A bit,' Charlie agreed.

'But not everything.'

'Not everything by a long shot. For example, I don't know how you knew that Elisabeth was going to meet General Heinegg that day. Can you tell me?'

The response was bland. Briedon was gaining confidence. 'I'm not sure I can remember,' he said. 'There were so many sources. Why's it so important after all this time?'

'I loved her,' Charlie said simply. 'She was special to the others, too. None of us believed she could have been turned.'

'How did you know I saw her with the General?'

'From people who were at Baker Street. And the archives,' he added, deciding to push his luck. 'I've seen your report – *and* the picture.'

'That's extraordinary,' Briedon remarked with what seemed a friendly smile, 'since I never sent it.' The eyes were suddenly cold again.

Charlie fielded the answer. 'Of course not. It was formally sent by Butler as Head of Circuit, but you were the one who got the information. You've just said you saw her with the General. Did you take the picture yourself?'

He nodded.

'Did you always take your camera?' asked Charlie.

Briedon laughed. 'In the war? Of course not. Films were like gold dust. It was forbidden anyway.'

'But you took it that day. So you must have known they were going to be there. Who told you?'

Briedon finished his Scotch. 'Say I could remember,' he answered, measuring his words, 'why should I tell you? I need to consider the benefit, don't I? To me, I mean. And the risk.'

'Risk?' queried Charlie – adding Briedon's own words: 'After all these years?'

'Oh, there's risk all right,' Briedon asserted. 'As you're well aware.'

'Where's the risk?'

Briedon studied him. 'I think you know. I think you know more than you're telling me.'

'Then why have I come to find you? Why am I asking questions?'

'Because you don't know everything, but you know there's risk.'

'I don't know who from. Duclos?'

Briedon laughed. 'Duclos maybe. Maybe not. I don't know everything either.'

'OK, let's accept there's risk. Let's talk about the benefit as you said. What did you have in mind? Cash?'

'It comes in handy.' But he was doubtful.

'You've got a wife and kids, haven't you?'

Briedon was surprised he knew. 'You've gone to a lot of trouble,' he said.

'And I've told you why. Elisabeth wasn't a traitor – I'm positive of that.'

'Look, I saw her with a German general. She was a member of

the Resistance. I recorded it on film. Add that to everything else we knew – two drops by Lysander when the Gestapo were waiting on the ground, and everything pointed to her telling them.'

'You could have told them yourself.'

'That was before I was in contact with them. I was forced to help them, you know. I had no choice.'

'It's beside the point,' said Charlie. 'I just want to know who told you Elisabeth was meeting Wolf Heinegg. I'm prepared to pay for it – quite a lot – or help in other ways. Protection. A secure job. Maybe something I haven't thought of. Negotiate, Monsieur Briedon. I've influence and resources. You're in a strong position.'

Fear was back on Briedon's face. 'That's what concerns me,' he said. 'My strong position. Why, monsieur?'

'I've told you.'

'Not enough to convince me. Please answer the question, monsieur: why was she with a German general in occupied Paris? There can only be one answer, can't there?'

'No,' said Charlie, 'there's another. If I told you she'd met Heinegg in 1933 when he was only a captain and there was no hint of war, that they'd been very close, that there was a child . . .'

Briedon gave a short laugh. 'Makes it worse, doesn't it? Gives her more reason to betray us. It's not as though the affair had come to an end, is it? I don't know how you've come to terms with that yourself . . .'

His words found their mark. It had been desperately hard for Charlie, but he was still sure there was an explanation.

'For Christ's sake, she was Jewish,' he exclaimed.

Briedon seemed unimpressed. 'Listen, a woman in love can do anything. I don't suppose Heinegg was deporting Jews, but she could have wanted Germany to win, couldn't she?'

'No,' Charlie insisted. 'That's not possible.'

Briedon gave him a pitying look. 'Face it, monsieur. She spent hours in a hotel room with him.'

'OK – and I'm offering you one hell of a lot to tell me how you knew.'

Briedon studied him. 'You ought to hate her, monsieur. Why don't you hate her?'

'For God's sake, what does it matter?'

241

'Because that'd make sense.'

Charlie could hardly contain himself. He was closer than he'd ever been to the truth about Elisabeth, he was sure. This tubby little man opposite him knew what he'd been trying for months to discover – and was almost tempted to tell him. Almost. 'Listen, monsieur,' Charlie pleaded, 'I trusted Elisabeth – and still do. OK so I'm crazy, but you knew what'd happen when that report got to London – and it did. We were ordered by signal to execute her.'

'I heard she died in action.'

'Does it matter? The fact is she was innocent of the charge that your key evidence seemed to prove. Despite everything, I *know* that. For God's sake, surely that's reason enough to want the answer to my question?'

Briedon shrugged. He was clearly sympathetic, but the doubt was still there – probably not about Charlie's purpose now, but about the risks if he talked. Maybe it had been a mistake to mention the signal. For if Elisabeth was innocent, it must have been important for other reasons that she died – reasons that Briedon might not know. Like Charlie, he'd been used.

Briedon looked at his watch. 'I've got to go,' he said. 'Give me a couple of days to think about it.' Charlie's anguished disappointment must have been obvious. 'I've got to take account of everything,' said Briedon. 'Friday evening. Here. About this time. Say 6.30. Thanks for the Scotch.'

As Charlie watched him leave – this podgy, awkward figure with a rolling gait – an exhausted depression slowly spread through his body as though it were being gradually deflated. He got up and went to the bar. 'Scotch,' he said. 'On the rocks. A triple.'

6

It was another hot day and Charlie took his jacket off, carrying it over his shoulder, hooked on his finger. Marie's Park Avenue duplex wasn't far from his apartment on Fifth Avenue, so he had worked at home all morning before taking a stroll in Central Park to plan his tactics at lunch with her. There were the usual cyclists, even joggers, on the shaded paths, despite the heat. People were eating sandwiches on the benches. Office girls, taking early breaks, were stretched out on the grass in the sun.

He came to the lake and stood near a tree. It was cooler by the water, easier to think. There was a new scenario that he hadn't even considered until his meeting with Mastorakis. Even then it wasn't the Nazi funds that he had said Marie controlled that had alerted him, but the question he had thrown in as an aside: was she connected with the Elisabeth business?

The more he thought about it, the more he realised she could be. She had been grabbed by the Nazi myth. She was Meisinger's widow. She and Elisabeth had lived close to the Party leaders. Say Elisabeth had known something that no one else knew – could she have suddenly seemed dangerous to Marie that late in the war? It was unlikely: they had been close friends and Elisabeth had always admired her; but it provided a motive.

This wasn't why he needed to see Marie, but it added another aspect. He glanced at his watch. It was time to go.

'Charlie!' she cried as he was shown into the huge sitting room with the Chippendale furniture and Tang Dynasty bronzes, and the Van Goghs on the walls. 'I've been wild with impatience ever since your call. No one in years has insisted on meeting me without his wife – and not in a restaurant, in case we're seen. Anyone would think you were still in the OSS. But I've guessed. It's the girl, isn't it? She's divine, I'm told. Is she madly in love with you?'

'You never change, Marie,' he teased. 'You want all the gossip.'

'Well, is she?'

'It's not her I want to talk about. It's Elisabeth.'

She looked disappointed. 'OK, honey,' she said with a resigned shrug, 'in that case, let's get a drink. Gerard,' she called to her butler, 'two of your best.'

She gestured at a seat as the martinis were prepared. 'So what's with all the cloak-and-dagger stuff?'

'I've just found out about Wolf.'

She smiled ruefully. 'Well, I guess that was on the cards. From what I hear, you've been looking hard enough.' She held up the glass Gerard had handed to her. 'Here's to you, Charlie,' she said.

He drank with her, knowing he must take care to keep a clear head. 'Marie,' he asked, 'why did you tell Leah you could think of no one Elisabeth knew whose name began with W?'

For a moment, she was disconcerted. 'What was it going to gain, Charlie? He was a part of her life it was best you didn't know about.'

'Why?'

'Just seemed that way,' she answered. 'I mean, what did you do when you heard about Wolf? Shout hooray and do a couple of somersaults?'

'I've read his letters to her,' he said.

'Christ almighty. What did you do that for?'

'There were things I wanted to find out.'

'And did you succeed?'

'Too soon to tell. It's all on file in here, though.' He tapped his forehead. 'It's how I got to know that Wolf is Nikki's father. That's right, isn't it?'

'If you know, why ask me?'

'Confirmation. There could have been other contenders – maybe a drunken night with Pierre.'

Marie had changed as he spoke. The exuberant lady who loved parties, the vivacious hostess, was gone. Shrewd cold eyes were openly studying him. He could believe she'd been entrusted with investing millions. 'Yes, Wolf's her father,' she said quietly at last. 'What exactly is it you're after, Charlie?'

'I want to talk to Wolf. So does Nikki, of course. Are you still in touch with him?'

'I meet him occasionally,' she answered. 'We have friends in common. He comes to New York from time to time.'

'What does he do for a living?'

'Oh, this and that.'

'Like selling arms?'

'Charlie, when are you going to come clean with me? Maybe I can help you, but I've got to know what's behind all this. Wolf has to take care. You know about the indictment, I expect.'

'I hear he wasn't even there when the crimes were committed.'

'That's right. But every time he's about to apply for dismissal of the charges, some paper runs a story on the Nazis in Brazil and he backs off. He figures he could be set up as a scapegoat. It's ironic. He always loathed the Party. He's a good guy. You'd like him. Certainly he'd love to meet Nikki – he talks of her often. But she's such an obvious lead to him that he had to be careful.'

'He had trouble with a daughter before, didn't he?'

'You know about Ingrid, too? That was bad. Walking in the fire, that was.' She looked perplexed. 'Charlie, what is all this? A romantic appraisal, like people look at dead poets? The secret past of Elisabeth Ferrier?'

'Kind of.'

She regarded him sceptically. 'You're kidding me, Charlie. No one reads letters like that unless what's in them is pretty important. You level with me and maybe I'll level with you.'

He got up and walked over to the big windows and looked down at the traffic in the avenue forty floors below. Like toys. Like the train he'd brought back for Tim. 'I hear you're a big wheel in European investment,' he said with his back to her.

'I play a bit. I like the area. The government's pouring money in. Got to come good, hasn't it?'

'I hear it's more than playing. You're a power in the land. I bet Mr Meisinger would have been impressed.' He wasn't being tough. He said it lightly.

She laughed. 'Who told you about that? Did Elisabeth tell you?'

'No. She always called you Marie Cayzer.'

'It's how the world knew me. I still worked for the *Trib*, had quite a reputation – which made it easy. So did the timing. I was in New York when he died in Berlin – just before Pearl Harbor. Well, then we were in the war. It was no time for reminders about Mrs Meisinger.

'You could have gone back to Berlin.'

'Sure, but Nazism was losing its appeal for me. I didn't like what I was hearing. I was an American citizen. My roots were deep. Very few people know now about that brief time in my life.'

'I heard in Paris.'

'That figures.'

'By the way, Leah said she met von Eysebeck at one of your parties here.'

'She might have. What of it?'

'Nothing much, except that he was Wolf's bitter enemy, wasn't he?'

Her shoulders lifted in a worldly shrug. 'He does things for me,' she said. 'Like Wolf does in a way, though he's a few steps removed. They still hate each other.'

He swung round. 'Are they both in the arms business?'

She shook her head with a great big smile – the old Marie. 'You're not cut out for this, Charlie. No wonder you haven't found out anything – and I've a pretty good idea what you're looking for. Tell you what, I've got a letter for you. It'll hurt a bit but, after Wolf's letters, it's small stuff.'

She got up and went over to a Sheraton bureau, took an envelope, already opened, from a drawer, withdrew the letter inside and handed it to him. 'It's from Elisabeth – about you. And a bit more. Gerard,' she called out, 'we'll be ready for lunch in five minutes.'

Charlie unfolded the rice paper with fingers that he realised were trembling, only to be shocked as he recognised the writing he'd seen so often. He started to read:

Marie darling, this is the first letter for a long time and I can only write now because I've been recalled to London for talks. I think of you so much. Berlin seems such an age ago and we've taken such different routes, you and I, but I cling to the rewarding fact that our friendship has endured beyond politics, beyond war, beyond distance.

I'm in love again, which may not surprise you, though you of all people know just how much of me Wolf came to own. But life had to go on, didn't it? And Nikki's there, of course. She's pure delight – has my eyes but his stern jaw. Maybe she'll be a tank commander one day!

What you'll hardly credit is that Charlie is a boy of twenty, a New Yorker, quite different to anyone I've ever known, and I'm obsessed. How can I, a woman of the world of thirty-five, be obsessed by a boy of twenty? I can't help touching him. When I'm apart from him I think of him all the time – which is hard sometimes, for often he's in great danger.

That shows you what I've become. I feel about sixteen, except that I know so much more than he does, than any of them do. They're all as brave as hell but they're kids, even my Head of Circuit. By contrast, you and I in our early twenties were veterans.

Charlie looked up. 'I'm a veteran now all right.'

'But Nikki's not, I take it?' countered Marie. 'She must be about the age you were then.'

'She's pretty smart. Had to be. Lived on her wits for a long while.'

Marie smiled. 'You like her, don't you?'

'We laugh a lot.'

'But you're just good friends?'

'Bit more maybe. We've got Elisabeth as a kind of bond.'

'You're not fooling me for a second, Charlie. Hope you did better with Philana. You're crazy about the kid, it's obvious. No, don't argue – just finish the letter.'

She stabbed a finger at the pages in his hand and he went on reading:

I saw W in Paris a few months ago. About Nikki, but it was the first time since Charlie. In secret, of course, but we're used to that – though it's dangerous now.

We tried, you know – to make love, I mean, to see what remained. Neither of us meant to. Not with Charlie. W's got a girl, too. It seemed a good idea, though, but there wasn't a trace any longer, which after all those years left us saddened. For death comes so soon, especially in war, and passion is its opposite, the illusion of stopping time, that awful clock of destiny. Oh God, see how pompous I've got!

Again Charlie stopped reading, shock making him breathe faster. He'd been in Paris with her on that trip. She'd said she had to see someone about Nikki – which wasn't exactly a lie, was it? It was the sort of half-truth that he himself was so often telling now.

Marie was looking at him. 'I told you it'd hurt. Still, no doubt about her feelings for you, eh?'

He nodded and returned to the letter:

Saw Claude briefly and he told me he'd learned from a secret source that, through Switzerland, you're still controlling . . .

He turned the page, but the next page was missing. 'Still controlling?' he asked. 'Controlling what?'

'You've seen enough,' said Marie. 'More than I intended. Come on, let's go in to lunch.'

7

Terry wandered casually into Charlie's office. 'The big chief's just arrived outside – demanding a pow-wow. The smoke signals say the US Cavalry are over the hill.'

'What about that tanker of his?' asked Charlie. '*Pacific Star*. Did you see her yesterday?'

'She's OK. At half a million she's a gift. What's he want in return, Charlie? He's got to be trading favours at that price.'

'He doesn't like tankers.'

'Maybe *you* shouldn't like this one.'

'What do we say? Thanks but no?'

'Not on your giddy life. I want her steaming for Rotterdam. Just make sure you read the small print, Charlie. Shall I show in Sitting Bull?'

But there was no need. Mastorakis showed himself in, flinging open the door and filling the entrance. 'I can't wait outside for ever, Charlie,' he said. 'Do you think I've taken time that's costing millions to come over just for the coffee?'

'Sorry, Costa. You should have called. I'd have seen off all the problems.'

Mastorakis closed the door firmly behind Terry. 'Charlie, I don't like what I'm hearing.'

'Who's been telling you things?' asked Charlie.

'Several people.'

'Like?'

'René Levallier. He's very important now with this new appointment. Got sources of information everywhere. He knew your Elisabeth, you know.'

'Sure. She and Lucille were childhood playmates.'

'He says there were secrets in her life which weren't too savoury. Criminal friends, even crimes.'

'She was a journalist. They mix with all sorts. What was his point?'

'That going around asking questions with this kid of hers was dangerous. You could muddy the water. I don't want a widow for a daughter, Charlie.'

'He said that?' Charlie asked with a lightness he didn't feel. 'That I might get killed?' Spoken aloud for the first time, the words caused a frisson.

'That was the message. For heaven's sake, what are you doing, Charlie?'

'I said I'd tell you when I could. You're so impatient.'

'That's how I made my fortune – by being impatient.'

'You made your fortune because you're a cunning old fox. Know what we talked about with René?' asked Charlie. 'Vacations in Deauville. And you say my life's in danger?'

'It's not what you talked about, it's what's come back to him on the air waves. And no one's fooled by the cover of the girl, Charlie, including me.'

'I thought everything was to do with girls . . .' The phone rang. 'Lena,' he said into the mouthpiece, 'I don't want calls.'

'It's Paris,' she answered. 'Monsieur Duclos. He says it's important.'

'Charlie Dawson,' said Duclos when he was connected, 'I hear you've been using my name without my permission. Don't you ever dare do that again – not if we're going to stay friends – and I wouldn't want me as an enemy.' He rang off before Charlie could reply.

Charlie was shaken, but fought to stop it showing. 'Where were we now?' he said. 'Girls . . .'

'I wish it was girls,' said Mastorakis, 'but you're into something dangerous, Charlie, and you've got to back off.'

'OK, Costa . . .' Anything to get him to talk of something else. 'About this tanker, *Pacific Star*. Terry likes it. What about the papers – and the payment?'

Mastorakis stood up. 'No rush, Charlie. There are a few technicalities, like you'd expect when ships are cheap. Some debts, which I'm dealing with. I'll send you the papers shortly and you can let me have a cheque then. Meanwhile you can go ahead and put a crew in. You've changed the subject, haven't you? Very deft. But don't be too tricky, Charlie. I'd get drastic to protect Philana.'

Charlie nodded. 'I don't doubt it, Costa.' He moved past him and opened the door. 'I swear I'll tell you everything soon.'

Mastorakis stared at him grimly – a bear of a man, in a state of frustration. 'Mind you do,' he said and stalked out of the office.

Charlie returned to his desk, thinking about René Levallier. What had he heard? Maybe Sonya could find out. The telephone rang again. 'Miss Ferrier from Paris,' said Lena.

'Charlee?' The sheer delight he felt at hearing her voice shook him a little. It seemed like months since he'd left her, but it was less than a week. 'Are you there, Charlee?'

'How you doing, honey?' he asked.

'I'm not missing you a bit. Did you think I might be?'

'I thought it possible.'

'You missing me, Charlee?'

'A little – like all the time.'

'How's it going with your Philana? You getting the sweats, Charlee?'

'You're asking too many questions again.'

'Of course, I forgot. You said you didn't get the sweats with Philana. Did she like the sapphire?'

'Sure, it went down well.'

'Did she ask about me, give you any trouble?'

'A little, like you'd expect.'

'Not too much, I hope. Charlee, Max called me about the screen test. He's got a producer keen. But I won't do it if you don't want me to.'

'Do *you* want to? That's the important thing.'

'You didn't want me to at La Galère, did you?'

'We were busy.'

'Was that the only reason?'

'Darling, I can't run your life for you. The movie business is a tough world but a lot of people seem to like it. If Max thinks you'd be good, why not give it a whirl?'

'You don't mind?'

He did, as she knew. It was a world of attractive men, powerful men. 'I can't mind, can I?' he said.

She was silent for a moment. 'OK, I'll give Max your regards. And Charlee, I like it when you call me darling. You just did, you know.'

'I know.'

'I thought it might have just slipped out. Have you made any plans yet about coming back?'

'I only just got here. I will soon.'

'I was kidding just now, Charlee. I'm missing you very badly. Call me soon, won't you?'

'In a day or two.'

'I'll be waiting. Goodbye, darling.'

'Goodbye, darling,' he said.

'That sounds good,' she said and rang off.

He was due at Marie's. She had called and said she would like to talk to him again, and suggested a cocktail at five. It was early for him to drink cocktails, but it suited him that afternoon. It was Friday, the day he'd arranged to see Roger Briedon at 6.30 in the bar on 91st Street.

That was a meeting that did need care, he reckoned. Briedon would have done some thinking, talked to people, as he clearly had to Duclos. Charlie unlocked the bottom drawer of his desk and took out the gun and the shoulder holster he'd bought. He removed his jacket, strapped on the harness so that the holster was under his armpit, and put the jacket back on again. He smiled as he thought of what Mastorakis would have said had he known. It was a Colt .38 – not too brilliant as a weapon, they said, but it was familiar, what he'd had in the war.

He left the office and walked for a few blocks, thinking of Nikki. There was a girl ahead of him who looked like her. He was always seeing girls who looked like her – until they got close. She was so often in his mind, sometimes at the oddest of moments – in meetings, at dinner when he was talking to people, when he awoke in the middle of the night. Always it was the laughter that he remembered.

What would he have done, he wondered, if he hadn't got Wolf as an excuse, as Sonya had mocked? End it? How? Well, it's been lovely knowing you. We'll always be great friends, won't we? Let me know if you need anything more.

Sonya's sceptical look came back to him. It wouldn't have been like that. He was hooked. They would have made love every time he was in Paris – and somehow he would have been in Paris more often than before and Terry would have been making more cracks about talking to his chair. And maybe it would have ended in one of the ways that Sonya had listed in Nikki's apartment on the day of Wolf's letters. And maybe it wouldn't, because there was an element that didn't exist in other love affairs. Elisabeth.

The holster under his armpit was causing him discomfort. He'd get used to it, he supposed. He looked at his watch. It was later than he thought. Turning, he used his other arm to hail a cab.

8

The stranger in Marie's apartment stood up as Charlie entered. He was tall – about six foot two – with broad shoulders, a full beard and thinning brown hair that was grey at the temples. He had an easy smile as they shook hands.

'I thought you'd like to meet Otto,' Marie said. 'He's been a friend of Wolf's since they were cadets together. He knew Elisabeth, too.'

'Otto Grolmann?' enquired Charlie.

'How did you know my surname?' he asked. His English was fluent but strongly accented.

'I've seen some of Wolf's letters,' Charlie answered. 'You were involved, I think, with the Black Forest business – when they were discovered, I mean.'

Otto nodded wryly, amused by the memory. 'Wolf forgave me. I had no choice but to tell Rehmer. I knew where they'd gone – as von Eysebeck had told him.'

'Otto sees more of Wolf than I do,' Marie put in. 'He'll pass on any message you want.'

'I live in Germany, you see,' Otto explained. 'Wolf's in Germany a lot.'

'Charlie's got very friendly with Nicole,' said Marie. 'Too friendly, I suspect, though it's not strange. She looks like her mother.'

'Wolf would give anything to see her,' said Otto, 'but you know his position, I gather – which is why he hasn't tried to find her before. She could have been such obvious bait for a set-up. Marie tells me you'd like to meet him, too. Maybe you can help.'

'I'd like to.'

Always there was a kind of half-smile on Otto's face, coupled with an odd look of caution. Charlie got the feeling that he could move very fast if he needed to. 'The question that might bother Wolf,' Otto went on, 'is exactly why you want to talk to him, Charlie?'

'He sounds an interesting guy. We loved the same woman – and one that was pretty rare. That gives us a lot in common.'

Otto reached in his pocket for a silver cigarette case. 'Smoke?' he said, flicking it open and offering it to Charlie, his gaze steady. 'I think Wolf would need a better reason than that. I'm sure he'd like to meet you, too, but he has to take care about his social calls.'

'Point taken,' said Charlie. He was filling in time while he thought, wished Marie had warned him who he'd be meeting. It was deliberate, he guessed. She wanted him on the wrong foot. It was too soon to give Otto the real reason he wanted to meet Wolf. He knew nothing about what Otto had done immediately after the war – or Marie for that matter. So he'd got to come up with some other reason why Wolf should see him – a reason that would convince Wolf. 'I can see he's got to be careful,' Charlie went on. 'It concerns some of Elisabeth's papers that Nikki's got.'

'Papers?' asked Otto, trying to contain his interest. For the first time, Charlie noticed that his eyes were grey. There was the light line of an old scar on the side of his face. 'What kind of papers?'

'Letters. A diary even. She was still writing that when I knew her right there in the field, though the Vercors was different because it was so remote.'

'It was against the rules?'

'Of course. She told me it was notes for a novel, and I never got a chance to look at it then. Naturally there's nothing in it that would be any use to an enemy, but she mentions W pretty often. And there's quite a bit in it I don't understand. I think maybe Wolf might fill in the gaps.'

'Charlie, you're not telling us anything,' Marie put in.

'I'm giving you the basics.'

'There's more, isn't there?'

'There's always more, Marie. If you could answer my questions, I wouldn't bother Wolf.'

'How about trying us?' said Otto.

'I've told you enough, I think, to convince Wolf to see us – with arrangements that he can control.'

'Us?'

'I'll bring Nikki, of course – if he'd like that.'

'What about this mystery that concerns Elisabeth,' said Marie. 'Why you're seeing all her old friends?'

'Wolf was a mystery, let's face it. Wolf was a hell of a shock.'

Otto inhaled and the smoke escaped slowly from his nostrils, his eyes searching Charlie's face like radar. 'Can we just talk for a moment about you and Elisabeth? She joined your unit, yes? How long did you know her?' he asked.

'About a year.'

'And it became very important, so Marie tells me.'

'It was something I could never know again.'

'She was a lovely girl,' Otto agreed. 'You were very lucky – as Wolf was.' He smiled at the thought of her. 'You were with her when she died, I hear? Ambushed, I believe?'

'That's right.'

'It must have been tough. Any other casualties?'

'One of our maquisards was shot in the leg. But all of us in the unit were OK. We pulled out fast.'

'Except Elisabeth.'

'She was very exposed at the wrong moment.'

Otto was silent, thinking. 'I'm sorry to interrogate you, Charlie, but you understand, I'm sure.'

'Go ahead.'

'Tell me,' he said, 'did she ever speak of Wolf?'

'No – though that's hardly surprising.'

'Of course, it would have made her suspect. She wasn't ever suspected, I suppose?'

'We heard that the Gestapo had taken Nikki – wrongly, as it turned out. Anyone was suspect in that position – even Elisabeth.'

'Did you know she'd worked in Berlin?'

'Oh yes, but years before.'

'That didn't make you wonder? Or London? Didn't it make London wonder?'

'They cleared her.'

'And never changed their mind?'

Charlie was tempted to reveal the truth, but decided against it. He shook his head. 'What are you trying to tell me?' he asked. 'That they *should* have changed their mind?'

Otto's expression was bland, with just a hint of amusement. 'I'm asking questions, Charlie,' he said, 'not trying to tell you anything.'

He got to his feet – with a movement that was both lazy and controlled. 'I must go. It's been a pleasure to meet you. I'll report to Wolf.' He shook Charlie's hand warmly, and kissed Marie on the cheek. She went with him to the door, where he turned. 'Oh, Charlie,' he said. 'That gun. It shows, you know. You need to adjust the harness.' Then he turned and went into the hall. Charlie noticed that he had a slight limp – so slight that he hadn't seen it before.

Marie came back into the room. The usual smile was absent from her face. 'Why are you carrying a gun, Charlie?' she asked.

'I'll tell you that,' Charlie answered, 'if you tell me what you control in Switzerland.'

The smile was back. 'No wonder she loved you, Charlie. But you want to take care, you know. You're playing with big boys.'

'How do you know?' asked Charlie.

She avoided the trap. 'I've always had a nose for news,' she said.

There were more people in the bar than when Charlie had met
Briedon there earlier in the week – perhaps because it was Friday.
Even so, the barman recognised him as he ordered a Budweiser.
'You were in the other night with that tubby guy, weren't you?'
he said. 'I've got a message for you. He'd like to meet you at his
apartment instead of here. He's expecting an important phone
call.'

'You know him then?' said Charlie. 'Didn't realise he was a
regular.'

'Comes in sometimes. Not exactly a regular. Hasn't been in
the city long.'

'See you again then,' said Charlie. 'Later maybe.' He left the
bar, feeling apprehensive. Bars were safer places to meet than
apartments and, if he was in danger, as he was being warned on
all sides, was it wise to walk into what might be a trap? Yet, he
was certain that Briedon had at least part of the answer to the
question that had dogged him for months. Briedon must know
who tipped him off that Elisabeth was meeting Wolf – and where.
And that person must have wanted the evidence passed to
London. Could he pass up the chance that Briedon had decided
to come clean?

He walked the four blocks up Columbus to West 95th,
pondering the pros and cons. The discomfort of the gun, lessened
since he had adjusted the harness, was reassuring. He was glad
he'd got it. Oh, Elisabeth, he thought, if you could only have
known what you started.

He crossed 94th, glancing up the street towards the Park. He
could see the trees above the fast traffic of Central Park West.
The evening was warm, but muggy – the end of a cloudy day. It
dawned on him then that no one knew where he was. Should he
call someone just in case? Who? Terry? He'd have left the office
and wouldn't be home yet. Mastorakis? He'd call out the Fire
Brigade. Philana? She'd call her father. Marie? How could he
trust Marie?

He thought of friends. How would he put it? Just wanted you
to know I was going to Apartment 44, 52 West 95th Street. Why?
Well, it's just possible something might happen that'd make it
relevant. What kind of thing? I can't explain right now but . . .
Dangerous? Of course not. Whatever made you think that? The
fact I rang? Yeah, I suppose you must think it a bit odd but . . .

oh, forget it, pal. The moment he put down the phone, they would call the police and the sirens would be on.

He heard one behind him now on Columbus. The car roared by him, its light flashing, the siren wailing as it passed, then fading with the distance. He felt as though he were playing a role in a film. The sirens, the gun, the fear.

He turned into West 95th Street. It was a street of run-down apartment blocks – peeling paint, rust, eroded brickwork. Scene 37, shot 14. At Number 52 there were a row of entryphone bells, some with names, some without, beneath a cracked plastic cover. A couple were jammed in their sockets. He pressed the bell by Number 44 with little hope that it would ring in the apartment. Nothing happened, so he pushed the entrance door. It was no surprise when it gave to his touch.

He went up the stairs, covered with worn linoleum, to the fourth floor, a bit breathless by the time he reached it. A lesson there, surely. Here he was, risking his life, buying handguns, and he wasn't even fit. How had he got himself into this?

He walked along the passage to number 44 and his fear sharpened, for the door was ajar. He knocked, but there was no sound. For a moment he wished he'd rung Briedon from the bar. He might have dropped some hint of what he could expect. But if Briedon was there waiting for him in the silence, maybe with a gun raised, a knife in his hand – or if anyone else was – he wouldn't have given him any warning.

There was a smell of cooking – stew, soup, something like that, for the evening meal. 'Monsieur Briedon,' Charlie called out. 'Are you there, Monsieur Briedon?'

There was no answer, yet Charlie sensed he was there. He felt for his gun – a little self-consciously. It seemed ridiculous and unreal, like a game, like a film. Yet he'd bought the gun for real, hadn't he? For situations exactly like this. He drew it delicately from the holster, aware of his lapel brushing the back of his hand as he did so.

Then he moved cautiously into the apartment – at first into a small, dingy hall and then, by pushing another partly open door, into the living room. The shock of what greeted him was like being struck. A sharp intake of breath, the thumping of his heart, sheer cold fear.

Briedon was lying on the floor, face down, his arms stretched forward as though he'd been reaching as he fell for the support of the table beyond his fingers. He'd been wearing a white shirt and blood was seeping from a hole in his back, soaking into the material as if it were blotting paper, so that a whole area of his torso was wet crimson. Already it was dripping on to the carpet beside him.

It was a long time since Charlie had seen anyone who looked dead from bullet wounds. The sight was obscene – far worse than casualties in action because it was so alien to the setting. It just didn't happen in private apartments, did it? Thoughts began to flash through his mind. Disappointment – he'd expected so much from this meeting. A horrified kind of sadness because he'd liked Briedon. And then the sudden chilling perception that whoever shot him might still be there, watching him, gun aimed; that he, too, might soon be lying on the carpet with blood oozing from a hole in his back.

He glanced quickly around the room, but there was no sign that anyone else had been there. Nothing seemed out of place. He went into the small kitchen, directed by the smell. There was a pot on the stove, its contents simmering. He turned off the flame and went back into the hall to check out the rest of the apartment, still with the gun in his hand. There was just a bedroom and a bathroom – again with no sign of disturbance. He even explored a cupboard.

He returned to the living room and bent down over Briedon's body to confirm that he was really dead, though the extent of the bleeding left little doubt. He wondered what to do. Call the police? They'd ask why he was there, why he was carrying a gun. They might hold him, in which case Mastorakis would hear about it and his bevy of attorneys would be swarming all over and the press would make hay with pictures of Philana.

Yet, if they discovered he'd been there and failed to report it, he could well find himself as suspect number one. How could they find out? Fingerprints? All he'd touched was the stove and the cupboard in the bedroom. He remembered the barman who'd given him the message. But he didn't know Charlie's name – or Briedon's – and the bar was three blocks away. All they'd get was a description. There was nothing to link him to Briedon.

It was only then, as he wrestled with the problem, that the thought occurred to him: poor Briedon could tell him nothing now, but there could be another lead in the apartment – documents, letters maybe? He put his gun back in the holster and looked around the sparsely furnished room, wondering where Briedon would have kept correspondence. There were two drawers in the table. He opened one. More fingerprints! Letters all right, but addressed to Soissons, all about business, plus a few bills and a card from one of his workmates. He was in Miami having a great time.

The second drawer was no more productive – a tablecloth, mats, a screwdriver and pliers, a map of the city.

Then Charlie noticed a jacket slung on the back of a wooden chair. Why hadn't he seen it before? he wondered. He found the wallet in the inside pocket – in smooth brown faded leather, worn at the corners. Folded within it was a telegram that had arrived in New York from Paris at four o'clock that afternoon. 'Sorry I could not speak to you today stop will call you 1815 Friday stop until then do not play violins of autumn – Verlaine.'

Verlaine was a nineteenth-century French poet, and lines from his work had often been used for coded messages sent by SOE to the Resistance after BBC news broadcasts. It was a codename, therefore, that bore the colour of Elisabeth. The violins, presumably taken from a poem, were also some kind of cipher. The telegram could be useful as evidence – especially if links could be found. Who was Verlaine, for Christ's sake? Almost certainly the man he was after. Or the woman. So Charlie slipped it into his own wallet and returned Briedon's to the pocket of his jacket on the chair.

Again his mind reverted to the police. He'd stolen a document from the dead man. What if the killer had alerted them by phone? They could walk in the door and find it on him as well as the gun. Anyone could walk in. Not just the police. Even a friend would be enough to involve him.

There was a moment of panic. He must get out – then he remembered the fingerprints. He ran into the kitchen, wiped the gas burner control with his handkerchief and the drawer handles of the table in the sitting room – then dashed into the bedroom to remove any traces on the cupboard doors.

He left the apartment, trying not to hurry. He went down the stairs and out through the unlatched entrance door into the street. It was deserted except for a man walking along the far sidewalk and, fifty yards behind him, a boy. Charlie strolled towards Amsterdam since the street was one-way westward, so that any police in cars heading for Briedon's building would only get a back view.

As he reached the avenue, he heard the siren behind him. He resisted the temptation to look back, though it needed a huge effort. The siren stopped, which meant the police car had.

Charlie was about to hail a cruising cab but thought better of it. Cabdrivers who had been working the area around this time could be questioned. So he waited with three other people for the downtown bus. After twenty blocks he got off and hailed a cab. He directed the driver to his home, but then after a few minutes told him to stop at the Plaza Hotel, which was on the way. Briedon's death had changed the whole picture. He needed to consult Sonya.

It was after midnight in Paris and she'd gone to bed early, as her sleepy voice indicated. 'Sorry,' he said, 'but I've got some pretty shocking news. Briedon's been murdered – just before he was due to meet me.'

'Oh no!' she exclaimed. 'My God, Charlie, you're going to have to start taking a lot more care. René Levalier asked about you today. I had to see him on a story. He said the Sûreté had heard from London about your enquiries with Nikki. You ruffled some feathers, it seems. He thinks it's linked with Marie Cayzer and Wolf and Nazi funds.'

'Christ, the links are remote.'

'Same characters. See it from their angle. They're going after Wolf more seriously, raising the priority. René likes you – he said he was concerned, hoped you weren't going to end up in the Seine.'

Charlie felt very cold suddenly, as he had with Duclos's threat. Involuntarily, he shivered. Seeing Briedon's body had been traumatic. The image of it was still with him in vivid detail. So was the fear. The gunfire was getting close. Still, he forced a jokey answer, as they would have done in the Vercors. 'That's all I need to hear. Been one of those days, hasn't it?'

She recognised the tone of his response. 'It's not that funny, Charlie. Maybe we should tread water for a while.'

'When we're making progress?'

'Where to? Think about it, Charlie, and call me again tomorrow.'

Charlie put the phone down but kept his hand on the receiver. What Sonya had said about Wolf had made him think. He needed

Wolf now. When people started getting killed, Charlie was out of his depth. Wolf was clearly a kind of gangster. He'd know what to do and, after those letters to Elisabeth, surely he'd got to care. Charlie dialled Marie's number.

'Have you used that gun yet?' she asked.

'Wouldn't know how,' he answered. 'It's just my latest neurosis.'

'You're worrying me, you know.'

'I just heard something interesting from Paris. Do you reckon Wolf knows that the Sûreté have raised his priority? They're going after him, it seems.'

'What's this, a gesture of friendship – a sprat to catch a mackerel?'

'It's now more urgent that I meet Wolf. I need him, Marie. Truly.'

'What's changed the tempo? A couple of hours ago you were pretty cool.'

'Please, Marie – just get a message to him that I have to see him.'

'How can I help you if you won't confide in me just a little?'

'Marie, it's vital.'

'Well, I'll tell you something. Soon after you left, Wolf called. Weeks go by and I never hear, but he called. He's intrigued, Charlie. I think he'll see you, but he wasn't committing himself. You'll have to go back to Paris. He won't be there long, so it'll be on spec, may even be a wasted journey. Want to risk it?'

'God yes.'

'Philana will go berserk.'

'I'll make it up to her.'

'I'm going to Paris myself on Wednesday – as I always do at this time for the Collections. You'll be staying in the Bristol as usual, I suppose, so I'll contact you there. And Charlie . . . you'll sure owe me after this.'

'I'll start saving.'

How could he swop jokes at a time like this? he wondered as he put down the phone. For a few moments, he stayed in the booth, overcome by a sudden wave of fatigue. He thought he was going to cry. Shock, he supposed. His feelings were confused – excitement at getting closer to Wolf, who seemed to promise so much, horror of the past hours that was growing as numbness faded, and sheer panic that lay in him just below the surface.

He forced himself to leave the comfort of the booth. He had to get back to normal life. He thought of going for a drink but he knew he couldn't cope with the trivial talk of lone men in bars. He walked through the lobby – familiar territory that he'd trodden so many times before – and joined the short queue at the entrance waiting for cabs.

Philana greeted him with a bright smile, put her arms round his neck and kissed him. She was already dressed to go out. 'You haven't forgotten we're dining with the Graysons, have you?' she said. 'You had, hadn't you?' she laughed.

'Just for a moment,' he admitted.

'You're not looking too marvellous,' she said, studying him anxiously. 'You feeling all right?'

'Sure,' he said, 'fine. Bit tired maybe.'

'Like a drink before your shower?'

'That's a good idea.'

They went into the living room and she prepared it for him. There had been no recurrence of the outburst a few days back. She was back to the role of loving wife and he had taken her message to heart – tried not to be a stranger, tried to be there for her. But he knew his performance wasn't adequate. He had too much on his mind.

'Anything interesting happen today?' she asked as she dropped the ice cubes into the glasses.

'The usual hassle,' he said.

She approached him with the glasses in her hand and he thought how pretty she looked, her blonde hair held back by a diamond comb, his sapphire on her finger. 'You sure nothing happened today?' she said as she handed him his drink. 'You don't usually come home looking so pale.'

'Sure I'm sure,' he answered, thinking of what she would say if he told her the truth. Nothing had happened – other than escaping from the police because he might be accused of murder. 'You're looking lovely. Give me a kiss.'

'Will that put the colour back in your cheeks?' she asked with a smile.

'I reckon so. Set me on fire, I'd guess.'

'I'd love it if that were true.' She leaned forward, her own glass in one hand, and kissed him with parted lips. He responded warmly, holding her by the shoulders so she lost her balance and fell laughing on to his lap, still kissing him. Her drink spilled on his trousers. 'Doesn't matter,' he said, his mouth still touching hers.

The kids came in, having heard he was home. 'Oh look,' Rhona exclaimed. 'Mom and Dad are having a game.'

'You can say that again,' said Philana as she got off his lap, smiling. She straightened her dress, touched her hair to repair minor damage.

For a moment, he wondered if the remark was pointed, but she looked so happy he realised it wasn't. 'Will you have a game with us?' asked Tim.

'He hasn't got time right now,' said Philana.

'Tomorrow maybe,' Charlie added.

'It's so lovely for us all to be together,' she told him, 'and to be laughing. You won't have to go back to Europe for a while will you?'

'Maybe not,' he answered doubtfully and the laughter drained from her face.

'When?' she asked.

'Well . . . it may have to be later this week.'

There was silence then. Not even the kids said a word.

Nineteen

Philana was gripping the wheel tightly as they drove downtown in the heavy early evening traffic, looking steadily ahead with a troubled expression. She had run a comb through her hair before they left, but without her usual care, and it remained unruly, a few strands lying across her cheek.

Observing her in profile, Charlie was struck again by how beautiful she looked, moved suddenly by a wave of sympathy. He knew how impossible the situation was for her and was impressed by her dignity. He put his hand on her knee. 'I'll call often,' he said, but she didn't seem to have heard – just stared grimly through the windscreen.

Her decision to drive Charlie to the airport herself – instead of riding with him in the back of the Cadillac – was a last-minute impulse and he knew there was a special reason. There had been no quarrels since the day he got home after finding Briedon's body, no insistent questions as to why he was returning to Paris so soon. But the vitality seemed to have gone out of her. They had made love once or twice but there was a distance between them.

She told her father that Charlie was going and Costa had been on the phone demanding his presence as usual at the Twenty-One. 'I've a right to know,' he declared, glowering over his champagne, the furrows of his forehead forming deep folds. 'You've only been back a few days. Something vital must have happened to demand so urgent a return.'

'I promised, Costa: you'll be the first to know.'

'It's the girl. She's putting the pressure on.'

'It's not the girl.'

'She's called you, I know she's called you.'

'About a screen test. She wants to be a star. And *how* did you know?' Bugging would be excessive, even for Costa, but it was always possible.

'How?' he asked. 'It's what I'd expect. But if it's not the girl, then the trouble's serious and you're going to force my hand, Charlie.'

'How many more times, Costa? I've a duty, an obligation, which must for the moment be kept secret.'

'From me?' Tears appeared suddenly in his eyes.

'Even from you.'

'Considering what I've done for you?'

'Costa, my gratitude is overflowing, but I'm thirty-six, a father. I don't have to tell you everything I do.'

'This is different, you know that.' He paused, watching Charlie. 'Well, don't ever say I didn't warn you,' he added darkly.

As they crossed the East River by the Queensboro Bridge, Philana seemed to grow tenser, her hands so tight on the wheel that her knuckles were white. 'Charlie,' she managed to say at last, 'do you want a divorce?'

He realised then why the scene wasn't being played out at home. When you're driving you don't have to look at a person when you ask them a question – not even a question like that.

'No, darling,' he answered, 'I don't want a divorce. And you really must try to stop worrying.'

She turned her head then for an instant – a brief searching glance to be sure – before looking back at the road. 'Whenever you leave, I can never be certain you're coming back.'

'I'll come back.'

'If you're alive,' she said. 'I found your gun, Charlie. Why do you need a gun, for God's sake?'

'I've had it a while. You never know when you're going to need one. Don't worry, darling – I've forgotten how to use it.'

'You're lying to me, Charlie – and it makes me scared. And a little jealous.'

'It'll be over soon. And everything will be back to normal.'

'I don't believe that. Nor do you. Well, do you?'

'All right, nothing's ever certain. But I'm pretty sure it will.'

'Let's hope so,' she said forlornly.

When they got to the airport, she gripped his hand for a second. 'Be very careful, won't you, Charlie?'

'I will,' he answered as he kissed her.

'I love you,' she said. 'We've got a lot going for us, haven't we?'

'A lot,' he agreed. 'I love you too.' He walked towards the

glass doors of the terminal building, then turned and waved. He didn't like himself. I'm not cut out for this, he thought. But he'd told Costa the truth. He wasn't going back for the girl. The girl was there, though.

After midnight the stewards turned off the main cabin lights, but Charlie lay staring at the night sky through a gap in the curtains, sleepless yet lulled by the monotonous roar of the engines. He thought again of Briedon, who had started to obsess him, partly because he'd liked him, partly because his death had changed the gearing. They were on a new track now. Before, there'd been what seemed defensive moves – the warning off of Thelma with the threat about her child, Frank Charlwood's sudden change of mind, Briedon's disappearance from Paris – but murder was different. In a way, Charlie felt he'd killed Briedon himself, that if he hadn't traced him Briedon would be alive now.

The day after he talked to Marie, she'd called him again – at the office. 'I just heard about a Frenchman who got killed yesterday,' she said. 'Know anything about it, Charlie?'

'Should I? I'm not usually *au fait* with New York murders.' Was he casual enough, maybe too casual?

'Name of Briedon. Sporting journalist, once worked for Duclos's paper, they say. Just wondered if that was why it was suddenly so urgent you met Wolf.'

'What could Wolf have to do with a sporting journalist?' he asked.

'No idea. I thought you might know.'

'Any clues in the paper?'

'It's not been in the paper. Not yet. Sometime, Charlie, you're going to have to start telling me, you know.'

'See you in Paris, Marie,' he said and put down the phone, wondering how she'd found out if there was nothing in the papers yet. Then it occurred to him that she'd said it to fool him, to put him off the scent. If he suspected she was involved with this whole business, even at the fringes, he wouldn't expect her to be asking aggressive questions to which, in fact, she already knew the answer; so he'd think his suspicions were groundless. The same went for Wolf. Why should she help him? Why should she help him to meet anyone?

Charlie had thought a lot about Verlaine. The name alone, written on a telegram, had made him tangible. Until now, the search had been for someone vague – a powerful presence. There were suspicions. Duclos, Marie – but no hard evidence to tie either of them to Elisabeth's death. Verlaine could be someone else, might not even know them, though Charlie doubted that. He was sure they were involved in some way. He wondered what kind of man – or woman – Verlaine was, and tried to build up a picture of his life, his motives. Were there children? A wife? A home? An office? What did he do for leisure? A yacht at Monte Carlo? Racehorses at Chantilly?

One thing seemed certain: Verlaine knew Charlie, or at least knew his movements, his plans – and this was unnerving. Charlie needed to know his enemy. That's why he'd prefer it if Verlaine was Duclos, formidable though Duclos could be. Certainly the costume of Verlaine fitted Duclos – which is why he'd asked Sonya if she could arrange for them to see him, face him out. Duclos was an old pro, but he might show something of his hand.

Charlie turned from the cabin window and tried to sleep, letting the noise of the engines fill his mind. He dozed for a while, but he was awake again soon with the dawn and the first shafts of sunlight.

'Seems too easy,' said Charlie as Sonya drove him into Paris from the airport. Duclos had agreed to see them as soon as they could get there. He was busy the rest of the week.

'Does it matter that it's easy?' she asked.

'I like to know why.'

'I told you. We had lunch – the first time in months. I made it casual. Charlie's doing some research you could help with, I said.'

'He couldn't have bought that, so why's he seeing me?'

'Who can tell? To find out what you know maybe. To please me since I seem to be back in favour.'

As they went up the stairs of the *France Aujourd'hui* building, Charlie asked: 'How's Nikki doing?'

'You mean why wasn't she at Orly to meet you?' Sonya mocked. 'She's in London with Max and a big producer. The great screen test. They're flying in this afternoon. So's Romy. Max said Romy's worried about something, but he wouldn't say what on the phone.'

She led the way through the noise of the newsroom, and at the far end of it Duclos's secretary rose to greet them – then ushered them into the ordered tranquillity of his big office.

Duclos greeted Charlie as though he were an old friend, and for a moment Charlie wondered if he'd imagined that brief call in New York, with its curt and chilling warning. 'Now tell me,' said Claude sceptically as he filled three glasses with champagne, 'about this research you're engaged in.'

'It's good of you to give me your time,' said Charlie easily. 'You were pretty mad at me the last time we talked.'

Duclos laughed. 'You shouldn't have done what you did, Charlie. But then sometimes we all do things we shouldn't.' He replaced the bottle in the ice bucket on a side table. 'In his day, Briedon was good, you know. Not great, but he could write exciting copy. Did you ever get to meet him, Sonya?'

'He was spirited away, wasn't he?' she answered.

Duclos didn't react. 'Never was reliable,' he said. 'That was his trouble, why he stayed small-time.' He turned. 'Charlie met him, didn't you, Charlie?'

'Did you know he was dead?' Charlie asked.

He gave a brief nod. 'Roger always knew some unsavoury people. Fighters usually do. He was a fighter before he was a journalist. There – you didn't know that, did you?'

'Why's he dead, Claude?'

Duclos's expression was quizzical: it was a stupid question. 'He must have upset someone, mustn't he?' he asked.

'Do you know who?'

'Why should I know that?'

'Because you had an inside track to him. He called you only hours before he died.'

'That was to check on you. You'd used my name as an intro, hadn't you?'

'You've known him a long time. Back to Elisabeth's day. Then the war. You must have realised what he was doing in the war.'

'I had an idea,' he agreed.

'And I bet you have an idea who'd want him out of the way now,' Sonya put in. 'He was only a little guy. Who could he hurt? You know, don't you?'

Duclos laughed, pleased by her charge. 'You give me too much credit, Sonya. But I could make enquiries. I'd need a reason, though. Why would I want to know about a seedy little sports writer who'd long been over the hill?'

Charlie said nothing. He wandered over to the big window with his glass in his hand, and looked out at the cloudy Paris sky. He was tired after the flight and it was too soon for this kind of meeting, when you needed all your wits for the nuances.

He stifled a yawn, turned wearily to face Duclos. 'Do you ever see Wolf Heinegg now?'

Duclos laughed at the sudden mention of a secret name – then shook his head. 'No, Charlie, haven't seen Wolf in years.'

'You knew him well though, didn't you?' said Sonya.

'You're both at me, aren't you? It's like the Gestapo.' There was a look of supercilious amusement on his face. 'Yes, I knew him well,' he went on. 'He was often in Paris in the thirties – and later, too, though I hardly saw him then.'

'You knew about him and Elisabeth?' asked Charlie.

'Oh yes.'

'Did you tell Briedon about them?'

Duclos looked puzzled. 'Why should I do that?'

'My very next question.'

'You're looking tired, Charlie,' said Duclos.

'I didn't sleep much on the plane.'

'Your questions are very blunt. I'm not sure I like it.' He sipped his champagne, watching Charlie. 'No one talked of Wolf,' he said. 'Those were different days. Love affairs were secret – gossiped about, but barely admitted. For most people. But Elisabeth was rash. She'd bring him to parties and behaved – well, she left no doubt she was sleeping with him. Her friends tried to be loyal, but it was hard for them, the Levalliers especially. Sonya will understand that, won't you, Sonya?'

You bastard, Sonya thought. You can't resist it. 'Why me especially?' she enquired.

'Oh, I don't know.' He looked at her – then went on: 'To start with, the Levalliers were loyal to Elisabeth. But Lucille's sights were always high – and so were René's. Both were scared to death of scandal. The Wolf affair – or rather Elisabeth's flaunting of it – created a rift between them. For a while, she and Lucille didn't even speak. Then war began to loom and that put an entirely different complexion on it. Even now you won't find anyone who wants to talk of Wolf.'

'So who talked to Briedon?' asked Charlie. 'Someone told him she and Wolf were meeting. This was after the occupation of Paris, Claude.'

268

'I never heard that,' said Duclos. 'And don't look at me like that, Charlie. I didn't tell him.'

'Did you know they met after the war had started?'

'Know?' Duclos shook his head. 'But it wouldn't have surprised me.'

'Despite her work in the Resistance?' queried Sonya.

'Despite anything. We're talking of love, of passion. Go back in history and look at what people risked for love. Mark Antony. Catherine Howard. Abelard. What's a war?'

'A true romantic,' she teased, 'hidden beneath that shell of cynicism. Why didn't you tell Nikki who W was when she asked?'

'What do you expect? Yes, Nikki, he was your mother's lover – an enemy general, your real father, now wanted for war crimes? You think I should have told her that?'

Charlie had wandered over to the bookshelves that covered one wall of the room. As he ran his eye over the volumes, Duclos asked him: 'Why not tell me what's behind all this, Charlie?'

'I think you know, Claude,' Charlie answered, still scanning the shelves.

'I don't *know* much. I can guess some of it. When you brought Nikki here, I asked myself: What exactly is Charlie after? Months later I ask the same. It has to centre on Elisabeth because she was the link between you all – Nikki, Sonya, the Vercors comrades still so close, even poor Briedon. Well, you've found out about Wolf, but you're still sniffing the trail like greyhounds, aren't you?'

'So why after all this time? Answer: Elisabeth's death. It had to be that: there was nothing else. You discovered some new aspect that changed everything, that was crucial. So what could this be? Well, how did she die? Even why did she die? Which brings us to the signal, doesn't it?'

Charlie still felt a frisson at Duclos's words. The signal was an Allied secret, still classified. To admit to knowing of it was to invite suspicion. It hadn't slipped out by mistake. Duclos had lobbed it in as a tactic and Charlie didn't respond at once. He'd found what he'd been looking for among the books – six volumes of Verlaine's works. 'What signal, Claude?' he asked idly as he drew one of the books from the shelf – *Romances sans paroles*.

'Oh, Charlie,' Duclos said reproachfully, 'what's the point in pretending? Isn't the signal why you're here?'

'All right,' said Charlie, looking at him then, with the book open in his hand. 'What about the signal?'

'*You* tell *me*. In April something started to disturb you about the signal?'

'That's true,' Charlie answered calmly. 'It disturbs me more now – after what happened to Briedon.'

'Didn't that make you nervous? Is it worth the risk, Charlie?'

'It's something I've got to do. And, when you get down to it, what *is* the risk?'

Duclos shrugged. 'The truth, if there is a truth, could make you vulnerable – more vulnerable than Briedon.'

'Except that anything I know, the others will all know, too. You realise that, I'm sure.'

Duclos laughed, but his colour seemed higher. 'And you suspect this may concern me?'

'You're on the list. You must be. The two factors that condemned Elisabeth were Wolf and Briedon. You knew all about Wolf. You spoke to Briedon before he died. You were even aware that he was tempted to open up to me.'

'No,' said Duclos. 'I didn't know that.'

Charlie looked down at the title page of *Romances sans paroles*. 'Fond of Verlaine, are you?' he enquired.

'Quite,' Duclos said. 'I studied him at the Sorbonne. Along with others, of course.'

'Verlaine was a favourite?'

Duclos sighed. 'This is hardly the time to discuss my taste in poetry. I hope you believe what I've just told you.'

'That you didn't know Briedon meant to tell me the truth?' asked Charlie, replacing the book on the shelf. 'I'd believe that,' he went on, turning to Duclos, 'if you could explain how Briedon learned when Elisabeth was meeting Wolf – and where.'

Duclos smiled and sipped his champagne. 'If I could explain that, it'd mean I wanted her to die – and I swear I didn't want that, Charlie.' There was a fervency in his tone. 'That you must believe,' he added.

'Sorry, Claude, I don't,' said Charlie, 'but what I still want to know is why?'

'I don't know that,' Duclos whispered. 'If I did I'd tell you.'

2

'Know what's beautiful about this business, Charlie?' Max said, 'It's finding someone you think the camera will fall for – and then seeing it make love to her, linger tenderly on her lips, gaze at her eyes, feel her hair, caress her ears, her neck, her breasts. And then you know that for once you've got it right. It was like that with Nikki, Charlie, I kid you not. Nikki is going to be big. Believe me, this girl is a treasure.'

They'd met in the Ritz Bar, which always made Charlie feel slightly uncomfortable. The macho shadow of Ernest Hemingway, one of the hotel's most famous patrons, hung over the long counter. You got the feeling the barman would only serve you if you'd been charged by a Rhino. It suited Max, though. He enjoyed its aura of the celebrated, standing with his back to the window that overlooked the Place Vendôme, his imagination running wild.

'We were only a minute into the test,' he went on, 'and already Craig had cast her in the picture. "Magic", he kept whispering. "Just magic." She was, too. She knows how, Charlie. No one's told her. All she's been taught was to wiggle her bottom in that grotty club and serve Boeuf Bourguignon in the café. But everything was small with her, as it needs to be with the big screens. Acting school would have ruined her. She knew by instinct. No wonder I feel like a kid who's just had his first orgasm. And the timing – she's a gift from the gods. I was in trouble, no question – still am, but the future's looking good.'

'What's gone wrong?' Charlie asked.

'That Gresham deal was lousy. Remember all that garbage Sally was dishing out at Romy's about Ollie's vision? Thank God I never actually signed a contract.'

'So you're all right then?'

Max's face twisted into a look of uncertainty. 'It's not as easy as that. There were letters, even a bit of money put up. Ollie's out and they're trying to screw us to the wall. I've saved Romy from the wreckage, since she was never in the Ollie deal. I've kept Nikki out, too. They're the first clients of my new agency – and they're beauties, Charlie. But, boy, if either goes lame, I'll be dead, no kidding.' His eyes brightened suddenly. 'Ah, here she is,' he exclaimed, looking over Charlie's shoulder, 'my brilliant discovery.'

Charlie turned to see Nikki standing in the doorway – radiant in a white silk cocktail dress that had clearly cost a fortune. She was looking around the bar for Max, taking her time as though she'd lived in luxury hotels all her life, a casual hand on the arm of a tall, bulky man of about fifty. Her impact always took Charlie by surprise – but this time she was more stunning than he'd ever seen her and the sharp response in his groin almost hurt. He switched his attention to her escort, and was shocked by the spasm of hostility, primeval in its nature, that rose up in him.

She saw him then and froze with her eyes wide, as people are sometimes caught in press photos. 'Charlee,' she exclaimed in delight. She hurried towards him and kissed him warmly. 'You're back,' she said. 'I didn't know you were back. Max, why didn't you tell me he was back?'

'Because I didn't know either,' Max answered.

'I'm going to be in a movie, Charlee,' she said. 'Isn't that wonderful? It's about a girl who kills her mother's lover. Craig says I'm going to be a sensation. Isn't that right, Craig?'

'It sure is, honey.'

Max introduced the two men. 'I've just been telling Charlie about the test,' he said.

'We're all very excited,' Craig confirmed.

'You're a darling, Craig,' said Nikki, clinging to his arm and kissing him on the cheek. 'Did you know that?'

'I had a suspicion,' he answered with a smile of easy assurance, 'but it's good of you to confirm it.'

'Charlee, he made it so easy. He understands exactly how a woman feels, don't you, Craig?'

'Well I've been dealing with actresses a while now,' he answered as if that was pretty simple so long as you had the gift.

'We were trying this scene with a young actor,' she explained, still clinging to Craig's arm. 'This was from the actual script, Charlee. And Craig told me exactly what to do. Your reaction to him is very big, he said; if you were honest with yourself you'd admit you already wanted him badly. Your stomach's in turmoil. If he doesn't kiss you you're going to die. And you know what, Charlee, I felt just like that, didn't I, Craig?' She looked up at the producer with her big eyes wide as though he was the one she wanted to kiss her.

'The camera thought so,' said Craig. 'It came through electric on the screen. I hear you found this lovely, brilliant young girl in a Left Bank café, Mr Dawson. That could come in useful for the promotion. A trifle *déjà vu*, perhaps, but nice all the same.' He consulted his watch. 'Afraid we're running late, honey. We ought to be saddled up.'

'Already?' she queried, the star overtaken by the demands of her public. 'It can't be that late. You should have told me you were coming back so soon, Charlee.'

'So that you could have fitted me into your busy schedule?' he asked with a smile he didn't feel. 'Don't worry, I'll call and make an appointment.'

She gave a slight, wounded shake of her head. 'That's naughty, Charlee,' she chided from on high. 'You know I didn't mean it like that. I can't wait to hear all about New York. When can we – ?'

'Honey, the green light's flashing,' Craig cut in. 'Mr Dawson will be in touch, I'm sure. Good to meet you,' he said to Charlie, and swept her out of the bar like the celebrity he was planning to make her.

For a second after they left, Charlie could hardly speak. 'Don't worry about her, Charlie,' Max assured him. 'She'll be on the phone to you in the morning.'

'Who's worrying?' asked Charlie. 'This is going to be a hectic trip.'

'Charlee . . .' It was a whisper and she was behind him. 'I just realised. I didn't kiss you goodbye.' As she put her lips to his cheek she said: 'Come and stay with me tonight.'

'You look pretty tied up to me,' he answered.

'Only for dinner – with Craig and the director. I'll be home by ten. I'll plead a headache.'

'I don't know that – ' he began, but she cut in: 'Please, Charlee. If you don't I'll never speak to you again. Call me anyway. Promise me that at least.' She turned and ran out of the bar – not like a star this time, but like a young girl.

Charlie turned back to Max to find him speaking on the bar phone. He replaced the receiver. 'Romy doesn't want to join us here as she said,' he told him. 'She'd like to see us in her suite instead.'

'Well,' declared Max, 'this is a surprise.

That was an understatement, no question. Romy was playing it cool, appearing totally unruffled in a lacy silk blouse, but the anxiety was coming through. 'Hallo, Charlie darling,' she'd greeted him warmly. 'How lovely to see you again. You'll both remember Mr Maitland, of course.'

James Maitland, the writer they'd last seen on Sheikh Jassim's yacht, was standing by the window of Romy's living room – keeping his distance from the greetings, but watching, with a cigarette held to his lips. Again Charlie found him hard to place – too self-effacing, with his blond moustache and rosy complexion, to be a hard-nosed author of exposés. But the way he'd stood up to the Prince had shown that he was no light-weight.

'I'm not sure I should be talking to him at all without my lawyer,' Romy went on, 'but you can decide, Max. Let's all sit down. Then Mr Maitland can tell you about his book. He's been making progress, haven't you, Mr Maitland?'

'It's almost finished,' he agreed as he took a seat well away from the others.

'You must work fast,' said Charlie. 'It's only been a few weeks.'

'Much of it was already roughed out by then,' he explained.

'I've read his manuscript,' Romy went on.

'A draft,' corrected Maitland, 'that can be changed.'

'It's provocative,' she said. 'It claims I was Khalid's mistress, which I'm not exactly keen about. Far more important, it gives a vivid version of how Mr Maitland thinks my husband died in Nuremberg in 1937.'

'That was an accident in your bedroom, wasn't it?' asked Max.

'In the Prince's bedroom,' corrected Maitland. 'The Prince killed him during a fight.'

'That's absurd,' declared Max. 'Publish that and we'll sue you for millions.'

'What about the Prince?' Charlie asked. 'You've sent him the manuscript too, I take it.'

'Of course. His reaction was the same. We'll defend on grounds that it's justified, as we can show.'

'Are you sure you can afford it?' asked Max. 'The cost of libel actions can be in the stratosphere.'

'They can also turn books into huge bestsellers,' countered Maitland.

'Money doesn't seem to be a problem for Mr Maitland,' Romy remarked. 'He has rich friends. Even so, he's offering a curious deal. He's agreed to amend the book . . .'

'If we pay, I suppose,' snorted Max.

'I said curious. That wouldn't be curious. His condition is that I end my association with you, Max.'

Max's face, usually so impassive, displayed astonishment, touched – Charlie noted – by a hint of fear. This was something he couldn't afford. 'Does he now?' Max said. 'Why should he want that?'

'He declines to say,' Romy replied.

Max let out a roar: 'It's those Gresham bastards!'

'I doubt it,' said Charlie. 'Was a similar offer made to the Prince?'

'Pretty similar,' agreed Maitland.

'You mean you want him to take his horses away from Duncan Stewart?' Max queried. 'Why, for God's sake?'

'My friends are unhappy,' answered the writer. 'Mr Dawson here is embarrassing them. They want you both to use your influence with him.'

'Who the hell are these friends?' demanded Max.

'That, I fear, I can't disclose,' said Maitland.

'Let me get this straight,' said Charlie. 'What you're saying is that if Max and Duncan were to persuade me to stop being, well, embarrassing, as you said, then you'd drop this demand?'

'That's right.'

'You wouldn't insist that Miss Lagrange changed her agent?'
Maitland nodded.

'Or that Prince Khalid changed his trainer?'

'Correct.'

'And you'd cut the scenes in Nuremberg from your book?'

'You understand completely.'

'And what was the answer you got from the Prince?'

'What I expected – that he'd employ what trainer he chose.'

'And what answer do you expect from Miss Lagrange?' asked Charlie.

'Oh, the same,' Maitland answered with a boyish smile.

'Well, I'm glad you're clear about that,' said Romy firmly.

'To start with,' Maitland added. 'Then when she reads the scenes again – and rereads them and thinks about it – she'll begin to wonder. After all, there are plenty of agents, aren't there?'

'You're wrong,' Romy insisted. 'My debt to Max is enormous.'

'Perhaps,' conceded Maitland, 'but I think you'll come round to my way of thinking. The same, I think will happen with the Prince.'

'You're wrong about that, too. You saw what happened on the yacht. He told you he wouldn't be blackmailed.'

Maitland's smile was almost girlish. 'It's hardly blackmail,' he suggested. 'Not technically. You want me to change my book. I'm considering the request. Of course, if the truth is published as I've written it, then it could lead to the Prince's prosecution – and to yours, as an accessory after the fact.'

Romy seemed to wince. 'How has all this arisen? Who's told you these lies?'

'Ask yourself who knows, Miss Lagrange.' This wasn't hard: von Eysebeck was an obvious source. 'I checked it out, though – with his help in Germany. The case is strong.'

Romy was staring at Maitland with an anger that was both pained and confused. She didn't understand why he was doing this to her. But the young man appeared unmoved. She switched her gaze to Charlie. 'Who are these people you're embarrassing?'

'I don't know,' said Charlie. 'I wish I did.'

'Or how?' queried Maitland with an amused look on his face.

'Oh, I know that,' said Charlie. 'What I don't know, Mr Maitland, is why you're mixed up in this. You're a writer, for Christ's sake. What are you gaining from it? Why should you agree to change your book even if I complied with the demand?'

An enigmatic smile came to Maitland's face. 'For me, there are other compensations.' He stood up. 'Well, I'd better leave you now to talk about it. I've told you my schedule, Miss Lagrange, and you've got all my telephone numbers. Good evening, gentlemen.'

When the door closed behind him, Max said: 'I've got to thank you for that, Romy. It was really moving, but you must feel free to leave me if you change your mind. It'd be a great blow, but I'd understand, you know.'

'Max darling, I wouldn't think of it,' she said but, looking at her at that moment, Charlie wouldn't have put money on that. In fact, he guessed, she was thinking of it already.

3

You have to touch wood all the time, Leah reflected later, to placate the Fates. You just never know when your life will be transformed.

The irony was that that day, as she waited for Hugo at the corner table in La Coupole, she'd had a special sense of wellbeing. Everything seemed so good. It was the time of the Prêt-à-Porter or Ready-to-Wear, that was always staged after the big haute couture houses had showed their collections.

Not that Leah, or any other rival designer, would be allowed near the 'Prêt', but Paris was still the hub of world fashion. You had to stay in touch with what was new, and the small fashion shops, the nightly parties, the rag trade restaurants like La Coupole were humming with gossip about the trends.

Leah's own collection – a small one planned for London mid-season – was already designed and being made by the girls back home. There was still time, though, for minor changes or even one or two new numbers. By and large, however, she was happy about it. She knew it was good and she was looking forward to the press response to the dozen new skirts she was showing. Hugo predicted that the fashion writers would be dismissive but would give them good coverage.

Hugo was late but Leah didn't mind, for friends kept stopping at her table to talk about what was emerging in the show – the 'shape', the colours, the hems, the necklines. She was enjoying the excitement of the place – until a journalist named Gwen Harding sat down beside her and said: 'Seen this?' And there on the fashion page of the London *Daily Mail* was an article headlined: 'Will you be showing your pretties this Xmas?' about a small special collection by Dawn Chambers that included what she called 'microskirts'. There were pictures of girls modelling these – among them an action shot, showing that not much movement was needed for naked thighs to be revealed. The piece was mocking – 'Just show me the girl who'll walk down a London street in one of these!' it demanded – but it praised Dawn for being brave and suggested flapper fashions of the twenties had met the same negative response before they were accepted.

For a moment, Leah thought she was going to be sick. Her heart was thumping. Anger such as she'd never known was surging through her. Words like 'betrayal' kept coming into her mind. She wanted to break something – a plate, a glass. How had Dawn done it so fast? Even when Hugo had talked to her so stupidly, Leah's own plans were well advanced. But the result was there in front of her – and it would rob her own collection of the whole impact she'd hoped for.

'Do you feel like making a comment?' asked Gwen. 'You and Dawn are friends, aren't you? Do you think she has a hope of getting away with it?'

'Who knows?' Leah managed to get out.

'Do you think we're ready for fashions inspired by the twenties?'

'Possibly.'

'How about your own collection? Would you consider anything so extreme?'

Leah forced a smile. Oh God, would this woman please go away? 'You'll have to wait and see, won't you?' she said.

It ended fairly soon. Gwen Harding moved to another table in search of more rewarding material, and Leah was able to leave, blurting out an excuse to the head waiter that she'd forgotten an appointment. For a few seconds she stood in a state of shock on the pavement of the Boulevard du Montparnasse – then began to walk without any special purpose except to get away from La Coupole. Absorbed as she was, she didn't notice a man in dark sun-glasses get up from an outside table and follow her along the street. 'Miss Grant,' he said as he caught up with her, 'may I please have a quick word with you?'

She looked at the stranger in alarm – at the glasses, the blue shirt, the felt hat. His accent was strange – Bordelais, she suspected, from the south-west coast. 'You don't know me,' he went on, 'and I'm not the press, but I do have to say something to you. You're a friend, I think, of Charles Dawson. In the war together, weren't you? In that famous little group in the Vercors. Radio operator, I believe.'

'Yes,' she said cautiously. 'That's right.'

'You've got to stop him, you know. As a friend, I mean. I hear you're all close still, see a lot of each other.'

She didn't understand. 'Stop him doing what?' she asked.

'All these enquiries. Talking to people, asking questions. It's starting to upset my associates. So you must get him to give it a rest.'

'I don't know what you're talking about,' said Leah.

'I think you do, Miss Grant.'

'Then you've been misinformed. And even if I did, I don't have that kind of influence with him. He does what he wants.'

'I think you underestimate his respect for you. And you've got a right to be heard in this matter, haven't you? After all, Elisabeth Ferrier was your friend too, wasn't she?'

'Oh, it's about Elisabeth, is it?'

He shook his head in disbelief. 'Now come, Miss Grant, you knew that.'

'She's been dead a long time.'

He nodded. 'Exactly. And it's how she should stay – as I urge you to impress on Mr Dawson very strongly.'

'I don't think you understand. He won't listen to me.'

'It's you who don't understand, Miss Grant. It's crucial that you should persuade him – crucial to your interests, to your business. Do I have to say more?'

The fear cut through the numbness. This couldn't be happening, not on top of what Dawn had done. She shook her head to clear it. 'I'm sorry. I've just had a bad shock and I'm not sure I believe this. What can you do?'

'I can put you out of business.'

'But how?'

'Persuade Charles Dawson – or you'll find out, won't you? Good day, madame.' He crossed the boulevard to a little red Peugeot that was waiting at the curb – and, as she watched, the car disappeared swiftly in the traffic.

4

The old song was haunting, rising above the noise of the party. The trumpet blared. The black singer was good as he belted out the lyric of 'Mack the Knife' – Kurt Weill's famous adaptation of Macheath, the highwayman from *The Beggar's Opera* by John Gay. With its laughing menace set to that precise and heavy beat, it added a tension to the occasion, like background music in a film – all those people tanned from Mediterranean vacations, elegant women, powerful men, pretty girls. A wow came from the horn, rising high in the register.

Charlie wasn't in a party mood. It was only a few hours since Leah's hysterical call which, following so soon on the Maitland threat and a talk to Duncan, had made him deeply anxious. The technique was clever – putting pressure on the others rather than on himself, the old tactic of divide and rule. And it was tantalising because he was clearly too close. But to whom? Duclos? Someone else? And how? And, always, why?

Sonya, however, had urged him to come to the reception with

her since she was duty-bound to attend and the annual *France Aujord'hui* event was always staged with style. 'It's a good idea for you to be in view just now, for he'll almost certainly be there.'

'He?' Charlie had asked. 'Who's he?'

'Whoever's behind all this.'

And as Charlie stood there, alone for a moment, surveying the crowd, he thought of what she'd said and wondered if the man *was* there, if maybe at that very moment he was watching *him*. Duclos saw him then and gave a sardonic but friendly smile, a light wave. The words of the singer seemed to be coming over louder, as the band got into the number. In his *Threepenny Opera*, Kurt Weill had turned Gay's womanising highwayman into a crook with style and a lethal jacknife, and set a story to Brecht's dramatic music against the decadent hopelessness of Berlin in the twenties. To Charlie that day, it seemed acutely pertinent – almost Elisabeth's time in Elisabeth's place. And what would she have thought of it all? The old question. She'd have laughed, he guessed.

Charlie could see Elisabeth's daughter on the far side of that crowded room. He had known she'd be there. Max and Craig wanted her to be seen around to promote her career; and she was the kind of pretty young girl Duclos liked to dress his life with, in amongst the politicians, corporate VIPs and established stars.

Nikki was aware he was watching her, despite all the guests between them, the smoke, the passing waiters. She knew precisely the effect on him as she touched Craig, put her arm in his, responded with that eager little laugh to his banalities.

Craig was the new element in their strange relationship, with its ever-changing hues. 'I just can't help it, Charlee,' she had said with the frankness he found engaging. 'I love to see that look on your face as I do it. What do you expect? I'm a minx, aren't I?' They'd been lying in bed as they talked that first night after meeting in the Ritz Bar. 'But I'm yours whenever you want. You know that. You're Number One and always will be. And it's good, isn't it? Or are you complaining?'

'Have you slept with him?'

'Not yet. Oh, Charlee, don't look like that – please.'

It was the 'yet', of course. He had guessed why she'd asked him to come to her that night. She needed to be sure her hold on him was still secure. 'You do think some funny things, Charlee,' she said. 'Even if it's true, it's not so bad, is it? It's been horrid without you. You've been with your wife. You could have changed. Anyway, you make it sound like scheming. You didn't really think that, did you?'

'Maybe not,' he said.

'Wasn't I as passionate as I've ever been?'

'Marvellous,' he answered.

'Well then,' she rebuked. After a pause, she asked: 'Would you mind terribly if it happened with Craig?'

'Mind?' he asked casually. 'Why in the world should I mind? I'd just want to kill him that's all – slowly, with my bare hands.'

She giggled. 'Oh, I do love to hear you say that, Charlee. I'll try not to – really I will.'

'Will it be very hard?'

She gave a sigh. 'It'll never end, Charlee. Not between you and me.' It was a kind of answer – and all he could expect.

Max wandered up to him as he watched her with Craig. 'He's a nice guy, you know,' he said. 'And good for her. You should see them working together, how he brings her out. She's a different bambino.'

'Must be great,' said Charlie.

'Now, Charlie, don't be like that. You've got no plans for her – she's just a piece of ass, isn't she?'

'No,' said Charlie. 'That she's not, by Christ.'

'OK, so you were obsessed with her mother and you're obsessed with the kid. But she's got to think of her future. Craig's taken with her. If she plays her cards right, he could marry her. She's the same type as his last two wives.'

René Levallier was standing suddenly in front of Charlie – in a suit that could have been sculptured for him. 'Well, if it isn't Monsieur Dawson. You didn't take my advice then. You're still here in Paris.'

'I've been back home. Didn't Costa tell you?'

'Well, that was a fleeting visit, wasn't it? What have you found out about Elisabeth?'

'Quite a lot.'

'There's much to find, of course.' The perfect smile. Again the wow of the trumpet. 'Remember, if there's anything I can do to help,' Levallier said. 'There could be ways that are open to me now.'

For a second Charlie didn't understand. 'Records, for example,'

Levallier added, 'that may be still be classified as secret. Officials who'd be frank if I asked them. Things like that.'

'Of course,' Charlie said. 'Your new appointment. Forgive me, I should have congratulated you.'

Levallier shrugged as though it had never been in doubt. 'We were fond of Elisabeth.'

'I heard that Wolf caused problems between you,' Charlie ventured. 'With Madame Levallier in particular.'

A worldly smile, well controlled. 'You knew Elisabeth. A dear girl. She loved to challenge the established order. But you have to choose your timing. Her death was so tragic – *and* perplexing.'

'Perplexing?' echoed Charlie.

'No one else died during the raid, did they? We must meet again soon. Another lunch perhaps. Lucille enjoyed the last one.'

He moved on with a gesture of one hand, the white cuff revealing a large monogrammed cufflink in jade.

Max returned to Charlie's side. 'Thought any more about what Maitland said?' he enquired.

'Yeah.'

'And about what happened to Leah?' Charlie nodded. 'Come up with any answers?'

Charlie glanced at him. 'Not yet, Max but I'm getting very close.'

'And what do I do if Romy gives way – you know, says "Goodbye, Max"?'

'She said she wouldn't think of it, didn't she?' Max just looked at him, the bags heavy under his eyes, and he shook his head sceptically. 'Great number this, isn't it?' said Charlie as the singer returned to the sinister theme verse about Macheath and the jacknife he used with such gloved skill. The trumpeter took it in sweeps to a trembling high C, and the drummer ended it with a pounding flourish that provoked involuntary applause.

'Why, Charlie, I was just going to call you,' said Marie from behind him; and he turned to see her there with her big proprie-torial smile, all white teeth – in a black dress, a diamond brooch, a string of pearls – and, with Marie, you could be sure they were real.

'I've spoken to Wolf,' she went on.

A spasm of excitement that surprised him. 'What did he say?' he asked.

'He's agreed to meet you. La Vie Nouvelle tomorrow night at

ten. That's a club in the Boulevard Raspail. He wants you to take Nikki with you, but neither of you must tell a soul. Is that clear, Charlie? No one. Can you rely on the girl?'

'Oh yes – in a case like this. What do I do? Ask for him?'

'No. He'll contact you.'

'How will he know me?'

'He'll know you, Charlie,' she said. 'Will it end all the mystery – meeting him, I mean?'

'I don't know,' he said, watching her carefully. 'It must help, though.'

Marie's gaze was searching. 'When are you going to tell me, Charlie? I might have the key to the riddle. Always my ear's close to the ground, you know. It concerns Elisabeth's death, doesn't it?'

'So you know that much.'

'But she died in action, didn't she?'

'The point's not how she died, but why she died. Got any ideas?'

She shook her head. 'I don't know. What I do know is that the going's getting hotter. You heard what happened to poor Leah at La Coupole?'

'Yeah,' he said. 'It shook her. Shook me too.'

She smiled sadly. '"Et ces voix d'enfants chantant dans la Coupole." You don't recognise that, Charlie?'

He shook his head. 'Should I?'

'It's from a famous poem by a famous poet. One I thought you'd know.'

'Why did you think that?' he asked.

'Because it's Verlaine, Charlie. Because it's Verlaine.'

5

'I must be getting old, Duncan,' said the Prince. 'Horses are starting to have more appeal for me than women. Just look at those two coming now. Have you ever seen anything more beautiful?'

Both men were mounted and the string were working the Limekilns gallops where the Bury Road meets the Icknield Way. The two boys were with them on ponies. Others were watching, too – a couple of men with binoculars by a car in the road, a man riding a hack at a walk on a line parallel to the gallop.

They could be tipsters for the press, spies for the bookmakers or the big punters. The lands known as Newmarket Heath were owned by the Jockey Club but they were all very open. Usually the trainers knew the watchers, but not always.

The lads were working a straight mile and a quarter – just a couple of horses at a time, on the bridle but very close – and it was a while before these two horses were near enough to make out clearly, coming as they were out of the sun. 'That's Kestrel on the right, isn't it?' said the Prince.

'That's him,' confirmed Duncan. 'Moving well.'

The two horses passed them, with Kestrel moving easily, about three lengths ahead. 'Looks better every time I see him,' said the Prince. 'You're doing so well with him, Duncan. I'm glad I told that hack writer what he could do with his book.'

'I appreciated that enormously, Prince,' Duncan told him. 'I can think of a lot of owners who'd have taken no chances, I can tell you.'

'I've met his sort before,' Khalid said. 'You can't give in to them. What's the immediate plan for Kestrel?'

'Just one more race this season, I think,' Duncan answered. 'Doncaster probably. If he takes that, it'll have given us three good wins and make him a clear contender for Epsom next year in the ante-post market.'

Ken rode up to him. 'Sorry to interrupt, Father, but there's a man who wants to speak to you.' Duncan glanced at him in irritation. 'I told him you were with an important owner,' the boy added quickly, 'but he insisted. Wouldn't take a second, he said.'

Duncan looked at the stranger. He'd seen him before that morning – the man who'd been walking his horse beside the gallop. 'Don't mind me,' said the Prince. 'Go and see what he wants.'

Duncan rode over to him. He was wearing a check cloth cap and was about forty, with a complexion weathered red. 'That Kestrel looks exceptional,' he said.

'Good of you to say so,' said Duncan, 'but I'm with – '

'Could go a mile and a half without any trouble, couldn't he? That's providing his legs hold up.'

'What do you mean?' Duncan asked.

'Fragile animals, these thoroughbreds. Pity if anything happened to him. Of course, you're a friend of Charles Dawson, aren't you?'

'What of it?' asked Duncan, though fear was already tensing his stomach.

'Together in the war, weren't you? A kind of bond between you still, they say. Why not tell him to stop being silly?'

'I don't know what you're talking about.'

'Thought you'd say that, but you do know, don't you? Just tell Dawson, will you? That's a lovely colt . . .' He gestured at Kestrel, who was being walked towards them alongside the horse he'd been working with. 'I'd like to see him do well, meet his potential. So would you, wouldn't you?'

Abruptly he turned his horse and cantered away. 'Hey, come back!' Duncan shouted after him. 'I haven't finished with you yet! Follow him, boys,' he ordered, then thought better of it. 'No, don't! Come back, Ken.' His youngest son was already off in pursuit. He obeyed his father's order, but slowly so that he could see where the man had stopped. 'There's a box waiting for him, Father,' he said as he trotted back to him. 'About a mile up the Bury Road.'

6

'Don't turn round . . .' The words came from behind him and he froze. 'Stay as you are just for a moment . . .' The voice, coloured by a slight accent, was familiar, but Charlie couldn't place it. He did as he was ordered though, standing in the middle of the room. 'Now take off your jacket.'

'Is all this really necessary?'

'Please . . .' Where had he heard that voice before? 'Just do what I ask.' And Charlie did, holding the coat out, not knowing what to do with it.

The evening had been bizarre from the start. They had been expected at the club. There was a table reserved in the cocktail lounge, but Thierry gave no sign that he knew the reason they were there. He welcomed them in his usual friendly way, kissed Nikki warmly, shook Charlie's hand and gracefully conducted them to their seats, where he took their order for drinks. It was as though they were ordinary members enjoying an evening out. The girls were friendly, waving to Nikki as they passed, but kept their distance.

Nikki had found this disturbing. She had been wildly excited at the prospect of meeting Wolf. 'What do you think he'll be like,

Charlee?' she'd asked. 'What do I call him? Papa? Do I embrace him? I mean he does know who I am doesn't he?'

'Don't worry about it,' Charlie told her. 'He'll handle all that.'

Then Thierry came over and said that Jean-Paul had asked to see him. 'And me?' she asked eagerly.

'Just Monsieur Charlee for the moment,' Thierry said. 'Why don't you go and talk to Véronique at the bar?'

He conducted Charlie to an office on the lower floor and opened the door. The room was empty. 'Jean-Paul won't keep you a moment,' Thierry said and closed the door behind him. Charlie looked around him. There was a modern desk and, behind it, a big high-backed leather chair; also a large sofa, a cocktail cabinet, pictures on the walls of girls – scantily clothed, one or two nude. A second door, with opaque glass, was in the far wall, leading perhaps to a bedroom. It was from this entrance, at a moment when his back was towards it, that the stranger had emerged – with his quiet, chilling orders.

'Glad you're not carrying the gun,' he said. 'You can turn round now and put your coat back on if you want.'

Charlie knew who it was then. Otto, whom he'd met in New York, was sitting in the leather chair behind the desk. 'So we meet again,' he said with a smile. 'Have a seat please. I'm told it's become more urgent that you meet Wolf.'

Charlie pulled up a wooden chair. 'Marie said he'd be here tonight.'

Otto leaned forward, his elbows on the desk, fingers clasped. 'He is,' he said. 'You're speaking to him. In New York, I fear, I misled you, pretended to be my friend. I've learned to be careful.'

'You've convinced me,' said Charlie.

'You mean your gun? I'm nervous about guns.' The blue eyes were smiling. 'I like you, Charlie, but it's too soon to trust you. Now, what about those papers you spoke of last time? Did you say there was a diary?'

'I was pretending too,' Charlie answered. 'As an incentive. There is a diary, but I understand it well enough. I needed to see you for a better reason. What do you know of Elisabeth's death?'

'What you told me. It was hard to believe when I first heard. Elisabeth always seemed so indestructible. That's what *she* thought too, wasn't it?'

'Maybe she *was* indestructible, in fair play, but the cards were marked.'

286

Suddenly Wolf was alert, his eyes unblinking as he studied Charlie – a hint of the tank commander. 'What do you mean?' he asked.

'She didn't die in action. We were ordered to kill her.'

The grey eyes widened as he stared at Charlie. The colour heightened in his face, making the scar seem even whiter. But he said nothing. He got up and began to pace the room slowly, the limp more marked than it had seemed in New York. 'The games are over, Charlie,' he said at last. 'You're not going to play with me like you've played with Marie.'

'I had to. How could I trust her?'

'How can you trust me?'

'I know what Elisabeth meant to you.'

'Do you?' he asked.

'I've an idea,' Charlie said, reluctant now to repeat he'd read Wolf's letters.

Wolf was standing facing him, his head framed quaintly by the scissored legs of a nude on the wall behind him. There was nothing about him to suggest that he'd written to Elisabeth with such passion, that he'd even loved her. There was alarm in him, caution. 'What do you want of me?' he asked curtly.

Charlie was surprised by his response. He had expected an immediate offer to help, the barriers down between them. 'I thought you'd care,' he suggested.

'I care,' Wolf said. 'But I've cared too much. Got numb, I guess.'

'Was she an enemy agent?' Charlie asked.

'Elisabeth? Of course not.'

'Then why was London convinced she was?'

'How should I know? In war people often get things wrong.'

'I'll tell you why. Proof of contact with the enemy was passed to them from Paris. Whoever sent it wanted her executed. I'm looking for him. Will you help me?'

Wolf moved to the chair he'd been sitting on, leaned on the arms from behind it, his eyes searching Charlie's face. 'How far have you got?' he asked.

'I'm quite close,' Charlie answered. 'A man was murdered in New York only minutes before he could tell me. Three of the others who were with us in the Vercors are under pressure to make me give up . . .' He broke off.

'But you still don't know who?'

Charlie shook his head. 'I found a telegram on the body of the dead man. Signed Verlaine. A few words that looked like code.' He paused but Wolf offered nothing, just went on gazing at him. 'I hoped you might have a notion. Who'd stand to benefit from her death?'

There was a movement of his shoulders – the start of a shrug. 'Who indeed?' He started to pace the room again – this muscular man, standing six feet two, with his beard and strong features. 'I had no idea she was murdered,' he said. 'That's been a shock. You're right in thinking she meant a great deal to me – way back, though, when I was a different man.' Just for a moment his face was sad. 'She wouldn't approve of me now. It went on between us a long time, survived many tests. You've learned something of it, I expect.'

'I know that the High Command never quite knew how to handle it,' said Charlie.

Wolf laughed. 'It was tantalising for them – a woman of such influence that if she'd only share their great, noble Aryan vision she'd be invaluable. They couldn't understand why I couldn't convince her; they thought she didn't love me. Yet our affair went on. We took great risks – both of us. Himmler himself told me they'd thought of taking her in . . .'

'A foreign national? A journalist of her stature?'

Wolf looked pained. 'What could anyone do? We thought France might act when we took back the Rhineland – but the troops just stood there, didn't they? Even Elisabeth couldn't cause a war.'

He sat on a corner of the desk, hands deep in his jacket pockets, his eyes amused. 'When she joined the Resistance, she became a target again – almost as tantalising. By that time I was prominent in the Army. The SS couldn't mess with me too much, though at one stage they threatened to take Nikki. I said that if they did I'd go to the Führer. The Führer had always liked Elisabeth. I warned Elisabeth, told her to get a message to me at once if anything happened. She did hear something, but it was a false alarm, some other child.'

'She could get messages to you?' Charlie asked.

'She could get messages to me.' He met Charlie's eyes in mild challenge. 'Oddly,' he went on, 'it was my brother generals who persuaded me to arrange a meeting. We'd met once since the Occupation – to talk of Nikki. That was the excuse. We were both traitors. A strange sensation – to make love as enemies.' He saw Charlie's response. 'Sorry,' he said, 'that was insensitive. The generals wanted peace – not Armageddon. Germany could hardly win. Elisabeth seemed a good way to offer it.'

'You mean you met her to pass a peace offer to the Allies?'

He nodded. 'She was ideal. She had prestige. She knew everyone. She could get to Churchill himself if need be.'

'When was this?'

'February '44, I think. Maybe early March. She was on a visit to Paris.'

Charlie remembered that day in Paris. Elisabeth had been very late back to the safe house, arriving long after dinner – and been unusually withdrawn. At first she hadn't wanted to make love and, when they did, there was a desperation. She had even cried, which she had never done before.

'Did you sleep with her?' Charlie asked.

Wolf shrugged. 'We lay together – for old times' sake. But what had once been there had gone. Mainly we talked about the peace offer, but she couldn't see how she could pass it on without admitting she'd met me.

'I remember saying to her idly that I was going to be near Annecy in three weeks' time and wondered if there was any way I could see Nikki. I'd be with Rommel, who was attending a meeting in Chamonix. Then I realised what I'd revealed – to a member of the Resistance! I saw the look in her eyes. "There," I said, "I've given you a great chance – to get our most famous general. What a coup that'd be for you, wouldn't it?"

' "Yes," she agreed.

' "Your local *réseau* could find out where and when the meeting will be. Of course, it'd be traced back to me. The generals know we're meeting."

' "What would they do?"

' "Execution."

' "Their best tank general?"

' "There are others. It's not '34 now. Most of the tank regiments are being taken over by the SS – true zealots, loyal to the Führer. So my life's in your hands," I said. "What so different? You've always had my heart."

'She raised herself on her elbow. "The conflicts of war," she said. She kissed me then, on the lips, but lightly. "Don't worry, darling," she said, "I could never do it. We'll win the war without it. After all, you and your generals think so, too, don't you? That's why you're offering peace."

'She got up then and I stayed in bed and watched her dress. She combed out her hair and put on her beret. She could see me in the mirror. She gave a little shake of her head as though she didn't understand how we found ourselves in that position – and blew me a kiss as she left the room.

'I thought it was the last time I'd see her, but we did meet again a couple of days later in a hotel, just for an hour or two to settle something about Nikki. But we didn't lie together. We knew that part of our life was over. It was just business.'

For a moment, the two men were silent. 'It's a sad story,' said Charlie. 'In a way.'

Wolf sat down at the desk. 'Let's get back to the issue. If you're so close, Charlie, you'll have got a theory – suspicions at least?'

'Hardly enough for murder. Von Eysebeck's been involved on the fringes.'

A contemptuous laugh. 'Not murder.'

'You've known Marie for a long time?'

'Since 1933.'

'You'd trust her then?'

Wolf hesitated. 'I don't trust anyone – not entirely.'

'You work with her, though?'

Wolf stroked his beard, amusement in his eyes. 'Sometimes our interests coincide.'

'Elisabeth had learned about her operation in Switzerland. Could she have become a danger to her? That was just before the invasion. The Allies wouldn't have liked what Marie was doing.'

'Could she have organised it from America?'

'She was in touch with Zurich through Portugal. From Zurich contact with Paris would have been easy. She knew all about you and Elisabeth – and you were crucial to the evidence.'

'You mean I was used?'

'We were both used,' said Charlie. Wolf threw him a questioning look. 'When the order came, we had a ballot,' Charlie added. 'I was the unlucky one. There was no choice. I shot her.'

Wolf winced. 'My God,' he said. 'My God, that must have been the hardest thing you ever had to do.'

'It's made me very angry, determined. That's all.'

Wolf shook his head slightly. 'It's made me angry too, Charlie,' he said softly.

'I thought you didn't care any more.'

'I've just started caring. I'll make enquiries. We'll work together. We'll be partners.' He stood up with a sudden movement and thrust out his hand and Charlie grasped it. 'If you want to contact me, call this number in Düsseldorf,' he said, writing a number on a piece of paper. 'Say you're . . . say you're Mr Churchill.' He grinned at the notion. 'Now I'd like to meet my daughter. How much of this does she know?'

'She thinks her mother died a heroine's death,' Charlie answered and told him what she knew.

'Is she in love with you, as Marie says?'

'It was inevitable, I suppose.'

'And you're married. Well, I'm in no position to criticise, am I?'

'If I was Nikki's father I wouldn't encourage it, but it's complex. Elisabeth's an integral part of it.'

'She's still with us, isn't she?' said Wolf. 'Ironic – a bond between you and me.' He picked up the phone from the desk. 'I'd like to see Nikki now,' he said. 'Will you send her down?'

Her knock was light and she stood there, looking at her father. An odd sound came from him, as though his throat were constricted. His eyes dampened. 'My God,' he said, 'it's uncanny. You could *be* her.' He moved from the desk and held out his arms and, with a little cry, she ran into them.

It was an intimate scene and Charlie had no part in it. So he left them, closing the door behind him, and went upstairs to the bar.

7

Leah rose early. She could never sleep late before a collection – even a small mid-season one like this. Hugo hadn't stirred as she got out of bed. She took her clothes and dressed in the spare room, made a cup of coffee and left home for the five-minute walk to the shop.

It was not long after dawn on a cloudy day, and there wasn't much traffic yet – or many people about. There was a parked milk van ahead of her – a man and a boy, working the doorsteps on each side of the street, with bottles in metal carriers. It made her think of her childhood when she had always awoken to sounds of the milk deliveries. They'd used horses then to pull the vans, trained to keep up with the milkmen as they moved along the road. The man grinned at her, wished her a cheery good morning.

She turned into the King's Road and thought again about the stranger in the Boulevard du Montparnasse. In fact, he was always there in the back of her mind like a dark shadow, a voice with a Bordelais accent, coming back to her repeatedly as a catchy tune comes back. She had done as he told her – pleaded with Charlie to stop his searching, or at least to reduce it, take a breather, go back to the States. Hugo had talked to him, too. Charlie had told them both that he was sorry he couldn't, but thought it would all be resolved soon. Hugo, being Hugo, had grown abusive. 'If anything happens to Leah, I'll never forgive you, Charlie,' he said.

'Easy now,' Charlie answered. 'Nothing's going to happen to Leah. That's not what the man said.'

'Or the business,' declared Hugo.

'Or the business. What can they do? Set fire to the shop? You're insured, aren't you? So what'd be the point?'

'I mean it, Charlie. If anything happens, I'm going to beat you so blue that even your Nikki won't recognise you.'

'Now, Hugo, that sort of talk doesn't help.'

Of course, Hugo had this instinctive response to anything linked to Elisabeth. The mere mention of her name was enough to infuriate him – even more so, strangely, since he'd told Leah about the way Elisabeth had got him and his father out of Germany. Also, she knew Hugo felt badly about the Dawn business. Not that he ever said so: he wasn't that kind of man.

She had spoken to Dawn about the way she'd sprung her sudden collection, or rather Dawn had spoken to *her*. Leah hadn't complained, but she'd been cool. 'You sound a bit put out, sweetie,' Dawn said. 'But I told you what I was doing, didn't I? Well, perhaps not in so many words, but I gave you the message like a good friend.'

'I'm glad Hugo was such a help to you,' Leah countered and immediately wished she hadn't.

'Now, sweetie,' Dawn cooed, 'that's really a little ungenerous. Just a touch of the little green god, eh?'

Hugo had made the best of it, insisting she shouldn't cancel the show which had been her first thought. After all, the new skirts wouldn't be the biggest sellers: they were just something for the press, weren't they? Her collection was terrific – girls would be falling over themselves to wear her designs. But she ought to keep the short numbers in – just to emphasise the trend. His enthusiasm had convinced her, and by that morning she was excited, as she always was before a show.

She arrived at the shop and took a careful look at the display in the window. She always enjoyed that, though they'd be changing it later, dressing it with one or two of the numbers from the collection. She unlocked the glass front door, relocked it behind her, walked through the showroom and down the stairs to the workroom that adjoined her office.

The door of this was open, which was odd, for normally she kept it closed, and as she went in she had a feeling that something wasn't quite right about the workroom. Then, from the doorway, she saw the open window, unlatched, with the glass broken.

She turned back into the workroom and realised what was missing. The clothes for the model girls to wear in the show should have been hanging on rails, beneath dustcovers – positioned at the side of the staircase outside the line of vision of anyone descending. But now Leah could see that there was nothing on the rails. The dustcovers lay in a crumpled heap on the floor. The clothes had gone – only hours before they were due to be displayed on the catwalk.

It took a few seconds for her to take in the reality of what had happened, then she grabbed the phone to call Hugo. Oddly, her first thought was that Dawn was involved somehow.

'What do you mean, darling?' Hugo said. 'Dawn's not a burglar.'

'She stole my idea, didn't she?'

'Now come on, darling. She was thinking along the same lines as you. OK, she rushed her show to get in first, but now you're talking about a break-in. It must be that man in Paris.'

'Oh my God,' Leah cried, 'what are we going to do?'

'You're going to make a cup of coffee, sit down quietly in your office, and wait for me. I'll be there just as soon as I've phoned the police.'

Leah had two calls that day – in the chaos of phoning everyone who'd been invited to the show. One was from Dawn, who said: 'I've just heard the news, sweetie. I'm devastated. It's unbelievable. Who'd do a thing like that?'

'We've got an idea,' said Leah.

'That sounds sinister, sweetie. In fact, it makes me think. I had a reporter on the phone about a week ago. At least, he said he was a reporter – from the *Standard*. He was talking about the collection – my collection, I mean. Then he mentioned you. Well, they often put us together, don't they? And he asked if you had a collection imminent too – or whether you'd be waiting for the London showings in October. Well, I said you had an early one – I even told him the date. Sweetie, I hope I didn't do the wrong thing. It was only after the call that it struck me as odd. I mean, anyone who worked for the *Standard* would have known, wouldn't he, or could have found out from the Fashion Desk?'

The other call was brief. She recognised the Bordelais accent at once. 'Well I warned you, didn't I, Miss Grant?'

'Why?' she screamed. 'Why have you done this terrible thing to me? I did what you asked. I spoke to Mr Dawson. My husband even threatened him. But we couldn't persuade him.'

'Then you must try harder, mustn't you?' said the caller and hung up.

8

Duncan hadn't taken lightly the threat on the Limekilns. He had called in a security firm to set up a twenty-four-hour patrol of the yard and alerted the police. The boxes on both sides of Kestrel's, which had been fitted with heavy padlocks, had been scrubbed out and fitted with special alarm bells. The horse's lad slept on one side, and Ken and Rob were taking it in turns to spend the nights in the other. No new staff were taken on. When Kestrel went out with the string, outriders on hacks rode each side of him on the way to the training grounds and kept strangers away while he was waiting to work.

For a few days all the precautions seemed unnecessary. No one came near the yard. Nothing unusual happened at the gallops. The security patrols had nothing to report.

When he heard about Leah's burglary, Duncan called in a director of the security firm and the Newmarket police chief to make sure no aspect of security had been overlooked. They were both confident. There had, after all, been no protection at all to Leah's premises. A child could have got in, the police chief asserted.

Then, after a week, Kestrel was pulled up during the morning's work, slightly lame in his off foreleg. No one thought anything of it. Every week horses would strain a tendon or a hamstring, hurt a heel. The legs of thoroughbreds were almost absurdly fragile for the speed and weight they had to bear. Bob Williams, Duncan's favourite vet, was called in to examine Kestrel – a matter of routine for a horse of that value. He would return tomorrow, he said.

Duncan had insisted from the start that his two sons should play a prominent part in Kestrel's protection. He kept them out of school and gave them daytime duty rotas. It was good experience, Duncan reckoned, and they mixed easily with the lads.

He trusted his lads, but it was always possible that one might be attracted by a large bribe, and they were the obvious way to get at a horse – especially through his feed. Eighty horses had to be fed three times a day and, although Kestrel was treated as a special case under tight supervision, there was quite a mêlée.

The day after the vet's first call, Rob had been on duty all morning and Ken was due to take over the afternoon shift at 12.30 – but at fifteen he'd just fallen for the first girl ever to take his fancy. She was free for an hour until 1.30 and Ken begged his brother to stay on for the extra hour – promising he'd repay the favour. Rob, easy-going as always, had agreed.

At one o'clock, when the lads were at dinner, the vet had returned for a routine call, as he'd said he would, though he hadn't actually arranged a time – and it wasn't Mr Williams himself. It was a man of about thirty-five named Fraser who said that Mr Williams wasn't feeling too well that day. Rob had never seen him before, but there were several vets in the practice, so it didn't strike him as strange.

He cleared Fraser's access to the yard with the security guard and went with him to Kestrel's box. The vet felt the swelling. 'Doesn't seem too bad,' he said, 'but Mr Williams wants him to have a shot – a relaxant for the muscles.' He prepared the injection, gave the hypodermic a little squirt to clear any air bubbles, and pierced the horse's skin with the needle. He was in no great hurry as they left the box, asking about his next race and hazarding a guess that he'd be back at work by the end of the week.

Half an hour later, just after Ken had taken over from his brother, he visited Kestrel's box. He was appalled to find the colt lying sprawled on the straw, half on his side, one forefoot thrust forward, totally still. Desperately the boy unbolted the door, rushed into the box and bent down to examine the horse more closely. He wasn't dead, but his breathing was so shallow that he probably soon would be.

Ken felt the shadow as someone stood in the stable doorway, blocking the light. He looked up. He had never seen his father so angry, and he was scared.

'I couldn't even leave you with security men to support you!' Duncan shouted.

'But Father – ' Ken began.

'Don't try to make excuses. You've failed in your duty. You've let the whole family down.'

'Father, please – ' the boy tried again, close to tears.

'I just want the answer to one question,' demanded Duncan. 'Who's been near the horse?'

'Rob said the vet came.'

'What vet?'

'Someone from Mr Williams.'

'Not Mr Williams himself?'

'I don't think so.'

'What do you mean, you don't think so? Weren't you here?'

'No, Father.'

'That's all I need to know. Ring Mr Williams and get him here at once. Tell Vincent to come here with Frank. Then go to your room and stay there. I'll talk to you later.' Duncan was bending down by the horse, cradling his head on his knees. Vincent was the head lad. Frank looked after the horse.

'But Father, you're not being fair,' Ken insisted. 'Rob was here. No one's failed.'

Duncan was examining the horse's eye, holding back the lid. 'Do as you're told, *now*!' he ordered.

'Yes, Father,' said Ken as Duncan wrenched Kestrel's teeth apart to look at his tongue. The boy ran to the house, no longer able to hold back his tears.

Duncan didn't follow him for over an hour. By then Williams had examined the horse and taken a blood sample. 'He's not dying,' he said. 'He's been sedated. What did you say the man's name was?' he asked Rob, who had been summoned to the box.

'Fraser.'

'What did he look like?'

'Thirties. Fair. Not very tall.'

'It's odd,' said Williams. 'I had a journalist on the phone. Said he'd just joined the *Sporting Life*. He'd heard a rumour that Kestrel had gone lame. He knew he'd won both his races, and was wondering about Doncaster, where he'd be fancied on his form. Would he be fit? he asked. I said I was sure he would, since it was only a knock. He was interested in the treatment, as sports writers often are, and I told him. I said I'd be seeing him again today, but it was pretty routine.'

'So he knew a vet would be expected,' said Duncan.

'He knew when, too. A woman rang this morning and spoke to my secretary. Told her they'd got a bit of a problem at the Smith yard, nothing too serious, and was I visiting the Fordham Road today? Naturally she checked my appointments and told her. So he knew enough to get here before me. The caller rang back and cancelled. I bet you we'll find that no one rang from Smith's.

'My guess is that someone just wanted to put the horse off colour for a bit, interrupt the training programme – in a dramatic way! I'd say he's had a shot of Etorphine. Know what that is, Rob?' he asked the boy.

'No, Mr Williams.'

'Called Elephant Juice in the trade, as your father knows well enough.' He glanced at Duncan, but he was too shocked for light banter. 'What they use for sedative darts for wild animals. Needs delicate handling. Very small doses are useful for geeing up horses, but more sends them to sleep. More still and the effect's the opposite and they're climbing over the ceiling.'

Williams picked up his bag and left the box. 'Odd business,' he said as he walked through the yard with Duncan. 'He knew what he was doing – if I'm right, that is. Couldn't be a warning of some kind, could it?'

When Duncan returned to the house, he found Annette waiting in the kitchen. 'You realise Ken's still in his room?' she asked.

'Oh, I forgot about him,' Duncan said.

'He said he had nothing to do with it. Is that true?'

'Apparently. The boys swopped rotas.'

'I hope you'll apologise. He's very upset.'

'I'll have a word with him.' Duncan went upstairs to Ken's room. 'Sorry to have got it wrong, old chap,' he said.

The boy managed a smile. 'Give a dog a bad name, I suppose, Father.'

'Sort of.'

'I think I'd have let the vet in, just as Rob did. Then you'd have thought I was running to form, wouldn't you?'

'Well, maybe there's a lesson there,' said Duncan. 'You need to look good in the Form Book.'

'A lesson for sons?' asked Ken. 'Or for fathers?'

The tears welled in his eyes and Duncan was moved. He embraced the boy. 'You've got a good point there,' he said, 'and it's been well noted by the trainer.'

It was then that Duncan was called to the phone. 'How's the colt?' he was asked by the voice he recognised.

'Now listen to me – ' Duncan began.

'Just do as I said,' the caller told him, 'and the horse'll be running next year. Otherwise . . .'

'Say I can make some headway with Charles Dawson.'

'If he sees sense, you mean?'

'Yes.'

'Then call a number I'll give you and leave a message. Just say: "Mr Smith agrees." It's an answering service who don't know the identity of their client, so there's no point in the police checking the number. And, mister, no other tricks. Dawson had better be serious, or the colt will die.'

9

Charlie stood at the window looking at the trees in Hyde Park. He felt like an animal at bay – isolated, panting, running a little scared.

All five of the old Vercors group were there – summoned by Duncan to a suite at the Dorchester. But this was no reunion. This was crisis. The bond between them was fractured – the damage clear in the façade like cracks in an old building.

Kestrel had been the breaking point. The Prince had backed Duncan over Maitland's book, but horses were different. He'd put the ten best with another trainer – including the star colt.

Leah was still in a state of shock. Max too was shattered. Romy had weakened, as Charlie had expected, under the threat of scandal. Those Nazi revelations would have been too much in France. The telegram had come that morning. 'Dreadfully sorry but sure you'll understand. Writing darling.'

Duncan had stood in front of the fireplace, looking very solid in his tweed suit, his hands behind his back. 'It's the end of the road, Charlie,' he said. 'You've got to drop it.'

Charlie had looked at him for a second and shaken his head. He'd glanced at the others in turn. They agreed with Duncan. Even Sonya thought that things had gone too far. He had moved to the window to distance himself from them all.

He needed time to compose himself. Out in the Park the leaves were turning. In a few days, they'd be falling. A London autumn. He looked up at the sky. Scudding clouds revealed the sun for an instant – a bright moment before others covered it, dulling the light. The sky was darker over Battersea. It'd be raining soon.

He understood the reaction of the others well enough, and felt for them. He'd even expected the showdown. Why should they risk so much? Charlie would have done, of course. His ships could have been sunk, his marriage destroyed; his resolve would have been unshaken. But he'd become a zealot. Life was easy for zealots.

'You've got to laugh, haven't you?' he said at last without turning. 'Remember how it was in April? Jesus, that's only five months ago. There we were in Paris, talking about how close we all were, like a family with a secret language.'

Charlie's words weren't loud. 'Remember what you said, Duncan? Wouldn't miss a reunion. Not even the Prince could make you do that. Then Leah talked of how Hugo had tried to stop her coming with a trick about an order. In sixteen years, we said, nothing had changed. It was as if we'd only left the Massif a week before. But something's changed now, hasn't it – and it's certainly not Elisabeth, or what she did for us all.'

'You're being unfair, Charlie,' said Duncan. 'We're not fighting a war any longer.'

'Yes we bloody are!' Charlie swung round. 'I'm fighting a war, Duncan.'

'You can't win it,' he answered. 'No one can.'

'I'm going to win it. You watch.'

'What's winning?' asked Leah. 'A prosecution?'

'Perhaps. If I can get the proof.'

'And if you can't?'

'Then I'll think of something.'

'Charlie,' Max interposed in a tired voice, 'you don't even know there was a crime. You're just guessing.'

'I know,' said Charlie. '*You* know, for Christ's sake. Why the hell are you getting all this action if there was no crime?'

'OK,' Max agreed, 'maybe there was a crime. But even if you solve it, how can it help Elisabeth? She'll still be dead. So where will it have got you?'

Charlie hesitated. 'At peace. Knowing we've honoured her, done the right thing.'

'Mighty fine sentiments,' Max mocked, his eyes angry in his immobile face. 'It's easy for you. Nothing's happened to your business.'

'Do you think that'd make a difference to me? Seriously?'

Max shook his head. 'I'm in big trouble, Charlie,' he said.

'I know, Max,' Charlie said.

'I can't afford nostalgia.'

'I understand what you're going through. I'll do anything to help.'

'How can you help?' asked Leah. 'Except by stopping, as Duncan says.'

'Money, Leah. Influence. Any favour you care to name. You want me to bear your loss?'

'It's not just the money, Charlie. It's the prestige, doing what you need to do – a career, I suppose.' She looked so distraught that Charlie put his hand on her shoulder.

'I know,' he assured her.

'When you get right down to it,' Duncan said, 'it's revenge you're after, isn't it?'

Charlie stared at him, suddenly angry. 'Don't knock revenge, Duncan. Why do the police hunt murderers for years? Because a society needs it – and I sure as hell need it.'

'It was sixteen years ago, Charlie,' Leah said. 'A different world.'

'So it doesn't matter?' he queried. 'Is that what you're saying, Leah?'

He'd shamed her. 'No, of course not. I owe her so much, but how long's it going to go on, Charlie?'

'Not long, I'd guess. I'm near. I've met Wolf and he's agreed to help. That's important.'

'Because he's a crook?' Duncan challenged.

Charlie faced him out. 'Possibly. I'll use anyone's help to find out who murdered Elisabeth.'

'*You* murdered Elisabeth,' said Max. It was almost a whisper, but he was breaking the rules and, for Charlie, it was like a punch in the face.

'How can you say that?' he retorted in quiet fury. 'Remember Duncan's order? Whoever had to do it must never never breathe a word. All our fingers were on the trigger. I'm surprised at you, Max.'

Max avoided his eyes. 'I'm a realist,' he said defensively, 'fighting for my life.'

'You were used to kill her too, Max. Get that straight.'

'Now let's cool down a bit,' urged Duncan. 'I've got a compromise, Charlie. We all loved Elisabeth, but we've got to think of our future – and she'd expect us to. Say you give it a break for a few weeks. Go back home to Philana.'

'Don't be dumb,' Max put in. 'He won't do that. Not with the kid in Paris.'

'I'll call the number as instructed and say Mr Smith agrees,' Duncan went on. 'That'd take the heat off. I could probably save the horses. Max could talk Romy round. Leah could rework her collection. Then you can pick up the chase again later.'

'That's worth thinking about,' said Sonya, speaking for the first time and mainly for Charlie.

'It's Sonya speaking,' Max reminded him. 'Nothing's happened to Sonya yet either.'

'I'm expecting to be fired any minute,' she said.

'So what do you say, Charlie?' asked Duncan.

He shook his head. 'Sorry – I'm not letting up for a minute. The trail may go cold.'

'What trail?' demanded Duncan. 'There is no trail.'

'You wouldn't have said that if you'd seen Roger Briedon lying dead on the carpet.'

The telephone rang. Sonya, who was nearest, picked it up. 'A call for Mr Dawson,' she said. 'New York.'

'Charlie . . .' It was Terry's familiar voice. 'Am I glad to have got you! That pa-in-law of yours has gone bananas. Right out of his skull. Know what he's done? Filed a restraint order in the Marine Court here to arrest *Pacific Star*.'

'You're kidding,' said Charlie.

'Wish I was. She's due in Rotterdam today. By now they're probably nailing the order to the mast and no one'll be allowed to touch her until the court says they can.'

'On what grounds?'

'Theft. He says you haven't paid for her.'

'That's true, as you know. He said there were problems and we'd settle the payment later. Meanwhile I could take her.'

'That's not what he's saying now. He's pressing the police to prosecute. Wants you arrested the moment you re-enter the country. If you don't come back, he'll go for extradition.'

'He's gone crazy. I'll call him.'

Charlie put the phone down. 'Mastorakis should be in a madhouse,' he said as he dialled the New York number. 'He's putting the police on me. Hope that makes you feel better, Max. Costa,' he said when he was put through, 'what the hell's all this about?'

'You've stolen my ship.'

'I can hear you laughing, you crazy old bugger.'

'I'm not laughing. I'm sad. My daughter's husband steals my ship.'

'You said I could take it, that we'd deal with the details later.'

'I don't see that in writing. I see no cheque.'

'That's garbage, Costa. What are you trying to do?'

'Get you in jail. That'd be best for everybody, especially Philana.'

'It won't do the family name any good, her husband in jail.'

'Better than her husband dead,' answered Costa and rang off.

'He's afraid they're going to take me out,' Charlie told the others. 'Thinks I'd be safer behind bars. If he'd listened I'd have told him what I've said before. Anything I know, you'll all know. So there wouldn't be any point, would there?'

'Oh yes there would,' Duncan asserted. 'That's what we're saying, Charlie. You can't rely on us to help any more.'

Charlie looked at Sonya and she gave a kind of helpless shrug. 'OK,' he said. 'That tells me. From now on, I'll go it alone.'

Twenty

I

It was late morning and, though quite cool, the sun was out and the women on the broad pavements of the Champs-Elysées were still in their summer dresses. They were at Fouquet's and Nikki, in yellow which set off her black hair, was so breath-taking Charlie couldn't take his eyes off her – as she acknowledged with a small smile.

She had acquired a new poise, making her seem even more her mother's daughter. Elisabeth had always had a sense of control, even in the crises. That day, though, Nikki was in one of her quiet, introspective moods. 'When I'm away from you, I get afraid something's changed,' she said. 'When I'm with you I know that nothing has. You're built into my life now, Charlee – and I'm even more scared.'

He took her hand, wondering what was coming. They hadn't seen each other for a couple of days, since he'd been in England, and she'd rung saying she had something to tell him. 'Scared?' he echoed. 'What do you mean?'

'Why didn't you say you were going to London?'

'I tried to reach you,' he said, 'but you were too busy with your new life. It was a last-minute thing.'

'Business?' she asked. 'Or Thelma?'

'Not poor old Thelma again,' he sighed.

'She's not old,' she said, looking at him, her eyes wide. She mouthed a silent kiss. 'You'd never tell me what that was about. There's so much you won't tell me, Charlee. Are you surprised I'm scared? Max was with you in London, too, wasn't he?'

'That's where his office is, remember?'

'Sonya's office isn't.'

'She had a story. She often goes to London.'

'I bet you saw Leah and Duncan as well.'

'We had one of our get-togethers,' he agreed.

'Was my father there?'

'Of course not.'

'Why "of course"? I was his long-lost daughter, yet he sent for you first.'

'He wanted to make sure it wasn't a set-up. I told you.'

She looked at him doubtfully, then shook her head. 'I think it's the same secret. Oh, Charlee, I wish I didn't love you. No, I don't mean that. But you'll be very careful, won't you? For my sake?'

'What is all this? Someone been talking to you?'

'No,' she answered, 'not even Max and he never stops talking. I asked Sally.'

'And what did she say?'

'That there was something odd about the whole Elisabeth business. She's an awful sourpuss, Sally is. What's so odd about it, Charlee?'

'She was special to us. You know that. Her death was terrible.'

She was watching him. 'Something new's happened. I think you're in danger. I had a dream,' she said.

'We all have bad dreams sometimes.' He wondered what she'd have said if she'd known that the police had been enquiring for him at the hotel – just making sure he was staying there, they'd told the friendly desk clerk, an unofficial check requested by the New York Police Department.

Charlie had called Costa again. 'I'm placing the two million with lawyers in escrow,' he told him, 'pending production of the documents.'

'Don't waste your time,' his father-in-law said. 'I'm not selling to a thief.'

'Costa, will you stop being so dumb.'

'You're going to jail, Charlie. The gendarmes will be waiting for you just as soon as I can fix it.'

Charlie knew it would take some time to fix – even for Costa with his short cuts. But he needed time himself. Maybe he should move in with Nikki. Evasion in the maze of little streets round Saint-Séverin would be easier than at the Bristol. But she would be really frightened harbouring a wanted man.

He took her hand. 'What's this you've got to say to me?' he asked.

She hesitated. 'It doesn't seem so important now,' she said. 'You didn't want me to make love with Craig, did you?'

He felt the old stab of jealousy. He sipped his drink. 'I'm in no position to make rules – as I said.' His voice was calmer than he'd thought it would be.

'But you didn't want me to, did you?' she pressed.

'Of course not but – '

She cut in: 'No buts, darling. Just say the words: 'I didn't want you to.'

He smiled. 'OK, I didn't want you to.'

'Darling.'

'Darling,' he added obediently.

'Then you'll be pleased. I said no, Charlee.'

Charlie was so relieved he felt ashamed. 'Was he upset?' he asked.

'A little, I think. Not many girls turn him down. Not girls like me who are just getting their first chance.'

'Have you still got the part?'

'I think so, though he did talk vaguely about still casting.' She grinned. 'See what I've done for you – risked my chance of being a star.'

'You'll be a star.'

He had disappointed her. His response was too muted. 'Don't you realise what I did for you, Charlee?' she asked.

'Did you want him?'

'I only want you, Charlee. You've spoiled everyone else for me. But you've missed the point.'

'The point is did you want him?' he insisted gently.

'Say I did want him. Would that make it all right for you? Wouldn't you think of me lying there with him, saying the kind of things I say to you, doing what we do together – '

'Don't, Nikki,' he said. 'It's unthinkable.'

'Knowing with another man the joy we know together,' she challenged, 'crying the things I cry at climax – '

'Nikki, stop this. You know how I feel. I adore you. But I can't escape the fact that I'm in your way.'

She gazed at him tenderly, then a bit desperately. 'I want you to be in my way, but I want you to know what it's like. With Craig, it was a big decision. Think of what he was offering, Charlee.'

'Darling, you're independent now.'

'Why is it I weaken whenever you call me darling? Other people throw it around as though it doesn't mean a thing.'

'What is this?' he asked. 'Women are saying no all the time.

You're a lovely girl. You knock over every man you meet.' Suddenly he understood. 'I've got it. Doing it would have been no big deal. *Not* doing it was the test.'

She was furious. 'Sometimes I hate you, Charlee,' she said.

He kissed the back of her fingers, feeling he'd been too rough. 'He won't back out, darling. He's not going to cast you in an important movie just because you sleep with him.'

She looked away. They were seeing it from different points of view. 'Max'll know if the role's still mine,' she said. 'I asked him to meet us here. Have you quarrelled with Max, Charlee?'

Charlie paused. 'Not exactly quarrelled.'

'And the others? Oh God,' she said anxiously, 'not Sonya surely?'

He was saved from answering by the sight of Max making his way towards them between the tables. He was unhurried, seeming slightly bowed, his long face gloomy. When he reached them he acknowledged Charlie silently with a raised hand, Red Indian fashion. 'I've just been with Craig,' he said to Nikki. 'You've got to be nicer to him, honey. He's giving you a big break, you know.'

'You mean I've got to sleep with him?'

'Well, maybe not every inch of the way but . . .'

She turned to Charlie. 'What do you think of that then?'

'What I've just said.'

'Charlee's just told me that you don't get cast in a major movie by sleeping with the director.'

'He has, has he?' said Max. 'He's a great student of human nature is Charlie. OK, you've got to be right for the role, but who knows what other kid might be right too.'

'So,' said Nikki, her eyes on Charlie, 'say I take my clothes off to make sure as Max is urging . . .'

'Now I never urged that, honey . . .' Max said.

'You want me to say "Please don't," right?' said Charlie.

'Is that so hard?' she asked.

'It's not hard, but I want *you* to decide. Is Craig worth it?' Charlie asked. 'For the fame, for the money, for what? Anyway, Max, surely those days are over, aren't they?'

'Those days will never be over, Charlie. You did a great test, honey,' he said to her. 'I've got total faith in you, my cherub. We'll sell you. But you need the right vehicle and this is it, baby. So just oil the wheels for me. You don't have to open your legs, but play along a little, will you? Be fun – anyway until we sign. Why not join him now at the George V? He wants to take you to lunch.'

'This minute?' He nodded. She shrugged and stood up. 'Tell me, Charlee,' she asked, 'wouldn't Maman have done it? Anything for a story.'

'She'd have had to like the guy, I think, or she'd have used a different method. She'd have got the story all right, but not many people made your mother do something she didn't want to, I can tell you. Elisabeth grasped life. She was in charge.'

Nikki's eyes suddenly filled with tears. For a second she closed them. 'Did she grasp death too, Charlee?'

She started to walk away, then turned – her pain showing in her face. 'Will I see you tonight?' she called out.

'We'll have dinner,' he answered.

Max watched her as she left the café. 'French women walk so beautifully, don't they?' he said.

'I didn't know you were back in Paris,' said Charlie.

'Protecting my investment,' Max answered. 'With Romy gone, she's all I've got. Craig's pretty sour.'

'Because she hasn't come across?'

'He expects to have a rapport with a young actress he's working with so closely. And you know how Nikki goes on. Like she's not wearing knickers, like she's screaming for it. Then when he takes her tiny hand in his, she suddenly gets morality.'

'She doesn't realise half the time what she's doing,' said Charlie. 'In some ways she's still a kid.'

'Well *you* know don't you, Charlie. One look from you and she's on her back because you had this big thing with her mother – and that sure seems to set her on fire. Maybe makes you burst into flames, too. Do you think of Elisabeth when you're screwing her?'

'Don't talk like that, Max. Not about either of them.'

'Forgive me, I'm just a crude bastard,' Max jeered in falsetto. 'Does she know yet what happened to her mother? What really happened?'

'You know she doesn't. We've talked of it often, haven't we?'

'I don't want to talk to you at all, Charlie. The only reason I'm here now is because the girl's my future and you control her. So I need you. I wish I didn't. It's like needing a case of TNT. You got any further with the great quest?'

'Give me time, Max,' said Charlie standing up to leave. 'We only left London yesterday.'

'Time's running out, Charlie. I'm a desperate man. So you better show some fast results or you know what? I'll tell the girl – every fucking detail. As it happened in glorious Technicolor.'

Charlie felt so cold suddenly that he shivered. 'You do that, Max, and I'll never forgive you.'

Max's dark, passive face creased into a rare smile. 'How do you think she'd feel then about those nights of wild ecstacy, Charlie – knowing you drilled her mother full of holes? And don't say you didn't. I saw you. Boy, we'll show that scene in close-up.'

'You bastard,' said Charlie. 'I'll hound you. I may even kill you.'

'Give up, Charlie,' urged Max, 'like Duncan suggested. For a while, at least, so we can mend the fences. Give up or for Christ's sake win – but fast.'

2

René had left the curtains drawn – thick and heavy, blanking out the light except for a beam from the slit where they joined. It was afternoon and they could see each other easily enough, but he was in an odd mood. His desire was as strong as ever, but it was contained, sensual, lingering, so that the needing was prolonged. As a man he was so changeable. Sonya never quite knew what kind of lover she was going to find.

They lay in Lucille's great bed with the covers thrown back. He had savoured her whole body, unhurriedly, starting by taking each of her toes in his mouth – then lightly kissing the inside of her calves, licking the cavity behind her knees, brushing her open thighs with his lips, moving ever higher until he could part her with delicate fingers so that his tongue could reach within her, stroke her, flick her. Gently, he took her in his teeth. 'Not hurting am I?' he asked.

'It's incredible,' she answered.

'Don't come yet, will you?' he said.

'I'm not promising,' she whispered.

It had been one of those times when it was almost perfect in the sense that there was nothing he could have done to her or she could have done to him that could have improved the complete-ness, the union, the heights that they attained – which on reflection would strike her as strange, as part of some grand plan by a deity with a sense of humour. God's joke, as Elisabeth would say.

Sonya had never before been in the Levallier mansion on the Avenue Foch – and she had only been invited that day because Lucille was in America and the house was closed and the servants absent. René, in his new position, had the use of an official apartment. He had suggested they went to his home since he was expecting a phone call that he didn't want to go through the Ministry switchboard.

'You might find the visit amusing,' he had said. He had taken her on a tour of the ornate living rooms, looking unused like a museum with the soft furnishings covered with dustsheets. They had ended up in the imposing master bedroom, with its paintings on the wall that were sensual but tasteful, Empire furniture, curtains and covers in soft shades of pink and blue. When he'd suggested they made love there, she'd wondered about his motive.

'Wouldn't you prefer it in a different room?' she asked. There were another fifteen, not counting the servants' quarters. 'Some-how a bed seems more a wife's than a husband's.'

'It's the best bed. Will it bother you?'

'Not if it won't bother *you*,' she answered. 'I've never met Lucille.' He'd kissed her then and begun to unbutton her dress and the discussion was over. But it made her wonder about him as she lay there naked. Was it, deep down in his subconscious, a deliberate slight of his wife? The thought didn't linger. After all, his wife would never know.

The telephone rang – his important call. 'Do you want me to leave you?' she asked.

'You don't need to,' he said, 'but it'll take a while and bore you to death.'

'Then I'll go exploring,' she said. She didn't dress, since she would be returning. Instead she put on his shirt that had been lying on the floor. She caught a glimpse of herself in a mirror. With the tails reaching almost to her knees, she thought she looked rather fetching. So did he. He smiled approvingly as he began to speak on the phone, and she blew him a kiss as she went through the doorway.

She wandered from room to room, wondering again at the size and elegance of the house. She'd always known René was rich, but the sheer weight of his fortune was somewhat underlined by the magnificence of his home.

She opened yet another door with the pannelling picked out in gold leaf and found herself in what could only be his study – a wall of books, some volumes that looked ancient and were doubtless of great value; a huge desk in walnut, set so that René's back, when he was working, would be to the tall French windows – covered that day by drawn curtains, like those in the rest of the house.

She examined the books, looking instinctively – as Charlie would have – for the works of Verlaine. They were there, of course, and she pulled one out and flicked through the pages. She put it back, noticing that there was a gap in the set as though a volume had been removed.

She wandered to the desk, moving round it to switch on the lamp. Everything on it was antique – even the blotter with its leather corners, the pages virgin white. She noticed that a side drawer had a key in it – again a sign that the house was currently unused, since the key wouldn't be there if it protected anything private.

Idly she turned the key and pulled open the drawer. It was empty except for a small book bound in leather. She took it up. It was a volume of Verlaine – part of the set on the shelves. She opened the flyleaf – and was shocked to her bones, her heart pounding, the nausea rising.

She was looking at the crucial words in the telegram Charlie had found on Roger Briedon's dead body in New York: 'The violins of autumn.' They were written on a slip of paper clipped to the first page. The phrase had struck Sonya as though it had been ringed in red – but in fact it was an item on a list that clearly formed the basis of a code. Written alongside each, where the meaning wasn't obvious, were the short messages they were intended to convey.

The code was crude. She was acquainted with codes. During the war, signals had usually been in numbers or letters, representing words in some prearranged form. A message could have been sent to Briedon in that pattern – a group of figures linked to the words of Verlaine. The figures 22, for example, could mean the second word on the second line or indicate individual letters. The instruction in that wire had been very simple. Briedon had asked what he should do. Don't play the violins of autumn meant: Don't do anything until telephone contact is made. But the police, who would be certain to find the message, couldn't know that, couldn't pursue it. The time of that call had been stated so that Briedon would be in his apartment, and alone, when the gunman arrived.

It was a few moments before Sonya could take in the horror of what she was facing – or the implications. Her lover was Verlaine. Her lover had ordered the death of Briedon and, almost certainly, arranged the murder of Elisabeth. On this day of all days, it was hard to absorb, for she felt closer to him, more in love with him than she had ever been before. But she knew she must force herself to confront the truth. She tried to consider the options open to her. Should she steal the book? No, for that would reveal what she knew and set both herself and Charlie up as targets. That in itself seemed inconceivable. That he would kill her – the man she'd just permitted to possess her, the man who'd known the most private, personal part of her in the most intimate way possible!

She realised she would have to return to René. His phone call would be over soon. She put the book back in the drawer, closed and locked it. Somehow she'd have to contrive to behave normally, even to make love again. Could she? It seemed impossible, but he'd expect it – especially after what had gone before.

She could pretend to feel unwell, she supposed, but the performance would have to be good – as it would if she went back to his bed. Any wrong note and he might remember the volume in his desk, and guess she had been in his study.

She shivered. In that huge empty house with no servants, she'd be exposed. No one knew she was there, and if René suspected she'd seen the Verlaine code his hand would be forced.

What she did now would clearly be vital. It was then, as she was standing beside the desk, that the door to the study began to open. She leaped to the bookcase, an instinctive move to distance herself from the drawer, and pretended she'd been examining the volumes on the shelves. 'You have a marvellous collection of – ' she began, expecting him to appear in the doorway. But it wasn't René. It was Lucille.

The two women looked at each other for a moment without

speaking, both shocked. Sonya had only seen press photos of her, usually in ball gowns, but in the flesh she had a presence, as though born to the aristocracy. Cool, unperturbed – perhaps, unbelievably, a little amused. 'I know who you are, of course,' said Lucille, 'though I hardly expected to find you in my husband's shirt. It's attractive. I should wear it again. Do you feel it gives me an advantage, that you're – how shall I say – underdressed?'

Sonya's laugh was mirthless. She was confused, experiencing fear, shock, embarrassment now. 'A little, I'd say,' she answered. 'Plus finding me in your home.'

'And my bed, I gather. That's going a little far, don't you think?'

'He needed to be near the phone.'

Lucille strolled towards her, elegant in a fawn velvet suit that was exquisitely cut. She sat on a corner of the desk and folded her arms. 'You're more attractive than the picture in your column. They should do something about that.'

'I'll pass on your message,' said Sonya. She felt even more uncomfortable. 'May I sit down?' she asked.

'Take the master's chair,' Lucille said agreeably.

Sonya sat at the desk, crossing one leg over the other. 'We thought you were in America.'

'I came back early – to find out what was going on. He's keen on you. Do you want him?'

Sonya was appalled. Want him? How could she possibly want a killer?

'Divorce is out of the question, of course – a man in his position. But something less, perhaps . . .' Lucille's voice trailed off. 'I could end it completely. I know the truth about the Frankfurt corruption story. But there'd only be someone else.'

To Sonya, the scene had the quality of a nightmare. Then suddenly she realised that Lucille's return was a means of escape. 'What do you want exactly?' she asked.

Lucille shrugged. 'I may hate you a little,' she said, wandering over to the bookshelf, 'but I'm used to it now. You were with Elisabeth in the Vercors, weren't you?'

'Yes.'

'I used to worry sometimes about René and Elisabeth, but then she fell for Wolf. You know about Wolf, I hear. Poor Wolf.'

'Why poor Wolf?'

'Rich, powerful, a huge organisation rooted in the post-war black markets. It's warped him, so he's doomed to be always running. He should never have fled after the collapse. He wasn't guilty – not of war crimes. But he's guilty now, which is why the chase is hotting up.'

'If he wasn't guilty then, why – '

Lucille turned to her. 'He's become a gangster. Tell that nice Charlie to be careful of him. René and Wolf were friends once. Now they're enemies. Frankfurt saw the final bitter parting. Now you'd better go back to him, hadn't you?'

'With you here?' Sonya exclaimed, the fear returning.

'He doesn't know that,' Lucille answered. An artful little smile played about her mouth. 'I'll tell you what. I'll go and phone from a café, say I've just arrived. That'll avoid any dramas. By the time I get here, you'll have gone, won't you?'

The thought of being left alone again with him was unnerving. 'You'll call quickly, won't you?' Sonya asked. 'This won't be easy.'

'Within minutes, I promise.' She studied Sonya for a second. 'Why is it I like you?' She shrugged, lifted a hand, the merest gesture of farewell – and left.

Sonya stood outside the bedroom door for what seemed like a long time. She could hear him still speaking on the phone. Despite Lucille's return, she was very scared and it surprised her a little. She was a journalist, she'd been in dangerous situations, conducted hostile interviews; yet the very thought of turning that handle was making her heart beat like a hammer.

At last, by sheer will-power, she made herself open the door and stood hesitantly in the entrance. René smiled at her, waved while continuing to speak. She studied him with new eyes – seeing the face of a killer. Even now, after all that had happened, he looked immaculate. His hair wasn't ruffled. The bedclothes were smooth. 'Call me back then,' he was saying. 'I'll be here for some time.' He glanced at her as he said it and she was disgusted. He put the phone down. 'You should always wear shirts,' he said, 'except now. Take it off.'

Just exposing her body to him, which she'd done so often, now seemed a gross violation of her privacy. It was as though he was a stranger. But she forced herself – undoing a couple of buttons with trembling fingers and letting the shirt slip from her shoulders to lie round her feet. She felt a need to cover her pubic hair like the nudes in old paintings – but resisted it.

'I've missed you,' he said. 'I like you to be near me. What have you been doing?'

'Looking around,' she said casually.

He pulled back the covers for her. 'Come here,' he said softly.

She lay carefully beside him and his hands at once began to roam. 'Can we lie quietly just for a moment?' she said. 'Reaction,' she added. 'It was tremendous just now, wasn't it?'

'Next time it'll be even better,' he assured her. 'We're in the mood.'

My God, she thought. Please, please, Lucille, will you phone?

Minutes went by that seemed like hours. Soon he got restless; he began to fondle her. At first she tried to check him, but he said 'No rush. I just want to enjoy you,' and it would have been unusual for her to insist. God, she thought, I'm lying with the man who killed Elisabeth. The revulsion in her was barely controllable. At one moment, as he moved his hand between her legs, she shuddered – and was terrified he would feel the movement. Oh God, Lucille, when are you going to phone? Perhaps she'd run into a friend, changed her mind about returning at once.

'What's the matter?' he asked.

'Nothing,' she answered.

'You don't seem very keen.'

'I'm a bit tired. It was tremendous before, as I said.'

'Kiss me,' he whispered. How could she kiss him? He turned her face towards him with his hand, and she submitted, revolted, accepting his tongue, his wet lips, clutching him in her horror – which only served to excite him. Phone, please, for God's sake phone.

He parted her legs then and entered her. She shut her eyes. Please, Lucille.

The phone rang. Never had she heard a sound that she wanted more. He let it ring a few times. 'Shall we leave it?' he said. Was this horror never going to end?

'It might be important,' she suggested.

'No one knows I'm here.'

'You just asked someone to call you back.'

'He won't be calling yet.'

Oh God, answer it, please. Hang on, Lucille. You know he's

here. She had to be careful, couldn't be too pressing. 'Perhaps he's thought of something he had to ask you,' she said. 'Could be vital. I shan't go away. We've plenty of time.'

'Oh, all right,' he agreed, turning to answer it. Another appalling thought: Oh God, don't let it be someone else.

He reached for the phone. 'Hallo?' he said. The caller didn't answer. I'm going to die, Sonya thought. 'Hallo?' he repeated. 'Who is that? . . . Lucille? . . . Where are you? . . . What are you doing in France so soon?'

'My God, Lucille!' Sonya whispered as though in fear of discovery. She started to get out of bed, the relief flooding through her; but he stayed her with his hand.

'Where are you, darling?' he asked. 'At the airport? . . . Why didn't you warn me? I'd have met you . . . Where are you now? At Jeanette's? When shall I see you then? . . . But that's marvellous . . . No, I'm not doing anything important. I just came in to make a call, do a few things . . . Why don't you go to the apartment? . . . Oh I see. Well, I'll see if I can find some champagne . . .'

Sonya slipped from his grasp and leaped out of the bed. Hurriedly she started to dress as he put down the phone. 'She'll be about half an hour – has to pick up some clothes here. We've still got time.'

'Why has she come back early?' Sonya asked.

'I don't know,' he answered. 'Odd, isn't it?'

'Well, you can't just lie there,' she said as she drew on a stocking. 'You've got to dress, too. We've got to make the bed.'

'I'm sorry about this, darling.'

She smiled at him. It was a big effort. 'That's all right. Not your fault.' She couldn't bear to look at him for more than a few seconds. She turned her back, searching for her other stocking.

When she was ready, he went with her to the front door, offered to get her a cab. 'Don't worry,' she assured him, 'I feel like a walk.'

'Aren't you going to kiss me?' he asked.

She brushed his cheek. 'We shouldn't dally,' she said. 'She could be here any moment.'

He looked at her uncertainly. 'It's upset you, hasn't it?'

'A bit, but you're not to blame, are you?' She started down the entrance steps, then turned. 'Call me,' she said, because it was what she would usually say. He wasn't convinced. Even allowing for Lucille's sudden return, there was something wrong with the way she was behaving, but he couldn't pinpoint what.

She didn't wait – just waved and hurried away along the Avenue Foch.

3

It was about half an hour before dusk and Charlie paid off the cab where the girl had said at the junction of the Route de Suresnes and the Route de Madrid at the head of the Lac Inferieur. He was in the heart of the Bois de Boulogne and, as ordered, he began to walk, heading west, in the open ground on the north side of the water.

He was to keep walking, he'd been told, until they met. Wolf, as he had cause to know, never took chances. The Bois was heavily wooded, which would give him cover that was thick and easily accessible, but in the clearing which Charlie had been directed to he could see if he was accompanied – or being followed. Not the club again, Charlie guessed, because Wolf feared repeated patterns. That way, others could be waiting.

In the park, in the dimming light, Charlie felt exposed. There was hardly anyone about. A couple far ahead along a lane with a dog. Movement among the trees. Cruising homosexuals perhaps, but maybe others more sinister.

'Charlie . . .' Wolf's voice came from behind him. 'Just keep on walking. Why the summons?'

'I know now who I've been looking for.'

'And who was it?'

'René Levallier. But I still don't know why.'

'I can tell you that. There's a tree trunk ahead, on its side. Stop there and sit down. I'll join you in a moment.'

Charlie sat down and waited. He still couldn't see Wolf but guessed he'd moved back into the trees to watch for a little longer. At last, he appeared – rather suddenly from behind him, walking softly on the grass.

He sat down on the bench, leaving a gap between them so that, to an observer, they could have been two strangers. 'Now,' he said, 'what makes you so sure?'

It was two days now since Sonya's panic call. 'Charlie,' she'd said in a small taut voice that was most unlike her, 'I've something vital to tell you.' Half an hour later, she was in his suite at the

Bristol – and for once she wasn't poised and controlled. She was a woman in a state of near-shock. 'I've been with René Levallier,' she said. 'I've never told you about René, but it's been going on a few months now. Today I've been in his home. He had to take a long phone call so I started to look around the house and found myself in his study and . . .' Slowly, she told him the story, including her terror at the end. 'So there's no doubt, is there?' she ended.

For a moment, he hardly seemed to have heard her. He stood at the window, looking down into the street. He felt nothing. No sudden joy, no excitement, no relief even. For months he'd devoted himself to the search for this man – the ghost-like presence behind that terrible night by the rail track, the mind that had planned Elisabeth's death, fed to the SOE the material that would force their hand, known that someone in the Vercors circuit would have to slay her in cold blood, with bare bloody hands as Charlie had done, which he would never forget or forgive as long as he lived, and which he had sworn to avenge. And now he'd found him. It was then – as the old vivid memory came back to him of the Sten jerking in his hands, of his poor beautiful Elisabeth falling, lying, dying – that the fury suddenly swept through him with a force that left him panting. He swivelled suddenly. 'Why?' he shouted at her. 'Why?'

His vehemence shocked Sonya for a second. 'Charlie, I don't know.'

Slowly, his rage ebbed a little. He shook his head, as though to dull the image so that he could think. He moved over to where Sonya was sitting, bent down, and put his arms round her. He just held her, tightly, their cheeks touching. 'Sorry, pal,' he whispered. He stood up. 'Sorry,' he repeated, taking control of himself. 'That was selfish, wasn't it? It must have been horrific for you there today – a sort of betrayal.'

She nodded, her eyes filling with tears. He held out his hand and she gripped it, holding it against her chest. 'I never really suspected him,' he said, 'though I wondered. I couldn't see his motive. I couldn't see Duclos's motive either but, like you, I could imagine him having one. Same with Marie. But René? Did he have the power to organise a killing in New York, a burglary in London, doping a horse in Newmarket, financing Maitland?'

'He has a lot of power,' she said quietly. 'It's vital to him. He used to talk of how much more he'd gain with his new appointment.'

'Different sort of power,' Charlie said. 'Heads of state, politicians, civil servants, corporation presidents . . .'

'It was always more than that. How did he get so wealthy? René's involved in all sorts of things. Remember that story about corruption in Frankfurt that Claude grilled me about? I sat on it.'

Charlie looked at her in astonishment. 'He got to me somehow,' she said. 'What he'd done didn't seem so bad the way he described it.'

'But you've been around, honey.'

She shrugged. 'Don't grill me, Charlie. I'm pleading guilty. Lucky I *am* guilty – otherwise, I'd never have found the Verlaine, would I?'

He smiled – in sympathy, approval. 'It's a huge break, Sonya. I'm in your debt for the rest of my life.'

'*Your* debt? I thought we were a team. She was *our* Elisabeth.'

'Didn't look like that the other day in London.'

'They were anxious. Understandably. And they weren't in love with her, aren't still in love with her. What are you going to do now?'

'I'm going to contact Wolf.'

In the Bois it was getting so dark he could hardly see Wolf's face. 'And the whole code was based on Verlaine?' Wolf queried when Charlie had finished.

'That's the way it looked. "The violins of autumn" was in the telegram in Briedon's pocket. He was the man I found dead in New York. He wanted to tell me the truth, I know he did.'

'And you still don't know what that is?'

'I don't know why Elisabeth died.'

'I do,' said Wolf. '*Now* I do. You've told me. Did you know that René collaborated with us during the war?'

'I'd never heard that. Doesn't exactly surprise me, though.'

'Mind you, I don't know what it means really when you get to that level. What choice did he have? He was in a key ministry. But he took it a lot further than he had to. He actively worked for us in secret, set up contacts with the Resistance. Sometimes the SS would pretend he'd offended us to preserve the façade. They even arrested him once and held him for a few days. That was how he could be my go-between with Elisabeth. When

Nikki needed money, René fixed it. If I needed to get a message to Elisabeth, René fixed it. If I wanted to meet her, René fixed it.'

He paused and his cigarette glowed red in the darkness. 'So why did he want Elisabeth to die?' Charlie asked.

'I've just told you.'

'Then I didn't hear you.'

'Because she knew, of course. She knew he was a collaborator on a grand scale, though no one else did. She knew he'd made millions out of working with us. Not quite in the class of Pierre Laval, but more than enough to be condemned to death – the bastard.'

'I hear you've quarrelled. You were friends once, weren't you?'

'Once,' he agreed, 'but he's got greedy now. He double-crossed me and it's worrying him. That's why I've suddenly acquired new status with the police.' He paused. 'Well, we must consider what to do, what we've got in the way of proof.'

'The key,' Charlie answered, 'is the photograph of you and Elisabeth together. In Occupied Paris she was with an enemy general. There were other charges, but after that they'd believe anything in London. Briedon admitted to me that he took the picture. How did he know you were meeting?'

'René, of course. He arranged it for me, arranged all our meetings. But what can we prove? We can't prove he had Briedon murdered, let alone Elisabeth. You can just about prove that Briedon was taking orders from him. You *think* Briedon was tempted to talk to you, but you don't *know*. You *think* it was a contract killing, but you don't *know*. Could have been someone off the street.'

'I do know,' said Charlie. 'Even if I can't prove it, I know.'

'Forget Briedon,' said Wolf. 'Stay with Elisabeth. What crime did René commit? All he did was pass to London information that was true. Perhaps, as a loyal Frenchman,' he added sardonically, 'he thought the Allies should know that one of their key people was on intimate terms with General Wolfgang Heinegg.'

'He murdered Elisabeth.'

'He didn't issue the order, Charlie. That was issued formally by Baker Street. No court could find René Levallier guilty of any crime.'

'He can't get away with it,' said Charlie.

'He won't.' He said it softly, a voice in the dark, a glowing

cigarette, the scent of tobacco smoke. 'I know what to do now.'
He was silent for a few seconds. 'We'll kill him.'

4

It was 5.45 in the evening. Sonya was early – too early – sitting
alone in the Brasserie Joséphine, where she had so often met
Charlie and Nikki. She felt vulnerable, exposed – in every sense.
She sipped the Campari, wondering why she'd agreed to do this.

She knew that Charlie was near – watching her from a distant
table, using a copy of *France Soir* for cover; that Wolf was
waiting, too, with a car nearby, engine running. What she didn't
know was when or how he was going to act. It depended, Charlie
had explained, on how René arrived. If he walked, they'd
probably take him before he got there. If he came by cab or in his
official car, then she was to have a drink with him, discuss a
personal problem – that her feelings for him were growing too
strong perhaps – then suggest they walked to her apartment in
the Palais Royal ten minutes away. It would happen on the way.
A car would draw up beside them, René would be bundled in
and it would roar off into the traffic. When questioned, she
wouldn't know why or by whom he had been seized.

She didn't like it, and she knew Charlie didn't like it either. In
the war, it would have been different. But they'd both become
accustomed to peace, to living by the law. Even her memory of
that traumatic afternoon in the Avenue Foch had dimmed. René
was a murderer, corrupt, venal. But she'd met quite a few
murderers, as journalists do, done pieces on them. 'Passionising',
as Claude had always called it, making them live. Mostly, they
were pretty ordinary people, who went home to their wives for
dinner, loved their children.

René was hardly ordinary – a man of fine intelligence, humour,
sensitivity. He'd understood her needs and changing feelings,
versed as a lover in playing a woman as though she was a violin,
as the old saying went. She had loved him – more than she
realised. It didn't just stop because you discovered something
about a man you didn't know before. Something? She sipped her
Campari. It was more than something, she thought. Elisabeth.
Always the soul-searching came back to that – to the debt, to the
love. If only it could have been settled in court, by sending for
the police. God, René was clever.

When she had called him, he seemed relieved. 'I've been

worrying about you,' he said. 'You were in an odd mood when you left.' He was surprised when she suggested they meet in a café instead of her apartment. 'There's something I've got to talk to you about,' she said. 'It'll be easier in a café.'

'Well, why not somewhere better?' he asked. They could go out to the Bois or meet at Fouquet's maybe. No, she said, she needed to be near home – which she knew would set his mind working. For it could be because of work, or because of him – somewhere to go when they'd finished the serious talking.

She sipped her Campari again, and noticed a man standing in the doorway of a shop reading a paper. He glanced at her and went on reading. She wondered if it was Wolf. She hadn't met Wolf. Charlie had insisted on that. Better that she knew as little as possible.

She'd been surprised that Wolf was handling the matter himself. He was running an international organisation, with echoes of the Mafia. Surely staff did this kind of thing? 'He knows René,' said Charlie. 'Doesn't want anything to go wrong. It has its personal aspects, too. René double-crossed him. They're rivals, enemies.'

She noticed another man leaning against a tree. He was tall, and was also reading a newspaper. He put it down and began to pace up and down, as though he was waiting for someone who was late. He hadn't looked at her, though. Wolf didn't know what she looked like, she thought – then remembered that she'd been asked what she would be wearing, and maybe, like Lucille, he'd have seen her picture above her column in the paper.

This was getting absurd. Like a film, as Charlie had felt as he walked to Briedon's apartment in New York. But this was real life. René was going to die, probably by a bullet, as Elisabeth had died because of René. Well, there was logic there, a rightness, a tooth for a tooth – if that was a rightness.

Poor Lucille, she thought suddenly. Lucille was real life too. So was that afternoon in the mansion – when René had made love so exquisitely, when the mood was perfect and all the elements had merged and she'd gone to a height she had never known with a man before.

She knew then that she couldn't go through with it. She was only a decoy but she would still be killing him by proxy – as it had been with Elisabeth with all their hands on the trigger. She looked at her watch. Ten minutes before he was due. He could still be in the apartment – the official one where he'd said he'd be. Guiltily, she looked around, sensitive to the eyes that must be on her. Well, everyone had to go to the toilet. She walked into the interior of the café, half expecting that Charlie would follow her, found the phone, and dialled Levallier's apartment.

Lucille answered. 'I've got to be quick,' Sonya said. 'Tell René not to come.'

'Come where?'

'He knows. Lucille, it's vital.'

Sonya rang off, then walked over to Charlie, hidden behind his newspaper. 'It's no good, Charlie,' she said. 'I can't do it. I'm going home.'

Wolf, pacing the flagstones idly, had seen her go inside, and had watched her return and talk to Charlie. They had left the café together, walking in the direction of the Rue des Capucines. He guessed what had happened, had been half expecting it.

The question was: Had she succeeded in warning René? Probably not. It was late. He was almost certainly on his way. He would get there and find there was no sign of her. He would probably have sensed trouble already. So what would he do? He would phone her apartment, get no answer. So he'd go there. Even if he had got her message, he would probably do the same.

Wolf signalled to the car. The timing was on the tight side but, since she was walking with Charlie, he could get there before her. Thank God he'd insisted that Charlie should get a set of keys from her. Just in case something went wrong, Wolf had said. The apartment, if only as somewhere they would walk to, was a feature of the plan. In operations like this, every possibility had to be considered. He hadn't been a Panzer general for nothing. Decisions often had to be instant, all the possibilities had to be thought through – predicted as far as they could be before a battle.

His Mercedes moved fast along the Boulevard des Capucines, and down the Avenue de l'Opéra, weaving through the traffic, until it stopped at the Palais Royal. There were three men with him. He got out, entered the main courtyard of the ancient building, once the home of aristocrats, now converted to apartments. He'd been there already to study the geography, and he ran up the stairs to the second floor. He let himself in, did a quick survey, decided that the best place for him to hide if necessary was in the cupboard in her bedroom. Would she need to come to the bedroom? He doubted it. She wouldn't change or even repair her makeup. Not at once. She'd have a drink with Charlie. They'd both feel like a drink after the drama of the past hour.

He heard them arrive. As he had predicted, she poured Charlie a drink. She needed one, too, she said – a proper one this time, and strong. All the indications were that they'd remain in that big living room with its view of the Gardens. So Wolf positioned himself beside the door – and waited for René.

5

Max lounged on the sofa in his shirtsleeves, his feet up. They were waiting in Craig's suite in the Hôtel George V. Craig and Nikki were held up. He looked at his watch. 'How much longer, for Christ's sake? It's past 5.30. I need a drink.'

'Surprise me,' said Sally. 'Just once, it'd be good.'

'It'd be good if you weren't such a cow. What the fuck have I done now for you to talk like that.'

'Exist,' she answered, enjoying the impact of her brief brutal answer.

'I don't know why you're still around,' said Max bitterly. 'The ship's sinking.'

'I like it on deck, I suppose. Enjoy the pain. Must be into bondage.' She paused, seeing the hurt in his eyes. 'You want a drink. Order some champagne. Would Craig mind?'

'He'll forgive us. You do it, chick. I need a piss.'

He went through the bedroom to the bathroom, without closing the door. As he relieved himself, he heard her calling room service. He went back into the bedroom, took up the phone. He asked for Charlie's number and lay on the bed as he waited for the answer.

'Hallo, Max,' Charlie said. 'You've caught me just going out – is it urgent?'

'Just need to know how we're doing, Charlie.'

'On the point of cracking it, Max.'

'Be precise. I've heard that song before.'

'We know who it is, but I'm not telling anyone who doesn't need to know, Max. There's a good reason.'

'I don't believe you.'

'And *I've* no time to argue.'

'Don't forget what I said, Charlie.'

'Nor how I answered, Max.'

'Now listen, Charlie . . .' But the line had gone dead. 'Fuck!' Max swore – then realised that Sally was in the room, perched on the arm of a chair. 'Where's that fucking champagne?'

'On its fucking way,' she answered. 'I said to use fucking roller skates.' She knew he didn't like to hear women swearing. It was 1960. 'Fucking' was man's talk, banned usually, as she'd often reminded him, in front of the female sex.

'That was Charlie, wasn't it?' she said.

'Bull's eye,' he answered.

'So who's who? You asked him who it was.'

He glanced at her, noting the determined look. 'Oh, some guy he's been looking for.'

'Why didn't you believe what he said?'

'*You* know Charlie. His mind's always on the kid. Nothing gets done. He was making excuses.'

She knew he was lying – and just looked at him so that he knew she knew. The bell of the suite door rang and she went through into the living room to answer it. 'Just leave the tray there,' she told the waiter and then went back to Max. 'Who was the guy?'

'Oh, you don't know him. Wasn't that the champagne?'

'Who was the guy, Max? What was his name?' Max was cornered. He had known the door was open, but closing it would have been like a flashing light to her. He had thought he could keep the exchange cryptic enough. 'You threatened him, Max. You warned him not to forget what you'd said.'

'Joke, honey. Why the hell are you making such a big deal out of this?'

'Because it's time I knew. For months, Elisabeth has been with us like she'd been asked to stay.'

'You've always banged on about poor Elisabeth. For Christ's sake, let's have the champagne.'

'Not until you tell me. She's got very close just lately. She's ruined your business.'

'*You've* ruined my business with that sod Ollie.'

'Rubbish. Romy didn't leave you because of Ollie. Add Leah's troubles. And Duncan's. Now you're warning Charlie. You've got to tell me, Max, or I'm going to the police.'

Max was silent, watched her defensively. Oh, what the hell,

he thought. Things can't get any worse. 'OK,' he said. 'Get the champagne.'

'Not till you've told me.'

Again he paused. Max was frayed, scared of the future, a little corrupt. He'd done some fast deals in his time. But through the wreckage that he sensed he'd become, the one thing that was sacrosanct, that was pure – dwarfing the contracts, the movies, the clients, the money, the women because it extended beyond self – was the bond with Elisabeth. Despite everything he'd said to Charlie in London, and his threat to tell Nikki, it was an oath of blood brothers, unspoken but binding – almost more binding because it was unspoken, because they all understood and accepted it without the words. But the oath was to keep silence, not to find her killer. That was the crucial difference that had provoked the quarrel in London.

Max would never have told Nikki, as he'd threatened, because it would have denied the oath. Its purpose was to stop Charlie – and Charlie, versed in their secret language, knew that was its purpose. It was posturing, like stags locking horns. So how could Max speak of it now to Sally?

'I mean it,' she said. 'I'll ring the police now.' She went to the phone. 'Operator, will you please get me – '

'OK, put it down,' he said. There was a reluctance in her, and she put the receiver back in a kind of slow motion.

'Well?' she demanded when he didn't speak.

'Elisabeth was killed in an attack on a railway line near Grenoble.'

'Well, I know that,' said Sally. 'God knows, we all know that. Now tell me something I don't know.'

He was lying on the bed in his clothes, his trousers crumpled, his tie twisted below its loosened knot, and he looked up at her, his bloodshot, hooded eyes suddenly filled with tears. 'We killed her,' he said. 'Will that do?'

For a few seconds, the shock held her quite still, as though she was made of wax. 'Oh my God,' she said at last before asking quietly: 'Why?'

'Because we were ordered to execute her.'

'You mean . . .?' She couldn't go on. Elisabeth had been the cause of much anxiety to her, but this was unbelievable.

'London was certain she'd been turned.'

'And you got Romy through her – your great start in the

agency. And Duncan got the Prince. And . . . Oh God, how *could* you all use her after that?'

'She kind of told us to.'

'Told you to? Did she know?'

'She knew something. Not quite what. It was in the air though.'

'How did you kill her?'

From one of his eyes a tear ran very slowly down his long lugubrious face. 'At the railtrack they were waiting for us. The fire was heavy. The order was to make it look like death in action. Earlier we'd drawn lots in a secret ballot to decide who'd do it. That person would never tell the others, but we'd all share it. Fate chose Charlie and, despite all the secrecy, he couldn't keep that from us because, for Christ's sake, she was his life.' He paused. 'He shot her in the back with a Sten.'

Nikki's scream from the doorway seemed barely human – a primeval shriek of anguish that went back a million years.

6

Standing behind the door of Sonya's bedroom, Wolf heard the entrance bell. He could sense Sonya's hesitation as she wondered if she should pretend to be out. The bell rang again. 'You'd better let him in,' said Charlie softly, 'and we'll take it from there. Behave as normally as possible – as though you did have something to say but changed your mind. With me here, he won't press it.'

'Don't leave me alone with him, will you?'

'Of course not.'

Wolf heard her get up and go out into the hall. He eased his gun from its holster. There were muffled voices, but he couldn't detect what anyone said – until they came into the sitting room. 'It's René,' said Sonya. 'You know Charlie, don't you?'

'Hallo, Charlie,' he said.

'Would you like a drink?' Sonya asked.

'Just vermouth,' he answered. 'What happened at the café?'

Wolf tried to work out from the voices and the action where René would be, hoped he'd go with her to attend to the drink, for his back would be towards the bedroom door.

He made his move – with the silence of long experience, swinging open the door that he'd left unlatched. He'd guessed

326

right. René was with Sonya as she prepared the drink, an arm lightly round her shoulders.

Instinct made René turn – only to stop in mid-action as Wolf ordered him: 'Don't move. Stay exactly where you are. I've a gun, of course.' The words were quiet – but adequate. René knew who it was. If Charlie and Sonya were surprised, they didn't speak.

Wolf said: 'When I say so, René, move very slowly beside the door and lean against the wall, facing it, both hands against it. I don't have to tell you not to try anything – you know me well enough, don't you, René?'

'I know you, Wolf.'

'Right, now do as I said.'

Nikki was panting as she ran along the Avenue George V. Her face was half covered by her hair, and tears of hysteria were still streaming down her cheeks. But she didn't care how she looked. Never had she felt so distraught, so alone, or known such agony. The world as she knew it had come to an end. She didn't know where she was running to – it was just a desperate instinct to escape, the kind that frightened herds must know as they react to fear. But as she tired she knew there was no escape. She came to the Place de l'Alma, forced to wait for traffic, her breath coming in strained noisy gasps.

She was in shock – still unable to comprehend the speed with which the change had overcome her. One moment she'd been with Craig and they were laughing as they walked into the hotel because she'd told him that Charlie always called her a minx. He said that Charlie had something there, making much of the French word 'coquine' with its vaguely risqué undertone – and she pretended he'd offended her, displaying that look as though she wasn't wearing knickers that Max had talked about to Charlie. Then Craig met someone in the lobby and told her to go on up to the suite and make peace with Max and Sonya.

She got there just as a waiter was leaving. He held open the door for her and she heard Max and Sally talking in the bedroom. Impulsively, she grabbed the bottle of champagne, planning to stand in the doorway of the bedroom and hold it up with some kind of high-spirited tra-la-la. Then she caught what Max was actually saying, and time had been suspended as she listened, refusing at first to believe what she was hearing, the horror growing inside her, until the final unbelievable blow that brought out that scream that wasn't hers. It belonged to someone else. It *must* belong to someone else, because she was asleep and this was a nightmare of nightmares and soon she'd wake up because even nightmares of nightmares always finally come to an end.

As soon as they realised, they went over to her. Even Max, who wasn't the world's greatest mover, had been off the bed in a second – explaining, comforting, assuring. But they couldn't alter the fact – unless they denied it, which she begged them to do. 'Please tell me that's not true,' she screamed. But they couldn't. Max said that Elisabeth wasn't a traitor, that it had all been a set-up by someone who wanted her killed. 'We were just pawns, honey, in some big scheme. For months Charlie's been searching for the man who fixed it, who used us, who used him. You've been helping though he couldn't tell you why. And he's found him, Nikki. He just told me on the phone.'

She hardly heard. These were details. 'Tell me it's not true,' she repeated. 'Just tell me you were lying to Sally. You often rile each other. Please, Max, say you were lying,' she pleaded. 'It didn't happen like that. She died fighting – in action, under the heavy fire I've heard so much about.'

But he couldn't. Not like that. 'It was all of us, Nikki. Not just Charlie.'

'It was Charlee,' she said, so softly they could hardly hear her.

'Listen, darling . . .' Sally began, putting her arm round her.

'Don't touch me!' Nikki cried, and another awful scream escaped from her.

Suddenly she had to escape. The voices calling after her were distant – echoing across a mountain chasm. She tore along the passage, encountered Craig. 'Hey, Nikki, what's – ' he began, but she'd passed him before he could even complete that short question. She raced for the fire door beside the lift and hurried down the stairs two at a time. She fled through the vast marble lobby, ignored the commissionaire, and raced down the avenue.

She waited in the din of traffic at the Place de l'Alma. 'Sonya,' she said aloud to herself. Sonya would understand. Sonya would tell her the truth. She saw an empty cab, hailed it. 'The Palais Royal,' she whispered.

'Are you all right, mam'selle?' the cabbie asked.

'East entrance please,' she answered.

She sat in the back of the cab, her chest heaving, her thoughts racing – so many memories of Charlee. That night when they'd first made love in the Vercors. No wonder he was haunted. How could he have gone back? 'Oh, Charlee,' she wailed aloud.

'You said something, mam'selle?' asked the cabbie.

'It's all right,' she answered.

He drew up at the Palais Royal and she thrust a ten-franc note into his hand. She ran up the stairs to Sonya's apartment and rang the bell. Oh, Sonya, please be there. There was no response. She rang again – and held her finger on the bellpush. Maybe she was sleeping. Perhaps a lover was with her. 'Oh God, Sonya, please!' she shouted aloud, banging on the door with her fist.

Inside the apartment, they knew who it was, and heard the note of panic. 'Wolf, that's Nikki,' Charlie said, 'and she's in trouble.'

Wolf didn't answer. He was moved by the anguish in his daughter's voice but at this moment it wasn't what he wanted. He wanted to take René out of the apartment under the threat of a gun concealed in his pocket and deliver him to the Mercedes that was waiting with the engine running. If they passed neighbours on the way, it wouldn't matter too much. But a hysterical girl? His own daughter?

'Sonya!' Nikki screamed again, banging on the door. 'Oh please, please be there!'

Wolf realised he had no choice. Soon the noise would attract attention in the other apartments. 'All right,' he said, 'let her in. René, move further from the door, both hands on the wall still.' He was talking about the door that led to the hall, but his main concern was the door to the flat, which Sonya was about to open – an obvious escape opportunity. 'Don't think of it, René.' He didn't have to tell René there'd be no noise, that his Walther was fitted with a silencer.

He didn't want to shoot him in the apartment. There'd be the problem of moving the body, of blood, clothing particles on the carpet – but if he had to, he would.

In the hallway, Nikki flung her arms round Sonya's neck. 'Thank God you're here,' she exclaimed. 'Sonya, I've just heard the most terrible thing.'

'We'll talk later, darling,' Sonya said. 'Just now we've got a crisis. Your father's here, but don't go to him. Just do as he tells you.'

Nikki came into the room – tentatively. Wolf watched her as

she entered – looking like a child in her distress. 'Stay where you are just for a second, Nikki,' he told her. 'Now very carefully come here behind me.'

René saw his chance. There was only an instant of opportunity – literally a second as she moved to obey her father's order – and René grabbed it, diving for her in a rugger tackle and rolling with her.

Wolf fired and René felt the blow in his right shoulder, but in the struggle with the girl he found he'd still got strength in the arm, although blood was seeping through his shirt. He was on his feet fast, holding the girl in front of him with both arms. She was struggling. 'Stop it,' René said, 'or you'll get hurt. Do as I tell you and you won't.' His right arm was round her neck and he increased the pressure slightly to emphasise his words.

Wolf was covering them with the gun. 'Now, Wolf, we're going to back away,' said René, 'and go through that door to the hall. Then we're going to leave the apartment. And all the time she's going to be between me and you. Don't try anything, either of you,' he added to the others, 'or I'll break her back. Now, Sonya, get me a key to the front door.' She looked at Wolf and he nodded. Then she went to her bag, which lay on the sofa, and took out a ring of several keys. 'Take off the door key and put it in the left pocket of my jacket. Move slowly and carefully.'

René's plan was to lock the entrance after they'd passed through it – to slow the pursuit.

Sonya did as she was instructed. Maybe it was her proximity that decided Nikki to make her move. Or possibly it was René's lifting of his left elbow to give access to his pocket that weakened his grasp on her. Suddenly she wrenched herself free and leaped sideways. René's response was instinctive. For an instant, he was tempted to go after her as he had before, but he'd been lucky then, fallen in the right position to gain the cover of her body. This time he went for Wolf, knowing that in his concern for his daughter he'd be distracted by her movement. Wolf was bigger than he was, and stronger, but René had an innate cunning, well-oiled with constant use. He was also lithe and didn't have a limp.

The key was the gun. The gun made strength useless. So René dived for it, striking Wolf's wrist hard with the side of his hand to make him drop it. But he failed in his purpose. Both men were acting on instinct, honed by experience – and, as René attacked, instinct made Wolf tighten his grip on the gun. The shot from the silenced Walther wasn't loud, but its effect was huge. René felt the blow in his side, sending him spinning, but again he was winged – for the bullet passed through his soft flesh and found another target: Nikki, on the far side of him. She let out a cry as she was felled by the impact – and lay sprawled on Sonya's carpet in a position that, as Charlie, in his shocked state, vaguely recognised, was uncannily similar to the way her mother had lain in the mud by the railtrack sixteen years before.

For a second, Charlie didn't believe what he saw. Events had moved so fast, in a manner so unexpected, that he found them impossible to accept. That René should be lying there in Sonya's flat was bad enough, but Nikki! It was unthinkable! What the hell was she even doing there? Then, as she lay still, as Elisabeth had, horror pierced his disbelief. He leaped to her side. So did the other two, Sonya already reaching for her pulse. 'My God,' said Wolf in desolation as he bent down over her. 'Oh my God, what have I done?'

'She's alive,' said Sonya, tearing desperately at Nikki's blouse to expose the wound.

Nikki stirred, opened her eyes. 'Charlee,' she whispered. 'Charlee . . .'

'I'm here, honey,' he said.

'Tell me . . .' she managed to say, 'tell me you didn't . . .'

'Didn't?' he echoed.

'Kill her . . .'

'I love you, darling.'

There was almost a smile. 'Darling . . . not enough, Charlee. Tell me please . . .' But he didn't answer her. And even if he had, she would not have heard, would never hear him again.

7

The Cimitière du Sud in Montparnasse is enormous, stretching half a mile from north to south and a quarter of a mile at its extremes from east to west – a vast field of the dead, marked by rank upon rank of elaborate stone memorials and divided into unequal parts by a road, the Rue Emile Richard. It was here on a cold, bright morning in late September, with the trees already partly stripped of leaves, that they buried Nikki.

A small crowd was in attendance, a mixture of Nikki's few friends from before she met Charlie and those whose links were closer to her mother. The Vercors group were given pride of place. Annette and Hugo had flown in with Duncan and Leah, but Charlie hadn't urged Philana to join them.

Jean-Paul was there with Thierry – and several of the girls from La Nouvelle Vie. So were the *patron* and his wife, standing apart from the others, together with Clothilde. The VIPs were present: Claude Duclos, Lucille Levallier, Hélène Prévost – even Marie, who had never even met Nikki. In a way, it was as if Elisabeth was being interred as well.

The mourners gathered at the graveside bowed their heads as the curé recited the prayers, and Sonya threw a handful of earth on to the coffin as it was lowered into the ground.

For Charlie, the scene was so poignant that it lacked reality – as though the film had come to an end and they'd left the cinema; or at least that someone would tap him on the shoulder and tell him that none of it had happened.

Images of her kept coming back to him as the brisk fall wind blew cold through his hair. He knew again the shock when he'd looked into Elisabeth's eyes on the night he found her in the café; he heard the taunting innocence when people took her for his mistress; he recalled their high spirits as they sang together in the open Bugatti on the road to Deauville, played the next day like kids on the beach.

He thought of the moments of sadness, petulance, joy, challenge, of wisdom even – the strange mix of a child with flashes of maturity, as she'd shown with the Prince, displaying the sureness of a woman of forty. He even found himself smiling at the way she'd looked when he called her a minx – and then, as the weeks passed, played with the word, wearing it, changing it, exploiting it.

He saw her again in the white dress with Craig in the Ritz Bar – playing the star-to-be – and he wondered once more at that dark day in the Vercors, under Elisabeth's long shadow; those bitter challenges about his wife, the jealous taunts about her mother as 'Sainte Elisabeth', her coming to him at last that night and the laying of the ghost with her cry of 'Maman, let me have him.'

And then he had a black thought: Had Maman decided at last to reject that plea? He looked at the coffin lying in its dark hole, topped by the scattering of earth – and felt a woman's hand in his. Sonya was beside him. He glanced at her and saw the tears in her eyes. 'Like a brilliant little shooting star,' she said softly with a brightness she didn't feel.

People were beginning to leave and Lucille Levallier approached Charlie. She looked wan and every bit of her fifty years, but elegant in her black coat. 'I'm so sorry,' she said. 'It's sadder somehow when they're young.'

He nodded, his lips tight, not really wishing to speak of it, and asked after René.

'He's on the mend,' she answered. 'It'll take a while, I fear.' His wounds were worse than they'd seemed at first. 'You thought it was René, I suspect,' Lucille went on. 'I mean who contacted London about Elisabeth, who started this awful tragic chain.'

Charlie looked at her with haggard eyes. 'Surely it was?'

She shook her head.

'I know he used the Verlaine code,' said Charlie, 'in a telegram to New York.'

'You're wrong,' she insisted. 'In the past he used the Verlaine code, but not since – not for years. It hasn't crossed your mind who else could have used it, has it?'

Grief had made him slow and he did not, to start with, grasp her meaning. When at last he did, he shuddered. 'You can't mean Wolf?'

'Why not ask him?' she said. 'It was their wartime code. He's behind you now.'

Charlie turned. Wolf, who hadn't been there before, was standing alone beside the grave as the cemetery attendants began to fill it with earth. Dressed in a grey worsted coat, he held a black Homburg in front of him – with both hands, a little humbly, in a private gesture of respect.

He looked up as they approached. 'It's a sad business, Wolf,' said Lucille.

'It's a tragedy beyond anything I can conceive,' he answered quietly. 'She was a lovely young girl.'

'Like her mother when you knew her. I've just told Charlie it was you, not René, who decided that Elisabeth should die.'

Charlie was sure Wolf would deny it. He'd read his letters. He'd seen the evidence of a love so strong that Wolf had even defied Hitler's personal order.

Wolf's eyes were strangely bland as he met Charlie's querying gaze. There was a deadness there, as though his emotions had been cauterised. And suddenly Charlie realised the logic of what

Lucille had said. René was not the only man who'd known when Wolf was meeting her, who could have alerted Briedon for that crucial, damning photograph – on the last occasion, Charlie presumed now, the second meeting when they hadn't lain together, as Wolf had put it in his old-fashioned words. 'Why?' he asked at last in disbelief.

'Same reason as you – duty. She'd have had Rommel killed.'

'I thought you had a deal. She told you we'd win the war without it – as your brother generals thought.'

Wolf's desolate eyes were on the grave. 'I knew the animal, Charlie, loved her still. I couldn't take the chance. Rommel would have been too big to resist.'

'It would have convicted her as well – as you discussed.'

Wolf shrugged with an effort, his shoulders bowed by sadness. He seemed a different man. 'She'd have thought of something,' he said. 'Some other way she could have come by the intelligence. That's what she was brilliant at – thinking up things. Surely you knew that.' He turned to Lucille. 'I suppose you suggested to the police that I might be here?'

'I told them you would be.' A thin, sad smile. 'They didn't believe you'd take the risk. I said you'd assess it. There'd be a balloon to whisk you away, a troop of soldiers for cover, your own special angel maybe.'

'Deserted me, it seems,' Wolf said with a forlorn gesture at the grave. 'Ironic, isn't it, Charlie? Between us, we killed Elisabeth – the two men who loved her most. And then I killed her child. She had a saying . . .'

'God's joke?' Charlie asked.

'She had quite a turn of phrase, didn't she?' Wolf said. 'But that one's not so funny. Not when it gets near the knuckle.' He gave a heavy sigh. On his face was the saddest expression that Charlie had ever seen.

'But why did you need to kill René?' Charlie persisted.

'We had a debt, didn't we, Lucille?'

'If you say so, Wolf,' she said.

'And he knew too much – about recent years, I mean – and he knew it was too much. With the power of his new job, the gunfire was getting heavy. That's when you have to attack, Charlie.'

Charlie turned away. They were standing at the central point of the cemetery – where the main avenues, each crossed by lanes,

334

converged at a statue of an angel with a plaque marked *souvenir*. It was then, after Lucille's words, that his attention was caught by the gendarmes at the southern end of the Avenue Principale. He looked along the next avenue to the west. More police were stationed there. He turned north towards the cemetery exit to the Boulevard Edgar Quinet. A police van was parked across the entrance and, from it, a small group of men was approaching, though they were still quite distant. Most were in plain clothes but a couple were in uniform.

Duclos came up with Sonya. 'Well, this is a sad occasion,' he said. 'She was such a nice kid. You'll miss her badly, Charlie.'

'It doesn't bear thinking about,' said Charlie. 'I haven't let myself yet.'

'I hear René's making good progress,' Duclos said to Lucille.

'That's true, Claude. The anxious days are past.' She glanced at Sonya. Was it over between them? She couldn't tell. It had certainly taken a battering.

'You know, I feel like an old sage,' Duclos went on. 'Knowing everyone so well, knowing so much, yet wondering how it's going to end.'

'Hasn't it ended?' asked Charlie.

Duclos shook his head. 'You should have asked Wolf.'

'Should have?' echoed Charlie in surprise and turned towards Wolf. But Wolf wasn't there. Charlie looked around that vast burial ground with its hundreds of monuments, most of them elaborate – huge crosses, obelisks, sepulchres, statues made of every kind of stone. Wolf couldn't have asked for better cover.

The posse from the parked van was getting near. They spread out now along the cross lanes, for they realised that Wolf, concealed from them for a moment by the people with him, had gone. Gendarmes from the other groups started to close in – presumably for a systematic combing. It seemed that Wolf would need that balloon – or his guardian angel.

The mourners watched in an awful fascination as the operation proceeded, the police moving along the rows of graves as others surveyed them on the lateral cross-lines.

Wolf gave them a game for a while – about twenty minutes – showing himself sometimes, even waving to them. He wasn't making it that easy, though. He only stayed a second in each position – before disappearing. They soon got the measure of it. He revealed himself and a shot rang out. The bullet hit the memorial where he'd been, chipping stone. Several times he was glimpsed, fired at. But it became obvious he was playing with them – not making a serious attempt to escape.

Then he seemed to tire of the whole affair. He appeared beside a large cross, hanging on an arm, giving them time to take aim. He dropped out of sight – only an instant before the shots rang out. But he was seen again, not far from his previous position, remaining as a target even longer this time. Again a scattered volley, the sound of the shooting echoing from buildings beyond the cemetery walls. At last they'd got him. The impact made him stagger. More shots – and he fell from view.

But he wasn't dead. He could even walk. Two gendarmes got him to his feet and they brought him, half hanging between them, to their superiors, who were still with the funeral group. The skin of his face was white, as though drained of blood, and his breathing was laboured, but he managed a smile for Charlie. 'Thought I'd got that worked out,' he said brokenly. 'There's a time to die and I've passed it.'

They didn't let him linger and Charlie felt a deep wave of sympathy. 'I ought to hate him,' he said to Sonya.

'You oughtn't to hate anyone,' she whispered. Just for a second she buried her head in his shoulder – then resumed control of herself. Together they observed the three who'd been with them in the Vercors. They were standing nearby with their partners – a group of six. 'Champagne,' Sonya said softly. 'That's what Elisabeth would have said. Let's all go and drink champagne.'

8

The Comet came in over Long Island Sound, veered out over the ocean for its approach, and Charlie looked down at that endless beach of sand fringed with white by the breakers.

He felt heavy with his sadness, numb with fatigue, as though he hadn't slept for weeks – how troops must feel after long spells in battle. But he was coming home like a scarred old veteran and there was a comfort, a kind of rightness in that. What lay ahead he didn't know. In a sense, he didn't care, for he didn't have the equipment to care. His emotional engines seemed to have stopped, had maybe even burnt out – needed time for a refit at least.

He thought of his last call to Costa. 'You can call off the dogs,' Charlie had told him. 'I'm coming back and I'm ready to talk.'

'The cops'll be waiting.'

'Who are you trying to save me from?'

'I don't know. I don't know anything yet.'

'I'm telling you – there's no danger now.'

'I heard there was a drama and people got hurt.'

'Yeah, Costa, people got hurt,' he said and knew again the desolation, the start of tears.

'I spoke to Lucille, but she didn't seem to know much, said you'd explain.'

'I'll explain,' he forced himself to say. 'And Costa, for Christ's sake, get that bloody tanker released at Rotterdam.'

'What's the matter with your voice?'

'It's a lousy line, Costa.'

Philana was waiting in the Arrivals Hall and looked oddly alone as he approached her, the crowd seeming to wash round her as though she were a fixture. She was wearing a blue coat with a silk scarf and she was smiling – but she didn't wave, and as he got closer he could see the caution in her. Who was coming back to her? That's what she was wondering, he guessed. Who, indeed? He hardly knew himself. Some kind of zombie, he reckoned.

She kissed him affectionately – but there was a coolness, a restraint. 'No kids with you?' he asked.

'They're busy. They lead an active social life.' He knew why they weren't with her. She wanted to be free to talk without being overheard by sharp young ears. They walked to the car in silence, followed by the redcap with his luggage. She had chosen to bring the Cadillac out herself, as she had when she'd last driven him to the airport to catch his plane to Paris.

'Want to drive?' she asked, holding the keys out to him.

'No,' he answered, 'you take it.' She'd find it easier driving. Then she wouldn't have to look at him with the difficult questions.

'How did you stop Costa coming with you?' he asked lightly.

'By hiding. I didn't return his calls.'

'That wouldn't have stopped your father. He'd have set up a twenty-four hour surveillance on the doorstep.'

'I was always out, wasn't I? I lead a busy life, too.' The chat, half joking, touched with intimacy, was a help. They both smiled. Her father was common ground that was not too sensitive. Even Charlie had grown fond of him.

She started the engine, pulled out from the kerb. 'I'm sorry about the girl, Charlie.'

She wasn't wasting time. Straight in. It was out of character. A measure of her anxiety. He found it hard to answer her. 'It was very sad,' he managed to say at last.

'I hear that Father's friend, René Levallier, was wounded, too.'

'He's going to be all right.'

'I'm rushing things, aren't I?' she said.

'Maybe.'

'Any point in leaving it? I want it behind us. If it can *be* behind us. A new life, if that's possible.'

'OK.' He couldn't stop the sigh – but it wasn't the deadening sigh of so many marital quarrels. It wasn't 'Yes, dear.'

She sensed the depth of his tiredness, but she wasn't talking to dead meat. She wanted a response. 'What would you say if I told you I had a lover?' she challenged.

He watched her as she drove, looking ahead – serene, despite the charged question, the wisp of hair on her cheek. What would he say? He didn't know. He'd been taking a battering. Could another beating hurt much more? He wasn't sorry for himself. It was a fact – the vacuum.

'I'd ask the usual questions, I guess,' he said. 'Who was it? How long? How serious?' Then he added: 'Is there anyone?'

'No, but it's what *I've* been living with, isn't it? All our marriage in a way, but lately in particular. You said you'd tell me. What's the story?'

'A murder story. I've been looking for the killer. The girl was helping.'

They came to a stop at traffic lights. 'Who was the victim?'

'Elisabeth.'

She looked at him in surprise. 'What do you mean? I've heard the story enough times. The raid, the enemy fire.'

'It was never quite true.'

'So who killed her?'

'I did.'

She just stared at him then without speaking, transfixed. A blare of horns behind screamed that the lights had turned green. 'My God,' she said and drove on. 'That explains a lot. But why?'

He told her then – just the bare outline. About the signal, what happened to the group – the colt, the collection, Romy; about René and Sonya and Nikki and Wolf. And when he'd finished, there was silence in the car. 'I don't know what to say,' she said at last, 'except . . . Well, you could have told me.'

'I couldn't. You'd have stopped me.'

'I tried.'

'You'd have tried much harder. I couldn't let you.'

She drove on in silence for a while along the Long Island Expressway. 'There's one more question.' He knew what it was. Did it happen with Nikki – what she'd feared? 'But I won't ask it,' she added.

'Later maybe,' he suggested.

They were approaching the East River and the Queens Midtown Tunnel, and the Manhattan skyline was there in front of them. 'You got plans to go back to Europe?' she asked casually.

'No,' he answered, 'not for a while. Quite a while, I'd say.'

She slowed down, faced him for a second – and looked back at the road. 'Then we've got a chance, haven't we?' She held out her hand, her eyes still on the traffic ahead, and their fingers locked.